The Step

by

Derek G. Field

Published in the United Kingdom by

Oakfield Publishing

www.oakfieldpublishing.co.uk

A CIP record of this book is available from the British Library.

First printed August 2012

ISBN-13   978 0 9573265 0 7

Acknowledgement

I would like to dedicate this book to my dearest wife, Yvonne. She gave me the inspiration to write the book in the first place. I had related so many tales of my past and the happenings before, during and after World War Two that she said that if I didn't write them down, then no one would know of my exploits or life as it was at that time. She said that even if it was not published, it would act as a history for my family to read, particularly my sons and my grandchildren. Yvonne would spend hours reading through the text, correcting spelling or typing and commenting on the manner in which I dealt with the facts. Up until now I had only had the experience of writing text books on anatomy, so my ability to tell a story in an interesting manner was put to the test.

Tragically, Yvonne suddenly became ill and within a month of her diagnosis, died. I was absolutely devastated as she was all that I wanted in life. Everything we did, we did together and we had reached the time in life when we had chosen the type of house in which we wanted to live, the area we wanted to be. We both had wonderful families which we could visit as often as we wished and had reached that time in life when we had enough money to do or go anywhere we wished, in fact we boasted about how lucky we were that we had all that we desired, but mostly, we had each other. We had gradually fallen in love following the death of her husband Peter, and my dear wife Anita. I would have stopped writing the book after Yvonne's death as I lost all my enthusiasm for life, until her daughter, Jo told me, that before Yvonne died she had asked her to encourage me to finish the book. I therefore felt that, for her memory, I should continue writing and the continuation of the editing of the book was taken over by my daughter-in-law, Jenny. Although she lives about two hundred miles from me, we worked out a system where I would send the text to her by e-mail, she would read, correct and comment, then she would read each chapter out on the phone adjusting as we went. I would, therefore, like to express my deep appreciation to Jenny for taking over this task with such kindness and enthusiasm especially as she and Yvonne were close friends. I would also like to express my thanks to Matthew, my son, who has not only maintained my computer, sometimes at very short notice, but has also modified it and kept it up to date and able to function in an acceptable manner. He also helped with editing the book and spent a lot of time submitting the text to agents and publishers. My sincere thanks also go to my close friends, Karen Barbour, Neil and Clara Baxter and the actor Michael Culver, who read through the rough final version correcting punctuation, spelling and grammar and giving advice on the content.

All that happens in this book is fact. I have changed it into a novel as I believe that it is a little boring to read through an account of someone's life unless it is extremely well written. I have changed all the names, bar two, to avoid people recognising themselves. Many of the characters in the book will have already passed away and so will be quite oblivious of their part, but those who lived in the area will remember certain episodes that took place at the time and will jog their memories. Some of the characters I have split into two to avoid losing some of the colour of their contribution and others I have combined to produce a more rounded character.

I sincerely apologise to any of my readers who feel that they recognise a person in the book who is similar to them in character. I can assure them that although the places still exist and may be recognised by people now living in the area, the characters are purely fictional but loosely based on memories.

Foreword

Each of our lives is a story. We may not feel that the events in that life are worthy of recording, but they are all part of history and if they are not told and written down at some time, will be lost to the world forever. Ivy, the mother of my wife, Yvonne, lived until she was ninety six. During the whole of the time that I had the privilege to know her, I was envious of her incredible memory going all the way back to when she was a child, living in Putney close to Fulham football ground. She had a very hard life being the eldest of twelve children for whom she would be responsible for much of the day. She lived through both World Wars and had vivid memories of devastation, hardship and hunger. Many, many times I said that I would like to interview her with a tape recorder and ask her questions about her past and her upbringing, which I could transcribe into print. Sadly, I never did this and all the wonderful information she held in her head went to the grave when she died.

My story is very much like many others who lived through the times of the Second World War. If they think back they will say, "Now I think about it, I did that", or "I was there". The act of writing it down on paper jogs all sorts of memories that have been pushed to the back of the mind and it is amazing how one memory leads on to another and another. I was surprised how many names of friends I knew well and even people I hardly knew came to mind during the writing of this book. People appear, in one's memory, as they were at the time of meeting them, they stay the same age as when you knew them. Their faces come clearly to mind and even their voices can be remembered. Sometimes they are a little better looking in one's memory than they were at the time and the feelings one had when meeting them are gone, but their character comes through clearly.

Yvonne and I visited the area where I was born and brought up, some years before I began to write the book. I was astonished at the changes that had taken place, a few were improvements, but many were disappointments. The schools I attended appeared to be half the size and the playing fields, if still there, were much, much smaller than before. Some of the schools were actually smaller because certain sections had been sold off for flats or offices and they offered a sorry sight compared with the lively school, full of children, that had been there sixty years before.

I hope that when you read this book and if you have enjoyed it, you may consider putting some of the events of your life down on paper for all to read and you may find that your memory will give you much information which you have put to the back of your mind. I hope that you will gain joy at the recovery of your past and others will benefit from the knowledge of your life and the way it was spent. I used to write an editorial for a magazine and many times commented on a saying I had heard, "Live every day as if it were your last, because, one day, it will be". I would like to add to this, get your memories recorded in some way or they may be lost forever.

Chapter 1

Deuteronomy,

"Do not forget the things your eyes have seen, nor let them slip from your heart all the days of your life. **Rather tell them to your children and your children's' children."**

Isn't it strange, how, even on a hot sunny day in May, a stone step can feel so cold? It was remarkable too how the cold could penetrate through a thin pair of shorts and bring such comfort to a body that could really do with lying in a bath of cold water or wallowing in a cool swimming pool. To the side of the step, where the sun's rays were being reflected into the porch, the stone was almost too hot to touch and yet strangely the heat was not being conducted into the rest of the step. David ran his hand over the smooth edge from the hot to the cold areas and noted the evenness of the top surface which had mainly been produced by his father sharpening the carving knife and his mother, scrubbing and whitening the step daily. Every Sunday morning Dad would sharpen the knife in preparation for carving the Sunday joint and every morning Mum would clean the step. Dad took great pride in the sharpness of the carver, which had been given to them on their wedding day and had been sharpened so many times by Dad and the knife grinder man who came along at intervals with his strange barrow which looked a little like a sewing machine. He would pedal rapidly and the stones would spin around in front of his face. He would then take the knife and sharpen it on the stone throwing off clouds of sparks. By now the knife was only about half an inch across having had about an inch of steel ground away.

Mum also took great pride in the appearance of the step. The glazed brick step below was far less important over recent years. In the past it had to be maintained with red cardinal polish, which was a job on its own. After applying the polish David's mum would buff up the surface to create a shine in which one could almost see a reflection of one's face. This was followed by about half an hour trying to clean the red polish off of her fingers. Nowadays, however, Dad had painted the step with a red paint and although not having quite the shine or the smell, was adequate. In fact David could rest his feet on the lower step and had little worry about spoiling the shine. His mind was far away on problems he just could not have anticipated.

He was trying to control the emotion that had been building up in him over the past few weeks. He felt so angry and cheated and yet he had no one to blame and no one to swear at. He honestly didn't know whether to shout and scream or just burst into tears. The latter seemed to be the way he felt at the moment, but he knew that young men of his age didn't cry. He had become a great believer in God over the past year or so, which was partly due to the fact that his heart throb was a keen church goer, but his belief was certainly under some serious strain at the moment. He was told that God was all good and anything bad was from the devil. Well, where was God now that He was needed and where were the miracles that He was supposed to perform? What a situation!

Was it only last month that he was sitting the final examinations in his National Diploma of Design and he had been involved in submitting designs and arranging for the decorations that were to deck the front of Sutton Town Hall to celebrate the Coronation of Queen Elizabeth? Was it only last month that the world looked as if it was going to be his oyster and that openings for his future career were flowing in and he was being confronted with having to make a choice of which route to take? Was it only last month that he was playing cricket for his local team St. Anthony's, and achieved the best bowling figures he had ever had with this club. He had taken seven wickets for a mere forty seven runs and had, with his accurate throwing, run another batsman out. He could see no way out of this predicament. There seemed very little to live for. Only the support of his family and his young girlfriend, Janet, gave him some reason for continuing to feel that life might be worth living and perhaps he should wait a little and see how things go.

He could hear the sound of children playing games in the road and on the green outside his house and music being played on the latest record player. It was a tune well known to him as it was played regularly at the youth club he attended twice a week and was called the Blue Tango. The sound production was very poor, scratchy and muffled and he knew that the fibre tip of the needle should have been sharpened before the record had been played. He knew all the celebrations were in aid of the Queen's Coronation and as all over the estate, the old tradition of holding the party in the middle of the street had been reverted to and all the roads had been closed for that particular reason. There were only one or two cars that ever used that road anyway and many of the motorists would be over in the St. Anthony's Arms drinking more ale than was good for them, dancing the knees up and singing all the old songs many of which originated in the First World War.

Suddenly his thoughts were interrupted by small feet running up his pathway.

"Mum said, would you like to come and have some tea with us on the tables in the road".

It was a little boy of about five or six years old who was holding tight on to the hand of an even smaller girl, whom David assumed was his sister. He couldn't recognise them although they seemed to be dressed in party clothes, the little girl in a dress that spread out from the waist and the boy in a smart white shirt with long sleeves and shorts He didn't know quite what to say to them, it was about three in the afternoon, although he wasn't sure, but he felt to join the whole group of children would be a little demeaning. This was such a kind

3

gesture but how could he respond without hurting the feelings of these very pleasant children and what sort of message could he give them which would not upset the kind mother who had sent them? He also wondered whether all the eyes of the mothers and children were on him as the noise of laughter and shouting had ceased. He thanked the children and explained that he had just had his tea and was quite full up, which was a lie as he had not eaten since dinner time and in this heat he was feeling quite thirsty. The children stood in silence for a while, the boy then turned around and began to pull his sister away. She, however, stood her ground and was not to be put off by this answer.

"Could you come and just join in the games then".

David, who was now approaching his seventeenth year and about to make his way in the world, felt that he was not yet equipped in life to deal with such an honest request.

"I don't think that I will know the games you are playing" was his feeble and inadequate reply.

"That's alright" she replied, "Me and Johnny can teach you and they are really easy, all you have to do is to follow us in and out of the paper hats and streamers. You'll soon get the hang of it and then you can do it all on your own and there is a prize for the winner".

David felt as if the ground had opened up below him and he imagined himself skipping between the hats and streamers and having the final humiliation of winning the prize. He tried to explain to the little girl that he didn't think that he was able to do all the running and jumping entailed in their games and perhaps they should tell their mummy, thank you but he was happy where he was. Johnny pulled at his sister's arm but his little sister stood firm.

"Mummy said we must not take no as an answer and we should not come back unless we have you in tow".

"Tell Mummy, thank you, but I can't come".

With that the two turned and ran down the pathway and out onto the small green that lay in front of the house. There was silence for a short time and then the music started up and he could hear the sound of laughter and small feet racing up and down the pavement and road. David stood up and rubbed his backside to get the blood circulating and ease the pressure from the hard step. This was a mistake which he later would regret, but at the time felt was necessary. He did contemplate going indoors and finding a pillow to sit on, but partly through laziness and partly because it would look strange taking a pillow off the bed and putting it on an outside step which may not have pleased his mother. He sat down again on the cold step and let his thoughts swing back almost thirteen years when he sat on the same step in the same doorway and about the same time of the year.

Chapter 2

David's first recollection was of sitting on that same step with its smooth, grey surface and the feeling of cold penetration in his short trousers. It is strange how certain places and certain feelings evoke memories that have been hidden in the depths of the brain for years and suddenly are woken up and become quite clear. The feeling was the same, but the surroundings appeared to be quite different.

Geoffrey Evans, a boy of approximately the same age, who David barely knew was also sitting on the step. He had just had his fourth birthday and was proud to show David the presents he had received. David was quite distressed to hear that his prize present from his mother and father was a Jew's harp. This he endeavoured to pluck whilst at the same time blowing and sucking through his lips. There was no tune but a twanging sound which every now and again was interrupted by a sharp clank as the spring hit his teeth. His only other present was a sixpenny piece given to him by his elder brother. David knew that they were a poor and quite peculiar family but when he remembered what sort of presents he had received on his birthday, he felt quite ashamed and very sorry for poor little Geoff. Later on in life, unknown to him, their paths would again cross. Geoff's day was made, however, when David's Dad emerged from the living room, with his old roadster bicycle, which he always left in the living room for safety and convenience for doing odd jobs to it like oiling the chain and cleaning the wheels. Dad picked up the Jew's harp and with admiring adulation from the two boys, began to play some of the old tunes. David was quite unaware that his Dad had such talent as he never heard him singing, except round the pub when he had had a few beers, or playing any instrument, except on that occasion.

Dad was a very quiet unassuming man, slight of build and fairly short in stature, but with an arm as strong as an ox. David remembered that he had ridden on his shoulders on many occasions and had a vague feeling of being taken to see an enormous fire which was burning miles away, but could be seen over the local park. David always imagined that this could have been the burning down of the famous Crystal Palace, but when he worked it out he would only have been a year old and this memory may have been of another fire or perhaps what he had been told had happened. Dad had taken the three children to see the fire and perhaps this had made such an impression on him that it had stuck in his memory. He was a very talented man being able to do all the jobs necessary in the house including carpentry, electrics, metalwork, painting and decorating. He was an expert gardener filling the front garden with masses of his mum's favourite flowers including roses of all colours. The back was filled with trays of seedlings, chrysanthemums for the autumn and vegetables. Even the side fences were covered by rambler roses and the back fence gave a home to two large chicken houses full of laying hens. Mind you David never saw him cook as Mum was in sole charge and was proud of all her cooking skills, which would come into their own in the next ten years.

The view from the step was quite different in those days. Around each of the greens, usually termed the small green and the large green, was a series of low railings, which consisted of a single bar about an inch thick and square in cross section held up by iron posts at about five feet intervals. The railings were constructed with the sharp angle upwards to prevent small or even large children balancing along them and bending the bar. This only added more of a challenge to all the kids in the street and anyone who could not balance for more than two posts was considered a sissy.

The little green had two very large oak trees at one end which proved to be ideal for climbing although involving a fair amount of risk. The tree nearest to the house was the most difficult to climb having a thick trunk and no really substantial branches for the lower six feet. This meant that the initial ascent must involve the climbing on another's shoulders.   The rest of the trunk was only sparsely covered with thin branches until, at the top the climber would be confronted with a flat horizontal surface about two feet across where the top had been removed. David remembered that, when he was about seven or eight he was challenged to climb this more difficult tree.   He was a good climber and managed to make his way up the comparatively thin branches.   On pausing to get his breath he observed that he was already well above the height of his roof top.   He completed the rest of the climb, but could feel his hands shaking and his heart pounding. He carefully stood up on the flat top and, being scared to move his feet, looked towards the north.   He could see many tall buildings in the distance, one with a large dome, which he assumed to be St. Paul's Cathedral although he wasn't sure.

At that moment he could hear screaming from down below and his name being shouted out.   It was Mum.   She was going frantic standing in the middle of the little green.   He remembered that he descended as quickly as he could taking care not to let go of the branch above before he had a firm footing on the branch below. When he eventually jumped to the ground he noticed that all his friends had disappeared and only Mum, looking red in the face, was there.   After receiving several swipes around his ears and his legs he was sent straight to bed.   Beyond this little green the big green had a line of large oaks and elms across its middle and on the opposite side to David's house there was a line of large thick bushes which not only prevented anyone looking across the green and seeing into the front windows, but also was an ideal site for making camps and hiding places.   Other than this, the grass on the greens were kept in good order by a small group of council workers armed with sickles and scythes, believe it or not the mower had not reached these parts in 1939.

David's parents Bill and Nancy Fellows had moved down to this estate in the November of 1934 with their two young children Jack, who was six and his little sister Betty, aged four. They had been living with relatives in Battersea and had been offered this wonderful opportunity to move to the country. In fact it was on to a vast estate of council houses built on the green belt to re-house some of the poorer people who were living a difficult life in and around London. They thought that it was marvellous. A brand new house that had a tap with running water in the kitchen and for the first time in their lives, an electric light in each room. In addition there was an indoor toilet, something of which they had only dreamed. The kitchen had a fixed bath with a cold tap, but alongside it was a copper for heating the water. Next to the back door was an indoor larder with vents, top and bottom for the free passage of outside air; ideal in the summer, but a real draft producer from October to April. Bill would fit pieces of ply wood over the openings during these months which really defeated the object of the larder. The front room had a modern fireplace with an oven above the fire, which, when the damper was out, could almost glow red in the heat from the fire. All in all, the world seemed perfect. The only problem was that Bill was employed at the Brewery in Wandsworth and the only way he could get there was on his bicycle. The journey must have been at least an hour and a half each way.

On Fridays Dad would cycle along the high street in Battersea and with his hard earned wages purchase some fresh fruit. This was a rare treat for the whole family and, as David remembered, was mainly shared among the three children. Finding the money to purchase food was always a difficulty and Mum managed to keep the "wolf from the door" by, as she would say, "making ends meet". It meant a fair number of suet puddings, bacon rolls and fry ups of the left-overs from the day before. Sunday, however, always saw a small piece of meat, either lamb, beef, or pork, sliced very thinly by Dad with an equal amount placed on each of the plates. This was accompanied by copious amounts of gravy, baked potatoes and cabbage, grown on

Dad's allotment and boiled in the saucepan for hours and then squeezed under a plate in the colander until all the water had been expelled. Mondays, however, was a miserable day when Mum did the washing. Early, before the children were out of bed, in would come the large washing tub, which was usually left hanging by one handle on a nail through the side fence behind the large cast iron mangle. The copper would be filled with water and a fire, usually made up of all the old wood and old shoes Dad could find. When the water was almost boiling, which took a couple of hours, Mum would ladle the water, with a saucepan, into the washtub and with a bar of green Fairy soap and a blue block, would scrub all the soiled parts of the clothes, sheets etc., and drop them back into the copper where the water was allowed to boil for sometime. The clothes would then be passed back into the washtub with the aid of a thick stick and a final wash on the scrubbing board was completed. After several rinses in cold water they were taken out to the old mangle, with the two large wooden rollers and passed through the mangle turned by a large wheel at one end. Turns were taken to rotate the wheel as ten minutes against the thickness of the clothing was very tiring. This was mainly carried out by the children as Mum was hanging the mangled washing up on the rope line which stretched from one end of the garden to the other. The routine occurred every Monday come rain, shine or cold and frost. Sometimes the washing would become stiff on the line with icicles hanging from the clothing and often the rope would snap with the weight and all the clean washing would fall onto the muddy garden. These occasions were the only time David saw his mother sit down and cry. The whole routine must start again and be finished before Bill arrived home for his tea of cold meat, pickles and bubble and squeak.

It was always traditional that the woman of the house should have the meal on the table as the man entered the house and it was part of Mum's pride to stick to this routine. The children would be looking forward to Dad's return and would sit around him, as he was eating his meal, and ask questions about his day, always hoping that Dad would have more on his plate than he could cope with and would perhaps leave a morsel of meat or potato and some gravy for the onlookers. He had the habit of leaving about three roast potatoes and a quantity of gravy. He would mash the potato in the gravy, adding salt and pepper and then would divide it into the number of children. It was funny how that mash always tasted better than all the dinners they had had.

Chapter 3

The estate was a brilliant idea at the time, built to house poor families in and around London; it was soon filled with young or fairly young couples. David imagined that a requirement of two small children was also a necessity for procuring a house. A small choice was given as to whether the couple preferred a corner or middle of terrace house, but most opted for the terrace as it turned out to be a couple of pence a week cheaper on the rent. The rent was to be paid weekly, into one of the "rent offices", which were found scattered throughout the estate. At David's end of the street there were at least twenty children and that was only ten houses. This was about the general spread of children throughout the whole estate which added up to thousands of children, all of school age. This had been well thought out as numerous new schools were built all of the same design with white walls, large windows and green painted woodwork. They were all surrounded by tarmac play grounds and backed up by quite extensive playing fields, a great asset in the years that followed.

All the children attended their local school so no one had to travel any real distance and as they all knew each other they would walk in groups and enjoy the short trip. While one of the schools would have a senior section for girls the next would have the same facilities for boys, so, from the age of eleven some of the boys or girls would have to move to the adjoining senior school. Those who were lucky enough to pass the eleven plus examination would have to leave the schools on the estate and travel to one of the grammar schools in the surrounding towns. Believe it or not, most children did not want to travel any distance to their school and even more surprising, many parents thought that to go to one of these schools was stepping above your station and preferred that their children stayed in the "working class area".

Life was good for the children; they played on the numerous greens, local parks and in the roads. This was quite safe as there was only the occasional car or motor bike and their engine could be heard long before it came into range of the children. Often the vehicle would stop until the game was finished or there was a break and the children would then let it through. If a game was started many more children would soon appear and ask if they could join in. There were skipping games in the road, organised by the girls. Betty, David's elder sister by four years was one of the main organisers. She and her two friends Fanny and June would tuck their skirts up into their knickers and then control all the younger children by putting them into two groups and anyone not behaving correctly was sent away and not allowed to join in. Although this skipping was mainly for the girls, many of the younger boys would be allowed to join in as long as they behaved well and didn't disrupt the game.

Football was usually played on the "big" green and organized by the boys. Jack, David's elder brother, took a major part in this and the game would often grow to massive dimensions with perhaps twenty on each side. There was no age bar and little boys would run around the green after the ball while the bigger ones pushed and booted their way through the crowd. Jack and Teddy, who lived next door, would choose one team and two older boys Tommy and Larry would choose their opponents. The game would start after tea, about five o'clock and would continue until it was too dark to play anymore. In the summer this may have lasted three or four hours with relays of boys coming and going. Many times it ended up in a fight and David often saw the big boys from one end of the road take on those of his end in a violent brawl ending up with cut lips and black eyes. The next evening, however, they would have become friends again and the match would be restarted.

One of the major factors in causing injuries were the laces of the ball. It took, perhaps , an hour to pump up the ball and re-lace it with the curved iron needle using a thick leather lace. This unfortunately protruded outside the curvature of the ball. Added to this was the weight of the ball which was made of leather and often soaking wet from the day before. Heading the ball, if it came your way at head height, was a must and if you caught it on the lace you could be up the hospital with a gashed head and the possibility of stitches. Another problem was that the ball could hit any of the windows of at least thirty four houses which surrounded the greens and at the sound of glass breaking forty boys could disappear in the wink of the eye. Only the girls remained and there was always one that knew the name and address of the culprit that had kicked the ball.

On one occasion Bill, with trilby on, fag in mouth and heading for the Arms, came out , joined in with the game, and on his first kick sent the ball flying into a neighbour's window. He was the only person left on the green when the irate woman came rushing out carrying a large cane. He apologised profusely and spent the rest of the evening getting a piece of glass, cutting it to the right size and puttying it into position. It was lucky he was such a handy man, but his very rare evening out was lost. The money he had been given by Mum to buy a few rounds of drinks was put back into the kitty and used as housekeeping.

Cricket was the other major sporting occasion to be held on the greens. Unfortunately, stumps were hard to come by so pieces of timber from someone's backyard were used. The bat which was provided by Dennis Moorhouse, gave right of entry to both he and his two younger brothers. All three were good batsmen and were obvious choices. They also always played in the same team which was going to be the winner in the end. Many times the ball was lost in the surrounding gardens, but luckily many of the local dogs were trained to go and look for the ball and most times found it. Regularly they would go down to the local park where each batsman played as an individual, the winner being the one with the highest score. Everybody took it in turns to bowl and the game would continue until everyone had batted and bowled. The game would often last for hours and was only stopped when, as the light went down hoards of hornets would invade the pitch and fly into the faces of the players. There was always a mad rush for the gates of the park swinging either a stump or a bat above your head to keep the insects at bay. Life was good, the weather always seemed warm and sunny in the summer. There was always snow and sledging in the winter. Many of the parents seem to have enough money to visit the pub and consume more than they should at tuppence a pint. They would normally arrive home worse for wear, holding on to each other and singing, at the tops of their voices, many of the old songs. Some would link arms and do the "pallais glide" along the street to the amusement of the children who had been left to play in the streets. There was no hint of the strife and hardships that lay only a month or two away.

Chapter 4

It was a nice, bright Sunday morning and Dad was up very early, had his breakfast of thick toast covered with pork dripping, left over from the Sunday before accompanied by a large cup of strong tea. He had loaded his old bicycle with a garden fork, spade and rake tied on along his cross bar. On his carrier at the back he carried a couple of well worn sacks and on the handlebars he balanced a box of wallflower seedlings, ready for planting in the allotment. By the time Jack, Betty and David had emerged from their beds following a playful romp in the back bedroom, Dad was already digging hard. His allotment was situated just beyond the estate, but backing on to one of the playing fields of an estate school, separated from the allotments by a very high fence. Being a hard worker and getting great satisfaction and produce from his allotment, Dad had acquired the adjoining plot on which he grew most of his potatoes and rhubarb. Up against the fence he had planted a cultivated blackberry bush, which added to the joys of the children's visits to the allotments as it was not only covered, at this time of the year with large juicy blackberries, but it was also the home of a blackbird. Deep within the thick, thorny shoots there was a nest and the eggs they had spotted earlier in the year had now become small chicks. Dad would very carefully part the thorny branches so that the three children could see the progress, but they were not allowed to get near the blackberry bush unless Dad accompanied them.

All three children enjoyed a trip to the allotment which was at least two miles from the house. David remembered, however, he could not walk both ways so he was given a lift back on the bicycle accompanied by a sack of mixed vegetables. During the week, and on Saturdays the children were allowed to take part in working the land claiming certain vegetables and soft fruit as their own. Each was allowed to mark a marrow with their name and as the marrow grew they had great delight in seeing the name grow larger and larger. Of course, all produce was taken back to Mum except for the occasional new carrot, fresh garden pea or tender, fresh runner bean. This was a little treat for some of the hard work that the children contributed to the production of the greatly valued produce, although David, even at his young age, knew that his Dad worked his fingers to the bone and suffered almost continual back ache with the amount of digging and planting he did. Most of the vegetables and flowers were planned almost a year ahead, when the Ryder catalogue arrived in the post. The whole family would sit around the large circular table which dominated the front room of the house. They would each have a turn at looking through the very colourful brochure, full of pictures of perfect apples, strawberries, cherries, pears, etc. in the fruit section, and full of very colourful flowers in the garden division and fine large and perfect vegetables in the main section. After Dad and Mum had chosen all the seeds they thought they would need for the next year's sowing, each of the children was then allowed to choose one packet of seeds which they would sow the next year. Beans, either French, broad, or runner were favourites as samples could be brought up early in the year in a milk bottle with some blotting paper and water in the bottom. They also gave a magnificent show when they were grown in the very rich soil of the allotment. The children also knew that Dad had a favourite way of planting his runner beans. He would dig a pit of at least two spades depth. He would then line the pit with the contents of an old mattress, which was filled with flock. He then threw in all the rubbish and waste from the vegetables he had grown the year before, which he had kept piled up at the end of the plot, mixing in all the manure which the milkman's and baker's horses had deposited on the road and had been collected in an old bucket by the children. Finally he would top it off with a good foot of heavy loam. His beans were the admiration of all the allotment owners and would provide the family with a second veg every day for about six weeks finally ending up with those that were left on the plants being saved for cultivation the next year.

17

That Sunday morning did not turn out as they all expected. The usual routine was for Dad to go ahead while Mum got the children up and gave them their breakfast. They would then be clothed in their "Sunday best", the only time that these clothes were worn, and hand in hand they would be dispatched off to visit Dad on the allotment. This was a special visit as it meant that the work was almost finished when they arrived and they were on no account to touch or eat anything dirty. They all knew that a full inspection would be made of the clothing when they returned and "God Help", as Mum would say, any of them that had spoiled their clean clothes. There was also an additional treat which they all knew happened every allotment Sunday and that was the visit, after packing up all the gear, to the small sweet shop, which was just down the road beyond the allotment site. They were only allowed to choose one small quantity of sweets, which were usually sold in quarters of a pound or even two ounces at a time. The shop was really only the front room of a very small house just off the road, but the children were fascinated by the weighing machine the quaint old lady used with round weights of all different sizes at one end and a chrome dish at the other into which she poured the sweets out of large jars lined up on the shelves behind her. She was always dressed the same whether it was Sunday or a weekday with her hair wrapped up in a turban tied at the front in a large bow and her ample figure was surrounded by an off white overall that had obviously seen better days. She always wore large carpet slippers that had holes in the front with her big toes showing through. Nevertheless, she always wore a smile and had a kind word for the children. Sometimes the sweets would stick together and she would shake them up and down or prod them with a stick. She nearly always poured into the dish too many sweets and had to retrieve some with her hands and put them back in the jar. They noticed, however, she always let the tray touch the bottom of the machine, which meant there were one or two more than the weight. She would then make a paper cone out of old newspaper into which she poured the sweets.

This Sunday they left the house, waving goodbye to Mum, crossed both the greens, and down the alleyway. They carefully crossed the only main road on their journey, which only had a car or motorbike using it about twice or three times a day. The whole area seemed a lot quieter that morning, very few people were walking along the pavements and those that were seemed to have something on their minds, for they all had their head bowed and seemed intent on getting to somewhere quickly. There was no sign of the ladies that normally stood at the gates of their houses and very few men were in their gardens cutting the grass or pruning the roses. However, the sun was shining and the birds, mainly sparrows, seemed to be having a wonderful time landing on all the privet hedges along the pavement and singing to their hearts content.

David remembered that the three of them had walked down the main road that led to the allotments, but were still about half a mile away when a terrible whirring sound started up and gradually grew into an ear splitting scream. It wavered up and down with an ominous rapidity. The children stopped and stood still in terror. David remembered that he burst into tears and Betty took him in both arms, but looking very frightened herself. Jack stood for a while and then grabbing both their hands said "Quick, lets run to Dad, it isn't far". Betty refused to budge and then pulling the other way said, "I want to go hone", and with that started to run home. Jack came alongside and took David's other hand and all three ran along the pavement back towards their home. The terrible wailing seemed to grow even louder and they were unsure if they were running into danger. Suddenly, as they crossed a small side road David tripped and let go of Betty's hand. He fell on the road grazing his knee, hitting his elbow hard and cutting his lip. Jack and Betty helped him to the side of the road and a lady from one of the posher houses, just off of the estate, ran over to them. She produced a handkerchief and wound it around David's knee, which was now bleeding quite profusely. She also looked quite agitated and said that they should run home as quickly as possible as war had been declared against the Germans. David had no idea what it all meant, but Jack seemed to understand and pulled the other two along as quickly as they could run. All the doors of the houses were now open and people were crammed on their front steps looking up and down the road and shouting to one another. One old lady was screaming and another younger woman shouted, "Run home as quick as you can, the Germans are coming". This made the children even more terrified and they ran even faster half panting and half crying. A man shouted, "If you hear the church bells begin to ring. The Germans are invading". As they rushed around the corner of the passageway they bumped into a woman running the other way. Believe it or not, it was mum.

She too had been struck with horror when she heard the siren start up. She, of course, knew what it all meant, but had been assured that a settlement had been reached and the crisis was over. Directly she heard the wailing begin, she had turned off the oven and the hob and run out of the house heading for the allotments. She was still wrapped in her overall, which in those days flapped over at the front passing one of the ties through an opening in the other side so that it could be tied at the back. She had slippers on her feet and her hair was heavily laden with curlers with a scarf wrapped around the back and tied in a double knot at the front above the forehead. She looked white faced and her eyes were almost staring. She threw her arms around David and Betty and hugged them tightly. Then David remembered that she picked him up and took Betty's hand and ran towards home. Jack ran ahead so that he could open the front door by the key which always hung behind the letter box so that they could all run straight into the safety of their house. How wrong they all were. All the neighbours were at their doors, with their children and some of the braver men had ventured to the gates and were discussing the future and what was going to happen.

They all strained their eyes on the passageway to see the return of Dad and the safety of his presence. All three of the children were becoming extremely worried as, although the streets were clear and all the front doors were open with their families standing on the door steps, there was no sign of Dad. David's mum decided, to take the children's minds off of the absence, she would get down to bathing David's knee. She removed the handkerchief carefully and began to remove the congealed blood from the edges of the wound with a soft damp, clean, handkerchief. She finally cleaned out the cuts, under great protest, dried the area and applied one of her many bandages, which she had made from an old sheet. Then came the time when David had to tell her of his shirt and elbow. He expected to get a clip around the ear for the damage to the sleeve of the shirt, but mum put her arms about him and kissed him on the cheek. This was quite a surprise as kissing was not done very often in those days. When all the medical repairs had been done all four of them rushed to the front door to look for the appearance of Dad. Mum stood on the doorstep, biting her nails and looking anxious. All the neighbours now knew of dad's absence and had their eyes trained on the passageway.

The siren continued to sound wavering up and down in pitch and all sorts of rumours were passing from house to house. There were, of course, no telephones in that area, so nobody really knew what the situation was. Dad had procured an old wooden radio, which was the envy of all the neighbours. It was powered by an accumulator which had to be charged at the local petrol station in the next town. This dad had done only a week before, so everybody waited for dad to come home as he was the only one who was allowed to switch it on. Mr. Stamp, Peter's father, who lived next door but one, offered to go down towards the allotments and see if he could find out what had happened, but mum felt that this was putting him at risk for no real reason although in her heart she was worried to death as it was approaching the time when dad usually came home for his dinner.

Suddenly they all could hear a sound of clapping and they spotted Dad slowly emerging from the alleyway, walking by the side of his bike. To the cross bar was tied all of his gardening tools and resting on the saddle and the handlebars were two large sacks, presumably filled with vegetables from the allotment. All the local neighbours started to cheer and Dad walked slowly, balancing the sacks on his bike, right up to the front gate, where mum flew out and threw her arms around his neck. He was more than a little surprised as this was another unusual performance in front of the neighbours in the street. When Dad explained, however, that, when he heard the siren he decided to dig up extra vegetables and dig the ground ready for sowing his winter veg., the welcome changed into a verbal scolding including many words that were new to David. The tirade was soon stopped when all the men of their end of the street came to the door and asked Dad if he would switch on his radio and could they come in and listen. It took a little time to find an audible signal but then they heard a voice of an announcer introducing the Prime Minister. The men sat in silence as they heard him say that although he had hoped for a settlement and that the Germans had moved out of Poland, he had had no assurance and therefore we were at war with Germany. All sat in silence for a while. An announcer, or person being interviewed was saying something about not panicking, but David had never felt such a depressed atmosphere ever before. Mr. Pope, from next door said, "I never liked the bloody Germans anyway, you can't trust them". He was a little older than David's parents and had served in the First World War. He belonged to the British Legion Club and used to march each year to commemorate and remember all of his friends that had died in that war. Everybody respected him and no one answered his comment knowing of his feelings on the subject.

Chapter 5

"Hello",

David was suddenly brought back to the present. He was a little sad at this interruption in his thoughts, they had been quite a contrast to the doldrums he had been in for some time now and although they were not all pleasant memories, those events were all now passed and gone and perhaps he should be concentrating more on his future and how he was to solve this terrible situation he was now in. Everybody seemed to be nice and many of them offered help, but none of them could solve his present problems and the more help he had accepted in the past few days seemed to deprive him of his independence. Only two people seemed to really understand how he felt, one was his elder brother Jack and the other was a curate from the local church.

"I'm Polly" said the young lady who stood in front of him. "My two young ruffians came to ask you if you would like to join us, but I think that they gave you the wrong impression and invited you to take part in the games we were organizing. I actually asked them to ask you if you would like to join us, that is the parents, for a cup of tea".

With that Polly came and sat beside David on the step. She was dressed in a summery dress with the arms bare up to her shoulders and cut in a loop down the front and the back. The skirt was about three quarter length and seemed to be made of some taffeta material as it made a squeaky noise as she lowered herself onto the step. She suddenly moved her bottom along the step so that she came up against David and then stood up again.

"Sorry", she said, "that step is hotter than I thought it would be".

David at first thought that Polly was being a little forward seeing as she hardly knew him, but then realised that he should have warned her of the temperature of the step where she was going to sit.

"I am sorry, I should have warned you of the difference in temperature, I just didn't know that you were going to sit down. I will move up and you can sit on the cooler area" and with that he moved sideways. Polly again sat down and to David's great pleasure she was bottom to bottom and thigh to thigh.

"So what do you think, will you come and join us for a cup of tea and a piece of coronation cake?".

"To be quite honest" said David, "I am not very sociable at the moment, you see I have a lot on my mind and I don't think I would be very good company".

"That doesn't matter, we have all heard of the trouble you have had over the past weeks and we all would like to do something to help. We all live around the large green and up a couple of the turnings and you could call on us whenever you like"

With that Polly put her arm around David's shoulders. She could only have been about twenty two years old, but by the feel of her arms and the firmness of her breast she had a very pleasing figure. He felt his heart beating at twice its normal speed and, although he remembered that he was madly in love with his girl friend, Janet, this seemed to be an overpowering feeling of desire which he could not explain. She placed her other hand on his thigh, which was now tightly up against hers and lent over and kissed him on the cheek.

David could feel his cheeks burning and it must have been obvious to Polly that he was blushing at this close contact. He also felt quite embarrassed that his sexual desires had been suddenly thrust into action and he knew he would be unable to stand for a while without revealing his feelings in a visible way.

"I can't come over at the moment" said David, "but I may come over in about half an hour".

"I have seen you with your girlfriend walking down our road with your arms tightly wrapped around each other. You pass our door at the same time each Tuesday and Thursday".

"Do you live in Sherridan Road?" asked David.

"That's right, number twenty-eight. We often sit on the front step and watch all the people passing along the road. We are always guessing what they do and where they are going. I know that your girlfriend lives further on down the road past the St. Anthony's Arms and as you don't come back, we thought that you must live down that way too".

David did remember that on their way home from the church youth club, he and Janet would often leave the rest of the group and walk home on their own hoping to find some dark area where they could stand and have a kiss good night. He also remembered a young girl and a young woman sitting on one of the door steps and even remembered saying hello to them at times. The young woman always wore a low cut dress and her breasts, which were well developed always showed a low and full cleavage. Her dress always appeared to be of a silky material and her hair was long, almost reaching down to her waist and held backwards in a head scarf, which, instead of being tied under the chin was tucked back under her hair on the same side. David had never seen this way of using a head scarf and even at the time, felt how attractive it was.

"Now I remember you" said David, "Janet and I always thought that you lived there with your parents and little sister".

"That's right, but you didn't see my little boy and girl because they were usually in bed asleep. You seem very fond of your girlfriend, are you thinking of getting married later on?"

"I hope so" replied David, "although she is still very young and I have run into this bit of a problem. I am not sure whether it has brought us closer together or whether the responsibility is going to be too great for her. It took me a long time to persuade her to go out with me, although I think that that was due to the fact that I was very immature myself".

"How did you meet up?", Polly asked.

"I met her at a youth club holiday in the New Forest. It was on the night before we were all to go home, when they held a special dance."

"So had you already got to know each other before then?"

"No, I didn't know her at all, in fact I don't think I had ever seen her before."

David's mind wandered back to the holiday, one of the best weeks he had ever spent away. Walks had been arranged through the forest, tournaments of snooker, billiards and table tennis had been arranged indoors, if the weather was poor, and tennis coaching, with two professionals had been fixed up on the courts which were in the gardens of Avon House, where they were staying. There was even a croquet lawn just below the patio and the young curate from the church took a great delight in beating all comers, to whom he would teach the rules when they had made a mistake. He had his more serious side when he took the short service each morning, but even then he spoke common sense and his short sermon was always about something to which they could all relate. In the evenings they held an informal sort of dance and social where David had got to know most the members of the club really well.

David remembered there were many bicycles at the back of the House and how all the boys had decided to go on a bike ride across the forest to visit a vicar who had once been a curate at St. Anthony's. It was a mad idea as the distance was far more than most of them could cycle. By the time they had all been given tea and masses of sandwiches and cakes some felt that they couldn't make the journey back. The Vicar had the answer. He had bought a very old Rolls Royce. David didn't know the year, but remembered that it had horizontal grill bars on the front. They had covered the top of the car with blankets and tied all the bicycles on the top. With that everyone had climbed inside and the Vicar drove them back to Avon House. They arrived to a volume of cheers from the girls, and of course, all the boys were beaming with pride.

Janet must have been among the girls that day.

Polly butted in on David's thoughts. "How old was she at that time?" she asked.

"She was just coming up to fourteen and I suppose that is why I had not seen or taken any notice of her before. Mind you, I was only just sixteen, but thought that I had now really grown up".

David admitted to Polly how he had been very shy when it came to asking girls to dance and tended to stand back. Many of the boys had regular girlfriends who they danced with and there were only one or two girls left over. He recalled suddenly seeing this young lady, Janet, sitting on her own and felt that he could at least have one dance. He went over to her and asked her if she would be his partner for that quickstep. Dancing then meant either the waltz, quickstep, or foxtrot. She had smiled, stood up and joined him. It was only then David saw that she was dressed in a plain, but beautiful pale blue dress. She had a broad, white belt around her very fine waist and her jet black, wavy hair was set off by a white carnation pinned to one side. She must have been wearing a small heel as she appeared quite tall, almost the same height as himself. They did the three dances together and David accompanied her back to her seat.

"So that was the beginning of a great romance?" Polly asked.

"Well, no. When the next record was put on the record-player I noticed, again, that she was just sitting out. I couldn't understand this as she looked an absolute picture. She was sitting with Miss Bowlingbrook, the club leader, so I felt quite safe in asking her for the next dance. I walked over to her, and with great politeness asked if she would like to dance again. To my amazement and embarrassment she declined. I remember that I stood for a while not knowing what to do, then I turned on my heels and went back to the other side of the room".

"Poor devil" said Polly. "I have often turned men down when they have asked me to dance, mainly because I can't dance, but I never realised how embarrassing it could be for the man. Mind you I don't think that they were quite the same type of person as yourself, and they didn't ask in the polite way you did. Never mind, go on".

Polly smiled and as she did so her hand moved higher up the inside of David's thigh. He noticed that her hands were very smooth and his heart began bounding when she started to squeeze the muscles on the inside of his thigh. She was a very nice woman and David was sure that she meant nothing by it and he hoped that she could not hear the booming of his heart. He tried to bring his mind back to how he had first met Janet, but he found it hard to concentrate and his train of thought seemed to have disappeared. Almost as if Polly knew of his dilemma she demanded, "So what happened then?"

David summoned up all the mental strength he could muster and continued.

"The next day we were taken home. I asked Janet if I could sit by her side and she said it was up to me where I sat. I remember she suddenly seemed very cold and obviously not interested in talking to me"

David remembered that about half way home things had started to go wrong. It was growing dark and the lorry had been bouncing along the quite bumpy road. It had obviously not been designed for carrying passengers. There was a sudden, bang, and the lorry veered all over the road. The driver managed to pull up on the verge and they all had to clamber out. Many of the club felt quite ill and some of the girls were sick. They had felt sick before hand but they thought that this was due to the fumes of the exhaust which were filling the back of the lorry. This breakdown on the side of the road improved the situation a little as everyone felt less queasy and after the wheel had been changed, which took about half an hour, they all climbed back inside the lorry and continued with their journey.

"Did Janet continue to sit with you?".

"No, she went to sit by her sister and Miss Bowlingbrook. There seemed to be a strange atmosphere at that end of the lorry and I was completely at a loss as to what to do about it. I felt really dejected and wondered what I had done to cause such a situation. All the rest of the group around me seemed to be enjoying themselves and it wasn't long before they all started singing amusing songs which I thought were a bit near the mark for a church youth club".

Polly tightened her hand around the inside of David's thigh and pulled it hard up against her. David could feel the silkiness of her skirt and the warmth of her leg up against him and he had to summon all the strength he had to go on with the account. He hoped that no one would pass near to his gate as they would wonder what was going on. At the moment the privet hedge at the front of the garden prevented anyone seeing the two of them sitting there. He was also very aware that his mother was in the kitchen and may come to the front door at any time. He swallowed hard and continued.

"I can't remember all of the songs, but one of them had a rhyme that went something like this. Oh Sir Jasper do not touch me, Oh Sir Jasper do not touch me. Oh Sir Jasper do not touch me, Cause I'm lying on the bed with nothing on at all."

David described how each time they repeated the verse they knocked one word off of the end so that the second time through it went Oh Sir Jasper do not touch... This went on until there was just the exclamation Oh where they emphasised the word with groans and gasps, the rest of the words were sung silently in their heads so that the tune continued. Suddenly, Janet's sister, Dorothy, had come to the front of the lorry and pushed in to the side of David. He had not spoken to her much before, but she was a very pleasant, well built girl with curly hair and a very kind, smiling face. He had noticed her before at the club and knew that she had a very regular boyfriend with whom she always danced and walked home at the end of the evening. She tried to explain to David that her sister was only very young and had no interest in boys; in fact she said that she was frightened by them. She said that she knew that things would obviously change in the coming years but at the moment he shouldn't be too unhappy that she didn't want to sit with him or talk to him.

"This, of course, I could readily understand and it made me feel a lot better".

" So, did you go over and explain that you understood to Janet".

"No. I just accepted the fact and thought I may be able to talk to her if I could just walk with her on the way home from the club after the lorry had dropped us off.   I was completely wrong there because when I approached her and asked to carry her case, she asked me to go away as her father was coming to collect her and if he saw her with a boy he wouldn't allow her to go to the club anymore.   So I went home after a wonderful holiday feeling really down in the dumps and with a pain in my chest" David had realised that must have meant that he had suddenly acquired very strong feelings for this very young, slip of a girl.

Polly released the pressure on David's thigh and moved her feet backwards ready to stand up.   "Poor David, that sounds as if it must have been the first time you had fallen in love.   I know how it feels, it's funny how something so lovely can hurt so much.   Now I had better go back to the party as they will wonder where I have got to.   I would like to hear more of the story later as it seems to me she is all over you when you walk past my door".   Removing her arm from around his neck and her other hand off of his thigh, she said "I know you won't come over later, so I will come back in half an hour and fetch you.   In fact we have some Tizer and cream soda which we will be wanting to get from our shed so don't let me down as we could do with a little help lifting the wooden crates".   With that Polly stood up and made her way to the gate.   As she reached the gate she turned and said "Now don't forget, I will be over in half an hour".

David felt himself shaking.   His heart was still going twice as fast as normal and his face felt hot and flushed.   He felt ashamed at his thoughts as he was sure that Polly was a very pleasant young woman who was showing him great friendship and all he could do was to think of the sexual pleasure she had given to him completely unwittingly.   She was a very warm attractive woman who aroused a feeling in him that he had been told was lust, but he must admit that it did feel good. Mind you, he would be very pleased to help them move the crates of drink for the children. At least he would be doing something to help someone else, even if it was only lifting crates. He had been so used to people offering him help, it would be nice to give a hand to someone else.   He wondered how he had been so open speaking to this young lady as he had only known her for a short time and had divulged many of the secrets of his heart which he had not been able to tell anyone else. He supposed that it was easier telling them to a complete stranger and she did seem genuinely interested in him. She was after all a very attractive woman and although his heart was still totally controlled by his love for Janet. She certainly had a certain something which attracted him. She was, of course married, and the mother of two small children and although he had told her all the intricacies of his love life he knew nothing of her. He decided that he would ask her about herself next time they met and not allow himself to be the centre of the conversation.

This account he had given Polly of how he met Janet took him back to when he joined the youth club in the first place and how he had come to go on the holiday. The only club he knew of was at the local church. He persuaded his two very close friends, Danny Cressington and Peter Stamp, who lived in two of the houses overlooking the little green and had attended the same school, to go with him. Now Danny and Peter were a little suspicious of joining an organization which they thought may lead them to making some commitment. They were all only fifteen years old at the time and although David had been to the youth club a few times with his sister and her friends the year before and had enjoyed learning to dance a little, he couldn't convince them that they might enjoy the mixing with other young people. David remembered the three of them going along to the vicarage one afternoon and knocking on the front door. They waited for a while, then knocked again. They were just about to walk away when a man in a long, black gown approached and asked them what they wanted. David explained that they were interested in joining the youth club and wanted to know what to do about it.

"That is easy" was the reply, "you just need to come along tomorrow night, that is Thursday, and see the youth club leader, a Miss Bowlingbrook. Just tell her that Father Goodlife sent you and I am sure she will be pleased to give you all the information you want".

So, that Thursday all three of them went to the hut that was behind the church and very gingerly went in. It seemed a hive of activity with someone setting up a record player, several older lads putting out chairs and a couple more playing snooker on a table at the far end. A rather nice young lady asked them what they wanted and if she could do anything to help. They explained why they were there and she led them to the small room in the far corner where they met Miss Bowlingbrook. She made them feel very welcome and said that they would be made to feel at home with all the members if they decided to join. The only small requirement was that they would have to attend the local church each Sunday for one of the services and would have to pay a sub of six pence a week. They were to go away and think about it and if they decided that they would like to join, they should come back the next week.

They all turned up the next Thursday, with sixpence in hand and joined. The only problem was that they were holding a discussion meeting that night and it was being conducted by the young curate, Father Kingswood and the theme was to be, "What part should the church play in the development of human relations". They spent the whole evening listening to boys and girls, a little older than themselves giving their views. Suddenly the curate turned to them and asked what they thought was the role of the church. The three boys must have looked completely taken by surprise as they all sat with their mouths open. Danny was the first to recover and said, quite forcefully, and as if he was speaking for them all.

"My dad said that the church was a waste of time, what was kneeling and praying going to do when houses need to be built and food ought to be found for the poor. All those in the church ought to get off their backsides and do a good days work".

All the girls had started to giggle and there was a lot of whispering and shuffling of feet. David recalled seeing the look on Miss Bowlingbrook's face, she had turned a kind of purple and her eyes were popping. Mind you, that could have been due to her pebble glasses. She was puffing and looked as if she were going to explode. They made ready to make a quick dash for the door when the Curate raised his hand with his palm facing towards the club members. Then, believe it or not, he said that he was in full agreement with Danny, and Danny's father, and what he had said not only applied to the clergy, but also applied to all those who attended the Church, young or old. He said that the Churches' role in the present age was to go out to the people and by their good works persuade more people to join the Church and come to the services. There followed a short silence and then suddenly all the group started clapping. After that they seemed to be more accepted by the group and some even started to speak to them.

David, Danny and Peter went to the Church for their first Sunday Service, but Danny and Peter found it too hard to accept. They found the chanting and the singing quite foreign and when they saw the Priest, Servers and all of the choir dressed in long dresses with necklaces around their necks they made a quick dash for the door. They already knew that they would have a hard time facing their other friends, especially the girls, who thought that they must all have been sissies.

The next week David went back to the club on his own, even though Danny and Peter said he was a sissy, and spent several evenings throughout the next couple of weeks just sitting and looking at the dancing and occasionally playing a game of table tennis. He didn't feel he was part of the club as nobody seemed to talk to him but he felt that he didn't want to be beaten. David heard them all talking about a holiday that they had arranged at a large house in the New Forest and was quite surprised when the Curate asked him if he was thinking of coming. It was going to be for two weeks in August and he forgot how much it was to cost, but he knew that he couldn't afford it. He had only the remains of his earnings from the paper round and that fell far short of the sum needed. He also knew that he could not ask his parents for the money as they found it hard to make ends meet; Dad earned only a low wage and he had five children to support.   David said that he was not interested as he usually went away with his parents, which was not true as a day at the sea side in a charabanc was their only holiday. The Curate said,

"Oh well, that's fine, but I am a little sad as I am sure that you would enjoy the break from the normal type of holiday".

The club had hired a lorry with a canvas top to take them to the New Forest and David felt a little sad when he stood outside the Church and waved them all goodbye. Father Kingswood, the curate was also left behind as he had to cover some of the services at the Church during that two weeks.   He said, however, that he was hoping to go down for the second week and he would be taking two of the club that could only make the second week. He also told David that the Church had funded one person to go to the holiday for a week and unfortunately no one had been able to take up the place. It would mean that one bed had been paid for, but would have to remain empty. He asked whether David had planned anything for the next week as it would be very nice if he could help the Church in filling the spot. David said that he would like to come, but he would have to have a word with his Mum and Dad to see if they would give their consent. With that they parted and David made his way home.

Believe it or not, David's parents were very much opposed to him going away for a week with the Church.   They said that they had never taken charity and were not about to do so now and anyway they were not too happy about him mixing with that sort of person as they had never been church goers and could see no reason for kneeling and saying prayers and singing hymns. David had the unhappy task of having to go up to the curate's house and explain to him about his parents thoughts on the matter.

The house was next door but one to the church and as he walked up the pathway of the curate's house he was feeling extremely nervous. He didn't know how he could explain to him why his parents disapproved of him mixing with the church people and particularly the young members of the youth club. He had no idea how he could turn down the generous offer of the weeks' holiday which Father Kingswood said that the church had already paid for and how he could avoid feeling that he was throwing it in his face. The door was answered by a large round lady in a white overall and wearing brown slippers. Her hair was pinned back in a bun and she wore glasses, which she had propped up on her head. David told her that he had come to speak to Father Kingswood about a holiday matter and was quite surprised to be shown into the front room of the house. He recognized it as the same type of house as Geoff's, the boy with the Jew's harp, and he was quite familiar with its lay out with double doors leading through into the back living room and a fireplace opposite the door through which he had just entered. It was furnished as a dining room and had a table by the front window and three chairs pushed under the three sides. The lady asked David to sit in the armchair on one side of the fire and went off to speak to Father Kingswood. He felt at a disadvantage sitting so low in the armchair so he got up and stood facing the window which looked out onto a poorly kept garden.

Suddenly the door opened and Father Kingswood entered the room. He was dressed in his black cassock and was also wearing a dog collar and although David was a little disarmed by the uniform he was pleased to see that he was smiling broadly and came straight to him with his hand stretched out in welcome. He said how pleased he was to see David and excused his dress, but he was to take a morning service in about half an hour. David said that he would come back later if it was inconvenient, but he brushed that aside and lead him to a small office at the back of the house, which was full of books, papers and newspapers. He asked David to sit down and sat in an armchair opposite.

He put David at his ease by saying, "I bet this is about the holiday, I hope that it is to say that you can come with us. I've now been released from my duties up here and been asked to cover the second week at Avon House". David explained to him that although he would like to go his parents had objected. He asked David why and, of course, he couldn't tell him the whole story about him not mixing with those sort of people. David said that he thought it was because they felt that they shouldn't take charity. Father Kingswood was very understanding and said that his parents were very much the same and felt that perhaps David's parents had interpreted the offer wrongly. He asked if he could come down to David's house and have a word with them. David told him that he thought that it would make very little difference but he could try if he liked. This was a big mistake! You could imagine what Mum and Dad thought about a visit from the priest. They said that the neighbours would think that someone had died or something and especially if he turned up in a car and parked on the other side of the small green opposite the house.

Father Kingswood did come down to visit David's parents and David remembered he opened the door to him. This time, thankfully, he was dressed in a sports jacket, flannels, a normal shirt and quite conservative tie. He asked whether David's parents were in and when he confirmed that they were, David asked him to wait just a minute to warn them that he was here. Ever since he had told Mum of the pending visit, she had polished and dusted non stop. The house had never been so clean and tidy and all Dad's cowboy books had been hidden away. When he told them Father Kingswood was outside they both looked aghast, then Mum whipped off her overall and rushed to the door to invite him in. After the usual introductions Mum invited him to sit down in the best chair by the fire and they began to chat about the weather and the garden. Then quite unexpectedly, Father Kingswood said to David that he had really come to talk to his parents and would he mind slipping outside. David was a little annoyed at this, but nevertheless went out into the back garden. He must have been there for about twenty minutes when Mum called him in and he was amazed to see them all sitting round the table drinking tea and eating some of Mum's cake. Father Kingswood then said that all was well, Mum and Dad were quite happy about David going to Avon House for the week and he would send details the next day. They would all meet at the church and they would go down in his car. David had no idea what had been said during that meeting, but Mum and Dad were almost glowing with pride and achievement. After Father Kingswood had taken his leave of them they spent the next couple of hours saying how nice he was and how down to earth he had been. He had treated them as equals, which they of course were, but how he had overcome the resistance there was to accepting charity, David didn't know.

Anyway, they all met up at the church the next Saturday morning and equipped with sandwiches and a drink, headed off for the New Forest. Henry and Doris sat in the back as they were a couple and wanted to sit together. David was pleased to sit in the front as he always liked to know where he was going. He had got to know Henry and Doris quite well over the last couple of days as they had been kind enough to ask David to go with them to play tennis at the local courts. He had never played tennis, but they taught him the fundamentals and he was just beginning to regularly get the ball over the net. They all got to know each other really well in the car and Father Kingswood had told an endless stream of funny stories and jokes on the way.

Suddenly David's thoughts were brought back to the present by a roaring sound which grew louder and louder and at the same time all the children in the street and the adults started cheering. Over the roofs of the houses came a flight of Spitfires. David did not now how many, but he estimated there must have been about six. A few moments later there was another loud roar and again a large volume of cheering as another flight came across the rooftops. David imagined that these may have been Hurricanes, but when there are a group of fighters it is hard to hear the difference. The only thing David guessed was that he thought the Hurricane was a little slower than the Spitfire. They must have taken part in a flypast at a procession, perhaps in London and were flying back to base. As the sound died away David remembered the feeling he used to get when the fighters and bombers flew over head to take part in the raids on Germany. He also remembered a little of the terror he felt at hearing the German bombers heading for London. That was a time when something was happening every day. To a boy of only four or five it was a mixture of excitement and fear. The neighbours seemed to unite into one family and the sharing of life with others was something which had never happened before. David's mind wandered back to the beginning of the war and how things changed and how people came and went without anyone taking too much notice.

Chapter 6

It was early 1940 and David was a little disappointed over the next few months. After all the excitement of that Sunday, when all the sirens were sounding and everybody had come to their doors and stood on their steps telling each other all sorts of frightening stories of how an invasion by the Germans was about to take place and how we were about to see aeroplanes flying overhead, nothing had happened. In fact, it was learnt afterwards that this warning had been a false alarm and no enemy planes had even crossed the Channel. It had taken place, however, at the time that Neville Chamberlain, the Prime Minister had let the nation know that he had received no assurance from Hitler that he would not invade Poland and so from that time Britain was at war with Germany.

The street was quiet with everybody busy about their business. David did notice that there were fewer men around than usual. Many of the jobs that had been done by the men, such as delivering milk and bread, were now being carried out by women. He even saw some of the council greens, on the corners of the roads, being dug by women. One old lady came round, one day, and, after knocking on all the doors in the road, gave the occupants a large reel of sticky tape. She explained that they had to stick a cross on each of the panes of glass of the windows. At the time, David was playing with his two best pals, Peter and Danny on the small green with an old tin can. They saw the crosses going up in all the windows and quite incorrectly assumed that this was to show that we were English and would let our aeroplanes know where we were.   In fact it was to prevent the glass shattering from the blast of either bombs or guns.

David, Danny and Peter had grown into very close friends.   They played regularly together and spent a great deal of time exploring the neighbourhood. Although there was always a threat of something happening their parents would allow them to wander off for hours exploring the park, River Wandle, the woods near the school that they were to go to later and the shops, where nothing could be bought but lots of information gathered. Danny would often have a few pence in his pocket, given by his dad, which he generously shared with his friends. He was a good looking boy with long, curly hair and a slight tan, which was always there even in the winter. He was always full of ideas of what to do and where to go. Peter, on the other hand, was much quieter. He had long blonde hair and sharp features. He was always getting in trouble with his Mum and Dad and received a beating very often for things that the other boys thought were very minor. In his back garden, however, his dad had planted an apple tree which had grown to some size and was covered each year with masses of apples. This, of course made him very popular with his friends.

David was always reluctant to leave his friends in the evening as he was normally required to go to bed early and they could stay up much later. Indoors, in the evenings, nothing happened. There was the same old routine of coming inside when the darkness started to fall, having supper, which was usually made up of bread, cheese that Dad had made out of the sour milk in a muslin bag, and pickled onions and red cabbage made out of produce from Dad's allotment, then a quick wash of the face and knees in cold water and then off to bed. There was one thing which was slightly different from the usual, however, on the hour, from seven o'clock onwards, Bill and Nancy would turn on the radio and they would sit with their ear close to the speaker and listen to the news. Each night they looked very worried, but usually brightened up at the end and said that they thought, and had been told by Mr. Stamp, who worked up at the hospital, that it would be all over by Christmas. David was quite upset by this as he and his two friends felt that they had missed all the fun.

Strange things began to happen. First of all someone had removed the large, ornamental iron gates to the local park. These were one of the joys of going to the park as they could all stand on the bottom rung and someone would push the gate open and closed to give them all a ride, in fact they had made it into a game and those pushing would get up such a speed that when the gate hit the stop all those on board would have to hold on for dear life to avoid crashing to the ground. The park field itself, which was about a mile across, well it seemed that way to David, had had tall triangular post erections placed at intervals of about one hundred yards. They were told that they were to prevent German planes from landing there, but all they seemed to do was to make a game of football that much more difficult.

One day, two men came along in a lorry. This was quite unusual as lorries normally went on the main roads. The two men took out metal saws and started cutting down the railings around the greens. David and his friends complained vigorously, as they had just managed to balance for the required two spans. The men took no notice and threw all the railings into the back of the lorry. They said that it would all be dropped over in Germany to teach them a lesson. One of the neighbours did remark that these greens could now act as a landing ground for enemy planes as he had seen a Tiger Moth land on the park a few weeks before. The men just laughed and drove off with the balancing bars in the back of the lorry. They were going round to all the greens and removing the railings.

Croydon airfield was not too far away and on Sunday mornings Dad would take the three children off for a walk over Mitcham Common. They would often see small planes flying low and suddenly rising up into the air at a fantastic speed. These visits to the Common were one of the delights that the children looked forward to. Dad knew the names of all the birds and would point them out as they went along. They would visit the ponds where they would study the fish and if there was ice on the surface they would throw stones and break it. After a long walk alongside the railway which crossed the common, Dad would pop into a large, modern pub on the main road and have a pint. They would all, then, walk across the golf course and back to their side of the Common. One more pint in the Goat, buy some winkles for Sunday tea and then back home across the park to a Sunday roast and vegetables cooked by Mum whilst they were out. Mind you, the meat seemed to be cut thinner and thinner each week and the piece of meat left over was made to last for two days and not the usual one.

All in all David's world hadn't changed much. He did notice on the Common, that a large area on their side had been cleared and barbed wire had been placed all around it. The wire was in coils and spiked down with metal rods and was impossible to get through. Inside they had noticed that large areas had been covered with concrete and enormous metal nuts and screws appeared to be sticking up from the base, but at the time they didn't bother to find out what was going on as it seemed too far away. Further up the road, on the right, just before the railway bridge and Mitcham Junction Station, rows of wooden huts had been built. Each one appeared to be supported on brick pillars about two feet high and the central hut had a tall flag pole outside with some kind of military flag flying. The huts had all been painted brown and green in stripes and their roofs were all green. There were very heavy metal gates at the entrance of the small side road and there were always two soldiers standing on duty outside armed with rifles which they held across their shoulders. Also, every now and again, one of the new modern fighters would zoom overhead either going towards or coming away from Croydon.They were much faster than the smaller planes, but they made a louder roar and made everybody look up. David imagined that the planes flew over that particular area of the common to keep an eye on the encampment although at the speed they were travelling it would have been quite difficult to spot any German spies trying to get through the barbed wire fencing.

One morning, during the week, when all was quiet, David, Peter and Danny were playing on the large green. They had just bought a pea shooter each and armed with berries from a local council green, were racing in and out of the bushes shooting berries at each other. Suddenly there was a roaring noise which grew louder and louder. One of the modern fighters came flying over the green and soared up into the sky. High up above were other planes with square wing tips. They seemed to suddenly break formation and started to dive. The boys could hear the sound of machine guns and other planes came to join in. They stood in wonder at the wheeling and turning of the planes in the air. Up 'til that time they had only seen small slow planes flying in twos or threes and just the occasional fast, two winged modern plane, but now, here in the air in front of them was a sight never to be forgotten. Danny, who knew a lot about everything was sure that the black planes were Germans and said that he could see the crosses on their wings. He was sure that he had seen one going down with a trail of smoke behind it although Peter and David hadn't seen any planes hit. The planes continued to dive and then soar up into the sky in a wonderment of circles and arcs. Their amazement was soon interrupted by Danny's mother racing across the road screaming for the boys to run across the field to home and at the same time the siren started up. They all reached their respective doorways and stood on the steps looking skywards. Their hearts were pounding and the excitement was tremendous especially when all the doors of the street opened and everybody craned their necks to view the battle overhead.

To David, the war had begun.

Chapter 7

Suddenly the world seemed to have changed. All the adults seemed to become one big family. All mothers kept an eye on any children that were in their area and all the fathers could be approached for help and advice when it was needed. Many of the younger men seemed to disappear for a month or two and then return to the street smartly dressed in army, navy or air force uniforms. David was very impressed by the eye-catching grey, blue of the air force uniform and already, at the age of five, decided that was the service which he was going to join. When the new recruits arrived home their first trip was to the St. Anthony's Arms where they were greeted with cheers and back slaps from all those present. They never had to buy a drink all the evening and they were often carried home dead drunk or held up by their young wife or girl friend, who knew that they must make the best of this short time together before they were shipped over the Channel or to some remote part of the country for more training. Bill treated these men with great esteem as he knew many of them would have to lay down their lives for the country and he made it quite clear to the children that their future freedom depended on these men and they should always treat them with great respect.

David noticed that his Mum and Dad talked a lot in the evenings quietly between themselves. This was quite unusual as normally everything was chatted about openly in the front room. Mum looked very sad and frightened, but Dad seemed to be more confident than David had seen him before. About a week later, to the great surprise and admiration of the children, Dad came home in a police uniform. He looked extremely smart having both a flat cap with a badge on the front, a blue steel helmet under his arm, a shiny silver whistle in his pocket and a truncheon hidden in a long thin pocket down the outside of his trousers. All three children had to try on the hat and helmet.

All had to hold and swing the truncheon and then follow this up with a blow of the whistle. The last joy had to be done as quietly as possible as Dad pointed out the other policemen would come running if they heard the noise.

Apparently, Dad had volunteered to go into the army, but, believe it or not, at thirty five, he was considered too old at that time. Nevertheless, the recruiting team had realised that Dad wanted to do his part towards the war effort and recommended him to join the War Reserve Police Force. This had been set up to fill the spaces left by many of the younger policemen joining the Armed Forces. They were not on a par with the professional police force, but would be called on to do the same duties. Just along the street lived Dad's sergeant whom he could call on at any time for advice and assistance.

One morning the boys went out to discover that a group of men were digging up one of the council greens on the corner of their group of houses. They were intrigued to find that the men were digging a large and very, very deep hole. Danny said that he had heard that it was going to be a new underground station for the shipment of arms, but as the other two boys didn't know what that meant they were inclined to believe it. After only a few days, Danny discovered his mistake when the men built a room, underground, and the roof was made up of a thick layer of concrete. There suddenly appeared a very strong door and just outside a high telephone post. All the sides were filled in with sand and all that could be seen were the steps leading down to the door, two layers of bricks and a large area of black asphalt over the roof. This was, they were told, an Air Raid Precaution shelter, and they should keep away.

Danny was still convinced that other things were going on in there and the boys would watch out to see who came and went from the only door. First of all there were lots of comings and goings. They saw, what they thought were secret radio sets going in, a large round, black metal structure, which looked like a heater, but this Danny said was only to mislead anyone watching. Finally, a whole group of men with black helmets with ARP written on the front and black uniforms went down into the underground hideaway. Danny again thought that this was ominous and David should report it to his Dad, who was, of course, high up in the police force. All their fears were dismissed, however, when Mr. Jones, the ARP Warden came around all the houses, introduced himself to all the families and told them that from now on, starting today, they must cover all their windows with blankets to stop any light being shown. This he said would prevent any of the German bombers being able to see where they could drop their bombs. He said that some rolls of black paper would soon be available, which he would bring round. He also said that he would be round later on that evening to see if all the families had obeyed the law.

Frantically the ladies searched for all the old blankets and curtains that they could find, with which to cover their windows. All the children helped to cut this to size and the dads got out their nails and fixed the blackout materials to the frames. By late afternoon most of the work had been completed and the outside and inside of the houses became dreary and dead looking. Later on that evening as all the family sat trying to listen to the radio, it was a favourite programme of the week, Tommy Handley in ITMA, there came a loud voice shouting outside, "Put out that light!" This occurred several times, then came a loud knocking on the door and an irate Mr. Jones stood there, red in the face. He gave Bill and Nancy a good telling off and said that he could see light coming from one of the cracks at the side of the window. Dad assured him that he would see to it immediately and he stood outside until it was done. Mr. Jones wasn't all that popular. Jack said that he wished Dad had been dressed in his police uniform, then Mr. Jones would have had a shock and not been so rude. All the children agreed that he was a very officious man and not to be upset in any way.

Two days, or rather, nights later, Mr. Jones came into his own. Bill had gone off on duty lasting from 6p.m. till 2 in the morning. It was about 9 o'clock in the evening and pitch black outside. David was ready for bed and Betty and Jack were playing draughts. Mum was at her usual occupation of taking apart old jumpers and cardigans, rolling the wool up into balls all ready for knitting into more jumpers, cardigans, gloves and socks. She was an expert knitter and would go at such a speed that David had difficulty seeing her fingers wrap the wool around the needles. Suddenly, and without warning, the siren began to wail. Mum had been told that she should take the children and go into the cupboard under the stairs for safety. They all thought that this was a little stupid until they heard the growing roar of aircraft. It grew louder and louder and they all raced into the cupboard standing close to Mum. David could feel her shaking and to add to the worry, Betty was crying and Jack was looking very white. David had never seen his brother and sister, who he held in great awe, so worried and frightened.

There began a whistling and screaming as if thousands of bees had been let loose and they heard the thump and bangs of heavy objects hitting the ground. There was the sound of the bells of fire engines and many men and women rushing around outside the house. There was, again, a loud knocking on the door and Mr. Jones shouting. Mum ran to the door and was amazed to find the front garden and the path outside on fire. In fact it was a blaze about five feet high and was a strange bright, silvery blue colour. The children came to the door and after their eyes had become adjusted to the bright light , they saw that there were fires everywhere, all over the two greens, two houses on the other side were on fire and the sky was bright as if it were daytime. Mr. Jones was shouting for help. He wanted as many people as possible to make up as much mud as they could, as pouring water on these bombs only made them flare up even more. He said, "The bombers have passed over, but we have got to get all these fires out as the large bombers will follow up and be able to see the target". Everybody put on their coats and rushed outside, the small ones mixed up the mud and the larger children and adults threw the mud onto the incendiary bombs. They were long and thin with a tail made up of fins at one end. Some had buried themselves into the paths and roads and some had gone through the roofs of some of the houses.

David put on his clothes and his dad's older helmet and rushed out to help Peter, Danny and many others to put out the fires. Mr. Jones and a couple of fathers were called away to see a lady round the corner who had one of the bombs, alight under her floor. It had come down between the two brick layers and was setting all of the floor on fire. They tried to clear out as much of the furniture into the front garden before the whole house went up in flames.

Luckily, for them, but not for others, the bombers did arrive with a terrifying roar which seemed to last for hours, but although there were still some houses ablaze, they passed over head and not a bomb was dropped. Minutes later, however, they could hear the roar of explosions taking place some way away and anti aircraft guns firing almost non stop. There was a bright glow in the direction of London and they all knew that they had had a lucky escape. They learnt afterwards that the incendiary bombs were most probably laid down as a marker for the line into London.

Dad did not come home that night, but after hours of worry, he appeared the next morning absolutely exhausted. He had been rescuing people from blazes and bombed out houses. He was pleased to find the house and family were all intact and then climbed into bed and slept all day. He told the children little of his exploits as he felt that this may upset them, but there were occasions when he would sit in the evening and recount a situation in which he had been involved.

Chapter 8

One day, while the boys were trying to light a fire in the bushes on the big green, Danny noticed that the fat old doctor, who nobody really wanted to see, went into David's house. He was accompanied by a lady in a uniform. Danny thought that this was highly suspicious, as he didn't recognise the uniform as being either army, navy, air force or police. This made the three boys approach the house with great care. Peter and Danny hid behind the hedge while David was sent in to check on the lie of the land. "If you are captured", said Danny, "shout out loud and we will run to the police box and phone the constable". David entered the house cautiously and was surprised to find no one down stairs. He could hear moaning coming from the front bedroom and decided that he would quietly creep up the stairs. He only reached the third step when the upstairs door opened and the lady came down. She took David into the front room and explained that his mother was very ill and did he know where his father and brother were. David explained that his Dad was at work and he had no idea where his brother was. The lady then went out into the kitchen, washed her hands and went back upstairs. David could not believe what was happening. When he left home this morning his mother looked fine, she had waved them goodbye and the only thing which was different was that she was normally smiling. This morning, however, she had tears in her eyes. David thought that this was because she knew that she would miss him.

He took out his marbles, which he had been collecting for a long time and which he stored in a cocoa tin, and started to roll them over the red patterned lino in the front room. He had invented a game where he would try to stop the marbles in one of the patterned squares close up to the skirting board. He had managed to get three in the box when he heard a terrible screaming from up above and his mother shouting. It seemed to go on for ages and he sat on the floor, too terrified to move. All he could think of was what would they all do if his mother died. Oh how he wished Dad was here, he always knew the answer to any problem.

After, what seemed like an eternity, David heard another crying, but this time it was completely different, very high and very shrill. He imagined that it may be the woman spy. His fears were overcome when the lady came into the front room carrying a blanket in which lay a small baby.

"Would you like to say hello to your new little brother? "said the woman spy.

Thus, little brother Bobby was added to the family. David went outside to tell his two close friends about what had happened, but was surprised to find that the hedge was not hiding two rescuers. He was very disappointed to find that they had given up waiting and were now having tea in Danny's house.

It seemed a cruel blow to David that they would now have to share the meagre rations with another mouth and he would most probably have to let him have some of his marbles. It also seemed even more worrying that even though so many things were happening at home, he was required to go to school. He had visited the school, which was situated about half a mile from his house, in Green Water Lane, when he went to meet his elder brother Jack and his sister Betty. They were well up in the school, Jack, who was coming up to eleven years old, was in the top class of the juniors and ready next year to move to a boys senior school. Betty, who was nine, was also in the junior school but only at that time in the middle class.

David remembered how, after the summer holiday of 1940, he started school proper and was obliged to spend the whole morning and part of the afternoon in the Green class, which was specially designed for the new children. They had funny ideas that all the children needed to sleep on the floor for part of the day and for that time they used to pull down the blinds and turn off all the lights. Luckily, Danny and Peter were in the same class, Danny being eleven days older than David and Peter being his senior by two months. At these quiet times they would make small bombs of the plasticine and throw them at each other or at a boy they didn't like. On occasions they would make paper darts and throw them around the room to the amusement of the other children. It wasn't long before the girls in the class told the teacher and all three boys would be sent down the corridor to stand outside the Headmistress's office. David remembered that she had leather straps on both of her wrists, but even so, would give each of them a slap on the palm of their hands. Danny was sure that she had been sent over by the Germans as she was always dressed in black and had thick pebble shaped glasses. She wore high, black leather boots and walked with a stick in her hand. Her office, set at the end of the corridor, was always filled with smoke and very often, the Headmaster from the juniors, whose office was situated vertically above hers, was sitting with her. Danny felt that this made him even more suspicious of their tie up with German spies. There were posters on the notice board which warned people not to tell anyone of any secrets, or speak of any secrets in public. These posters carried messages such as "Walls have ears" and "Keep your thoughts to yourself".

In the middle of the morning the children would be given a third of a pint of milk with a cardboard top through which they could push a straw. This always gave a welcome break to the childish stories they were read and at lunch time each child was given a small Cornish pasty, which, to some children was the only meal they would receive during the day. After the enforced sleep the children would be sent home. Very few parents came to collect their children and most had to make their way home on their own. Many, of course, soon gained new friends and they walked home together. David was lucky. Peter and Danny lived next door but one to each other. For them going home was great fun. They would run through the woods which were adjacent to the school and were on the way home. At the end of the woods was a small brook in which they could race small paper craft, or pieces of twig. Of course this was a little tame for the three of them so they would put their boats or twigs in the brook on one side of the road and then run full speed across the road to the other side to see which of the craft emerged first from between the bars of the storm drain. They would often follow the brook through the woods where it entered the local park, but this now meant that they must take the long way home, causing their mothers a great deal of worry.

One Saturday morning a football match was organized on the big green. Little did they know at the time that such a frightening period would evolve from such a simple game. Mike Morris, who lived on the corner five houses away from David, was picked by the opposing team captain. Mike was about a year older than David and was tall for his age with thick curly hair. Everybody treated him with suspicion as he was a Catholic and went to a different school from the rest of the boys. He was a very nice lad, good looking, quiet, but quite knowledgeable. He played good football and was an asset to the team he was in. About half an hour into the game the opposition came racing towards the home team's goal. Someone centred the ball and David leapt into the air to head the ball away. As his head hit the ball he felt a violent blow under his chin. Mike had tried to kick the ball into the goal. His foot had come up under David's jaw with such a force that it had made him bite his tongue, which he always had sticking out, between his teeth. When he came to, after a few moments, blood was pouring from his mouth. A group of boys carried him over to his house and into his kitchen where he vomited blood into the sink. Mum held his head over the deep basin and looked absolutely frantic. Dad, on seeing the situation, grabbed a pushchair, ready for Bobby, bundled David into it and started running towards the shops where there was the only phone. Luckily, as they reached the first set of shops one of Dad's colleagues in the police force came rushing over. On seeing all the blood he ran back to the nearby police box and phoned a police car. They raced up to St

Anthony's Hospital at the top of Ridge Hill with the bell on the front of the car ringing continuously.

David remembered being wheeled on a trolley at high speed down long corridors into a space ship room with large bright lights and everybody dressed like laundry men with masks over their faces. Someone stuck a needle into his arm and the next thing he knew he was in a room with two other children. The room had a large window and he could see the red sky and the tops of trees. When he woke a second time it was night time and a nurse was sitting by his bed. His tongue seemed to fill the whole of his mouth and it was quite impossible to clench his teeth together. He found that he had to breathe through his nose and this became very frightening especially as his nose seemed to be running all the time.

The nurse took his hand and rubbed the back of it. "How are you feeling", she said. It was then that David realised that he was unable to speak. All that came out was a mumbling sound. He was normally a great talker and was often told by his adults to be quiet. In fact his Grandmother, who did not like him too much, would often say to him, "Children should be seen and not heard". In fact that is about all she would say to him. She was always dressed in black with a woollen cardigan over the top part and a long black skirt down to the floor. She always wore black leather boots and a flat pork-pie style hat on her head, which was held in place by a ribbon under the chin. David was sure that she wore the same clothes day and night as he never saw her in anything else. She lived in London with David's aunt who seemed to like him even less than his Gran as she would spend all the time she saw him telling him off or smoking non stop. David never knew what he had done to the pair of them to make them dislike him so much but imagined that he had been naughty at some time. On the other hand, Jack and Betty were highly liked by the two of them and Gran thought that the sun shone from Jack's bottom.

The nurse leaned over David's bed with a glass of a lemony looking drink in her hand. "Do you think that you could drink a little drop of this? It will quench your thirst and help to reduce the swelling in your tongue" David lifted his head but found it quite impossible to swallow any of the fluid. "I know what will help" she said, and putting down the beaker on the side table, turned and walked out of the ward. A short time later she returned with a straw and putting it into the drink in the beaker held it up to David's mouth but with little success. He lay back on the pillows and within seconds was fast asleep.

The next morning he woke feeling a little better. His mouth was still full of tongue and he could feel the hard stitches in the top and the bottom but the pain was a little less both in his tongue and his jaw. He sat up in the bed and suddenly realised that he was very, very thirsty. He reached out and took the beaker of lemon drink with the straw and slipped it between the roof of his mouth and his tongue. He sucked on the straw and although it caused him to go into a violent coughing fit, he did manage to swallow some of the drink. He remembered that it was a very pleasant taste and spent some time drinking a little at a time. The boys in the next beds came over to him and asked him what he was in hospital for. He tried to tell them, but they were unable to make out what he was saying and after a short time they lost interest and went over to a small window into the next ward in which David noticed there were girls. One was tall and had long curly hair and spoke very nicely. She enquired about David, but one of the boys said, "We think he is not all there", which annoyed David intensely.

David drank as much of the drink as he could, but spent most of the day in bed. The next day, however, he woke early, was given a bowl to wash his face and hands and was allowed to get out of bed. To his relief, his tongue had decreased in size a little and he was able to mumble some words. When the boys heard that he had been injured in a football match and rushed to hospital in a police car, their attitude changed. They were full of admiration and even went as far as explaining it to the girls next door. That afternoon, he and his two new friends played with some of the toys that were available in the ward. They were in the middle of a game of snakes and ladders when they heard the sirens sounding. The girls started hammering on the window between the wards. They were pointing at the outside window and were obviously very excited. The three boys went to their panoramic window and to their horror saw masses of large black aircraft flying straight at the hospital. They started to count them, but it was impossible, there must have been hundreds of them. The sky grew dark with their number and they thought that they could not survive such an onslaught. They knew that they were German planes as they had the distinctive cross on their wings and they all seemed to be painted black. Suddenly all the doors of the wards opened and nurses, doctors, porters and cleaners all came rushing into the rooms and hurried the children into the corridors. There they raced along between beds and trolleys all containing patients. Some had tubes attached to bottles which were hooked on to either the top or bottoms of the beds. They were all heading for the centre of the hospital. It was a complete panic. The lifts were blocked by beds and the stairs were jammed by people carrying patients down to the basement. After about ten minutes they heard the non-wavering sound of the all clear and the panic ceased. The bombers had all passed overhead and not a bomb was dropped.

The next day outside the windows David saw men standing on wooden boxes and hanging on ropes, painting the outside of the hospital with stripes of green and brown. The hospital had been a shining white and stood on the top of Ridge Hill. It was apparently very visible from the air and was a marker for bombers heading from the coast into London. Again, they had had a lucky escape. David did wonder how long they could be so lucky. They all made their way back to their wards and the game of snakes and ladders continued. That evening David even went to the adjoining window and tried to speak to the girls, but due to his swollen tongue could only manage a mumbling type of conversation. He was greeted by roars of laughter from the younger ones. The older, taller girl with long curly hair showed great concern and tried to encourage him to speak more. David thought that she was very beautiful and kind and although he was only five years old at the time, he was sure that she was his first love. He felt that because she encouraged him to speak, it helped to reduce the swelling in his tongue and his road to recovery. He was discharged from the hospital the next day and never saw the girl again, in fact, he didn't even know her name. He had a deep hurting feeling in his chest and he felt extremely sorry that he hadn't even bothered to find out where this young girl lived or what school she attended. All he knew was that she was very kind and had done a great deal to help him overcome the difficulties he was having with his speech and communication with other children without looking and sounding as if he was also mentally disturbed. He had so looked forward to his mother coming up to fetch him and take him home. When she arrived she looked very nice in her new coat which Dad had bought for her the Christmas before last. Well he hadn't actually gone out and bought it for her, she had gone out on her own and spent hours combing the shops for the cheapest and nicest coat she could find as she knew Dad would have to struggle to find the cost from his allowance which remained after the housekeeping had been surrendered. Anyway, she looked warm and lovely to David as she hugged him tightly and produced the paper carrier bag containing his clothes. He was pleased to see that she had brought his favourite jacket, navy blue, short and buttoned up the front right up to the neck.

As they left the ward he waved goodbye to all the friends he had only recently acquired, wished them luck in the future and followed Mum down the stairs and out into the open air. He remembered how strange it felt breathing in the cool, clean air and even though he had only been there for a week, how strange everything seemed. This was not surprising, as things had changed dramatically in that short time and the world he was going home to would make him grow up quicker than his years, and the sounds and sights of the near future would leave a deep and memorable scar for the rest of his life.

Chapter 9

As David walked home from the hospital, with his mother, he noticed great changes had taken place and everybody was busy rushing here and there and lorries and horse and carts were carrying heavy loads of what looked like large, curved corrugated metal strips. On the large green, opposite the hospital, many older men and women were digging deep holes and the earth was being piled up at the sides. When they reached home Jack and Betty came in from the back garden to welcome him home but they were a little disturbed when they heard him speak as the stitches which had been inserted in the top and bottom of his tongue were still in place and his tongue was still a little swollen. They all went straight into the back garden where Dad was digging hard. His head was just visible above a large pile of earth and he appeared to be up to his waist in a square hole. He and Jack had been digging all morning and were both exhausted. Dad had been given the dimensions of the hole which was necessary and they were to expect their Anderson Shelter to arrive within a few days.

Mum had been told by the sister at the hospital that David was to drink as much as he could over the next week or so to help to reduce the swelling of his tongue. As was her want, Mum always overdid any instructions given and he was made to drink a large glass of water every hour or so. He remembered that in the hospital they had given him a large jug of very tasty sweet lemon squash and he was more than willing to drink this at anytime, he even shared it with the boys in the ward, but just plain water was not his favourite drink. Anyway, after polishing off the large glass full he went out in the street to see his mates, Danny and Peter. They were in Danny's garden, where several men were digging an enormously long trench. It seemed to be as wide as the hole that Dad was digging, only this time it stretched the whole length of Danny's garden and into two others.

David found Danny and Peter with three other small boys making a camp at the back of a garden shed. When they saw David, they ran over and welcomed him home. Danny said that he had so much to tell him that they ought to go into the camp as secrecy was vital. When David said how pleased he was to be home, his two friends burst out laughing and started to mimic the way that he spoke. This went on for some time and David was more than a little upset by their reaction, but when he pointed out the large gash across his tongue and the black stitches sticking out like wires holding the edges together, they looked aghast and settled down to some sensible talk. Danny led them into the camp, which was a low grey structure made up of an old blanket, the covering material of a flock mattress and a series of branches of a tree. They all climbed in under the hidden opening, including three other boys who were unknown to David, which meant that they were having to sit with their legs over each other.

Danny began telling some of the story of the last two weeks. It started with the tale of poor Mike, who had been the reason for his operation and stay in the hospital. Although it was not his fault, Danny said that he had been given a good clout by his Dad and been made to stay indoors, in fact they had not seen him since. Danny was sure that he had been beaten so hard that he was most probably either dead, or unable to walk. He said that the three other boys, Terry, Tommy and Billy were all in their class at school and had been made members of Danny's gang. They all went to school together as they had been told by the head teacher that they should stay in small groups if possible for their safety. Danny added that this was in case any of them were captured by the Germans. She had also said that, if they were nearer to home when a siren started up, they should run for home, but if they were nearer school they should run to the school. Danny said that he felt that it was safer to run home, unless you were at the school gates, as their mums could look after them better and they knew that they were safe. They decided that they would all meet outside the warden's shelter each morning and decide on their approach to the day ahead.

Over the next week they all met up and went to school together. Tommy was a little smaller than the rest of them and they all kept an eye out for him. His mum used to bring him to the corner and thank them all for looking after him on the way to and from school and he was always so pleased to be included in the group. David had a soft spot for Tommy as he seemed to look up to them all and was not put off by other boys calling him names. His dad was a sailor and was always away at sea. Tommy always said that soon his dad was coming home on leave and then he would bring him to the corner instead of his mum. The other two boys, although shorter than David, looked quite tough. Billy was very scruffy, he always had the same old jumper on which was a sort of brown colour, a pair of torn short khaki trousers and a pair of boots that may have been his elder brothers or his dad's. He always had a runny nose, which he never wiped so that it ran down into his mouth and was often a greenish colour. Nevertheless, he was a boy you could rely on if you got into a fight. Terry, on the other hand, was quite posh and spoke in a funny way. He always wore the same clothes, but his jacket looked strong and fairly new and his short trousers almost met his long socks at the level of his knees.

In that week the siren sounded twice while they were on their way to school. The first time they were just approaching the woods, which was just over half way. They all turned tail and ran as fast as they could to Danny's house. Unfortunately for the boys, the "all clear" sounded almost immediately and Danny's mum sent them straight back to school. The second time the siren sounded as they were approaching the school gates. They could have actually been there ten minutes earlier, but Peter suggested that they should slowly stroll the last hundred yards. At the sound of the siren they all ran full speed back home, but this time they went to Tommy's house. Tommy's mum was very pleased to see them all and offered them

61

drinks. Danny explained that they had gone to her house as it was the nearest and they were afraid of being caught by some stray fighter. Tommy's mum was very impressed and thanked Danny for his good judgement, which made him feel very proud. It was quite untrue, of course, as Tommy's house was the furthest away and Danny knew that she would not rush to send them back to school. Strangely, although there were no planes or bombs that they could hear, it was almost an hour before the "all clear" sounded and they strolled off to school.

The school playing fields had been covered by rows and rows of concrete shelters. Some were for the infants, some for the juniors and the rest for the seniors. The only seniors in the school were girls; senior boys had to transfer to another school in another part of the estate. Nearly every morning the school would have a practice evacuation of the classrooms to the shelters. At first they gave a warning of the time of the alarms sounding, but as time went on they would sound them at random. Danny was sure that the teachers had been warned as they never had too many books or papers out at the time of the alarm. He could spot the tell tale signs and would warn his group that an alarm was imminent. They then would carefully make their way to the side of the door and as the alarm started the boys would be out of the door, across the play ground, through the gates to the sports field and down into the shelter. They were always first and who should be waiting in the shelter but the Headmistress. After a week or two of this achievement, Danny, Peter, David, Terry, Tommy and Billy were all given a special gold star, which was presented to them at the assembly in the main hall in front of all the infant school. On showing the stars to Tommy's mum she was overjoyed and thanked the rest of the boys for looking after Tommy so well. She even gave Danny a tight hug, which made the rest of them a little jealous as she was a very attractive mum with a warm, soft bosom.

Going to the shelters was great fun at first. It meant missing quite a lot of time working in the classroom and although the teachers tried to keep the classes separate, it was good fun moving around from class to class. Later it lost all its attraction when the teachers got their act together and even started to bring work down with them so that the class could continue. At the end of each of the shelters were two portable toilets which were quite open for anyone to see. Some of the smaller children found it quite difficult to hang on until they got back into the usual school toilets, so they would have to pay a visit in front of the whole infant school. Many of the girls would giggle and point to the unfortunate boys who stood up to do their business. Later, when the practice became a reality and the siren went, the guns started up and the sound of aircraft could be heard, all the rehearsals became invaluable. The classes quickly emptied, the children ran fast across the playground and into the shelters. All took their place on the benches on either side of the shelter and they all sat and waited. Many times the aircraft came overhead and the guns would open up. Heavy booms could be heard and everyone sat in terror waiting for the next explosion. The only movement in the shelter was a column of children making their way to the end of the shelter to the toilets and there was always a group around them. Normally, within half an hour the "all clear" would sound and after a reasonable pause they would make their way back to the classroom.

It was about this time that David remembered that they had one of the first major local raids of the war. Most of the raids up until then had been aimed at London and the docks. They would see or hear masses of heavy bombers passing overhead. They would all huddle into the cupboard under the stairs and Mum and the baby plus all three older children would stand or sit in terror in the dark, hoping that the German bombers would all pass over without dropping any of their load. The siren normally went late in the evening and after hearing the heavy thuds of bombs being dropped a long way to the north, the all clear would sound and they would all return either to bed or to listen to the radio, that is if Dad had remembered to get the accumulator charged. They all knew that in the next hour or so the siren would go again as some of the stray bombers who had not completed their mission or had been damaged, would fly back overhead and, perhaps, drop the bombs they had left. On this particular occasion Betty, David and the baby had all gone to bed while Jack and Mum were still up. The siren sounded and almost before the baby could be removed from the cot and the younger children were up from their beds, there was an almighty burst of very loud explosions. The house shook violently and the ceiling in the back bedroom split across and came crashing down onto the dressing table and foot of the bed. Many of the windows shattered and Mum and Betty started screaming. Mum raced into her bedroom and snatched the baby from the cot. In the meantime Jack had rapidly climbed the stairs to get Betty, who was putting on a coat, she said, in case she would have to go outside and David was down the stairs and in the cupboard almost before the flashes of the explosions had disappeared. The terrible sound went on for about ten minutes with the house shaking and unknown objects throughout the house falling. Then, as suddenly as it had all begun, the noise stopped and the all clear sounded.

There was a knock on the door and Mum, baby in arms, went to open it. Mr. Stamp stood there in his shirt sleeves, the front was open to the waist, and his black, grubby looking trousers held up with thick braces and a belt which was undone at the front. He enquired if they were alright as he knew that Dad was on night shift and wouldn't be there. David was so impressed, even at his age, that anyone could be so kind as to check on the neighbours so quickly. After Mum assured him that all was well, although she thought that we had some damage to the ceilings upstairs, we all went to the door. All the neighbours were outside, many of them leaning on their gates, discussing the violent attack. They could see in the distance to the north a bright red sky and they could hear the thuds of bombs being dropped. Mr. Stamp turned to Mum and said, "Some poor sods are getting it. I'll go round to the Warden's Shelter and see what's going on". It was the first time David had heard Mr. Stamp swear in front of the children, but in these particular circumstances, it didn't seem too bad. Mind you it wasn't the last time they heard him swear; in fact it seemed to grow more profuse as the war went on.

When Mr. Stamp returned he said that he was getting a group of volunteers together to help the Warden. Apparently it wasn't enemy bombs which had caused all the noise and damage; it was the new anti aircraft guns that had recently been installed on the common, about a half a mile away. Many of the residents had had quite serious damage to their houses, but fortunately, there were very few people injured. There was the sound of an ambulance bell, but the Wardens had first aid kits and were administering bandages and dressings to those who needed them. In those times most mothers knew how to handle quite serious injuries and very few had to go to the doctor and a visit to the hospital was very rare. Everybody was extremely thankful for any help they received and there was always a neighbour who knew more than the rest. Mr. Stamp soon had his little band of helpers and he went off, still dressed as he was when he came to the door, obviously in charge and looking a little bumped up with his sudden importance.

By the time Dad arrived home the next morning, which was strangely a lot later than normal, they had cleared all the debris from the upstairs rooms and made a pile of it outside the front gate on the green. Dad didn't seem as happy as normal and the blowing the whistle and trying on the helmet did not go down in the usual way, with laughter and merriment. He sat at the kitchen table and put his arm around Mum and the children saying how pleased he was to see them all well. All three children sat with him while Mum made him a cup of tea. Jack was the first to break the silence and asked Dad if he knew about the guns being installed on the common. He said, yes, he knew that they were being installed, but did not know when they would be set into action. Jack then asked if he had been around the area when the raid started. Dad replied, "Yes, I was at first, but a problem occurred some miles away and I was redrafted to go and help to sort it out".

"Tell us what happened Dad", asked Jack, "we haven't seen you looking so down for a long time". The other children muttered in agreement and Mum said, "You might just as well tell us Bill as we won't get a minutes peace until the children know".

With that Dad started to tell them all about his nights work. "It was late evening when the guns first started. We had all taken up our first aid kits as we knew whenever there was a raid, even though no bombs dropped, there would be people who would be injured. I was summoned to the sergeant's office, where he told me that a land mine had been dropped over near to Worcester Park. The bomb disposal man was going in to defuse the bomb as it was very close to many houses and needed a policeman to take down the information which he would relay to him. I was taken there by police car and arrived in about fifteen minutes. The local Warden was very old, but had managed to clear all the houses of people and had made a cordon around the area with rope".

"Couldn't he have taken down the notes", asked Jack. He thought it was a strange thing that Dad had to go all that way when this Warden was already on hand.

"No, that was not his job and anyway he couldn't hear too well. I lay on the ground about a hundred yards away from the bomb at the side of a small thin man, who was dressed in an old raincoat, large brown boots and wore thick metal rimmed glasses. He obviously had worn a trilby hat, but this he had placed at the back of a pile of sand bags that were in front of them. He introduced himself to me by his christian name, Bert, and explained to me that this bomb was a large one. He had had a provisional look at it while I was on my way and said that it was controlled by a timing device. He had no idea how long they were usually set for, but they normally went off within a few hours. I asked him how it had landed in these gardens from a height without being smashed to pieces. He said that it had come down by parachute. He then explained to me that it did involve some risk and what he wanted me to do was to write down what he would shout to me, exactly as he said it. He would need to undo the timing device which was often sabotaged and then he would have to cut through certain wires in order to disarm the bomb. I said that I understood as we had had training in this type of operation. He then shook me by the hand, stood up and walked towards where the bomb had embedded itself into the garden. Some very brave men had dug most of the earth away from the side and this was obviously where the timing device was situated. He said nothing for a while and I was tempted to check to see if he was alright although we had been told not to move from our shelter, little though it was. There was absolute silence, which was suddenly broken by a shout of "Front panel open". There was silence again for about ten minutes and as I peeped around the sandbag I could see him pulling things out of his pocket and putting other objects on the ground. There was another shout of "Cutting blue wire". Again a long silence which was followed by several more shouts of different manoeuvres being carried out. I wrote them all down as he said them. I could feel the sweat trickling down my chin, but I knew what he must be going through... Anyway, all was well and I went back to the station to give in my report".

"Did he come back to speak to you Dad", asked Jack thinking that this story didn't seem to end correctly.

Dad seemed to have cut the story short near the end and there was a strange pause. Dad sat for a while as if he was deep in thought and then said, "No, he didn't speak to me, but all was well. Now kids, I am feeling a bit tired, I haven't slept all night and feel just about all in". With that he got up from the table and made his way to the stairs. Mum turned to the children and said, "Just keep quiet for a while. I am going upstairs to make sure your father is comfortable". She then followed Dad up the stairs.

They sat in silence for a while first of all feeling sorry for Dad and the hard night he had had to endure and then realising that all was not well. Jack then said, in a whisper, "I think Dad is a little upset and we should avoid making any noise for the morning". He asked the other two not to mention any more about Dad's exploits and said they should avoid playing the fool with the whistle and helmet. This they all agreed to and made a pact to be good for the next day or two. David only then realised the sort of job Dad had been doing and the danger he had to face when the demand was there. He also thought of that very brave little man who, without hesitation, approached and handled the most dangerous of bombs and risked being blown to pieces just to save others from the same fate. He wondered how many other men there were who did this kind of work and how they learned the art of dismantling a bomb which they had had no part in manufacturing. The enjoyable life they had had for such a long time had vanished and the world had turned into a frightening place and he could see no hope for the future. There seemed to be more bombers every night and they seemed to be quite helpless against them. Was an invasion imminent as most of his pals predicted, or could the British find some way in which they could stop this devastation and loss of life? To a six year old boy it seemed that the world was near to its end and he could see no way out.

Chapter 10

Over the next few weeks the whole estate was bustling with all sorts of people doing all sorts of jobs. Dad had finished the deep hole in the back garden although the loss of the russets apple tree and the very productive vegetable patch seemed a sad state of affairs. The rhubarb had been moved to another area which pleased Dad and he knew that it would be unproductive for a couple of years now and he would not have to suffer sour rhubarb and custard in the near future. Two men had arrived with a large horse and cart to deliver some of the sheets of corrugated steel that David had seen on his way home from the hospital and they said that two other men would return and help Dad and Jack set up the shelter. David had never seen such a large horse. It was twice the size of that which pulled the milk cart and had large, hairy hooves. It also seemed to have a very long mane and wore blinkers. It was a magnificent animal and when David said this to the men, they told him that he came from the brewery and would have to go back to delivering beer later on that day. The sheets of metal were very heavy and the two men and Dad had to take them around the next door's back gate and handle them over the fence into their back garden.

Nearly every night the planes would pass overhead and the guns on the common would start up. Now, of course, they were not worried about the noise or vibration of the guns and often stood on the step, the actual step that he was sitting on at the front door, and watch the flashes in the sky and the sweeping searchlights, which he thought must be situated in the same camp as the guns. They could hear the whistling noise of the shrapnel coming down from the exploding shells causing a sharp ringing as it hit the pavements and roads. They watched and waited for one of the planes to be hit by the guns but they always seemed to be lucky. On several occasions they saw flames coming from one of the aircraft and many times saw them caught up in the searchlights, but no actual hits seemed to occur. Many times there were two sirens, one when the planes were passing towards London and then again when they returned. They used to call them strays as they had left their squadrons and were making their own way home, obviously damaged in some way.

After the raid, and when the all clear had sounded, Jack and David would go out and collect some of the shrapnel from the roads and fields. It was often still warm and Jack said that it would have been red hot when it came down. One time they found a dark blue kit bag in their front garden. It had nothing in it, but it had German writing on the side and bottom. They wished that they could have known the story behind this find, but Dad said it was most probably jettisoned when the plane was heading back to Germany. Another time Jack found a knife which they all agreed looked foreign, but nobody knew. Jack saved all the shrapnel, bullet cases and other odds and ends in a drawer in the back bedroom and they all used to go up and admire the size and quantity that he had accumulated.

Another obvious change in the sky line was the number of barrage balloons. They looked like lines of elephants with large rounded bodies and enormous ears. They seemed to be tethered to the ground by long steel cables, but when the three boys went to discover what was at the end of the cable, they found a lorry with an enormous winch on a trailer. The one they had traced was situated on an area of marshland by the side of the River Wandle and when they approached the trailer, two men, in black uniforms and black steel helmets stopped them and asked them where they were going. Danny immediately shouted, "Run, run!!", and they all turned tail and ran for their lives. Later, when they reached the safety of the opposite bank of the Wandle and were near to some houses, Danny, through his gasping for breath, said that he didn't like the black uniforms and helmets and although the men spoke English, he thought there was something fishy about them. Anyway, the balloons grew in number and although once they saw a plane catch its wing on one of the cables, they felt that they were a waste of money.

One day, when they arrived home from school, two young ladies dressed very nicely in uniform, which was a sort of blue colour, were knocking on all the doors of the houses. All the neighbours were either standing or sitting on their front steps and the ladies were handing them khaki coloured bags with a shoulder strap. They went to Danny's house first and David and Peter went into his gate to see what was going on. They certainly didn't want to be left out if things were being handed out free. The ladies took out three boxes and gave one to Danny's dad, one to his mum and one to him. They then made them open the bags and take out the contents which seemed to be a short fat cylinder with a rubber face mask attached.

The ladies made Danny put the strap over his head so that the cylinder hung down under his mouth and the rest of his face was covered tightly by a layer of black rubber. There was a transparent slot level with his eyes so that he could see where he was going. As he breathed in, there was a sucking sound from the cylinder, but as he breathed out the rubber at the sides of his face flapped and made a rude noise. David and Peter could not stop laughing at this strange sight and when Danny started to dance around his garden making rude noises, everybody started to laugh, except for the two young ladies. They were very angry and after getting Danny to remove the gas mask they tore the whole gathering off a strip. They said that these gas masks may save their lives in the future and they must always carry the case with the mask in it, wherever they went. All except Dad, who had a large bulky case with a long corrugated tube, which went to a box on his chest. This was a special type of gas mask. They were all made to put them on and woe betide anyone who laughed, or even giggled. David's new brother was given a large pink rubber box with a window in the top. The ladies showed Nancy how to put the baby in the box and shut the flaps. David could see that Mum was very

71

pleased to retrieve her baby from the box, and would obviously only use it as a last resort.

In the evenings, when Dad was there, they would listen to the radio. They were particularly pleased when one of their favourite programmes was on. David remembered that they would tune in to Tommy Handley in ITMA, High gang, with Bebe Daniels and Ben Lyon or the Brains Trust and Dad particularly liked George Formby singing "When I'm cleaning windows". David couldn't remember when these were on during the war, but they were all very popular. During the day a new programme came on called "Workers Playtime". It was full of comics telling funny jokes and music to sing to. He used to like listening to this as it sounded as if things were not so bad and everybody was pulling together to make the best of the situation. It made him feel that the war would soon be over and they would all return to the wonderful days before the war when the sun always shone and the trees and grass were always green. Some of the songs that were being sung gave him great encouragement as well. Songs like "There'll be Bluebirds over, the white cliffs of Dover" and "Keep the home fires burning", gave him the feeling of a return to peace and plenty of food and even sweets and a feeling of safety from the almost continual bombing raids.

The paper of the day was "The Mirror", which had a whole page of cartoons. Names like Buck Ryan and Garth seemed to ring a bell, but one of the popular strips was "Jane", it wasn't so much the dialogue that interested them, it was the fact that sometimes she would be drawn nude. There was never any sign of the front of her torso, but, in those days, it was always worth hoping. The most important part of the paper, from the children's point of view was the map that depicted the progress of the armies, both Allied and Axis. There would be a rough map of Europe and arrows portrayed the advance or retreat of the forces. It was hard to imagine that these were real wars going on, it just seemed that that it was the progress of arrows, either black or white and they could cheer when the whites were advancing and they would boo when the blacks seemed to be getting the upper hand. There was a lot of booing in these early months of the war and very little to cheer about.

One evening Dad was out with the Police and Jack had been allowed to tune in the radio as a special treat. During one of the funnier programmes the siren sounded and as their shelter had not yet been put together, they all sat ready to go into the cupboard under the stairs. They turned off the radio and sat in silence listening for the first sounds of heavy engines. Suddenly there was a low moaning sound which grew louder and louder. There was a sound of high pitched whistles being blown by either the police or the warden, then the sound of heavy explosions. They all rushed for the cupboard and as they entered it the house shook and there was the sound of crashing buildings and smashing glass. The heavy explosions continued for a short time, but gradually grew less violent. The guns, however, continued firing for another ten minutes, then there was the sound of the all clear and they began to relax. They all went to the front door and stood on the top step to see what damage had been done. The houses all around the large and small greens were still intact, but they could see a bright red, glowing sky in three or four areas. They could hear the sound of bells ringing from either fire engines, police cars or ambulances. All the neighbours were at their doors and some of the men were heading off to see if there was any way in which they could help. The whole road was a bustle and everybody was frightened and worried. They knew how close they had come to having their house destroyed and how near they had been to being killed.

The next morning a whole group of children with Jack and Teddy, from next door, went to see what sort of damage had been caused. The first area they came to was just beyond the local shops. The road was cordoned off with ropes and there was a piece of red rag tied to the centre of the rope. There also appeared to be a white flag tied to the branches of the tree outside the centre house. A bomb must have hit the front of a house, or landed in the front garden, as the whole of the front walls of three houses was just a pile of rubble and the upper floor was hanging down over the stairs, which had more or less collapsed. There were the remains of several beds hanging over the edge of the upper floor and the bedclothes were flapping in the breeze. They all got as close as they could so that they could see what was going on. David looked up at the white cloth which was flapping in the breeze. He had a horrible feeling in his stomach when he realised that the cloth was actually the pyjama jacket of a small child. He pointed it out to Jack and Teddy who had not really looked up into the tree.

There were about ten men, some with helmets on and some in just their vests carefully digging in the rubble covering the front gardens. There had obviously been a fire as the remains of two of the houses was black and there was a nasty smell of burnt, wet rags. All the children stood in silence until a policeman came up to them and said that they would help the situation if they were to go away, preferably go home. They walked back to their street in silence and even though there was a lot going on around them, they felt too sad to take part. David couldn't get the picture of that pyjama jacket up in the branches of the tree out of his mind; no one would have climbed the tree to put it there. It must have belonged to a small boy about his age. He hoped that he was not wearing it when the bomb dropped although he knew in his heart that the explosion must have occurred during the raid the night before and he would have been in bed at that time. He was also very disturbed by the fact that the men in the front garden were not using shovels and spades, but were carefully taking the pieces of masonry off piece by piece and laying it to one side. A dreadful question came into his mind, "Was the little boy still under the rubble", and "Had he been there all night?"

Later that day, in the afternoon, a group of about ten men came along the street and started to erect the shelters. David was surprised how quickly they could put one up. It seemed that it all fitted very cleverly together. A series of large nuts and bolts held the "U" shaped pieces of steel together in a sort of arch shape. Then flat pieces were bolted to the front and the back. The front section had a gap for a door and the back section also had a gap for an extra escape panel. It was set about five feet down in the hole that Dad and Jack had dug. They looked inside and found that it was filled with a slimy mud. Later, however, a new group of men came round and lined the inside of the base with a wooden box. They said that more men would come round the next day and fill the sides of the wooden box with concrete. The door was fitted, the back panel was held in place by a long bar and even though it was not quite complete, the shelter was ready for use. It would certainly be safer than staying in the house if a raid took place. They were told that some bunks would be provided later, but if there was a raid they should go into the shelter as it was the safest place to be. David looked down into the shelter and thought he would rather face the bombs in his warm house than to dive down into this cold, damp smelly, dark tin box. How wrong he could be! After the lining of concrete was in place it looked a little better, but now it was dark, damp and very cold.

Nearly every night there was a raid over London. The drone of heavy bombers, the sounding of the siren and the sharp crack of the antiaircraft guns was a regular feature. Luckily for them only the occasional bomb hit their area of the estate and that was due to the fact that most of the bombs were meant for the docks east of London. Only the occasional bomber being in difficulties or have lost its way would then discharge its load on the way home. It seemed strange to David that with all the search lights with their beams sweeping the sky and the mass of shells that were exploding in amongst the planes, very few seemed to be hit. Another thing, there never seemed to be many fighters shooting at the German planes even during the daytime raids. Deep in his mind he felt that nothing they could do seemed to arrest the continual bombing of London and he couldn't imagine anything would be left of the city and the docks when the bombing was over and how about the people that lived up there, how would they survive the continual smashing of their houses and the fires that always followed the raids. They used to look out of their windows to the north and see the sky a fiery red which seemed to reflect on the billowing smoke that was spread like a cloud above.

The warden advised all the people in their area to use the shelters whenever they heard the sirens. Mum and Dad had made up the bunks in the shelter with blankets so that they were ready for use and regularly, when the siren went, they would all race down the stairs to the back door, which was always kept unlocked, across the tarmac area of the backyard and through the door into the shelter. They weren't allowed to use torches until they were in the shelter with the door shut as these lights, they were told, could be tell tale signs as to where people lived and the planes could either check their position, or drop their bombs. The shelter was damp and cold and everybody waited for the all clear so that they could leave the shelter and go back to their beds in the house. The race to the shelter, at any time in the night was becoming so regular that Dad and Mum thought it would be better for all of them if they started by sleeping in the shelter. Dad put a paraffin heater in there which was lit about half an hour before going to bed and they would all go into the shelter at the same hour, usually late.

David then found an enemy that he had not considered before and was equal to all the German bombers. The shelter became the home of some of the biggest, blackest spiders that he could imagine. To see one sitting on one of the pillows or found under one of the blankets frightened him more than the bombs. He couldn't imagine why he was so terrified of such a small creature that looked so ghastly and could run so fast. He remembered that he refused to go into the shelter and was only persuaded when Dad had been sent in and checked all the blankets, floor and inside walls and any unwanted visitors he would put into a pot and throw them into the garden. David didn't know at the time that his Dad had a horror of spiders as well and it must have been very scary for him to coax them into the pot. Danny said that he thought that these large, black spiders had been dropped by the Germans purposely to keep the people out of the shelters and make them easier to bomb. He also thought that they could be poisonous and would bite during the night when all were asleep. This observation of Danny's did not help a six year old boy terrified of these black, long-legged creatures, so he would strip the beds before climbing on to the bunks and search all the nooks and crannies for any foreign visitor.

The shelter did give them all a sense of safety, however, they were assured that only if a bomb hit the top of the shelter could those inside be killed. David told Danny that because they had joined all their shelters together they had made a larger target for the bombers to aim at and the chance of his shelter being hit was three times more likely than a bomb hitting his own. Danny always had an answer which would prove that theirs was the best. He said that if a bomb hit their shelter they could all escape into a neighbours garden, especially if the shelter became buried by the rubble and mud caused by a bomb hitting the house. Anyway, it became routine each night to go to bed in the shelter and even with the dread of the spiders and the sound of the bombers going overhead, they began to sleep quite soundly. Little did they know that it would not be long before they would have to share the shelter with a very much more dreaded visitor.

Chapter 11

The Spring of 1941 could have been a time for fun and games if it wasn't for this dreadful war. The world had certainly changed; all the normal things that boys did seemed to be spoilt by the fact that the future was so uncertain. Nevertheless, many things had improved. The friendship between the neighbours had grown so much that they all appeared to be one happy family. The mothers would help each other out at any time with shopping, looking after the children, cooking cakes, etc, whilst the men seemed to be available to do odd jobs in others houses if their men folk were caught up in some task to help the war effort. Any woman whose husband was away fighting on the continent or even further abroad would expect help from all the surrounding neighbours and people were always checking that they were alright. Many would be invited into others houses for a chat and a cup of tea, but most used to stand or sit on the outside step and spend hours discussing the future and the progress of the war. David liked to sit in with them and listen to the conversation as news was hard to come by and anyway there used to be odd bits of news about people he knew. The parents would send the children off to play when the conversation got round to anything really worrying and when they didn't want the children to hear. The children would gather on the road and play hop-scotch. The girls would draw out the chalk squares on the road writing the numbers in each and all the others would be sent to find "chippers", pieces of broken china, to throw into the squares.

Everybody seemed to be getting into a routine. Each day they would check the papers and see how the troops were getting on and how the arrows showing advances or retreats, was progressing. The news on the wireless was vital and there was always absolute silence when the broadcast was on. People went around either singing or humming the songs sung on the wireless by Gracie Fields, Vera Lynn and George Formby. Whistle While You Work and Workers Playtime seemed to bring some sense of safety to them all. The only part they found terrifying were the raids and the sounds of the sirens and the all clear. School was much the same. Many of the classes were now held in the long concrete shelters and learning anything was not easy whilst sitting in rows on either side of a central passage. If the siren sounded the children were encouraged to sing songs which the children knew, mainly hymns, such as "We plough the fields and scatter the good seed on the land".

The boys had their usual routine of going to school. Peter, Danny and David would stop on the corner for a short time to wait for the other three boys, particularly for little Tommy as he was always brought by his mum and she was always so nice and always thanked the others for looking after him. She was a very pretty mum and often put her arm around David and gave him a hug to thank him for being friends with her very precious son. Tommy was well liked by everybody although he was a little shy and quiet. He was always bragging about his dad, who he thought the world of. He was a sailor and looked after the communications. Apparently he could read Morse at a very high speed and Tommy said that he was very high ranking, although he didn't think that he was a captain. Anyway, he never knew where he was as his ship, The Hood, was one of the most famous and powerful ships in the British Navy. The boys always hoped that Tommy would be able to tell them some secrets of naval battles or sinking of German ships, but he never seemed to know anything of importance. Danny thought that Tommy's dad may be a spy and on some secret mission and that may account for the lack of information. This of course made Tommy's dad a very important sailor and Danny thought they should keep an eye open for him in the papers.

They all stuck to the same pattern of going to school. If they were anyway short of the school gates when the siren sounded, they would all race for Tommy's house, where they knew they would not be sent to school too quickly and they may even get a drink and cake. If they were at the school gates they would run to the shelter and just sit anywhere. That would mean that it would take at least half an hour to sort them all out and find the teacher that was in charge of them. Danny was only six, but even at that age he liked to sit with the girls and chat to them. Everybody, including the teachers, carried their gas mask in a shoulder bag and every now and then they would all be made to put them on and demonstrate that they knew how to use them. It was never necessary to have the practice race for the shelters now as the siren went quite frequently and anyway most of the lessons in the morning started in the shelters. If a raid took place at the end of school everyone was made to stay behind until the all clear was sounded. This would sometimes last for a half an hour after the end of school and all the children felt cheated of their time off. Danny went to the teacher several times to enquire if they would be allowed to come in half an hour late the next day, but was often answered with a clip around his ear. It was strange to think that very few parents ever came to meet the children from school and no child ever complained about punishment which was handed out to the children for misbehaviour. They all knew that if they told their parents of their misdemeanours that they would get another hiding at home as the teacher was held in high esteem and was always right. David received several smacks on the inside of his thighs or a ruler across the palm of his hand, but only twice received the cane, once across his hand, three times, and once on his backside by the head mistress, He couldn't remember what he had done wrong, it was often just for making a noise, or talking whilst the teacher was instructing the class.

One day, when the boys were to go out onto the remaining patch of grass to play football and the girls had a knitting class, David got into an argument with another boy. The boy was one of the gang leaders and had several followers. He pushed David over onto the floor of the changing room and they were immediately surrounded by a crowd of boys shouting and cheering. David got up and rushed at the boy, who was bigger than himself, and caught him a hefty blow on the side of his face. David had had many tussles and boxing practice with Jack and they had both become quite skilful in the punch game. Just as the punch was thrown, their teacher appeared at the door. She grabbed David by the scruff of the neck and dragged him back into the classroom amidst cheers and boo's from the onlookers. David was made to stand in the front corner of the girl's class room with a dunce's hat on his head. All the girls then laughed especially when the teacher gave him two needles and a ball of wool. "There we are" she said, "If you like fighting, perhaps you could make something for the soldiers". David had the final laugh, however, when he cast on fifty stitches and started to knit, one pearl, one plain at some speed. He knitted much faster than any of the girls and they all sat and watched. Betty, David's sister had taught him and Jack to knit, (only scarves of course), but little did she know that it would prove such a life saver in the end. David stayed all the afternoon with the girls and became quite popular.

As if things were not bad enough at this time, three things happened that made David's life less easy to bear. The first was an unfortunate situation, which, if it hadn't been for the nice people concerned would have been a major problem. When Bill and Nancy moved down to this area from Battersea, in London in 1934, David's aunt Lily, Dad's sister, Uncle Geoff and their three daughters, Jane, Doris and Sheila also acquired a house about half a mile away, on the same estate. At the beginning of the war Uncle Geoff, who was several years younger than Dad, joined the Navy and was immediately posted up to Scotland for training. This was going to take several months and as he had these three young daughters, they all decided to go up there to be with him during the training months. When he was drafted to a ship at the end of his period of training, Aunt Lily and the three girls came home. Unfortunately, whilst they were away squatters moved into their house and when they returned they were unable to get these people out. Dad went round with his uniform on and asked them to leave, but they refused. They said that they had the right to stay there and would not leave. There was no other answer than Dad had to invite Aunt Lily and her family to stay with him and Nancy. Mum found this very difficult and the only answer to the sleeping problem was for Jack and David to give up their room and sleep in the shelter, while Aunt Lily and two of the girls would sleep in their room and Sheila would sleep in with Betty in her box room. If a raid occurred during the night, which was quite often, they would all dive into the shelter and wait for the all clear. Mum now had to cook for three adults and six children and although they brought their ration books along with them, it was hard to make ends meet, as Mum would say. Luckily, after about three months the council found them a house where the occupants had moved away from the area to avoid the bombing, and Aunt Lily and the three girls moved out.

David and the family were just enjoying the space afforded to them by the vacation of the rooms when another more disastrous event occurred. David arrived home from school one day to find that his Grandmother and his Aunt Lu had arrived at the house and were going to stay. They lived in Balham and the bombing had been so bad that they thought that it was time to leave and stay with the eldest daughter, Nancy. This move by them into the Fellow's house was considered worse than all the German bombers dropping their entire load on their street. A bomb had fallen on the Hippodrome, which was at the end on their road and the whole place had burnt down, but David could see no reason for them to move into their house and ruin their lives. David had never got on well with his Grandmother; she was a very Victorian lady who didn't like children although she had had ten of her own. Perhaps that was the trouble. No child was allowed to speak in her presence unless she asked them to and David never ever saw her smile. Even David's Mum and Dad were frightened of her and she could make an atmosphere almost unbreathable with her cutting remarks. Of course, poor Dad could not refuse to let them stay as they had only just been relieved of Dad's sister and her family. Aunt Lu was Gran's right hand woman. Gran was always right and what she said went. Aunt Lu was a nasty piece of work and to add to David's dislike of her, she was a chain smoker and what with Dad's half ounce of Old Holborn with the additional lettuce leaf, the house smelt like an ash tray. Sometimes it was difficult to see across the room and as all the windows and doors had to be closed it became quite difficult to breathe. There was no where to go as they only had one living room and the kitchen so David would have to sit and put up with it.

David would complain to Danny and Peter and occasionally he would go into Danny's house for an hour or two. Danny had all sorts of ideas of how to solve the situation, but most of them were quite impracticable, like putting a skipping rope across the pathway to trip one of them up, or putting some poison in the tea. These were never put into operation. To add to the inconvenience, Gran insisted on having Bill and Nancy's room and moved in there with Aunt Lu. This meant that David and Jack lost their room again. Luckily Gran and Aunt Lu only came to the shelter once or twice and found that the racing down the stairs and climbing into a crowded shelter was not their cup of tea.

After about another two months they decided that it was as dangerous to live at the Fellow's house as it was to stay in their own house in Balham and now, causing more joy than they could imagine, they climbed onto the eighty eight bus and headed north. All the family helped them carry their belongings to the bus and David was as helpful as he could be, knowing that they would not return to stay again unless they were bombed out. David prayed that the Germans would spare Balham from their raids from now on and find their way to their real target, the Docks.

But the third disaster that occurred at this time was the worst of them all. One morning Tommy and his mum did not meet them at the corner of their street. This was not too unusual as sometimes Tommy would be sick, or his mum was not too well. They would just wait the next day for a little longer, but if they didn't show up, the other five boys would head for school. This particular morning, however, they were very surprised to see at the other end of the corridor, Tommy's mum sitting outside the headmistress's room. They went into their class, but Danny said he thought that he saw that Tommy's mum was crying. Peter and David didn't always believe Danny as he had a habit of exaggerating, but on this occasion, David could not see why he would say a thing like that. Time seemed to drag until the milk break when all three boys put up their hands and asked if they could be excused, which meant that they would like to visit the toilet. Feeling that the boys were up to no good, the teacher said that they could go, but she would come along with them. This hampered their investigation and they had to force themselves to pass water just to please the teacher.

At lunch time the caretaker came into the classroom and spoke to the teacher. She then asked the three boys if they would come to the front of the class. She said that she didn't know what they had been up to, but they were to go to the headmistress's office immediately. They walked very slowly along the corridor trying to think what they had done to be called to the head's office. This only usually occurred when there was a caning in lieu. They sat for a while trying to think of all the things that they had done which might merit this command to visit this area of the school which was normally out of bounds. Peter, who was the most sensitive of the three, said that he thought that it must be something that they had done in the race to the shelters at some time and they all tried to think back to any incidence which may have been seen by the teachers. They had all pushed others aside in the rush and the girls were always complaining. Danny thought that there was more to this than met the eye. He was convinced that it must be to do with the war, perhaps they had been selected to become plane spotters or to listen out for any children who may be linked with foreigners. David was sure that it was something to do with Tommy or his mum as that was the only thing that had changed in the past two days.   They waited for what seemed like an eternity then Danny decided to knock on the door.   A harsh voice shouted "Come in", and they all trooped through the door to face the headmistress.

Chapter 12

David was suddenly aroused from his dreaming by the sound of the latch being raised on the outside gate. He couldn't decide whether he had been dreaming or just deep in thought. All he knew was that his recollection of the war had become so clear that he imagined that he was back in 1941 and the memories were quite real. How many times had he sat on that step, particularly in the last couple of weeks, and enjoyed the freedom of wandering through earlier years and the comings and goings of himself, his family and his friends. He thought, at times, that he would not survive to the end of the war, but here he was now indulging in the pleasures of thinking back on what actually happened.

"Sorry, were you having a little doze?"

It was Polly, she had obviously not forgotten her promise of returning and asking for some help with the crates of soft drinks that they had stored in her shed. David was a little sad that these memories had been interrupted at such a crucial time. It was like waking from a very pleasant dream when you were just about to kiss a beautiful girl and you try to go back to sleep and continue where you left off.

"No, I don't think I was asleep. This lovely warm sunshine had lulled me into dreaming while I was still awake. I am glad you came back, did you want some help with the drinks?" With that David got up from the step and stretched. He must have been sitting still for some time because he could feel two painful spots under his bottom which had been resting on the hard step.

"Well, if you're ready to go, I thought we would just join the others for a quick cup of tea, then we can pop round to my house and get the crates".

"OK, I will just have to let my mother know where I am, I won't be a moment".   With that David opened the door of the porch which led into the living room. He glanced inside and seeing that the room was empty, strolled through to the kitchen, where there was a wonderful smell of cakes being cooked.

"I am just going across to the group of parents who are running the street party to help carry some crates of soft drinks from one of the houses.   I'll be back in a moment".

Mum had just removed one tray of delicious looking fairy cakes from the oven and was trying to prize them out one by one, without damaging the bases.   One or two had broken in half and the two pieces lay on the kitchen table.

"Would you like to try these broken cakes and see what you think?"

"No, the lady who has asked for help is waiting outside".   Mum was a little surprised as none of the family ever turned down the offer of the broken cakes, especially when they had just come out of the oven. She put down the knife she was using, wiped her hands on her overall and started walking towards David.   It was quite strange, although David's only thought was to help move the crates, he didn't actually want his mother to come to the door although he knew that if he said, "You don't need to come to the door", his mother would put two and two together and make five.   He walked back to the porch door with his mother at his heels and joined Polly, who had by now moved to the front gate.

"Hello, its nice of you to ask David to help out with the party, where is it you live?"

"Oh, only just up the road, don't worry, I'll make sure that he gets back OK", replied Polly.

David felt an absolute idiot, how could his mother make him feel so small in front of a young woman who was little older than himself. It was only a few weeks ago when he was completely free to go where he pleased, with whom he chose and do whatever he felt inclined. In fact he really had more freedom than most. His mother had taken on a very protective attitude now and was very careful about what he did and where he went. David went to the front gate and immediately Polly slipped her arm into his. Although David knew that this was just a friendly and kind gesture, he was painfully aware of his mother's eyes being upon them. He tried to remove his arm from Polly's grasp, but only half succeeded so that their hands became intertwined. As he closed the gate Mum called out, "Don't forget that Janet is coming round for you at seven thirty and you'll need to change and have your tea".

"Don't worry" called Polly, "I'll have him back long before then".

With that they walked off across the small green and onto the area of the big green which had been laid out with all sorts of games and tasks for the children. At the far end they came across a group of parents some looking after small infants who obviously were a little scared of taking part in some of the games. Polly went towards two canvas chairs which were empty, but before they sat down said, "This is David, he has kindly volunteered to carry the crates of Tizer from my shed, but before we get round to that I thought he would like a cup of tea with us".

At that several of the ladies got up and came over to them to shake hands and say hello. Polly went through their names, but David had a hard job to remember many of them. He did know a couple of them, Francis, Julie and Sophie, but the others were quite unknown. They were all very nice and said how pleased they were that he had come to help, although, David knew in his heart that they could have managed the carrying between them and he wondered if Polly had invented this task just to get him out there for the cup of tea. This, unfortunately, included a large slice of home made cake which one of the older ladies presented to him on a plate. Having no table he sat for a while holding the cake in one hand and the cup of tea on a saucer in the other. First he balanced the cake on his lap and after drinking half of the tea he tried to swap them over. Almost immediately the cup slipped over the saucer and spilt its contents between David's thighs. In seconds he was surrounded by ladies, one removing the cup and saucer, one removing the cake and another handing him a tea cloth to dry his thighs and shorts. They were all worried in case he had scalded himself, but he assured them that he was alright and after the necessary drying had been done, a new cup of tea was produced. This time, however, David refused the cake. Although David felt a fool spilling the tea as he had done, he was quite enjoying being the centre of attention for a while, an experience which seemed to have disappeared in recent weeks.

"Come on then, lets make a move down to my place and get the extra drinks before all the kids start coming back for refills"

Polly grabbed David's arm and accompanied by Julie and Sophie they crossed the small section of the large green and went down the road to Polly's house. David was surprised to see that her front door was open although many of her neighbours were at their front doors either leaning on their gates or sitting on their top steps. They were all chatting and laughing and joining in the festive atmosphere. They greeted the small group with cheers as they entered the front gate, through the front porch, living room and kitchen to the back yard. David was surprised to see that what they had been calling a shed was actually the large brick shelter that had been left in Polly's garden. It was fitted with a light and David noticed that along one side there was a row of deep shelves reaching right up to the ceiling.   On the top shelf was a line of wooden crates.

Polly pulled out a set of wooden steps and placed them in front of the shelves and climbed up to the top step.   She reached for the first of the crates and lowered it down to David.   It was immediately taken by Julie who began to carry it back to the party. The second crate was taken by Sophie who followed Julie.   Now came the difficult part, the second row of crates was at the back of the rack and Polly could not reach far enough to drag them forward.   She came down from the steps and David climbed to the top.   Polly held him from the back as he reached forward.   David felt her hands gripping his thighs and he also felt the front of her upper torso and her firm breasts pressing against his calves.   He slid the crate to the edge of the shelf and started to descend the steps still holding onto the crate to save it falling.   Polly did not move, she just let David slip through her hands until she was holding him around the upper part of his thighs and her breasts were up against David's buttocks.   Her hands had reached a position where she would know exactly how she had affected him and he stood on the bottom step unable to move.   He was completely overcome with embarrassment and pleasure as Polly slipped her hand up the front of his shorts and held him tight.   They stood like this for some minutes with David balancing the crate on the shelf and he felt Polly's warm, firm body clothed in its silky dress pressed up against the back of his thighs and bottom.   He slipped the crate into the lower shelf and turned to face her.   He had never had such a feeling in all his life and he realised that Polly was not just being helpful.   She crushed herself against him and he felt a slight parting of her legs.

David's mind was in a complete whirl and he was absolutely helpless in trying to resist his own temptation.   He had only experienced this kind of feeling a couple of times before in his life, once when he was trying to teach a female student to dance when he was at the Art School and she had misread the closeness of their pelvises to be an invitation to caress him in his private parts and the second time when he had first kissed Janet and felt her relax against him. They had both been times when his mind seemed to whirl and he felt a zinging feeling in his head. The first he knew was intentional and the student was quite aware of the effect she was having on him and if the place had been right, would have pursued her need. The second time was completely innocent, but this time David was very much in love with Janet before it happened. Both of these experiences had been charged with great emotion and a mixture of lust and love, but neither had been raised to the same intensity as this. He slipped his outstretched hand around her waist and onto her back and pulled her to his chest, which only increased his torment as he felt her warm, firm breast compressing against him. Polly let her head drop backwards and David was aware that her slightly open lips were about to engage with his. He closed his eyes and waited for the ecstasy which was bound to follow. They had had a talk by a Canon from another parish about six months before, when he had said that as Christians they should take great care of their commitments to persons of the opposite sex and should only meet in groups and should, at all times, avoid being on their own as a couple. He also said that kissing was a serious commitment and should only be undertaken when one was engaged to be married. Many of the girls took this to heart and would not kiss their boyfriends goodnight, which caused a series of rows and break ups that led to much heartbreak and tears. Janet was a devout Christian, even though she had only been in the church for a very short time and took the advice as gospel and refused to kiss David or even walk home with him alone, for some two or three weeks.

All his good intentions and all the learning about personal relationships, morals and faithfulness had been blown away and his mind and his body had one thought and that was to enter a new world, unknown as yet to him, but with passion, pleasure and satisfaction beyond belief. This shelter was a secret haven where they were hidden from prying eyes, what a change of usage from the safety it had afforded only six or seven years before when the German bombs were the invading menace.

Chapter 13

The three boys stood for a long time facing the headmistress's desk while she continued to write on a piece of unlined paper in front of her. The office smelt of stale smoke and David could see a cigarette end smouldering in the nearly full ashtray which was on the right of the desk. All the furniture was the light coloured wood the same as in their classroom only she had carpet on the floor and curtains at the windows. She continued to write with her scratchy pen and every now and again would lift her eyes just sufficiently to pop the pen into the ink pot which was sunk into the desk. Her hair was tied back in a bun and seemed to be held there by some sort of fishing net. It was pulled very tight to her head and made it look like a shaped, black ball. David noticed again that she wore leather splints around her wrists which were held in place by straps and buckles and it was only then that David saw that her fingers were twisted and deformed and she was having quite a difficult task holding on to the pen. Her fingers had the resemblance of gnarled oak twigs and he wondered whether they had always been like that or perhaps she had been tortured at some time. He remembered that she walked very badly and slowly and often used a stick.

"Sit down" she instructed. "There are some small chairs over by the bookcase". They turned and walked over to the bookcase by the door, each returning with a small chair. They looked at each other and for the first time felt afraid of what was to come. They had up to now, only been instructed to stand up when the headmistress entered the room and here she was now telling them to sit down. They sat down and waited.There was a long pause during which the headmistress kept her head down. After what seemed like an eternity she lifted her head and spoke.

"Mrs. Honeywell, little Tommy's mother came to see me this morning with some very bad news". David's mind raced ahead, he now knew that his hunch was right and he thought that she must have complained about the boys not waiting long enough in the morning for Tommy and his mum. He broke into the headmistress's conversation and said, "We waited as long as we could for Tommy, but we were afraid that if we left it any longer we would all have been late for school". Danny and Peter nodded in agreement, but before they could make any additional words of support, she cut them short.

"That is not the reason for me asking you to come to my office. Mrs. Honeywell has told me how kind you have been to her and to Tommy and how you have looked after him on the way to and from school. I am very pleased with the way you have behaved. Unfortunately, it is something more serious that she came to tell me and she asked if I could let you know and save her from the heartache of having to tell you herself. I expect you all know that Tommy's dad is in the navy?" They all nodded and David recalled how proud Tommy had been and how he always brought the conversation round to his dad and how important he was looking after all the wirelesses on board of his ship. "Well", she continued. "The ship that he was a sailor on was sunk and all the brave men on board, except for just a few, were drowned. Tommy's dad was not one of those that were picked up and he therefore was assumed drowned". She paused for a while to let the news sink in and then said, "I would be very pleased indeed if you would do me a great favour and not tell anyone in your class or at the school. I will say a little prayer for Tommy and his dad and mum in assembly tomorrow morning and to save you being quizzed by all the other children, I will allow you to go home early, in fact straight from here, to save you going back to class".

"What will we tell our teacher, please Miss?" asked Danny.

"Don't you worry about that, I will pop down to class and tell the teacher what I have done, there will be no problem for you".

With that, she stood up and walked around the desk. All three boys stood and then filed through the door, which she held open. She followed them down the corridor and when they came level with their class she stopped them and said, "Off you go then, just tell your mums and dads that you have been given a half day off for good work". With that she gestured as if to give them a push and unbelievably and for the first time ever seen by the boys, she smiled.

The boys raced off down the corridor, out of the door at the end and into the playground. They could not believe their luck. All thoughts of poor Tommy had gone out of the window and they were free to race home. As they were running down by the small stream that crossed under the road Peter, who was the quieter one and never really made any decisions shouted for them to stop. Between his gasps for breath he asked,

"What will your mum and dad say when you reach home and tell them that we have all been so good that the headmistress has given us the afternoon off? I know my mum and dad will not believe me and I may well get a hiding, or even the belt, for lying".

Danny and David agreed. Danny's dad was a little bit heavy handed when he believed that Danny had not told the truth and this he admitted was quite often. Only David thought that his mum would believe him, but he was afraid that she may send a note to the school to ask for an explanation. They all agreed that it would be sensible not to tell their parents and to go somewhere on the way home to take up some of the time. With that, they turned into the woods by the side of the stream and walked towards the park.

They spent most of the afternoon walking along the River Wandle searching for frogs spawn and making whistles out of broken off pieces of reed. They stood on the bank of the mill pond, which was at the back of the old leather factory and watched the large wooden wheel turning and splashing on the far side. It was a slightly frightening area as the old factory was made entirely of wood and they could see through the slatted walls the shapes of skins of animals hanging up to dry. Danny thought that he could hear the sound of animals being tortured and killed, but David and Peter could only hear the banging of hammers and the grinding sound of the water mill. They had been told that the pond in front of the mill was bottomless and on no account were they to swim in its dark and deep waters. Further up the river a new concrete bridge had been built and two huge, green corrugated doors barred the exit on the other side. The top of the corrugations of the gate was cut into sharp spikes and the bank on either side of the doors was protected by rolls of barbed wire. They crept across the new bridge and tried to look through the gap between the doors. They were securely padlocked with a thick chain passing through the post on either side of the gap, but they could not make out anything inside. Danny asked the others to lift him up on their shoulders so that he could look over the top. Even sitting on the others shoulders he could not see over the doors, so he carefully climbed up higher and gently held onto the jagged top of the doors. Inside he said that he could see hundreds of lorries and vans, he could not see any tanks, but he was sure that they were there.

Suddenly there was a shout from the inside and they could hear men's feet running towards them. David and Peter both turned to run and poor Danny had to grip the top of the door. He let go and jumped down and they all three ran like the wind down the side of the river until they reached the wooded area where the weir divided the main river from the escape stream. Here they hid in the bushes and waited for the sound of running footsteps. None came, but they hid for a while just in case the men were still out looking for them. It was only then that Danny showed the others his hands which were cut across the palms and both hands were bleeding quite badly. Danny and David had handkerchiefs which they wrapped around his hands. Having sorted out that little problem they found that they were now faced with something a little more dangerous. In their hurry they had raced along the opposite side of the river bank and were now confronted with one of three options. Either they went back to the concrete bridge and the prospect of being caught by the pursuing men, this they thought may get them into terrible trouble and who knows, could they be charged with spying and perhaps shot? Or, should they try to swim over the main part of the river, which looked deep and fast flowing at that point especially as the top six inches was flowing towards the weir. This was not an option as none of them could swim and the river was too deep to wade. Thirdly they had the risky option to balance across the top of the weir which was not very inviting as not only was the flow of water pulling towards the foaming water at the bottom, but the top was covered with a green slime which they knew would be very slippery. As the two first options were "no goers", they decided to balance across the top of the weir.

Danny was the one with all the courage and volunteered to go first. He took off his shoes, tied the laces together and hung them around his neck then stepped onto the top of the weir. He took great care and when he had reached the centre, he crouched down and looked back. He shouted to the other two to stay nearer the deep river side as the green slime was less thick. He then stood up again and slowly made his way to the opposite bank. The last three or four strides he tried to run and nearly fell into the deeper water. On reaching the opposite bank he turned to face the other two and said that it was easy, which was of course what one would say if you were now safe. Then came David's turn. His heart was thumping and he felt so frightened that he thought he was going to be sick. He also took off his shoes, tied the laces together and hung them around his neck. He then felt Peter's hand on his arm and when he turned he saw that he was shaking all over and looked as white as a sheet. Peter said, "I can't do it, I will have to go back". David thought that this was not an option and, putting on a brave face, said, "We will go across together, I will go in front and you can hold on to my hand, that will help us both to balance". Peter reluctantly agreed and putting his shoes around his neck they both set off from their side of the weir. All went well until they were about three quarters of the way across the stream. A man at the bottom of the weir shouted to them, they couldn't make out what he said, but it was enough to make Peter turn and with that he lost his footing and went sliding out of control down the weir into the bubbling water at the bottom. David made a dash for the opposite shore and they went racing down the river bank to look for Peter. Just below the foaming waters on the bank they saw a man pulling Peter from the water. Both were soaking wet and Peter was spluttering and coughing. After making sure that Peter was OK, the man gave all three of them such a telling off that it made their stomachs wretch with fear. He said that if he saw them anywhere near those gates again he would inform the authorities and they and their parents would be sent to jail.

They walked down the river to the little iron road bridge and then examined Peter. He seemed no worse for wear except that his clothes were soaking wet and the back of his trousers and shirt were covered with green slime. They tried to rub it off, but with little success. All this was forgotten when just as they were about to leave the river Peter spotted a small pond which was full of frogs spawn. They found an old tin and almost filled it with this valued find and with that they started up the road towards their homes.

Half way up the road there was a police box with a blue light at the top which was on. This meant that there was a policeman inside and this was confirmed by a bike leaning against the back of the box. Danny suggested that they should walk on the other side of the road in case the policeman had been told of their exploits down by the river, but just as they were level with the box the door opened and the policeman came out. They continued to walk up the hill with their faces towards the houses. Suddenly the policeman shouted to them from across the road. They began to run until David realised that the policeman was Dad's friend who had been so kind to him when he had bitten his tongue playing football. He called to the others to stop and went across the road to say hello. He was most interested in the progress David had made after biting his tongue and David showed him the scar which was just about healed. The other two came back to the box and when the policeman saw Danny's bandages he enquired as to what he had done. Danny said that he had tried to pull a milk crate out of the river and had cut his hands in doing so. He then turned to Peter and asked him how he had soaking wet clothes and green all over his back. Peter pointed out that he had fallen in the river while trying to help Danny pull the crate out. The policeman then turned back to Danny and said. "Let me have a look". Danny took off the handkerchiefs and opened his hands. "I had better clean those hands up" he said and opened the door of the box. It was very small inside, but in a cupboard at the side there was a first aid box. He took out a bottle of fluid and cleaned up the wound. After examining the cuts he looked at Danny and raised an eye brow. He then dressed the wounds with clean gauze and sticky tape. When all was done they said their goodbyes and headed for home with their valuable tin of frogs spawn carried by Peter.

They arrived at their homes a little early, but nobody seemed to notice. Danny's explanation about the milk crate seemed to satisfy his mum and dad and when he told them of his friend the policeman who had cleaned and dressed his wounds, no more was said. On the other hand poor Peter may have been believed that he had fallen in the river, but his mum and dad were not really interested in how he was, their main concern was the state of his clothes. He was rushed inside, stripped and thrown into a bath of cold water. He told them later, that his dad whipped off his belt and while he was still wet and naked, had given him six lashes with the leather belt. The other two knew that this was the truth as they could hear the screams coming from Mrs Stamp's kitchen where the bath was kept. Mum just gave David a smack on the inside of his thigh just because she felt so sorry for poor Peter and said that she held David responsible. The only slight give away was the tin of frogs spawn that Peter had taken into his house. He was questioned for a long time as to how he had acquired frogs spawn on the way home from school when they knew that the nearest pond was down by the River Wandle. Anyway, after some time questioning him the subject was dropped and the belt was replaced around his dad's trousers.

That night, when they listened to the BBC they heard the dreadful news that earlier that week several British ships had been sunk by a very large and powerful German battleship and that "HMS Hood" had received a direct hit in its ammunition compartment and had blown up. The announcer said that there had been only a few survivors. David knew that little Tommy's dad had not been one of them.

As the months went by they began to notice that the raids were getting a little less frequent than before and the siren seemed to only go in late evening just as they were about to go to bed. If fact they began to sleep in their own beds and only ran for the shelter when the siren went. Jack and David found it hard to suddenly jump up from bed and race down to the shelter and they became a little casual about the raids. They would be woken by the siren and mum shouting for them to come to the shelter, but they would stay in the nice warm bed hoping that the all clear would sound without them moving. They would lie half asleep until they heard the drone of the bombers. Only when the sound was getting close would they jump out of bed and race down the stairs. Air raids, sirens, bombers and bombs were all part of their life now and they felt that they had acquired some control of their lives. Jack started to make model aircraft, which he painted and hung by cotton thread from drawing pins pressed into the plaster of the ceiling. He made Spitfires, Hurricanes, Lancaster Bombers and many others. There were not kits in those days and he used to cut out the fuselage and wings from balsa wood which he bought in a shop in Mitcham.

The period of heavy bombers passing over their estate seemed to be easing up and they thought that there must be some turning point in the war when the Allies would get the upper hand. Every day there were reports of how many ships had been sunk, or how many planes had been shot down. The announcer always managed to convince the listeners that the Allied losses were always less than the Germans and this would give them a sense of false hope.

One morning later on in the year they were all out in the front of the houses playing a game of cricket. It was quite a wild game as there was one batsman and one bowler. All the rest were fielders. The pitch was the centre of the road and the stumps, which had been carved out of long stakes, were stuck in the sewage drain. In the middle of the game there arose a low grumbling sound, which grew louder and louder. No sirens had been sounded but the cricketers all knew that this was the time to run for the shelters. They all dispersed to their separate houses. Strangely there was no sudden volley of antiaircraft gun as was the norm when a squadron of German bombers went over and also, there had been no siren to warn them of the raid. It began to dawn on all of them that these must be RAF planes heading out towards the coast. They all came to their front doors and stood on the top steps waiting. The sound grew into a deafening roar as a mass of large aircraft came over the roofs, all in formation with smaller fighters taking up the outside positions. They could see the red, white and blue circles painted on the undersurface of the wings and they were indeed British planes. All the children ran into the street waving their arms in the air and cheering. Many of the adults, who were at home came to stand on the door step and wave their arms. Mr. Pope, still in his shirt sleeves and braces with a fag in his mouth and a dripping nose walked into the middle of the little green and looking up at the amazing sight shouted, "Give it to them lads. Give the bloody Germans some of their own medicine!" No one seemed at all shocked at this outburst from the old veteran of the First World War, as it was what everybody was thinking as they cheered the bombers. They all tried to wait for their return, as nobody actually knew how far it was to Germany, how large a country it was, and most important, how fast the bombers could fly. It grew dark and they all went indoors. Later that evening there was a lot of engine noise, not always overhead and there was no sound of the siren or the antiaircraft guns. They therefore assumed that they had returned, but how many and in what state nobody knew.

It was announced on the wireless, the next day, that a bombing raid had been made on a German City the night before and that the raid had been successful with very few losses. Dad said that the BBC would never tell the people if there had been heavy losses as this would make the public lose heart, but to David it all sounded good news and it felt that at last the tide had turned and perhaps it wouldn't be long before the war was over and they could feel safe sleeping in their beds again. How wrong he was! The worst was yet to come.

Chapter 14

The war raged on, bombers came from the south dropping bombs and creating fires and devastation all over the south of England but particularly on London. Bombers came over from the north in close formation with thunderous engine noise, but no explosions. Gradually, the planes coming from the north seemed to be outnumbering those coming from the south and everybody began to feel that the RAF was getting the upper hand. Most of the raids on London took place in the late evening or during the night and although this was more frightening it did allow the freedom of doing other things during the day when a chance of the siren going was growing less and less. Going to school hadn't got the excitement that it had earlier when a race for home was going to be an option. The boys still waited on the corner for Billy and Terry to join them, but little Tommy was now taken to school by his mum and they went a different way. There was talk of Tommy and his mum moving to the country in the near future, which made them a little sad as they had grown to like little Tommy and his very warm and friendly mum.

They began to enjoy the trip to school and used to leave home a little early so that they could spend some time throwing sticks into the river or play a game of "He or Tag", where you had to chase anyone in the group and if you could touch them, they would have to chase the rest. They could always find ways of making the lessons more interesting. Danny was an expert at inventing a new "wheeze" that could only be seen by the pupils and missed by the teacher. In the playground the games were becoming much more active and "Leap Frog" was one of the favourites, particularly the version where the children would break up into two groups. One team would line up with their heads between the legs of the one in front and the one at the front would hold on to a drainpipe for stability. This meant that there was a long line of backs for the opposing team to leap on. The aim was to collapse the other team as quickly as possible with fewer participants than the opposing team. Life seemed to be improving dramatically and the fact that there was a war on and soldiers, sailors, airmen and civilians were all losing their lives was far from the children's minds.

They still all listened to the BBC news each evening to hear how the war was progressing and each day now it seemed to be getting better. The Allied losses were said to be getting less and the German losses of planes and ships increasing. Dad said that we were to take the numbers "with a pinch of salt" as he thought that they were manipulated for their benefit. Nevertheless, one evening there was a report of a terrible attack on a place called Pearl Harbour by the Japanese. Many ships had been sunk and thousands of men had been killed. This didn't mean too much to David as he didn't know where Pearl Harbour was, whether the Japanese were on our side or not and it all was a long way away in the Pacific Ocean, which David did know was on the other side of the globe they had in the school room. David couldn't believe his eyes when he saw that Dad was smiling. Mum was a little annoyed and asked him to explain himself. Dad replied, "I know it sounds callous, and I am very sorry about all the loss of shipping and particularly the lives of all those poor sailors and their families, but that is the biggest mistake the Axis has made. America has not been in this war. Although they have been leasing us ships and planes and been sending food supplies over to us, they have not committed themselves into the fighting. Now they will have to respond and I think that they will come in full force and back our poor forces that have been holding out throughout the last couple of years". Before anyone could answer there came a knock on the door and there stood Mr and Mrs Stamp with Peter and his brother, Ben.

"Did you hear the news, Bill" asked Mr Stamp, "What do you think it all means?" Dad repeated what he had told all of the family and with that they went off to the neighbours who were standing in their doorways or sitting on the steps to spread the news. Luckily Dad was correct in his interpretation of the situation and the war now had another player and they all knew that it was a large wealthy country that had joined their side. Many of the men were guessing that the war would be over in a few months, some a year, and the bombing and killing would soon end. They had not understood the power and might of the German army and the tactics Hitler still had up his sleeve.

As Churchill, the Prime Minister, had said on the radio or as David remembered, he thought he said, "This is not the end, it is not even the beginning of the end, it is just the end of the beginning", and how right he was!

For a few months nothing seemed to change. They thought the streets would be filled with Yankee soldiers, sailors and airmen, but none appeared. The boys were a little sad as they had been told that the Yanks always gave all the children they saw packets of chewing gum and although this was not sweets, they knew it was the next best thing. All the older girls were told that the Yanks had lots of nylons which they gave away, but they were also disappointed. One major change that they all did notice, though, was that the bombers going south appeared to get more frequent and they would go out twice a day, in fact one very heavy raid during the day and another at evening or during the night. The Allied bombers going south was made up of much larger planes than before and they had a circle with a star in the middle under the end of each of the wings. David knew that this was the symbol of the American Air force. It was comforting to know that the Royal Air force that had taken such a major part in guarding the skies all over Britain for over two years now had been joined by one of the largest air forces in the world and their defending role had now turned into an aggressive one. The whole family were becoming so casual about the German raids on London that they all returned to their beds in the house and only when the siren went did they run for the shelter and even then Jack and David would wait until they could hear the engines of the planes.

The news didn't seem to improve over the next few months; in fact it seemed to become more and more depressing. It gradually dawned on David that they were all alone against an enemy who would stop at nothing to take over the world. Poland had been overrun by the Germans at the very beginning of the war and Belgium and France soon followed. It sounded to him that Russia, who he thought was their only ally, was also in great danger of being over run and he wasn't sure which side Italy was on. To a seven year old boy all these countries seemed to be on the other side of the world and he couldn't understand why Germany wanted to take over all that land and kill off all the people when they apparently had a large country of their own. Nevertheless, he knew that many men were being killed fighting and nearer to home many people were being bombed, not only in London, but in many cities all over Britain.

The luxuries they had all shared before the war, like sweets in the newsagents, bread in the bakers and meat in the butchers were almost forgotten. The only shop that seemed to have food in its windows was the greengrocer and the vegetables seemed to be mainly potatoes and cabbages. Luckily, Dad still managed to find time to cultivate his allotment and it was the source of many extra treats such as onions, peas, beans, lettuces, tomatoes etc. and of course he always had sacks of potatoes as a fall back. All the neighbours kept in with Dad as there was always the chance of a few vegetables coming their way when Dad had a glut. Poor Mum would spend most of her time queuing for their ration of meat for the week or at the bakers for a loaf of bread. David would go with her at times and hear her bargain for a little extra or cheaper meat and in all honesty he thought that the shop owners were a little afraid of Mum as she had a very determined streak in her. David also remembered the times she used to struggle home from the shops with two large, heavy shopping bags full of essential foods for the family. He felt quite sad now, to think of her, cold and often wet, unable to feel her hands due to the lack of circulation. Why didn't they recognise the strain she was under and help her more? She had always been a good looking Mum who was kind and loving. She was the envy of most of the children in the street and always had a good word for nearly everybody. Dad obviously adored her and they had a very loving and warm relationship which was passed on to their children in care and protection. They must have both been at their wits end trying to make ends meet on Dad's low wages and they must have always dreaded what tragedy may suddenly fall from the sky.

Early in 1942 Mum seemed to be putting on lots of weight and was becoming very round, warm and homely. David never put two and two together and came home from school one day to find another lady in the front room. She said that Mum was up in bed, asleep and he was to go out and play with his friends and not to waken her on any account. Jack was now at senior school and was never home until later as he usually played football with his pals after they had been dismissed. Betty had just gone up into the Senior section of David's school and was also home later than himself. So he went out to find either Peter or Danny. He knocked on Danny's door and when his mum answered, he was invited in. This was quite unusual as Danny's mother didn't like visitors coming into her house. She took him through the living room to the kitchen where Danny was having his tea which appeared to be dried egg fritters with Daddies sauce poured over them. There was a lovely smell of fried eggs and when Danny's mum saw how David was looking at the dish she offered him some. David had never eaten in their house before and the dried egg fritters tasted delicious. After they had finished, he and Danny went into the front room and played snakes and ladders. Even in a game of chance, like this, Danny always seemed to get the correct score on the dice to go up all the ladders and avoid all the snakes. One would have thought, with that luck, he would, in some way, be cheating, but David kept a careful eye on the handling of the dice and the way it was thrown and he knew that Danny would always be very lucky in life, or so he thought.

After Danny had won several games there came a knock on the door and, when Danny's mum answered it, David heard Betty's voice asking if she had seen her brother. David was summoned and hand in hand he and Betty made their way back to their house. Betty was absolutely bubbling with joy and was leaping from foot to foot. She would not tell David what was going on, but took him straight up to the front bedroom where David was presented with Mum, lying in bed, beaming all over her face, and holding a tiny baby wrapped in a small, white blanket. Betty went over to Mum and took over the small bundle and carefully held it in her arms looking down at the perfectly formed face. Mum had her hands just below Betty's, just in case. She had no real fears as Betty was one of the most kindly and careful girls you could come across.

"Come and be introduced to your new sister", Mum invited.

David came over to the side of the bed and looked into the small space and saw, what he had not expected in a million years, the face of his new sister. He thought it very strange that, when Bobby, who was now two, was born, he remembered that Betty spent the first two or three days crying and here she was now laughing and cuddling the baby. All he could think was that girls must be a little strange when they had this reaction to babies. There was one good side to the situation though David remembered. When Bobby was born, Mum had spare, large biscuits called rusks and there was always some over after the baby had been fed. There was lots of discussion as to what to call the new addition to the family and it wasn't till the next day, when Dad was at home, that Susan was decided upon as they all thought that this was a really modern name and would not be shortened. But strangely enough from then on Susan was always called Susy. She grew into a beautiful little baby with long blonde hair and bright blue eyes. She was always laughing and smiling and blowing bubbles. All the family were delighted with this valuable addition and even little Bobby, who was a tough little character, liked to take her in his arms and give her a fond cuddle. Betty was overjoyed with Susan's arrival. Apparently she had always wanted a little sister and this was the reason for her upset when Bobby was born.

No one realised the stress that Mum was now under. Her three elder children were now at school and although she knew that Jack and Betty were dependable and helpful, at times, David knew that he must have been a bit of a worry to his mother. In addition to this, she now had two very young children to care for and feed and a husband who was always available for police work and never knowing what sort of emergency he may be called upon to do. She had a well worn old pram, which Dad maintained in working order and she would place a small board over the back part of the pram and sit little Bobby on it with his legs hanging over the back between the handles. He was not the greatest little boy at keeping still and many times she would have to catch him as he fell to the pavement or grab his legs as he toppled back onto the baby in the pram. Thus, with the two large shopping bags hanging on the handles she would go off to the local shops to get the shopping for the family. David remembered that there were no such things as refrigerators in those days so this journey had to be made every day rain or snow. At weekends she would often be accompanied by Betty, who loved to push the pram and became so adept at it that Mum would trust her even crossing the roads.

One Saturday, Bobby decided that he did not want to go with Mum to the shops and when Bobby made up his mind there was no changing it. After pleading with this little two year old for some time Mum decided that he could stay at home as long as Betty stayed with him and kept a close eye on him. They all became engaged in some interesting task, Jack making another American aircraft, Betty reading a story to Bobby and David playing "Hit the tin can in the middle of the road with a rubber ball". Danny stood on one side of the road and David on the other. They would then place an old tin can in the middle of the road and each of them would try to hit the can and send it to the other kerb. After about an hour Mum came home and went indoors obviously to make the tea.   About half an hour later their front door was flung open and out came Mum in a high state of panic. She was followed by Jack and they raced across the small and large green and down the slipway towards the shops.   David rushed indoors to find out what all the fuss was about and Betty, who was crying explained through her sobs and tears that Mum had left the baby in the pram outside one of the shops.   She had met a neighbour and had forgotten that she had taken the baby to the shops.   Luckily, the baby was still fast asleep in the pram and it was outside the greengrocer's shop, where Mum had left it.

David began to enjoy helping Dad in the garden and on the allotment. He gradually learned how to get the best from the two plots.   At one time they had both been open farm land and therefore the upper soil was excellent.   Below, there was a layer of chalk and this helped the drainage.   The allotment and the back garden had been turned over for the production of as many vegetables as possible, except for one area which Dad always kept clear for the growing of a large patch of sweet William.   These were easy to grow and self-seeded every year. A large bunch of the flowers gave a great show of colour and would also sweeten the home coming of Dad if he was a little late due to a visit to the local on the way home.   The back garden was developing well around the air raid shelter.   The apple trees, although small, bore masses of apples each year and the rhubarb was flourishing, much to Dad's dismay. David would spend a little time following the milkman's horse and cart to collect the manure which the horse dropped all over the road and what with the droppings from the chickens in the pen at the end of the garden he developed a heap which could be dug into the garden and improve the soil.   He had seen Dad make up one of these heaps down at the allotment and copied him by growing marrows and strawberries on the top.

David seemed to have very little interest in school.   He knew that he had to go but he felt that it was a bit of a waste of time.   Play time was great and the hide-and-seek that they played between the shelters, although out of bounds, was exciting and enjoyable. Subjects like sums and writing he did because the teacher wanted him to and although he sometimes got things right he was nearly always being told off for not paying attention or "playing the fool". Danny and Peter were the same and only did what was required of them and no more. It wasn't until one of the younger teachers decided that they would all have an art class that things began to change. She had found some coloured pencils which had been stored away somewhere in the school and with pages torn from an exercise book set them to work on trying to produce an attractive pattern which would cover the page. Peter and David began to enjoy this challenge and set to work on their original designs. After about half an hour the teacher collected the drawings and pinned them to the board at the front of the class. To David's surprise, his stood out a mile being colourful and clear. Peter's was also quite pleasant, but the rest seemed to be rubbish. In fact some of the kids had only scribbled all over the page.

Danny had changed his piece of paper into an aircraft and was throwing it over the heads of the class; nevertheless, he had drawn all the signs on the wings and tail and made quite a good job of it. The teacher carefully looked through all the designs and finally selected David's as being the winner of the competition. She called him out to the front and presented him with a new pack of coloured pencils and a new small pad to draw on. He was, of course, delighted and felt that this was the beginning of his enjoyment of drawing, painting and design. All the girls in the class looked on with envy, but most of the boys blew quiet raspberries and called him a sissy. Peter's drawing was also commended and he was presented with a large eraser which could rub out pencil at one end and ink at the other. Danny was not given a prize, but all the class came to admire his plane and the way in which it was decorated. It certainly proved to cause the most amusement of all the designs.

It was about that time and on an evening that Dad had a few hours off, that Mum, feeling that Dad needed a break sent him off to the local for a drink with the other men of the neighbourhood. Dad used to like this small break and would consume a fair amount of mild and bitter. His sergeant was a popular man up the pub as he was renowned for getting things done and being fair when there was some sort of argument or row. He was a large man, maybe about six foot three inches tall and broad shouldered. He also carried a fair amount of weight around his middle and looked about twice the size of Dad. Nevertheless, Dad was his right hand man and whenever there was the chance for them to meet at the local they would always be popular and only needed to buy about half the amount of beer that they consumed. Dad changed into his civilian clothes, with his trilby set firmly on his head with the front peak pulled down over his eyes. Mum slipped some coins into his hand as he left the front door and waved him goodbye. It was strange that they never seemed to kiss as they parted, although in those days it was not considered right to show too much affection in public. In fact, even the kissing of the children was a rarity and only saved for special occasions such as births and deaths. Anyway, Dad, fag in the corner of his mouth and looking as if he had been released from prison for the evening, went striding off, across the small and then large green towards the alleyway leading to the main road. Here he turned up the hill and headed for the St Anthony's Arms.

Raids crossing this area of southern England had been getting a little less, although the bombing of London and the Docks continued. It was only the odd stray German bomber that had either lost its way home or had been damaged by the fighters or the guns that came back over the estate. The siren would go and the family would all race to the shelter, except for Jack and David, who would lie in bed until the last minute. On this particular evening, at about nine thirty, the siren sounded and the usual plan went into action. Almost immediately there was the thunderous noise of a heavy aircraft flying very low and sounding very menacing. Jack was still up, but David had just gone to bed. Jack helped Mum with the kids to get them into the shelter and then spotting that David wasn't there, raced up the stairs to pull him out of bed. They came down the stairs at a gallop, but were only half way down when there was a mighty explosion which shook the house. They continued through the kitchen and out into the yard and into the shelter. In that brief moment of crossing the yard David noticed a bright red sky and the sound of lots of people shouting. They stayed in the shelter till the all clear sounded and then emerged to a night with a sky so bright, it could have been day. Mum, Jack and David went to the front door and looked out to try to discover what was causing such a glow in the sky. It seemed to be coming from the area of the shops and people were running down the alleyway to get a better view.

Betty was told by Mum to stay in the front room and to listen out for the two youngsters. Then, David, Mum and Jack started walking towards the alley way and main road. David noticed that Mum was tending to race along and seemed frightened and anxious. They spotted Mr Stamp coming towards them and Mum enquired about the fire. He said that an oil bomb had hit the pub and the whole of the back part was ablaze. Mum took in a deep breath, then with her eyes rolled upwards and her mouth open, fell to the ground.

Chapter 15

"Mummy, Mummy, where are you Mummy?" It was Tracy, Polly's little girl calling from the kitchen of their house.

Polly pulled rapidly away from David and went to the doorway of the shelter.

"I am here, Lovey, in the shed. David is just helping me to get some more lemonade for the party. We are coming now".

"You seemed such a long time, I wondered what had happened to you. The others came back ages ago and I thought that you would be with them".

"David had to reach the crate at the back of the shelves and had to climb up to get it, so it took a little longer than the others. Anyway we are ready to go back now, if you could just help David to carry the crate it would make it a lot easier".

As David emerged from the shelter, which Polly persisted in calling a shed, with the wooden crate in his hands he felt hot and sticky. It wasn't so much the temperature in the shelter, but what had just happened. His heart was still beating twenty to the dozen and he was sweating profusely. He knew, by the glowing feeling over his face that he must be looking red and his hair was hanging in his eyes. He felt more guilty than ever when he saw little Tracy and wondered what had come over him to get into such a compromising position. All he knew was that he wished they had been left just that little bit longer and had the same sensation when one was awakened from a very pleasant dream just as things were going to happen. He didn't dare look at Polly who was now entering her kitchen on her way to the front door. She looked even more appealing as she walked in front of him, although she didn't show any signs of being any different than she was when they came down to her house.

Tracy put out her hand to the bottom of the crate and although she was taking no weight at all walked along with a smile on her face because she felt that she was helping. In actual fact, David had to carry the crate a little lower so that she could reach and therefore making the task of carrying it a little harder. They arrived at the large green just as half a dozen children came up for a drink and after putting the crate down on the ground, the bottles were removed and some of the tops opened for filling the beakers.   Polly, who had arrived just ahead of David and Tracy, had crossed the green to where the games were taking place to help with organizing them. David was filled with a feeling of being let down and remorse. He had hoped that Polly would sit for a while and talk, but she appeared as if nothing had happened and he didn't exist. He was about to head back to his side of the road when Tracy gripped his hand and announced to all those present that she had helped David carry the drinks from the shed.   With that, she sat down on the grass and pulled David down by her side.

"Mummy's looking after the boys playing football, she likes doing that".

"Does she like football?" asked David.

"No, but nobody else wants to do it.   Daddy likes football, but he is not very good".

David had not considered that perhaps Polly's husband may have come in and found the two of them in a compromising position.   He felt even more worried now about his indiscretion and what trouble it would have caused Polly if he had come home early. David had never before had any feelings of that kind towards a married woman. He remembered, when he was young, liking to be hugged by Tommy's mother, who he thought was very attractive, but it was never anything like this.

"Where does your daddy play football Tracy?"

"Here, on the big green. There are lots of them and they race up and down kicking a big heavy ball"

David remembered that he had seen a type of football being played on the green, but it seemed to be a wild sort of game, more like rugby with lots of twenty year olds crashing into each other and doing sliding tackles which no respectable footballer would dare to do. He couldn't remember, however, any of that sort of game being played for some time.

"When did daddy last play then Tracy?"

"Oh, not for along time, Well how could he, silly, he is a sailor and they can't play football on a boat".

At that point Julie, one of the women that David knew slightly, came over and just caught the last bit of Tracy's conversation.

"Yes, George, Polly's husband is in the Merchant Navy and spends a lot of his time away at sea. I think he is due to come home soon but Polly never seems to know exactly when as he doesn't write too often. Anyway, I am sure Polly has told you all that". Julie sat down on the other side of David and handed him a beaker of Tizer.

"You look very hot. Handling those crates is not an easy task, is it? I had to get more help to carry mine as the sharp edges cut into my hands".

"I helped to carry ours, didn't I David", cut in Tracy.

115

"Yes, you were a great help, I couldn't have managed without you", replied David.

Little Tracy's brother came running over to the three of them. He was trying to say something to them, but he was so out of breath that the words would not come out in an audible fashion.

"This is Sam", Julie said, "he is Polly's little boy and Tracy's brother".

"Yes, I met him earlier, but I didn't now his name was Sam".

"Mummy said she won't be long and she will come over to your house with you".

"Oh, tell her not to bother, I will head off now as I am going out this evening and I will need to get ready", replied David.

"Are you going somewhere nice?" asked Julie.

"Only up to our youth club to a social evening, but I will be going with my girlfriend and so I need to smarten myself up before she comes round".

"I think you had better wait for Polly to come back" said Julie, "she will feel upset if you have just gone. She was looking forward to meeting you and talking to you. Have you been going with your girlfriend for long, I have often seen you walking down the road with your arms around each other?"

"Yes, we've been going out, on and off, for about a year and a half now"

"She looks quite young".

"She is about two years younger than me, but very grown up in her ways. I wonder sometimes whether she really wants a boyfriend, she says that she wants to mix with everybody. Then, when everybody seems to have a boyfriend she is happy to go with me".

David didn't like to point out that when Janet had these "wanting freedom" spells, he was heartbroken and would walk or cycle up and down her road just so that he could get a glimpse of her. He did suspect that when they came together again he was most probably too keen and that may have put her off a little. Anyway, just recently, Janet had become very fond of him and they had begun to do quite a lot together. They had both attended the dancing classes at the youth club and had become partners. Janet had become a very good dancer and they had welded as a dancing couple. They would go out with a group of members of the youth club, visiting local dance halls and other clubs and she had become very affectionate to him. Kissing and cuddling had become the norm before they parted in the evening and David knew that he had a great desire to go further and he was sure his feelings were returned, but they had always managed not to go too far, as they say. They were always saying to each other that they would most probably get engaged some time in the future, so it would be worth waiting till later for the thing they desired, although David thought that he would have a hard time refusing if the opportunity arose. Janet had become very religious. David knew that one of the best ways of seeing her regularly was to attend church on Sundays, morning and evening and any special services that occurred during the year. She had become the teacher at the Sunday School and spent a lot of time caring for and laying out the vestments at the church. They had both become great friends of the vicar, youth leader and the two curates and would be available for prayer meetings and even some bible reading classes.

"That sounds very sad", remarked Julie, "I bet she was more fond of you than you thought, but didn't like to show it. Did you ever go on holiday together?"

117

"Oh yes, we had some wonderful times down at the Isle of Wight. We would go with the club by coach down to Portsmouth and then take the ferry across to Ryde. Many of the girls, including Janet, would feel quite sea sick on the crossing, but by the time we had all boarded the steam train to take us round to Shanklin, they had all recovered".

"I know the Isle of Wight quite well", interrupted Julie, "where did you stay?"

"In a beautiful old house run by the Girl's Friendly Society. The boys all slept in a dormitory and the girls in groups in large bed rooms. We were kept well apart at night as the youth leader and one of the curates was always on hand. During the days we would go on the beach, swim, play tennis on the courts and occasionally arrange a game of cricket against one of the other youth clubs that was also staying there. In the evenings we would have a short service and then follow up with a dance or social with a record player and we would all have a good time. It was all great fun and some of the best holidays I had ever experienced".

"Well, of course, you had your girlfriend with you, which must have added to your pleasures".

"Yes, that is true; it most probably made the holiday for me".

David didn't like to boast that by that time he had become very popular in the club. He took part in all the games that were arranged and in the cricket he was one of the main players as he played for his grammar school and his local team. He and Janet would attend all the dances and dance all evening. In any swimming races he always did well as he had been a competitive swimmer since he was nine. They had their exciting times including the time that a couple of the girls were being followed by an unknown man. He had apparently been

118

seen looking into the girl's windows at night and many of the girls were frightened to go to bed unaccompanied. The boys decided that they would put a stop to this, so they would take the law into their own hands and frighten the prowler off. They all dressed in black and armed with cricket bats and stumps they stood at all the entrances of the gardens, standing well hidden in the bushes. They stood there, perfectly still for about two hours, but luckily for them, no one appeared. They did this for about three nights and then decided that the man had obviously seen one of them and had decided that this was not a good place to enter. It was all very exciting at the time and added to the wonderful time they all had on the Island.

"Sorry to keep you waiting, I hope that the children and Julie have kept you amused. I had promised to take charge of the football match between the under sixes and I was nearly late. Never mind, it all went well and they all enjoyed it. Now you two", Polly was now talking to the children, "go with Aunty Julie to the apple dipping, I will go with David back to his house".

"There is no need for that", said David "you go with the children, I will be OK".

Polly put out her hands, and pulled David up on to his feet. Then she slipped her arm through his and turned towards the small green. Julie took the hands of the two children and after turning and giving a knowing smile to Polly, went off in the opposite direction. As Polly and David approached the small green Polly slowed down and gripped David's arm a little tighter.

"I am so sorry that I had to leave you so quickly when we got back to the group, but I had completely forgotten that I had promised to take charge of the football and they were all waiting on the other side of the green for me. Anyway, no harm was done. They thought I had just got tied up with some other organizing. "I suppose I had", she said, with a little giggle.

David dropped his head and muttered, "I am so sorry for the way I behaved, I have never done that before and I don't know what came over me. I felt suddenly very attracted to you and found it quite impossible to control my feelings".

"Don't apologise", said Polly, "I have always been attracted to you ever since I first saw you and have wanted to come that close for a long time. You had only seen me as you passed, but I would sit for a long time on my front step hoping that you would come that way home. Even though I saw you with your girlfriend, I thought that you may not have experienced that sort of closeness before".

"What about your husband, how would he feel if he knew what we had done"?

"Dear David. We haven't done anything. A little affection in this world is needed by all. You know I wouldn't let you go the whole way as that would make things very complicated and would most probably break up my marriage, but I am sure my husband must have times when he is away when he feels the need for female company and knowing him as I do, I bet he sometimes takes it. I may be wrong, but he is a Merchant Seaman and on a ship away from home and any females for weeks on end, so I can't really blame him. I hope I am wrong, but these young far eastern women are very attractive and very sexy, so he must be tempted. Anyway, don't think any more about it, I hope it won't put you off seeing me again if the opportunity arises. I know that I felt a great need for you when we were close and if it hadn't been for Tracy interrupting us, I don't know how I would have behaved, but that's bye the bye. Now go off and have a lovely evening and think no more about it".

David was amazed at the down to earth common sense this mature young woman had and found it impossible to reply. He just continued into his gate and up the front steps to have his tea and get ready for an evening out with Janet.

Mum knew something was wrong.   She had prepared a delicious salad, mainly with fresh produce from the garden and allotment.   She knew it was David's favourite tea and was a little surprised that he just sat and picked at the tasty beetroot, cooked that afternoon and the tomatoes, lettuce and cucumber all steeped in vinegar.   David was still shaking inwardly and could not get the turn of events out of his mind.

"Are you alright?"

"Yes, why do you ask?" enquired David.

"Well you seem a lot quieter than usual and you haven't made any remark about the tea".

"Oh, sorry Mum, I was just thinking of the games that were taking place on the big green".

"Did I see you go up the road with a couple of the ladies, earlier?"

David thought, Mum doesn't miss a trick, I bet she has been looking out of the window and had seen every move I made.

"Yes, I told you I was going to help to carry the crates of drinks from Polly's house".

"You seemed to be a long time coming back, I saw the other lady come back earlier carrying a crate.   It didn't look that heavy".

"Well it was", said David, getting a little angry.   "Why is it you can't just let me get on with my life and not keep questioning me over what I am doing"?

Mum looked very hurt and David could see that she was close to tears. He got up from the table and went over to Mum who had gone to the sink to start the washing up. He put his arm around her shoulders.

"Sorry Mum, I know you mean well, but I have got to stand on my own two feet and I feel that everything I do is being monitored".

Mum looked up to him and then squeezed his hand. "I am sorry", she said, "its just that I feel a little responsible for your situation at the moment and to be quite honest, I don't trust that Polly woman".

David looked down at Mum's kind, warm face and his mind went back to the time during the war when the pub was bombed and knowing that Dad was up there having a drink, had thought the worst and had fainted. David had held her head in his arms and felt that the world had come to an end.

Chapter 16

David knelt on the ground with Mum's head resting in his arms. What had happened to his Mum? He hadn't ever seen anyone dead, so he wasn't sure what the situation was. Mr. Jones, the warden, who knew it all and was considered to be a bit above his station, came running up. He was on his way to the pub to help with the fire. He was carrying a large box with a solid brass clip at the front. He proceeded to undo the clip and brought out a small bottle which he handed to one of the ladies, one of a dozen who had gathered around to see what all the fuss was about. "Undo the top and stick it under her nose", said Mr. Jones, "that should do the trick. I have got to go". With that he clipped up the box and went on running up the road towards the pub. Someone said, "Lay her flat and rest her head back on a coat". Another said, "I think she's a gonna, why waste the time". A youngish woman, who David knew as Mrs Brown seemed to take charge. She said, "Move back and give the lady some air. If you've nothing to do, go up to the pub and see if you can help there". She knew that most of them were just there to poke their noses in and the crowd quickly dispersed. She then took the small bottle Mr. Jones had left and after taking off the top, slipped it close under Mum's nose. Mum suddenly twitched and jumped. Mrs Brown put the bottle under her nose again and Mum turned her head away groaning at the same time. Finally she opened her eyes and looked absolutely lost. David gave her a great hug and shouted,

"Mum, Mum, its David, you're not dead".

Mrs Brown told her to stay where she was for a while and just take some deep breaths. Mum gradually came to and then spotted the bright glow just up the road. She sat up and tried to stand, shouting at the same time,

"Bill, my husband is up the pub having a drink, can someone find out if he is alright".

Seeing that Jack and Mrs. Brown, the lady who had administered the bottle to Mum's nose, were taking care of her, David ran off, down the alleyway and on to the main road leading up to the pub. As he ran up the pavement, he was joined by Peter, who had obviously followed his dad towards the burning pub. David felt a little better having his pal along with him and although Peter was a little reserved, his presence gave David a sense of security. As they drew level with the allotments next door to the Arms they were brought to a halt by a rope, which was stretched across the road and pavement. The crowds were about ten deep but David and Peter dived between the legs of the on lookers until they came face to face with Mr. Jones, who was keeping the crowd back at the same time as shouting instructions to the drivers of some of the fire engines and ambulances. He held his arm across in front of the two boys and wouldn't listen to their pleas concerning Dad. David tried to make his way along the fence at the side of the pathway, but a large woman grabbed him by the back of his neck and wouldn't let him go. Peter shouted, "I will try to draw their attention then you can get under the rope and run to the pub." With that he fell on the pavement and lay absolutely still with his eyes closed. The fat woman shouted, "Quick, the young boy has fainted", and with that she let go of David's neck.

David was amazed at Peter's cunning and as Mr. Jones ran over to take charge of the new emergency David ducked under the rope and ran towards the pub. The flames seemed to be more around the back on the other side. He ran across the front of the building, leaping over a whole mass of criss-crossing pipes, some leaking water into a large deep puddle which had formed in front of the public bar. It was the place he used to stand when Mum and Dad would go out for a drink on a summers evening or when relations came to call, unexpectedly. He made his way around the entrance to the saloon bar and down the small road where the wagon and horses came to deliver the barrels of beer. He was suddenly brought to a halt by a policeman who ran forward to prevent him going any further. David was absolutely delighted to see that it was his dad's colleague, the policeman whom he had met when he had had the accident and had bitten his tongue through.

"Get out of this area quickly and go home, what the devil are you doing in this restricted area, there is danger of an explosion".

David quickly said, "I am looking for my Dad, he came up here for a drink and Mum is scared that something may have happened to him". The policeman quickly pushed him over the fence of the pub and into the next field and said,

"Wait at the end by the road and I will make some enquiries,   I will come down there in a few minutes and let you know what I have found out".

 David stood at the end of the field by the road for what seemed like hours until finally the policeman, who was now without his jacket or his helmet, came running up.   "I am sorry David, I can't find out anything about your Dad. He isn't here and we don't think that he is in the building, but we will have to wait until later to find out.   In the meantime, go home and tell you mum that I will continue to make enquires and as soon as I know anything, I will let her know".

David ran as fast as he could down the road towards his school and turned right into the road which led around the back of the pub and back to his house.   As he ran along this road he could clearly see the blazing building and could hear the bells of fire engines and police cars.   When he reached his house he found that several kind people who lived in the alleyway had helped Jack and Mrs Brown to get Mum home, although Mrs. Brown had gone back to the pub to see if she could help.   Mum was half lying and half sitting on the settee.

Betty was by her side with her arm around her shoulders and someone, who David had seen over the shops many times, was making Mum a cup of tea. In fact there was tea for all which meant the whole ration for the month had been used up in one night. David explained that although he had managed to get around to the back of the private bar, which was on fire he had not got any news. He told Mum about the policeman and what he had said, but Mum kept shaking and muttering,

"Bill, Bill, please be alright". Jack then said something which made them all cheer up. He said,

"Dad never drank in the private bar, he only ever went to the public bar as the beer is a penny cheaper". They all knew that this was true; Dad felt that he was being cheated by paying more than the basic price for the beer, and anyway he wouldn't drink with the toffs, it was against his politics.

It was only after about half an hour, when Mr. Stamp came to the front door and asked if they had seen anything of Peter as he had been missing for some time, that David suddenly remembered Peter's clever idea and how he had left him on the other side of the pub surrounded by a mass of people. "I know where I left him. I will run back and see if he is still there". Mum told Jack to go with him and they both ran across the small and large greens, down the alleyway and up the road towards the pub. There was still a large crowd of people there, although by now the blaze was under control and some of the fire engines and ambulances had gone. Jack pushed his way through the crowd and came up against Mr. Jones, who was still shouting instructions and holding the crowd back. He certainly seemed to have a presence of authority and most of the people there seemed quite frightened of him. He, on the other hand, seemed to be enjoying his sudden importance. Jack shouted,

"Have you seen a little boy of seven, who fainted here some time ago".

Mr. Jones pointed to one of the houses about fifty yards away and said that he thought he had been taken there by two ladies. Jack and David knocked on one of the doors and an old man opened the front door. He was wearing his pyjamas. He looked lost and frightened and said that his daughter was not at home and could they come back later. Jack quickly knocked next door, where a couple of ladies said that they thought that the boy had been taken further down the road to number 253. David thought that this was all a little strange as Peter had only pretended to faint and there was really nothing wrong with him. On arrival at 253 they knocked and a young lady invited them in. To their amazement Peter was lying on a couch with his head on a pillow. The young lady's mother had a tray with cake and lemonade and was feeding Peter as if he was a baby. Jack explained that Peter's dad was worried about him and they should get home as soon as they could. On hearing about his dad worrying about him, Peter suddenly became alert and leapt to his feet. He thanked the lady and her mother and they all made their way back home. On the way, Peter explained that after pretending to faint he was carried to the lady's house and his head was bathed with water. He said that he couldn't come round too quickly as they would have been suspicious so he kept his eyes closed for a while and when he eventually did open them, they had produced lemonade and cake for him and as he wasn't allowed either of these at home because they were too expensive, he felt that he shouldn't be ungrateful, and accepted them.

When Mr. Stamp heard the story he gave Peter a heavy clip around the ear and told him to go indoors and get to bed before he returned or his life wouldn't be worth living and after Peter had raced off at double speed he turned to Jack and David and smiled with relief. It was the first and last time they had ever seen him show any emotion.

Susy and Bobby had both been put to bed and it was getting very late when there came a knock at the door. Mum immediately shouted "Oh my God". She knew that Dad had a key for the door and she would expect him to use it. Jack and Betty ran to the door and there, looking like a tramp, with his shirt torn and his face all black, was Dad. They threw their arms around his neck and hugged him tight. They all then went back into the house and Mum and Dad embraced each other for what seemed like hours. She said, "Thank God you are alright Bill, no one knew where you were and we thought that you might be in the burning pub. David did get around to the back of the pub and met your friend in the police, who knew nothing, but said he would find out what had happened to you".

After a cup of warmed up tea which was left in the pot, Dad sat down and explained what had happened to their night out. He and his friends were drinking in the public bar,

"There we are" said Jack, "I told you so".

Dad explained that when the siren went they didn't bother to take shelter as they were having a good time. Dad was about to buy his round when there was an enormous explosion which threw all the glasses across the room including the tables and chairs and all the men. Some were hurt by either flying glass or furniture. Some of the men went to help those in the bar that were crying aloud with pain, while Dad and his sergeant ran down the corridor to the back of the pub towards the private bar. The place was ablaze and they had to run back through the public bar and around the outside of the pub. They found that the private bar was burning, mainly over the outside. The bomb had come down in the garden at the back, close to the wall of the private bar and had covered the walls with a black oil that was blazing out of control. They opened the box of hoses that were stored at the side of a large tank of water, one of those that had been strategically placed for such an emergency. They were constructed of large pieces of black metal and must have been at least forty feet in diameter. In fact they were ideal for the local children to sail their home made yachts in.

Dad and his sergeant were trained in how to react and they recruited two or three more men to man the pumps while they went to the back of the pub and played the hoses on the flames. It wasn't long before the green fire engines turned up accompanied by ambulances and police cars. The fire men took over the pumps whilst others brought in the large hoses from the engines. Dad then went to help remove some of the injured from the bars and get them to the ambulances. Only a few people had been in the private bar. Dad said that he only saw a couple of bodies brought out on stretchers; the rest seemed to be able to walk or could be carried by friends or volunteers. He then went in one of the ambulances to help unload the injured at the hospital. When all the injured had reached the hospital and were being cared for, he then had to go to the nearest police box to phone in a report of the events of the evening. So what had begun as a night off at the local ended up as a long night's work and a lucky break to be in the right bar at the right time. Dad said that he knew that drinking in the public bar was not only cheaper but also a great deal luckier.

Mum made Dad a cup of cocoa and David noticed that she put a heaped spoon of sugar in it. This was a real treat as they had all had to have their cocoa without sugar for a long time now as it was so scarce. It was strange how Mum always seemed to have a little stored away so that she could bring it out on special occasions. All the children were sent to bed as it was well past their bed time, but not before Dad gave them all a sip of the nice chocolaty tasting cocoa. Mum looked really well again and sat looking at Dad with admiring eyes knowing that firstly, Dad most probably underestimated the danger he had been in and secondly he was doing a job which was contributing enormously to the safety of the local community. As David went up to bed he hoped that they would have a night free of another raid so that they could all settle down. He also thought, how comforting it was to know that they were surrounded by a well trained team of professionals, including the War Reserve Policemen, such as Dad and his sergeant, Mr. Jones, the Air Raid Warden, all the firemen, ambulance men and women and all the local people who seemed to know what to do in an emergency. People like Mrs. Brown, who lived down the slip way who could take over a situation and order people around her to get them to do the right thing at the right time. He thought that she must have an important job somewhere because she was much more forceful than his school teachers.

The next morning Danny, who had missed all the excitement of the night before for some unknown reason, joined David and Peter and went round to the shops, which were opposite the St. Anthony's Arms. They could get round to the side of the back of the pub, where Dad's police friend had pushed David over the fence into the field. They could see that the back of the pub was covered with a black paint-like material and all the windows and doors were gone. There was a large gaping hole in the garden up against the side of the pub, but the wall at that point was missing. The whole area was flooded with water and there were some of the broken pieces of hose pipe still left in the drive-in to the side of the pub. They then went over to the tank, which they found was completely empty. They were dismayed at this fact as it was only a couple of days before that all three of the lads had made fishing rods and had been fishing in that same tank. They had seen many fish and frogs in the water and wondered where they were now. They all assumed that the poor little creatures had been dragged out by the pumps of the fire engines and thrown into the flames with the water. They picked some buttercups and London pride which grew wild around the tank and threw them into the bottom of the tank as they thought it would be a good gesture seeing that so many fish and frogs gave up their lives to save the pub.

Peter told them that he was very surprised the next morning when his dad and mum greeted him with a smile and a plate of spam fritters for his breakfast. He had never known them be so thoughtful and kind and thought that it was most probably because of the events of the night before and the way he had fainted when he had seen the pub ablaze and thought that David's Dad was in the inferno. He said how nice the ladies had been when they carried him to their house and lay him down on their couch. He told Danny how they bathed his head with cold water and when he opened his eyes they had drinks and cake waiting for him. He thought it was best to stay there for a while as he had not had such treatment for a long time. David suddenly realised that Peter thought that he had fainted and had forgotten that he had pretended to swoon to draw the attention of Mr. Jones who would not let David pass the rope barrier. He decided to keep his mouth shut as Danny was enthralled by the story and obviously saw his friend Peter in a different light than before. The story was told time and time again and David noticed that it got more exciting every time, but he knew that he often exaggerated the facts and felt that he should not spoil Peter's night of glory.

David thought to himself, those ladies only lived about a block up the road from where Janet and her family live. He wondered if she had been living there at the time and whether she had any memories of the events of that evening. She was only two years younger than him and that would have made her about five. She was obviously too young to be out at that time, as seeing that her dad was in the army, he was most probably fighting the Germans on the continent, so her mother would have kept her and her sister indoors. He thought that he ought to ask her about the incident and see if she had any recollection of the night the Arms caught fire.

Chapter 17

Would the war never end? Summer passed into Autumn and then into Winter and still the German bombers came over dropping their bombs on many British cities, but mainly on London which seemed to be getting a pasting nearly every night. Still the sirens went regularly and still the occasional bomber would drop its load over the estate, leaving a trail of death and destruction. On several nights David would wake up to hear the heavy bombs being dropped a long way away and he and Jack would look out of their back bedroom window and see the sky over London a massive ball of red and yellow and they would know that much of the city must be ablaze. They had seen the same skies on many occasions before and wondered if there could be any more buildings left that had not been either blown up or burnt down. They had heard that the German's aim was to destroy St. Paul's Cathedral. This seemed quite pointless to them as it didn't house any arms or guns and would only be the destruction of a lovely old building. There had been an incendiary bomb which set the dome alight once, but it was soon put out and the Cathedral was saved. Some said it was an act of God, as no hoses could pump water high enough to reach the dome.

It was difficult to sort out the sequence of events that took place between 1942 and 1944, it all seemed a bit of a blur to David. He had become quite an expert on the sound of aeroplane engine noise and could easily tell the difference between a flight of fighters and a squadron of bombers. He and Jack could also, normally, tell the difference between a squadron of allied bombers from German bombers. This became quite useful at night as it would give them just that little more time to race to the shelter and alert the rest of the household. Jack continued to make his model aircraft and as each was painted in its distinct colours it was added to the horde of earlier craft hanging at different heights from their bedroom ceiling. The lower drawer of the chest was also filling with relics found in the streets and parks after a raid, mainly made up of shrapnel and bullet cases. The bedroom, although the largest in the house could only just accommodate Jack and David's double bed and Bobby's single bed, an old dressing table, plus the large Singer sewing machine, which had a treadle and large flywheel. This gave them great fun when they disconnected the leather band and by pressing the treadle up and down could spin the wheel at great speed.

It was during the same period that David experienced the loneliness and loss of his role model, when Jack was suddenly taken ill with some sort of breathing problem. He had had bouts of it in the past when he seemed to get short of breath and go into a kind of panic. This sent Mum and Dad into a complete flap not knowing how to help him. He had been to the doctors who had diagnosed it as asthma and although it was good to have a name for the problem, no one knew what it exactly meant. The doctor had said that it would disappear as he got older, but Jack's seem to be getting worse. Mrs. Stamp, who seemed to know about medical matters, told Mum that either he would have a change of life at the age of fourteen, as she said that all the cells of the body changed every seven years, or he would run out of breath one day and die. This did not cheer Mum up at all and when Jack suddenly had a panic attack and was gasping for breath, he was rushed into hospital. This seemed like the end of the world to David as Jack was his idol and all that he said and did was right and good. He lost a lot of interest in the studying of aircraft, tanks, ranks of soldiers, sailors and aircrew and even in collecting souvenirs. He did, however, keep a careful watch on the models made by Jack and kept them away from the sticky fingers of Bobby and Susy. Mum and Dad went to the hospital every day for a week until they brought home the good news that Jack was a lot better and they had arranged for him to stay with an aunty on Dad's side, who lived out in the country going towards Devon. It was actually in Newbury, but to David it could have been the other side of the world. He missed Jack and his guidance and felt that part of his world had come to an end.

Nevertheless, the group of children that lived in their area had all linked to form quite a little club and they would still go out onto the green, and down the park to play all sorts of games. Football was popular with boys and girls. Betty was always a good player to have on your team as she could barge anyone over and get the ball. Cricket and French cricket, hop-scotch and skipping were also quite popular and when it was beginning to get dark they used to play "knock down   ginger", which involved knocking on some unsuspecting persons front door and then all running and hiding. This was popular with the children, but not so much fun for the adults, who sometimes used to chase the children with a copper stick in their hand. David, Danny, Peter and a few of the other boys used to enjoy playing a cricket type of game where they placed one stump at the end of a pathway and would bowl a tennis ball, trying to spin it in from the left or the right. They would place a can about three feet in front to the stump and if you hit the can, you lost a life. This control of the ball would pay off in future years when David became very keen on cricket and made his way into the school teams.

Jack was away for about four weeks, but on his return Mum produced a very special tea and all Jack's friends were invited. There was great rejoicing in the house because Jack, even at this early age, had taken on a responsible role in the decisions concerning the house and the family and even Mum would turn to him for guidance in certain matters. David never really knew how far Newbury was from where they lived as Dad would get on his old roadster bike and cycle all the way there and back in a day. David now realised that even a good cyclist would find this quite a challenge.

David moved up through the infant and then into the junior school, but a lot of time was lost through raids and emergencies. Some of the teachers had left and gone to the country to avoid the bombing and it was hard to guess how many children would be in any class and whether they would be absent or late. David, Peter and Danny still worked as a trio with   certain additions, sometimes boys and sometimes girls. All three had a soft spot for Jane, the girl that lived next door to Peter, but she was only interested in Danny. All the girls seemed to like him. This pact that the boys had formed was quite envied by certain sections of the groups in the school. One particular group, or gang as they called it, was run by a tough, broad boy called Jerry Avern.

Jerry was a squat round faced boy with short hair and a ruddy complexion. He always wore a brown windcheater and black short trousers, which were creased and dirty enough to look as if he had slept in them and his boots must have been worn by several members of his family before being handed down to him. He had gathered a group of boys around him who were obviously scared of not being in his gang. Although short he commanded the group as his underlings and anyone not obeying his instructions was beaten up by one or two of his entourage. David, Danny and Peter avoided this group as much as they could as there was a nasty feeling every time he or his gang appeared on the scene, but in the playground and on the way home from school there was always the chance of crossing their path. One day, in the playground, Hughie Hitchinson, Jerry's second in command, came over to David, who was standing on his own looking at a game of tag taking part between a team of boys and another of girls. Hughie said that Jerry had told him to come over and tell David that he was to become a member of Jerry's gang. He said that he advised him to take up the offer as to turn it down would mean a beating up. David said that he wasn't interested in belonging to a gang as he was quite happy with the friends that he had. He knew that if a fight did occur he would have the backing of Danny and Peter and although they were not the toughest of boys they could give a good account of themselves. Danny was broad shouldered and quite muscular and although Peter was as thin as a rake he had a temper that even his elder brothers and sisters, two of each, would hesitate to arouse. David told the two of them of the threat that Jerry had given through Hughie and both of the boys agreed to make sure that they all went home from school together.

Nothing happened for a couple of weeks, although Hughie did come over and repeat the threat he had made earlier on. Then, one day, when Peter was off school with a cold and Danny was kept in by one of the teachers for playing the fool in front of all the girls, David found himself walking home on his own. Suddenly he was aware of a group of boys behind him getting closer and closer until one of the boys pushed him in the back. He started to walk faster, but they continued to jostle him. He decided that the best thing to do was to run down the hill, past the woods. He began to pull away from them until he suddenly noticed a line of toughs across the path in front of him. He stopped and realised the only way out was to run into the woods. He was not too worried about this as he knew the woods inside out and could swap from pathway to pathway quite rapidly. Alas, only about ten yards into the wood his path was blocked by Jerry and two other boys, one being his right hand man, Hughie. Hughie told him again that he was to become a member of Jerry's gang or he would be beaten up. David noticed that Jerry never spoke for himself, he always seemed to make others do his dirty work. By this time several other members of the gang had come up behind him, plus many other boys and girls who realised that a fight was imminent and didn't want to miss any of the fun. David said that he didn't want to join his gang and if any of the boys beat him up he would report it to his dad, who was a policeman. This was heralded by many of the boys laughing. One of the girls who knew David stepped in front of David and confirmed the fact that his dad was a policeman, although David knew that Dad would be able to do nothing about it and would say, "fight your own battles, it's the only way to learn".

Jerry said something to one of the bigger boys who stepped forward and pushed the girl so hard that she fell into a bush at the side of her. Then Hughie was told by Jerry to start the beating. He came forward,

David thought, reluctantly, and pushed David. David stepped back, but did not defend himself. Then Jerry shouted out, "Punch him in the face". Hughie Hitchinson then swung a fist that caught David a nasty blow on the side of the temple. He fell to the ground and lay stunned for a second or two. Then Hughie came running at him and dived on top of him with both fists flying. David's training with Jack on their bed in the morning, when they used to have friendly fights, suddenly came into action. He rapidly slipped to the side and held Hughie at bay. He shouted that he did not want to fight and wanted to go home. He was nearly in tears when a second blow hit him on the nose and all the gang started shouting for more. David fended off many of the blows as he was quite a good boxer until Hughie kicked him in the shin. David immediately saw red and hit Hughie with an almighty right cross, which knocked him to the ground. All the gang pushed Hughie forward and he again started lashing out with both fists, some hit the mark and some were dodged. There followed a period of punching, rolling on the mud and trying to throw each other into thorn bushes. David landed several heavy blows on Hughie's face and then caught him with a body blow to the soler plexus. Hughie fell to the floor gasping and David stood back expecting to be allowed to go home, but no. Several boys jumped on him and started hitting him in the face and the chest and David felt unable to concentrate on any one of the boys. One jumped on top of him and tried to pull him to the ground whilst the others tried to kick his legs away from him. When all seemed lost, one of the boys, on David's back was pulled off and thrown into a bush. One trying to kick his legs away was kicked violently up his bottom and went sprawling.

David swung round to see who had come to his aid and saw Mike Morris, the boy who lived about five houses away from David and had been responsible for David going into hospital after kicking him under the chin and causing him to bite through his tongue. There was a pause in the fighting and Mike said, "Anyone joining in will have to fight me first. Let them get on with the fight as a boxing match and when one gives in, the fight will end". Mike was quite a bit older than the rest and went to a catholic school further up the road. Hughie and David then started to box and David landed several hard blows to Hughie's chin. He fell on the ground and Mike asked whether he wanted to go on with the fight. He would not get up and David and Mike walked out of the woods amidst cheers from the quite large crowd that had gathered. David did not look back, but he knew that Jerry would not let such a defeat happen again. David was very reluctant to go to school for some weeks and made sure that he was always accompanied by his two pals, Danny and Peter. It was coming home from school which worried him most as Danny and Peter had been moved into another class and they were not always let out at the same time. David did, however, notice that Mike, whose school ended the day about a quarter of an hour earlier, was often just passing the gate as David came out and would walk along with him. David enjoyed this walk as Mike was a very intelligent lad and promised to teach him to play chess and how to take cuttings of gooseberry bushes and create new plants, when they had time.

One morning, as the three boys walked to the corner to meet Teddy and Billy, who still looked as if he had just got out of bed with a runny nose, hair all over the place and dirty knees, they were delighted to meet Tommy and his mum. David had seen them at times at the school gate, but always felt a little awkward as he didn't know whether she would burst into tears again. She looked very happy and put her arms around David and Danny's shoulders. It felt very nice as she gave them a tight hug. As they walked along the road she explained that she and Tommy were going to move to the countryside to stay with one of her relations until all the bombing had stopped. She said that they were very frightened when the bombers came over and she didn't want anything to happen to Tommy. They walked as far as the school gates, but instead of going in, they turned and went to walk home. Tommy's mum gave each of the boys a warm hug and kissed them on the forehead, then they walked away. David stood for a moment, not knowing what had hit him. He had never been hugged by a woman like that and felt a strange warm glow and a tingling sensation.

During the day they were asked by the teacher to write something which rhymed at the end of each line and ended up as a poem. She had read poems to the class quite often, but they were usually about birds or flowers, or sea and sky. David thought that he would write something which he could give to Tommy as a going away present so he based his poem on the war and the navy. He spent a long time playing with the words and just couldn't get them to fit into the line. When play time came along he asked the teacher if he could stay in the class and try to get the lines to fit as he wanted to give the poem to little Tommy. The teacher was so pleased that she said that she would stay at the front of the class and correct books and if he needed any help she would come to his desk and help him. He was very fond of this teacher as she was always smiling and had long hair, which was tied together at the back but hung down to her waist. She always wore a warm, pink, soft sweater and was never angry with any of the class, even if they were playing up. David finished the poem just before the rest of the class returned from play time and took it to the teacher to read. It went:-

The Navy is a great success,
Working O.H.M.S.
It guards the nation with its might,
It patrols the oceans by the night,
It guards the seas day by day,
It defends our England in every way,
And knocks the Germans off their feet,
As they come, fleet by fleet.

The teacher read it through and then seemed to read it through again. David felt quite proud of his attempt and wondered why the teacher was hesitating with her praise. She said, "David, what is ohms, is it something to do with electricity?" She pointed to the word on the second line which David had put all together. "No" he explained, "it means on his majesty's service, my brother told me that". She then smiled and said, "You must put a full stop at the end of each letter and make it a capital to show that it is an abbreviation". She then corrected the line and put her arms around him saying, "This is absolutely marvellous David. I am sure that Tommy will treasure it for the rest of his life". David walked back to his chair and felt the same feeling that he had experienced when Tommy's mum hugged him outside the school gates. In the dinner break he rewrote the poem on a new piece of paper and folded it in two. The teacher gave him an envelope to put it in just in case Tommy was not in when he went home.

Luckily, Mike was just passing the gates when David came out and they walked along together talking about different types of aeroplane and how to tell the difference between them and how fast they could fly. At the corner, just before the green, David left Mike and went down to where Tommy lived. He knocked on the door and almost immediately it was answered by Tommy's mum. She said that she had seen him coming in the gate. "Come in", she said, "We are just having a cup of tea. Would you like one?" David accepted the offer and was given a large mug and a thick slice of home made cake. He noticed that the room was very bare and there were some large cases by the door. In fact Tommy's mum pulled over one of the cases for him to sit on.

She said, "Thank you for coming round, you only just caught us. We are going to Morden to catch an underground train to London. I thought we had said our goodbyes at the school, but it is nice to see you again".

David explained that he had written a poem in class, that day, and wanted to give it to Tommy as a going away present. With that he proudly pulled out the envelope and gave it to Tommy. Tommy didn't know what to do with it until his mum said,

"Open the envelope then Tommy and let's see David's very kind and thoughtful gift."

Tommy ripped open the envelope almost tearing through the page inside and handed it to his mum. She read it aloud, but when she had read only five lines she burst into tears and ran out of the room and upstairs. David couldn't understand what was going on. Women were so strange. His teacher had smiled when she read the poem and put her arms around him, but Tommy's mum had burst into tears and he could still hear her sobbing upstairs. He didn't know what he had done wrong, but he felt that he should leave his tea and cake and go home. He said to Tommy,

"I am sorry I have upset your mum, I thought she would like my poem. Go up and see her and I will go home."

He went to the front door and let himself out. He walked down the pathway, which had privet hedges on either side and went to let himself out through the gate. Just as he was about to pull down the latch the upstairs window opened and Tommy's mum leant out and shouted.

"Don't go David, please come back and finish your tea. I will come down stairs in just a moment". David turned and went back. After about five minutes Tommy's mum came down stairs and rushed over to David, taking him in her arms and lifting him off the ground. She kissed him, again, on the forehead and after she had put him down she said,

"This is a wonderful poem, David, and a lovely gift for Tommy, which he will treasure. I am sorry I was such a silly cry baby in front of you, but it meant so much to me and it reminded me of Tommy's

141

dad. I will always remember you and your kindness, even though you are so young and if I can do anything for you in the future, perhaps when this dreadful war is over, just let me know. Perhaps you could come and stay with us sometime, in the country. I know Tommy would like that, wouldn't you Tommy?"

As David walked to his house he thought what a funny day it had been. He had been hugged by Tommy's mum twice and once by his teacher. Each hug had aroused a lovely feeling in him which made his cheeks glow and gave him a funny, but exciting, tingle all over. It had really been one of his best days, the two ladies that had given him the hugs were two of his favourites. His was a family where close contact in a loving gesture was quite uncommon. He knew that his Mum and Dad loved all their children dearly, but it was not quite the thing to do in those days.

Chapter 18

It hadn't been a very pleasent summer. There had been some short, sunny spells through May, but the hot and sunny months that David remembered in previous years had not yet occurred and he had spent much of his time, when not at school, sitting at the window watching the rain lashing down. Jack always seemed to be reading a book or making models of aircraft, whilst Betty would either be helping Mum with the cooking or making the beds, or knitting jumpers and cardigans. She was becoming quite an expert at all the different stitches and how to change from colour to colour and the speed with which she handled the needles was amazing. Bobby was always up to mischief. He was already four years old and had to be watched all the time as one never knew what mischief he would be up to. He was the apple of Dad's eye and would wait for him at the door. Dad would take him up in his arms or on his back and, while wearing Dad's helmet, would blow his whistle as hard as he could. It was lucky that Dad never let him handle the truncheon which was hidden down the outside of Dad's trousers in a secret pocket. Susy was always happy playing with her doll, whose eyes would open or close according to her position. When she was held upright her eyes were open and when Susy laid her down in her cot, her eyes would close. It wasn't till years later, when someone threw the doll at the wall that David found out how these eye movements were controlled.

During the early part of that year, 1944, the air-raids seemed to be getting less and the times that they had to rush to the shelter reduced considerably. They very rarely had lessons in the shelter at school and it was only on the very odd occasion that the boys would head for home because of the air-raid siren. In fact, this had lost a lot of its attraction now that Tommy and his mum had moved out. His house had been taken over by a very short, fat lady, who had a daughter about David's age. The neighbours and local children were really very unkind to them and would stand outside the house chanting rude rhymes. Apparently, although David did not know why it should provoke the groups of nasty onlookers, she, and her daughter were Jewish and this was not a popular religion to have at that time. On one occasion, the rougher element of the group ran up the privet lined pathway and knocked violently on the door shouting, "Come out you dirty Jew". With that the door opened and Mrs. Morris, as she was called, ran out and threw a plate at the retreating mob. After she had gone back inside, some of the boys crept up the pathway and threw stones into the back garden. Mrs. Morris came out of the front door with a copper stick, which was a thick piece of wood about three feet long. She swung it with all her might hitting one of the boys across the shoulders. It was only when a couple started throwing stones that she retreated into her house. To the relief of everybody present, two uniformed police came down the road at a slow policeman's plodding speed to sort out the problem. David was proud to see that one of them was his dad and the other his superior officer. Immediately, Dad gave David a threatening look and told him to go straight home, to stay indoors and wait for him to return when he would deal with him.

David did as he was told and when he explained to Mum that he was to stay in until Dad came home she sent him up to the bedroom to wait. David didn't know exactly what he had done, but by the look on Dad's face he knew he was in for a pasting. It must have been at least two hours before David heard Dad's key in the door and another half an hour before he could hear Dad's heavy police boots climbing the stairs. David moved to the opposite side of the bed to the door and waited for all hell to break loose. Strangely, Dad said nothing as he entered the door and quietly closed it. He was still in his police uniform which gave him a very authoritative presence. He told David to sit down and then told him something which made tears come to David's eyes and made him feel so bad that all the wonderful feelings of pride just disappeared. Dad explained that Mrs. Morris was called a Jew, because that was her religion.   She did seem a little mad because she had gone through terrible times that he could not imagine. She had come from Germany just before the beginning of the war escaping from a German army who wanted to kill her and her daughter.   They had taken away her husband and she believed that he had been shot through the head by one of the German soldiers.

She and her daughter Helen had hidden away in some waste bins until nightfall and then began to walk towards France. They had had to hide up many times and sometimes had no food for days.   She managed to get across to England and was put into a prison camp with lots of other German Jews.   It was some years before she was let out and allowed to live in a flat in London.   When the bombing became very bad she was moved down to their estate to try to find peace and some kindness in her life.   "What I saw today", said Dad, "was an utter disgrace and all those who took part, including you, should be ashamed of themselves. If this is what we are all fighting for, then we should give up and let the Germans in to kill all those they don't like". By this time David was crying openly and felt absolutely ashamed of the behaviour of the gang of boys.   Dad continued, "I expect you to find the boys that took part in the frightening of Mrs. Morris and let them know what she had gone through and I hope that they will feel as ashamed as you".   With that Dad opened the bedroom door and went downstairs.   David thought to himself that he would rather have had a beating than upset Dad like that.   He resolved that, he would in the next few days, seek out the boys and make them aware of the situation.   He knew many of them and he thought it would be best just to pick on those that he knew were not unkind and tell them to inform the others.

They were all amazed at the activity on all the main roads around the estate.   Army lorries were abundant, some pulling guns and some just full of troops.   Convoys of them would be heading south towards Sutton and David, Danny and Peter would wave and cheer as they passed them on the road.   They also noticed that squadrons of heavy bombers headed south nearly everyday, in fact sometimes twice a day and in the night. They knew something was going to happen, but they had heard nothing about this build up of troops. Dad guessed that the allied army may be going to make a landing in France, but even though he seemed to be in the know, he could not confirm anything. It wasn't till early June, when the rain was still coming down and making the summer even more miserable that Mr. Churchill made an announcement on the nine o'clock news that an invasion of France had taken place and our troops made up of many nations had landed on the beaches and were heading inland against heavy German opposition. All the family leaped up and down, including Mum and Dad and within five minutes there were knocks on the door. When David looked out he saw that all the front doors around the large and small green were open and hoards of people were running up and down the gardens and the pavement jumping and shouting and cheering. Many of the men had glasses of beer in their hands and some had formed a circle and were dancing what looked like the pallais glide. David sought out his two friends and they walked around the streets watching the mad behaviour of the crowds. He thought that this must be the end of the war and it would not be long before peace would arrive and the years of war and bombs and hunger would all be gone. How wrong they all were, the worst was yet to come!

Chapter 19

"Do you mind if I have a quick wash at the sink after we have done the washing and wiping up, only I expect Janet to come round in about half an hour and I am running a bit late". David was approaching Mum with the wiping up cloth in his hand with the full intention of taking the wet dishes from her and after drying them, putting them away in the large cupboard which backed on to one wall of the kitchen. Mum turned to him smiling and said, "If you hadn't spent so much time helping that young married mother, you would have had a little more time to get ready to meet Janet. I hope you are not going to tell her about your helping hand, I don't think that she will be so willing to believe your story". David could feel his face going red and tried to cover it up by turning away towards the cupboard. "Now, you go off upstairs and get your things ready that you want to wear tonight. I'll finish off down here and when it is clear I will give you a call". David put his arm around Mum's shoulder, she was always so aware of the situation and he marvelled at the common sense she always had when any problem arose.

"Thanks Mum, I won't be long".

He ran up the stairs two at a time and into the back bedroom. In the wardrobe he selected his white shirt, which he found neatly ironed and hanging on a hanger. The collar, which had been turned inside out to cover up the wear on one side, looked like new and he again was so grateful to Mum for the attention she always paid to all the children's clothes. He pulled out his dark brown suit recently acquired from Jackson's in Tooting and checked the trousers to make sure there were no marks on them. His mind turned to the first date he had had with Janet and how he had gone through the same routine before the couple who had persuaded her to go to the pictures with them, came round to call for him. He had spent many months asking her to dance and trying to make conversation with her, but always to no avail. After they had returned from the club holiday in the New Forest, she had avoided him as much as possible. David had been so taken by her looks and personality that he could think of nothing else. On the way home in the evenings after a night at the youth club, Janet would always walk home in a group which included her sister and her boyfriend and every time that David approached her, she would move away and keep someone in between them. One time, when he managed to get to her side and asked if he could walk along with her, she said that she was not interested in boys and particularly him. She just wanted to be a member of a group of friends and that was all.

When Norman and his new girl friend Bonny had persuaded Janet to accompany them to the cinema, David could hardly believe his luck. Bonny was a good friend of Janet's and could act as her chaperone. That evening David had been shaking so much that he found it hard to do up the buttons of his shirt and was all fingers and thumbs. When Norman and Bonny came to the door, David was waiting to go straight out, but Mum invited them in. This was most unusual as very few people, other than family and close friends had this privilege. Mum was obviously checking on who David was going with. She was quite upset to find that Janet was not there. They explained that they would call round to Janet's on the way.

David was shaking more than ever when they knocked on Janet's door and when her mother opened the door, David could hardly speak, his mouth was so dry. She greeted them with a warm smiling face and invited them in. She shook hands with all of them and turning to David said, "Now you will keep special care of Janet, won't you? She is still very young and she has not gone out with any boys before". With that, David was surprised to hear Janet, who was just putting on her coat, say, "Oh mum, don't be so silly, I can take good care of myself and anyway Bonny will make sure that I am alright". David didn't know what all the fuss was, as he knew that he would have done anything to make sure that no harm came to her. Janet's mum checked that she had the money for the bus and the pictures, and with that they started for the door. At that moment Janet's dad came down the stairs into the passage way. David was quite taken by surprise, Janet and her mother were quite petite, but her Dad looked like a giant. He had broad shoulders, massive arms and stood about six feet tall. He was dressed in a pair of old trousers and a tee shirt and what looked like army boots on his feet. He came face to face with David and said, "So you are the fellow who is taking our young Janet to the pictures, are you? Now you make sure you look after her and make sure that you come straight back here when the film is over, do you understand?" David could hardly open his mouth, he could hear the words, "Yes Sir", being said, but he couldn't make out whether it was him or someone else saying it. As they went out of the front door David felt a very heavy arm go around his shoulder and a mighty big hand grip his other shoulder. Then he heard the voice of Janet's dad say, "Are you alright for money, don't worry about Janet, she will pay for herself. Let her do that or she may not go out with you again". "I'm fine thanks sir, but thanks all the same."

David couldn't remember what film they had gone to see, he spent most of the time thinking of the beautiful young lady that was sitting by his side and longed to hold her hand, but didn't dare do so in case he was rejected. He remembered that at the interval they asked the girls if they would like an ice cream and felt pleased when both said they would. In the queue Norman asked David why he had not put his arm around Janet, "Hadn't you noticed that I had my arm around Bonny and she responded by giving me a hum dinger of a kiss. I imagine Janet is waiting for you to make some sort of move, then she might respond". After the interval, when the main film was just starting, David leaned away from Janet to clear his arm so that he could put it around her shoulders, but suddenly became a coward and came back to the centre of the seat. He spent perhaps another half an hour trying to build up his courage, but each time he began to make a move she leaned away from him. As the film was reaching its climax he thought to himself, it's now or never, and with that slipped his arm around her shoulders. She did nothing, she didn't turn to him or lean towards or away from him, in fact she seemed to be quite rigid. They stayed like that till the end of the film and as they stood up for the national anthem David removed his arm. Janet spoke very little on the way home and when they got to her gate she quickly ran up the path to her door without saying a word. Her mother opened the door and then after thanking them for bringing Janet back home so promptly, closed it again. That, thought David, was the end of his love affair with beautiful Janet. He remembered that he walked home feeling quite sad that he had made no headway in their relationship and could see no hope for any future in pursuing any sort of romance. But again, how wrong he was.

He was sure that it was the dancing that had made all the difference. Once a week the club would hold a dancing class when one of the better dancers or even, sometimes, a teacher, would run through some new steps for a particular ballroom dance. David had learnt all the basic steps when he had come to the youth club with his sister Betty a couple of years before. Betty had several friends who were always looking for partners and they soon taught David the fundamentals of all the main dances. In fact he enjoyed it so much that he would dance just about every dance that was held in the evening. This now paid off for, although he wasn't up to the standard of many of the members, he could lead and control his partner with some expertise. Whoever was doing the teaching would partner couples up and as they knew that Janet was very young and shy, they naturally put David with Janet. First of all David was holding too tightly or talking during the practice, although holding Janet in his arms was a great joy. They studied the steps and practiced hard and gradually they relaxed into the dance and felt very pleased when they performed the steps correctly and ended up in the correct position. Janet was a quick learner and each time they danced they added more steps to their repertoire. They would discuss how they would approach certain sequences of steps and would often sit together, at the side of the floor, talking about the club, other dancers and what they would like to learn next.   They learnt that, on Saturday evenings, some of the club would go to local dance halls to dance to one of the big bands of the day and it wasn't long before they were invited to join the group. They were now considered to be a dancing couple and although the ice was not really broken as far as personal involvement was concerned, David did have the pleasure of sitting with Janet on the buses and in the bars, when, in the interval, they would go for some refreshment.   He would even have the privilege of walking Janet home on occasions, although her sister and boyfriend were often present.

The club committee had voted to pay a visit to Winchester House, in Shanklin, on the Isle of Wight that year, which was a retreat for church youth clubs. All the club were pleased with this decision as it brought back happy memories of the holiday they had had together the year before.   David was in some doubt as to whether he should go as he only had a paper round and a lot of the income from that went to pay for the paints, paper and bus fares needed to keep him
It wasn't until Janet came to him one evening and asked him whether he was going on the club holiday that he thought seriously about it.   In fact she had said that she would like him to come and it wouldn't be the same without him. David couldn't believe his ears. He said that he would be going and also looked forward to being on the club holiday if she was there. He saved hard and even earned a little more cash by finishing his round early and going back to the paper shop to cover any paper boys that had not turned up that morning. Each week there was always an extra round or two which would earn him a few bob.   He was very reluctant to ask his parents for any cash as they had been very generous on many occasions in the past and had also agreed that he could carry on with his education at the Art School, even though they could have done with a little more money coming in.

151

That holiday was one of the best that David had experienced. He remembered the joy they had dancing in the room that overlooked the sea and standing on the cliff looking at the fireworks being let off from Sandown pier and listening to the warm strings of Mantovani and his orchestra playing the Blue Danube. Well, David thought that it was the correct orchestra and the tune, but he was not absolutely sure. It was certainly one of the warmest summers and they would lie on the beach sunbathing and occasionally, although not too often, David would slip his arm around Janet's waist. This was not really approved of as Janet thought that it might leave a hand mark on her waist or back and everybody would know how close they had lain together. When Janet was not on the beach or had preferred to go down to the village, shopping, David would take up his sketch book, which he carried everywhere, and make studies of the objects around him. His favourite subject was the older boats that had been left on the beach and were not now good enough to be used. Most of them were large, clinker, rowing boats. In fact he always felt that the best study he ever did was of one of the boats on Welcome Beach, he even slipped it into one of his paintings that he completed when he returned. Many evenings the club would stroll back from one of the villages and many times David would slip his arm around Janet and she would, on occasions, respond with a kiss. In fact they would take a little walk in the evening and would find a quiet spot away from the lights of the front and there they would put their arms around each other and kiss. Although David would have all the feelings of a young man with the girl that he loved held tightly in his arms, he never pushed his desires on to Janet. She was still very young and although she felt as if she was also getting the same desires, she always held back. One of their favourite spots was just along the cliff where the path leading from the front crossed the railway. He remembered that although it was dark and no-one could see them kissing and cuddling when a train came along they would have to stand away from each other and wait for it to pass.

That was the time when David first got to know Father Kingswood well. He was a very talented curate who knew all about aircraft engines, motorbikes, gardening, etc. and could play the piano well and sing to many of the tunes he played. He would sit at the piano in the recreation room and play many pieces by Chopin, his favourite composer. He took part in all the sports and would accompany David swimming way out into the Sandown Bay. It was often hard to remember that he was a man of the cloth and would change at the time of Church or Chapel Services and lead the congregation in prayer and worship. He would give his sermon on a topical subject and would always manage to bring in something involving the club, or the local community. Occasionally, even in a serious part of the service he would give one of the club members a wink or a smile. This was never disrespectful and many used to wait for the recognition or the quip. In fact when Father Kingswood was preaching the Church was usually full and all the members of the club would be there. He did a lot to improve the Christian knowledge of nearly every member of the club and they all respected him enormously. He was to become a lighthouse in a storm to David in the very near future, but at the time he was just one of those people in life who seemed to give everything and expect nothing in return.

Soon after returning from the holiday Janet and David met up to go to Church. They had begun this habit although David thought that it was overdoing it a little as they would attend every service. Janet had gradually become very religious and would spend a lot of time at the Church, teaching at the Sunday School, doing the vestments, etc. She was being encouraged by Miss Bowlingbrook, who was herself a devout Christian. This particular evening they noticed that although Father Kingswood was scheduled to celebrate evensong and to be giving the sermon, he was not there. After the service they enquired from Miss Bowlingbrook why this was and were told that he was suffering from acute sciatica and was unable to leave his bed. They decided to pay a visit to his house and were received at the front door by his housekeeper. She took them upstairs and there he was lying, propped up in bed and looking a sorry sight. After only half an hour he was laughing and joking and obviously so pleased to see them. It was at that meeting that David felt that he had really got to know Father Kingswood well. What a great friend he would turn out to be in the future.

"Sinks clear!" It was Mum calling from downstairs. David had done very little, he had spent most of his time sitting and thinking of the past.

"O.K. Mum, I'll be right down, I won't be a minute".

He quickly slipped on his trousers, did up the buttons of the flies and pulled the tab across the front and hooked it into the flat retainer. He then slipped on his shoes and after doing them up gave them each a rub up and down the back of the trousers of the opposite leg. He knew this is something that was discouraged, but it certainly brought a shine to the caps of the shoes when there wasn't the time to clean them properly. He raced down the stairs two at a time and was pleased to see that Mum had not only cleared the sink but had put the kettle on the gas so that he could use warm water. He poured the nearly boiling water into the bowl and after running in some cold water from the tap, took the bar of Fairy Soap and quickly washed his face and his neck. He splashed a little water under his arms to freshen them up and dried himself off with the towel hanging on the rack which hung from the ceiling. On returning to the bedroom he put on the shirt, put a decent knot in his tie and combed his hair. This shirt had cuffs and some months ago Jack had advised him to dress with the cuffs turned up, to keep them clean, and after all dressing was done, only then roll them down and secure them with cuff links. This he did and taking hold of his jacket went downstairs to get Mum's approval.

As he descended the stairs, he could hear a terrible noise coming from the kitchen. It sounded as if all hell had been let loose. On opening the door he could see Mum battling with Bobby at the sink. Mum and Dad were also going out that evening to visit one of the public houses with Uncle Andy and Aunty Doreen. They were coming over from their home in Earlsfield as he had free travel on the buses due to him being a trolley bus driver. Bobby was playing up as usual. He couldn't see why he should have to wash as he intended going down the park for a game of football and then taking part in one of the parties that were going on all over the estate. Mum thought that as Uncle Andy and Aunt Doreen would be there soon, he should at least look clean.

David went into the front room and saw Susy washed and dressed ready to go with the adults. She was never any trouble and seemed to take pride, even at this early age, in being clean and dressed in a pretty dress. She was sitting by Dad, who was listening to the radio and at the same time cleaning his shoes. These shoes had been polished so much over the years that you could almost see your face in the toe caps. The only thing David didn't like about them was that they were a light shade of brown. He looked up when David came in and was obviously surprised at David's sartorial elegance.

"Wow! You look good, I suppose you are going out with Janet this evening. You are a lucky fellow having such a lovely young lady to go around with. I hope you let her know how you appreciate her."

"Don't worry, I am sure that I make it quite clear to her what she means to me. We are just going up to the youth club this evening. They are holding a special dance to celebrate the Coronation, it is only two records, but we can put on records that we like and are easy to dance to. Anyway, I'll go and wait for her at the front door".

With that David went into the porch and opened the front door. He could hear the celebrations still going on over the green with children racing up and down and music being played. He felt a little conspicuous standing there as he thought Polly or one of her children may spot him and come over. That could prove a little embarrassing if Janet were to come when they were there. He decided to sit down on the top step He pulled the mat across on top of the step to protect his trousers and sat down. This always started him thinking about the past. He remembered sitting in the exact spot in 1944 on a Saturday afternoon listening to the laughter and shouting of his friends who were playing some wide game or other around the greens, when their celebrations of hearing about the invasion were shattered and their lives took a dramatic turn for the worst.

Chapter 20

It was Saturday afternoon and Mike had come over to David's house to teach him how to play chess. Mike had just been given a pocket chess set and was very keen on playing a game or two. The only problem was that no one else in the street had any idea how to play and thought it was a game only for the "toffs". Many of the children had not even heard of the game and thought it should be played in a similar way to draughts. Mike knew that David was keen to learn and was explaining to him the moves that different chessmen could make and how, if you made an incorrect start to the game, you could be "check mate" in only a few moves. They were sitting on the top step of David's front door, which was a very normal place to entertain friends as it was quite unusual to invite people indoors, even if it was raining. This day however, was bright and sunny and everybody was enjoying playing on the greens, or just standing at their front doors with the warm feeling that our troops had now invaded the continent and the war would be over in a few weeks. There had been no heavy bombers passing overhead towards London for some weeks now and most of the people on the estate had moved back into their bedrooms and the comfort of their beds and the shelter had been filled with bicycles, prams and garden tools, giving the thought that this is what peace must be like. Many of the children had not experienced peace before, and those that had, had forgotten about it.

David thought that he was doing quite well at his second attempt at chess. He had cleared many of Mike's pieces off of the board and he was just waiting for Mike to make one more error and he would take his King. Alas, Mike picked up one of his Knights and after doing a strange move of one forward and two to the side declared, "Checkmate". David was just about to complain that he hadn't seen that Knight down his end, when, above the shouting of the children on the large green, they heard a very strange throbbing sound. It sounded like one of the old motorbikes, with one cylinder but grew louder and louder. They dropped the pocket chess set and ran onto the green to see what was causing such a strange sound. It became almost deafening before, just over the rooftops coming from the direction of the shops appeared a plane. It was black and small with square wings and a pointed nose. On the back, about where the tail should have been was a cylindrical shaped section which was spitting a flame. They all stood still and in silence when suddenly one of the boys shouted out. "It's German; it's got black crosses on the wings. With that there was a mass exodus from the green, every child running towards his or her home. Many of the doors were already open and the kids ran straight in.

As David covered the thirty yards across the small green, he glanced up at the plane which was now passing over his roof and on its way towards Mitcham. He slowed down and watched as it sped on. Suddenly, and without warning, the engine stopped and the little plane seemed to go into a nose dive. There was an enormous explosion and they could see a column of smoke rising up in the distance. Many of the onlookers came out of their doors cheering and waving their arms in the air. They all supposed that the plane had been shot down and that was the end of another of their fighter planes. Dad, Jack and Betty all came to the door looking pleased. Dad said that he thought that the plane had run out of fuel as its engine had just stopped and he hadn't seen or heard any evidence of gun fire. David described the shape of the plane to Jack, who was quite an expert on German fighters and bombers, but he had no idea what it could have been. David thought how strange it was that the plane did not fire any guns at the crowd on the green, in fact it seemed to ignore them completely.

They were all enjoying the belief that another German plane had bitten the dust, when they were taken by surprise to see Mum racing across the big green, shouting and screaming for them to take cover.

Her shopping bag had obviously been discarded on the way home and she looked white and shaken. Dad ran out to meet her and tried to calm her down. All she kept saying was that the greengrocer had seen the plane and had said that it was a pilot-less plane, packed with explosive and no one could shoot them down and no fighters could catch them as they flew too fast. Dad put his arm around her shoulders as they came towards the house and David heard him saying, "Don't be silly, Nancy. How could a plane know where it was going if it had no pilot? Do you think any plane could find its way all the way from Germany, over the Channel and across the south of England without someone guiding it? I think that the greengrocer is spreading rumours and I will go over to him later and have a word with him".

"Anyway", piped in Jack, "we've got fighters now like the Lightening and the Mosquito which are faster than any of the German planes and they could catch them up and shoot them down long before they could get to here".

That was one of the rare times that Dad and Jack had been wrong. Mind you it was not surprising as no one had ever heard of a pilot-less aircraft before and as Dad had said, it seemed impossible that a plane could fly so far without anyone to pilot it.

They were just about to go indoors when the air raid siren began to sound.

"Bit late", chided Dad with a smirk on his face, "The Gerry had already been shot down or run out of fuel".

There were shouts from the road and they turned to see Mr. Jones, tunic undone and his black helmet on the front of his forehead, racing along the road on a bicycle. He was shouting and blowing his whistle. "Get in your shelters quickly, there are more bombers coming and they seem to be heading this way".

159

Dad was still not convinced, but he and Jack began to clear the shelter of all the old junk that had been thrown in it. They were casually taking the bits and pieces out and Mum was putting the kettle on to make a cup of tea, when, in the distance they could hear that awful throbbing sound. It was faint at first, but gradually getting louder. Dad and Jack began to throw out the contents of the shelter and Betty and David were clearing it away from the doorway. Mum came out of the house carrying Susy in her arms and pulling little Bobby by the hand. She ran straight to the door of the shelter and pushed the two children in. She then turned to Betty and David, grabbing them by the arm and almost throwing them into the shelter. Finally she almost dived in herself just as the plane came over the roof of the house. They slammed the door shut and listened to the very heavy crackling sound of the engine. It gradually grew quieter and then stopped. They all waited with baited breath until they heard the mighty explosion and the shaking of the shelter and the ground beneath their feet.

David found that he was sitting astride the front wheel of Dad's bike and the cover he had over his front light had pushed into the flesh of his back just above his belt. When they opened the door to let some light in, he was surprised to see and feel with his hand that it was bleeding. Because of the panic he hadn't noticed the sharp edge cutting into his back. They all climbed out of the shelter and checked that no else had been injured in the rush. Dad pulled out his bike and told Jack, Betty and David to continue to clear the shelter and make it habitable for them all. He told Mum to make up some sandwiches and some drink and get in ready to be taken down into the shelter if necessary. He then turned to Mum and said,

"I must go to see if I can help. After that I will have to report to the station and find out what is going on. I will try to get back as soon as I can".

With that, he carried his bike through the house, picked up his tunic and trousers on the way, slipped his helmet on his head and rode off down the road in the direction of the last explosion. It was very unusual for Dad to go out of the house with his uniform unbuttoned and no trouser clips around his ankles, but he was obviously very worried about the stories that were flying around and wanted to get the facts from the station.

When the "all clear" sounded Mum and the two younger children made their way indoors while the other three got to work on the shelter. It wasn't too difficult except for the bunks, which Dad had dismantled to make more room. They had almost completed the task when there came a call from Mum at the kitchen door. They all came in to find Mr. Stamp and Mr. Cressington, Peter and Danny's dads, were in the open door of the porch. Mum had already explained to them that Dad had gone to see if he could help where the bombs had fallen and then would go to the police station to find out some of the information that people needed to know.

They were wondering if there had been any news on Dad's wireless, but David explained that they never touched it in case they messed it up.

"Can you work the wireless, Jack", asked Mr. Stamp.

"Yes, I can, that is if the accumulator is still charged up. Dad did have it charged at the garage on Bishopsford Road last week, but we have been listening to it nearly every evening." Vera Lynn and Donald Peers, the two new young singers had been on quite a bit and the Squadronaires and Glen Miller were favourites of the boys. Mum was really taken by Donald Peers and his new song "In a Shady Nook, by a Babbling Brook" "Anyway, I'll see if I can find any news". Jack took the two leads from the radio and connected them up to the red and black of the accumulator. He then turned on the main switch at the side of the wooden casing and begun to turn the large knob

161

under the dial. The arm in the opening began to turn, but there were only whistles and bangs. After a minute or two Jack suddenly realised that he had not connected the wire that Dad had trailed all round the room on the picture rail. They found a knob at the back of the wireless marked "Ariel" to which Jack connected the wire. There was a loud bang and whistle and a sort of water rushing sound. Jack again turned the knob and miraculously, music could be heard. Jack said that he thought it best if he now disconnected the accumulator and wait for the hour when he was sure there would be a news bulletin, but he was interrupted by a voice coming on and David thought he remembered it saying,

"We interrupt this programme of music to warn listeners to heed the air raid warnings and proceed as quickly as possible to their shelters. Anyone who is away from the vicinity of their own shelter must be given entry to the nearest shelter. We are being attacked by pilot-less aircraft which are full of explosives so if you hear the distinctive sound or the siren, take shelter immediately. Keep tuned to this station for further information and advice. Please let others, who have not heard this broadcast, know about the warning".

David could not remember, after all these years, what the actual words were, but they certainly struck dumb all that were present. They left the house with their heads down. Mr. Stamp who was still in his dirty trousers and rough shirt with its sleeves rolled up and with his braces showing went off down the street to call on all the neighbours to warn them and let them know the bad news. He was always there when he was needed and was always willing to give up his time to help others and how valuable would this help be in the coming months!

Chapter 21

It was after ten o'clock that Dad arrived home that evening. All the children were still up, Bobby was asleep on the settee and Susy was being held by Mum as she was very restless. The other three were wide awake and had been worrying about the safety of Dad. It wasn't hard to stay awake during the summer as the sun was still shining and it would be another hour or so before dusk. The summer time had been extended to double summer time to give more hours for the farmers to work in the fields and produce more food. This meant that the time was two hours in advance of Greenwich Mean Time and as there were only a few hours of darkness the sun was well up by the time they went off to school the next morning.

Dad was greeted with hugs and kisses and in the commotion little Bobby woke up, and after grumbling and crying for a short time, saw Dad and requested a blow of the whistle and the placing of the helmet on his head. Dad refused the former and granted the latter and after a quick hug around Dad's neck, Bobby lay down on the settee and went off to sleep again. The others waited for Mum to make Dad a cup of tea and then told him about the broadcast and the dire warning that had been issued. They also told him of the many soundings of the siren throughout the evening, but only once had they heard the dreaded throbbing of an engine followed by a violent explosion. They told him that they had cleared the shelter of all the rubbish and made up the bunks although they thought that Dad should have a quick inspection to see if they were safe. Jack explained to Dad about the use of his radio and how he had been asked by the neighbours to try to get it going. Dad knew Jack was a very capable lad and although he was only fourteen, he may at any time be called on to make important decisions if Dad wasn't there.

"Just be a little careful how much you use it as the accumulator will have to be charged up again soon and I am not sure how much time I will have to go down to the garage" was Dad's only reply.

The four of them were dying to know what Dad had discovered about the strange pilot-less aircraft and what sort of damage they were causing and did he get to the one that had fallen Morden way.

"Lets deal with one question at a time, and then I will tell you all what I want you to do. First of all, I was wrong about the planes. They don't have a pilot and are guided by some sort of system set up before they are launched. The funny noise is due to them being powered by a different type of engine, but I don't know anything about this. I was right about it running out of fuel. It is designed to do this over the London area and at that point it falls like a massive bomb, as it is packed with high explosive. It is officially called the V.1 by the Germans, but I have already heard people refer to it as the "Doodle Bug", I suppose that is due to it looking like some sort of insect and others are calling it the "Buzz Bomb" and I suppose that is due to its noise and the fact that it is really a flying bomb".

"What about the one that fell Morden way?" asked Jack.

"I was coming to that", said Dad. "When I arrived the fire engines and the ambulance were already there. Two houses, in the middle of a terrace, had completely gone. Two or three houses on either side were badly damaged and one was on fire at the back. We spent most of the time trying to get people out of these damaged houses. Some of them were badly injured and we really needed more ambulances. Two police cars turned up and all those that could walk, but needed to go to hospital, were taken by the police. There was rubble everywhere, bricks, cables and furniture. I think that those in the two houses didn't stand a chance, they were not in their shelter, which was still intact. We only hoped that many of them had been, like us, outside looking at the bomb and were well away from the blast, but who knows. They will find that all out later"

"So what did you want us to do", asked David.

"I want Mum, Bobby and Susy to sleep, tonight, in the shelter. You older ones can sleep in the house as long as you race to the shelter at the first sound of the siren. On second thoughts, perhaps Betty, you should go into the shelter with Mum and the children just in case she needs some help".

"Where will you sleep Dad?" asked Betty.

"I am afraid that I am on duty tonight, as usual and I won't be able to get home until tomorrow morning. That is why I want you to do as I say, just in case there are any more "Flying Bombs" to come. I will have a word with Mr. Stamp as I go out and ask him to keep an eye on you".

They were all very sad that Dad had again got to go out into the darkening night and all felt more than a little apprehensive at the story of the earlier events. Nevertheless, all the older children who knew the situation assured Dad that they would do as they were told. Betty helped Mum to get Bobby and Susy into their beds in the shelter and after having a hot drink of cocoa in the kitchen, went to join them. Mum repeated the warning Dad had given to the boys about coming to the shelter at the first sound of the siren. The boys then put on their pyjamas and made their way to bed.

They had only just got into bed after a last look out of the back window, when the siren began to sound. They immediately raced down the stairs and out of the backdoor. They stood by the side of the shelter listening and looking up to the sky. Mum had opened the door of the shelter just in case they needed to dive in. After half an hour of getting cold the "all clear" sounded and they made their way back to the house. Within half an hour of getting into bed they were again aroused by the siren. Again they raced down the stairs, out of the back door and stood by the shelter. Again, nothing. The "all clear" sounded after about fifteen minutes and they went back to bed. David couldn't remember what time it was, all he knew was that it was very dark. They were awakened by the sound of Mum screaming out their names at the top of her voice above the sound of the siren and a frightening roar of that throbbing engine. Off went the sheets and blankets and the two of them descended the stairs in groups of four or five at a time. David remembered that he had almost leapt onto Jack's back at the bottom. They left the back door open and raced for the shelter where Mum was standing with the door open. At that moment a dark shape, like the Devil, appeared over the roof and although it must have been higher than it seemed, it looked as if it would clip the high oak tree that was in the front of the house but could be seen from the back garden. They literally dived into the shelter and Mum slammed the heavy door shut and pulled the metal bar across. Within seconds the engine stopped and they waited in silence. It seemed ages until the shelter was shaken by an almighty explosion. Dust fell from the top of the shelter and the door gave a mighty bang.

David remembered that they all sat in silence for some time trying to hear what was going on outside. Mum, Jack, Betty and he were all a little shaken up as they knew that the flying bomb had only just had enough fuel to over-fly their house, but someone very close had received a direct hit.

"The bomb may have reached the park or the common", whispered Jack with a sound of hope in his voice. "There are also the woods next to the park, it may have been brought down by the trees".

They knew, however, a little later when they heard the bells of the fire engines, ambulances and police cars that their hopes were in vain. Just then there was a loud banging on the shelter door. Mum rushed to pull up the bar that held the door in place and pulled it open. There was the kind Mr. Stamp, still in the same shirt and trousers with his braces all twisted over his shoulders as if he had put them all on in a rush, standing there with a paraffin hurricane lamp in his hand.

"I just came to see if you were alright. Bill had popped in to see me on his way back to the station and asked it I could keep an eye on you. Are you all alright? We were a bit worried as we had heard screaming and we saw no movement of the door of your shelter".

"That is very kind of you to take the bother to check on us", replied Mum, "It was me screaming at the boys as they were still in bed when the bomb came over".

Just at that moment the siren sounded again, which was very unusual as the all clear hadn't been sounded for the end of the raid. Mr. Stamp left them quickly, climbed over the fencing between the gardens and went back to his own shelter. Mum allowed the boys to climb out and try to fathom out what was going on. In the distance they could again hear that ominous roar. This time they could see the flame in the sky heading north, but well wide of their area. The noise of the engine gradually died away and about a minute or two later they heard the sound of a distant explosion. Jack and David went through the house to the front door and stood on the top step. Many people were at their doors and quite a few men were rushing across the green towards the turnings behind their house where the first bomb would have fallen, but nobody knew what had happened or whether it had hit any houses. Mr. Stamp, Mr. Pope and Teddy, Jack's friend from next door were standing by the gate. They all agreed that it would be best to stay close to their shelters for the rest of the night just in case further flying bombs came down around the local streets.

David and Jack went back to the shelter and after telling Mum that they hadn't found out any information of value, began to push their way into the already cramped quarters for the rest of the night. They

167

were amazed to see that Bobby and little Susy had not even woken up and had been quite oblivious to all the commotion that had occurred. None of the others slept very well as the siren went off about every hour and there wasn't always an all clear. They did hear more "Buzz Bombs" go over, but none were that close. They did however hear the thud of the explosions as they hit the ground. The temperature in the shelter gradually increased as the night went on and they were a little worried to open the door as the raids seemed to be so frequent that they appeared to be running into one another. The inside was completely dark as there was no light except for the paraffin lamp that Mum only lit occasionally as for one, they were short of paraffin and for two, one of the dangers of being in such a confined space was that of fire.

They were awakened in the morning by a knocking on the door and to their surprise and delight, it was Dad. He was still in his uniform, but looked out on his feet. They all left the shelter and went into the kitchen, where Mum brewed up a pot of tea and put a saucepan on the gas stove to heat up and cook some porridge. Dad told them to leave the shelter door open to give it an airing and so that it was ready for a quick entry in the case of another air-raid siren. Jack told him of their adventures of the night before and how Mr. Stamp had popped round to check that they were alright. He also told him of the "Flying Bomb" that had come down at the back of them. He said that he thought it could have only been a couple of streets away by the sound of the explosion. David did notice, however, that he did not tell him of Mum's panic when they stayed in bed and their rush down the stairs. The funny thing was that although Mum was standing next to the gas stove, stirring the porridge, she didn't say a word.

Whilst they were all eating their porridge, which David found quite tasteless, as there was no sugar or any sweetener in it, Dad began to tell them of his experiences during his night duty. He said that there had been complete panic during the night as these "Flying Bombs" were falling all over London. More had fallen on the southern home counties and he had been told, by an army bomb disposal officer that they believed that this was due to the fact that they had not got the range of the fuel quite right   Dad said that many of the bombs had fallen on the estate and he had spent most of the night helping people out of damaged shelters.   Unless the bomb fell very close to the shelter, or even a direct hit, they had saved the occupants from serious injury.

"That is why I want you to be in range of a shelter, where ever you go" ordered Dad.   Anyone must give you sanctuary if there is a raid and there are larger ones built by the shops and on the corners of the streets".

"Did you see where the bomb came down behind us" asked Jack.

"Yes, I was on my bike riding down Gladstonebury Road hill, when I heard the throbbing sound way behind me.   I began to pick up speed, but the noise grew louder and louder.   I started to panic and pedalled for all I was worth.   When I looked round I could see the plane still heading my way.   I suddenly realised that if I turned around and rode back along the road I could pass under it before its engine cut out.   I slammed on my breaks, leaped off of my bike and mounted it again riding towards the plane.   It quickly flew over my head and within another minute I heard its engine stop and after a short pause, a loud explosion.   It was then that I heard the one that fell on Shillingbury Road, so I cycled back up the hill and went to help there".

"What was it like", asked Mum.

"There was a massive pile of rubble where three of four houses had been.   Part of the house still standing was on fire, through a gas main being ruptured, but it was soon put out by the fire brigade.   Most of the people were uninjured as they had been in their shelters.   One of the shelters was buried by the rubble of the house and some of those inside were injured quite badly.   They had quite a job getting to them

169

as they had to remove all the debris before they could open the shelter. They had to remove a panel from the side to get to those inside".

At that moment the siren began to wail and they all rushed to the shelter. Dad stood outside to listen for the bomb, but after about a quarter of an hour the all clear sounded and they came out to resume their breakfast. The siren sounded many times on that Sunday. Between the raids everybody met outside their houses to discuss some of the experiences of the night before, or what they were going to do the next night. All agreed that they would sleep in their shelters and many of the men decided that they would stay up and keep watch with Mr. Jones, who seemed to be enjoying his very important role of spreading information and advice. Later on that afternoon, he came along the road on his bicycle shouting through a megaphone. He was telling everybody to sleep in the shelters and to stay as near to their homes as possible. One piece of news that made David and his pals happy was that he said that no children should go to school the next day as school would be cancelled. Nevertheless, they must wait for further instructions, which would come at some time the next day.

Danny was not one for being told that he should stay close to his home and the possibility of being involved with helping his dad to work in the garden and being asked by his Mum to do some jobs in the house. Sunday was always a day to go out and enjoy the freedom of no school and no jobs. He persuaded David and Peter to accompany him to the site of the bomb that had dropped in the street down by the woods. It was quite easy to slip away as all the adults were deeply involved in telling of their experiences the night before and many were waiting for Mr. Stamp or someone else to return and let them know what the announcement by Mr. Jones meant. The boys made their way down Salby and Selton Roads to Wimbourne Road. Half way down Selton their progress was stopped by a rope across the road with red rags hanging from the sides and middle. There were quite a few people standing looking down the road and as the boys made their way to the front, mainly between the legs of the adults, they saw a scene of complete destruction. The road was littered with the remains of beds, wardrobes, settees, kitchen furniture etc. The houses that had stood on the other side of the road had completely gone and in their place was a massive pile of rubble. Out of the middle of the rubble projected the remains of a chimney stack which was snapped off near the top. There seemed to be clothes, sheets and blankets and newspapers blowing all over the site. In amongst all this confusion were men, some in ARP uniforms, many in fire-fighting gear, some in police uniforms and others in just shirt sleeves. It was a little difficult for the boys to see all the devastation due to the height of the hedges on either side of the road they were in. So Danny approached the policeman on the other side of the rope and explained to him that his Aunty and Uncle lived in the house just around the corner and could he and his friends just go to the corner and see if the house was still alright. At first the policeman refused to let him cross the rope, but when Danny pleaded with him just to go to the corner, he said,

"Just go to the corner, have a quick look and then come back".

Danny asked if his two friends could come too, but the policeman gave a definite "No". With that, Danny climbed over the rope and ran down the street to the corner. He made his way to the middle of the road where he got a good view of the bombsite taking in all the information he could so that he could let everybody know what he had seen. At that moment a man came running into the road towards Danny and there seemed to be an exchange of words with the man gesticulating towards the barrier. Danny came running back and went straight to the policeman and after speaking to him, jumped over the rope and told everybody to retreat up the road as quickly as the could as the man had told him that they could smell gas and they believed there were still some people unaccounted for. The crowd raced backwards and the policeman removed the rope and tied it across the road further away. Peter said that he didn't know that

Danny had an Aunty living in that road and why hadn't he been to see her before. Danny shrugged his shoulders and said,

"Well, I thought that they lived there".

When they arrived back in their own street Danny was in his element telling all of them, adults included how he had seen a whole line of houses absolutely flattened. He described the scenes in detail and even the dreadful sight of the tail of the flying bomb sticking out of the rubble with the swastika painted in black. The other boys hadn't seen this part and wondered whether this was part of Danny's vivid imagination. They didn't mind too much as he always told a good story and when he described how he had smelt gas and had warned the policeman to get the people to move further up the street he appeared to be a hero.

That evening and night the siren sounded more frequently than they had ever experienced before. It gave the impression that every time the all clear was sounded it was followed by the continuous warning siren. They all stayed in the vicinity of their own or a known air raid shelter and at night, they slept in their shelters. The fact that these were pilot-less aircraft frightened most people as they had never heard of this before and what amazed them even more was that they couldn't fathom out how the flying bombs knew where to go. They realised that they were being targeted only by the fact that they were not fuelled quite correctly and as soon as the Germans realised this they would give them that little bit more fuel to get them to fly as far as London. What David didn't know was that London had been hit by many of these "Doodle Bugs" and he heard later that over two hundred of them had reached their target during the first twenty four hours. They had, however, grown accustomed to the dreadful droning noise that the engines made and they also knew that if the noise continued the bomb had passed over, but if the noise stopped you should be close enough to a shelter to dive in. Being aware of the pattern of the "Doodle Bug" gave everyone a little more time to move to somewhere safer and many would stand outside and watch the devilish plane roaring across the sky with the flame spitting from its cylindrical tail.

In the morning people gathered at corners of streets, on the greens on the front steps of their porches to discuss the number of bombs each had heard or where they had dropped. There was a kind of strange milling around with people passing on little bits of information and sometimes frightening others with stories which weren't always completely true. The majority of the groups were made up of women of all ages, some times with children, worried sick as to what they could do to protect their families. Men were few and far between as most of the younger males were fighting in the Armed Services and others, like Bill, David's dad, would be involved in rescuing bombed out victims or supporting the Home Services such as the fire brigade, ambulance or police services. Later on that morning Mr. Jones came along the street on his bicycle with a megaphone in his hand. He first blew his whistle and when everybody had stopped talking and turned to see what all the fuss was, he made this statement:-

"Due to the increased hostilities, it has been decided that all children must be evacuated from the estate. For the first phase, all children between the ages of eight and thirteen will be evacuated as soon as possible. Someone will come round to each household and take the names of children in that age category and they will give you all the necessary information then. If you have children of that age begin to prepare them for evacuation and listen out for further announcements".

With that Mr. Jones put away his megaphone and cycled off around the corner. They were very impressed by his speech although Danny said that he was sure that he had been practicing this ever since the beginning of the war. Most of the groups stood dumb obviously selecting, in their minds, the children that must go. There were so many questions to be answered. Mum spent a long time talking to the other women in the group and after about half an hour she came back to David and asked him to go in doors. They walked out into the back garden and Mum called Betty to come and join them. Jack came out too as he was keen to know what the situation was. Mum explained to David and Betty that it looked as if it might be just the two of them who would be evacuated first, she thought that Jack may be a little too old to go although she hoped he could go as he could keep an eye on the others. David said that although he had heard the announcement, he didn't really know what evacuation meant. He didn't dare ask his friends as they all appeared to know and he didn't want to look a fool. Mum explained that it meant that they would be taken away to somewhere safe, away from all these bombs, most probably into the country. Betty began to cry and said that she didn't want to go anywhere without Mum or Dad and she would prefer to stay with the bombs. Mum explained that they had no real choice and anyway she would be much happier to know that they were safe. Even so, she put her arms around Betty and gave her a great hug and David could see that Mum's eyes were full of tears.

After another night of sirens, all clears and Doodle Bug engine noises they awoke to a beautiful sunny morning. After breakfast David rushed outside to call on Peter and Danny. They sat on the kerb at the side of the road to discuss their future trip. Peter and David were devastated to hear from Danny that his whole family was moving out and going to stay with an Aunty he had who lived down in Devon. He said that he had never been there before, but his dad had told him that it was a small village surrounded by orchards and he would be able to go and pick apples whenever he liked. There was fishing and rocks to climb and his dad had said that there were old mines down there where he could explore some of the workings underground. Not to be outdone, Peter and David said that they had heard that they were going to a farm which was close to the sea where they could swim as much as they liked. They ignored the fact that not only could neither of them swim, but they had not even seen the sea. David was feeling quite happy about the evacuation as he knew his elder sister, Betty, would be with him and Peter and his young sister, Rita, would all be together. What an adventure! He couldn't understand when he went indoors, why Betty was still crying and looking very sad.

Later on in the morning a lady came to the front door with a large clip board. She was a teacher from one of the schools and she said that she was compiling a list of the children in the household who would be evacuated in the first phase. She noted down the names of Betty and David and told Nancy that she must wash and iron all the clothes they would need to go away for some time, as nobody knew how long this emergency would last. She left a list of all the items that they would need to have with them including gas mask, identity disc, ration book, etc. and she also warned them to be ready, with their cases packed as the order to evacuate would come soon, but without warning as they did not want the enemy to know the date and the time. Finally, she told Mum that Jack was not eligible to go as he was fourteen and would soon be required to start work.

That evening Dad cut the kit bag, which had fallen on the front garden during the incendiary bomb raid several years before, into two, sewing a bottom in the top half and making a top to the lower half. He then painted out the German writing with white paint. The next morning he painted in large black letters David Fellows on one and Betty Fellows on the other. Mum then began to pack them with all the clean clothes that each of them possessed , leaving space for the rest, which she would wash, dry and iron that day just in case they were called on to leave the next morning. Mum was obviously relieved to feel that at least two of her children would be going to an area of safety and erroneously thought that she and the two younger children would perhaps join them a few days later. There was an air of excitement all around the estate and children were roaming around the streets checking on who was going and who was staying. Some had been told that they may be evacuated to the country. Some thought that they may go to seaside resorts and others said that they had been told that they were going up into the mountains of Scotland. Nobody knew. Dad said that they should wait until the morning of departure and then they would be told the truth.

That evening they had a very welcome, but unexpected, visit from Dad's younger brother Uncle Andy, the trolleybus driver. He was involved in moving some buses out of London and moving them into the southern counties. He said that something big was afoot, but he wasn't sure what it was. He had seen many buses on the way and they were all heading south and he thought that it may be to bring back some of the wounded soldiers from the front. He was always a mine of information and the children would always gather around him to hear of his latest exploits, but this time, they guessed that he may be wrong. Anyway he kept them amused by his tale of the happenings of the night before. He said,

"I was driving my trolleybus into Fairgreen, at Mitcham where we turn around and head back to Battersea, when I suddenly lost power. I tried to glide to the side of the road, but got stuck right across the road. I knew what had happened, one of my bloody...." Mum gave a "shush" and said "Remember there are children present". "Sorry" Uncle Andy said and went on, "I jumped out of my cabin and walked to the back of the bus. All the passengers inside were shouting because, you see, they had no lights. Anyway, I grabbed the ropes on the back of the bus that are attached to the arms and found one of them was tight. That means that the arm has come off the wire and is sticking up in the air. I pulled it down to the level of the wire, but of course, in the dark I can't see the wire. Just at that moment the siren began to howl".

"So what did you do?" asked Dad.

"What could I do? I pulled out my torch and began searching in the air for the wire. Suddenly, as if in my ear, some one shouts.

'Put that bloody light out you stupid fool, didn't you hear the air raid siren. Why are you shining a light into the sky, if the Jerries see it they will know where to drop their bombs'"

"Oh, I bet you felt a bit foolish", Mum interrupted.

"No, I shouted, don't call me stupid you imbecile , how am I going to find my arm in the dark and move this bus off of the street and secondly, how can the Jerry pilot see my light when there are no soddin' pilots in the planes.   It was only then that I saw that the shouting voice had come from a police officer".

After having a cup of tea with the family he said that he thought it was time for him to head for home.   They all went to the front door and stood on the steps to wave Uncle Andy goodbye, but just as he reached the gate the siren sounded again.   He waited there and they all listened out for the dreaded roaring of a Doodle Bug.   Within a minute the spitting rocket engine could be heard, growing louder and louder until over the housetops they could see the flaming tail of the bomb.   They all ran through the house and stood in front of the shelter.   They all watched as the devil plane roared overhead and disappeared north.   With the final words of "Some poor sods in for a packet", Uncle Andy left for home.

All through the night and the next day the raids continued and there was no more news of the evacuation.   Mum had both of the kitbags packed and the children were ready to say their goodbyes and go as soon as the word came.   Betty was still a little upset as she didn't want to leave Mum and the younger children, but when Mum explained that they would most probably be with them in a few days, she calmed down.   Many bombs had fallen on the estate and everyone felt a little apprehensive as to who would survive the time to the evacuation and would a bomb claim any more victims before they went.   They just had to wait.

That evening, about eight o'clock, there came a knock on the door. It was the teacher from a local school who had been round before. She told them that the evacuation was to take place the next morning, early. They were to be at Tweed Valley Junior School at eight o'clock sharp with their bags containing all the items on the list she had provided. Mum asked where the children were being taken to, but the teacher said that she did not know, but they should ask tomorrow. She finished by saying,

"Please keep all this information to yourselves, do not spread it around not even to your next door neighbours. Secrecy is essential" and with that she moved on. Naturally, they waited for about half an hour, about time for the lady to clear the area, and rushed to the Stamp's to hear of their news. They had been given the same information, but did not know where they were going. After a short discussion they decided that it would be best to make it an early night and they would meet to go to the school the next morning. David knew he would not sleep much that night, what with the siren going so often and the excitement of the evacuation the next morning. He really didn't know what it all meant. He realised that he would just have to wait until the morning and do as he was told.

Chapter 22

David remembered that he didn't sleep very much that night. Part of his problem was the excitement of what was going to happen the next day and secondly the siren never stopped sounding. Several times they had heard the Doodle Bugs passing overhead and the occasional thud of a distant explosion. At six o'clock he was fast asleep when Mum leaned over and gave him and Betty a shake. They quickly climbed out of the shelter and went to the kitchen to wash and have breakfast. It was a beautiful summer's morning with the sun already above the horizon and the sound of many sparrows and other song birds singing away as if the war was over. By seven o'clock they were ready to go. Mum had washed and fed the two youngsters and after strapping Susy into the pushchair, Betty and David picked up their kitbags and left the house. Little Bobby was told to hold onto the pushchair so that Mum could keep an eye on him.

Outside the house they met Peter, Rita and Peter's mum. His dad had said his goodbyes the night before and had decided to stay in bed that morning. Peter's elder brother was away in the Navy, but his elder sister stood on the top step to wave them goodbye. Jack said that he would catch them up at the school and unfortunately, Dad was on a night shift and hadn't yet come home. There was certainly a sense of excitement in the air as they paraded across the greens and down the alleyway heading towards the Tweed Valley School, which was on the way to the hospital. They could see many other children heading the same way and realised that they would not be on their own. They turned right into Thornhill Road and after crossing the main road that lead to Dad's allotment headed up the fairly steep road towards the hospital, which they could see in the distance. After crossing several minor roads they turned right into Tweed Valley Road and they were brought to a sudden halt. They were stunned to see that the road ahead was a complete bombsite with houses on both sides of the road smashed to just piles of bricks and what remained of people's possessions spread all over the road, gardens and rubble. Although the way through was barred by many fire engines and ambulances and dozens of men and women working to move the bricks and concrete, they could see that the area of devastation spread right up the road. Strangely, there were some houses, which although badly damaged, were still standing in the middle. David had never seen such devastation before and he and Peter agreed that this bomb must have had double the amount of explosive.

They walked up to the rope which had been drawn across the road where two ARP men were redirecting all the parents and children who were heading for the school at the end of the road. They were instructing the parents to follow the signs to get to the school, which they were pleased to say had not been hit. They followed the detour around a block of houses and came to the large green area which ran all the way from the hospital, across two main roads, through the woods, next to David's school, right down to the park at the bottom. Surrounding the top part of this green they were amazed to see, what appeared to be to them, hundreds of buses of all shapes and sizes. They made their way into the playground of the school through the gates on the end of Tweed Hill Road and were immediately on the end of a long queue of parents and children some carrying cases, some shopping bags and others kit bags similar to those of Betty and David. The noise was deafening with children shouting to one another and parents trying to manoeuvre themselves into the fastest part of the queue. An ARP warden came up to keep the milling mob in order and the boys were pleased to see that it was Mr. Jones. He was being his bumptious self and was ordering everybody around, which, in all honesty, was needed. When he saw David and Peter he came over and explained what was happening. They were keeping everybody in a line so that they could get them straight on to the first bus they came to. When the bus was full it would set off on its own, each having a different route. They were not keeping the children in the school, as first planned, due to the danger of the school being hit and the buses were not travelling in convoy for the same reason.

"Can you tell us where the children are being evacuated, Mr. Jones?" Mum enquired.

"No, that I am afraid is a secret. They are worried that the Germans may hear of the evacuation and try to attack the buses or trains"

"So you do know that they are going by train somewhere" Mum asked.

"No, I only know that I am to get the kids on to the buses as quickly as possible, I don't even know where the buses are going". With that he turned to go, but Peter caught him by the arm and said, "Was that bomb at the end of the road a bigger Doodle Bug than normal Mr. Jones"?

"No, it was a bit of very bad luck, two bombs fell on the same road last night. As the rescuers were getting to the first bomb, a second one came down. They reckon it was a million to one chance. Anyway I must go". With that he went off down the queue ordering everybody to get in line and not to push. They had to smile, Mr. Jones was in his element and seemed to be enjoying every minute of it.

They very quickly made their way to the front of the school, but found that the queue wound right round to the gates that led on to the large green. Ladies at the side of the group ticked off the names of the children and any that were not on the list were made to leave the school by the side gate. Names were pinned on to their outer clothing and finally they were divided up into sections. Unfortunately, the section ended at Peter and Rita. David and Betty were in the section behind. They were very upset and asked to be moved into one section and after a lot of argument two children from behind David were moved up ahead of Peter. They moved towards the buses where lots of adults stood waving and crying. Mum turned to Betty and said,

"Now you look after little David for me. Make sure you stay together, don't let anyone split you up. You are a big girl now and I expect you to take charge if any decisions need to be made. Do you understand?"

Betty stood there with tears in her eyes and David just heard her reply in a very sad voice. She then threw her arms around Mum's neck and gave her an enormous hug. Mum's eyes were flowing with tears as she released her arms from around her neck and bent to hold them both tight, one in each arm. It was hard to realise now that Betty was only twelve years old at the time and he was eight. The next bus pulled up and the lady in charge of the boarding of the bus shouted out,

"Now hurry along quickly, we want to get as many buses away as soon as possible before Jerry decides to send any more of those "Doodle Bugs" over. Make your way to the top of the bus at the front and sit in the first seats you get to. Fill up the top from the front".

Mum again asked the young woman if she had any idea where they would be going, but she assured her that she had no idea and no one else would know as they were only given the information about that part of the journey which involved them. She did say, however, that each child would be given a lettercard when they arrived at their new home which would let the parents know where they were. She then started counting the children on board. Peter and Rita were first and they were followed by Betty and David. They ran to the front of the bus and sat in the four front seats. Peter and David thought that this was great as they had the best view of where they were going. There was a nasty smell of stale smoke upstairs and they thought that the bus had only just come off of its normal run. They opened the front windows ready for the off. The bus was soon full and the engine started up. There was a double ring on the bell and they started to move forwards. They all rushed to the kerb side windows and waved frantically to their mums or dads who had come to see them off. The bus moved slowly up the road towards the hospital and then turned right towards the Rose pub. At the island it went down St. Anthony's Avenue towards Morden where they would go on Saturday mornings to the cinema. There was a lot of noise on the top deck with some children shouting, some crying and some singing. Eventually, they all joined in the singing and the popular army song of the time was changed slightly to fit in with their present position. It went:-

We don't know where we are going until we're there,
There's lots and lots of rumours in the air.
We heard the teacher say, we're on the move today,
We only hope the blooming headmaster knows the way.
We've been marching up and down the playground square,
And now we're on the road to anywhere,
We hope the driver's knowing, where we are going,
'Cause we don't know where we're going until we're there.

As soon as the last line was sung the first was started up again and the song went on and on. All the children were now joining in and there was quite a party atmosphere building up. This was enhanced by the young lady, who was from the school, and the bus conductor coming around to all the seats and handing out lunch boxes, small bottles of milk and an apple each. When they had finished the lady shouted out,

"Now put this box, milk and apple in your bags because this may be the only food you will get 'til this evening".

Little did she know that Peter and David had already opened theirs and the sandwiches and rock cake had already been devoured and the bottle of milk was half empty. Due to this interruption they had no

183

idea where they were heading.   There seemed to be more and more buildings and many shops and old houses and David felt sure that he had gone that way when they went to his grandmother's house, which was near Clapham.   Then the bus reached a steep hill and the driver changed down the gears to get a little speed up.   At that moment Betty spotted the remains of a burnt out theatre and suddenly realised that this was the theatre at the end of their grandmother's road.

"We are heading into London", she shouted.   This made everybody stop talking and singing and look out of the windows.   Most of the children had never been to London and they were amazed at the closeness of the houses and the lack of fields around them.   They could see all the buildings that had been destroyed by bombing and all the windows, especially of the shops, that were boarded up.

Peter said that he couldn't understand how they were being evacuated to London when they all knew that it was the place that Hitler wanted to destroy.   He said that he would tell his dad and he would come and bring them home.   He said, "It's safer at home than up here".

The bus drove on passing bigger and bigger buildings, some looking quite grand. Then they were amazed to be going over a bridge crossing a very wide river with what looked like churches and cathedrals on either side. By this time many of the children had become very quiet and were beginning to feel the first signs of homesickness. They passed through war torn London gasping at the size of some of the buildings and the amount of bomb damage.   They slowed down along a street full of shops that were all closed, some with no fronts to them and many utterly destroyed until they pulled over to the left and began to drive up a slope in front of what appeared to them to be a massive, brick cathedral.   The bus stopped outside some large arches at the front and two men in uniform jumped on the bus.

David remembered that he said, "Do you think that they are going to put us all up in a cathedral and hope that Hitler will not bomb it because God will protect it?" No one answered. The lady came upstairs and said that they must all move as quickly as possible, down the stairs and follow the children in front of them. The men would lead them into the front door. Betty took David's hand and they entered the front of the building. Again, they were all amazed at the size of the large hall they had entered. It had columns of brick and wonderful patterns on the ceiling. They were hurried to the doors at the back and could not believe their eyes. Under an enormous arched roof was a line of platforms and standing between the platforms were several huge steam engines gushing out steam from between their wheels and black smoke from the funnel at the front. Behind the engines were many carriages which were also blowing steam out to the sides and the noise was deafening. Never, in all his life, had David ever seen such a sight. Steam and smoke from the engines was rising in massive clouds up to the arched roof and in the dim light struggling through a few patches of glass in the roof and from the far end of the platforms, it looked like and sounded like the furnaces of hell, or how he imagined hell to be. There were masses of children heading through the openings towards the platform all with their bags of different shapes and sizes and all with their gas mask case over one shoulder and across the chest.

Betty took tight hold of David's hand and they stood in a long queue on the approach to the platforms. In front of them were Peter and Rita. Peter was only a few months older than David, being eight in June, and was obviously very worried as he was supposed to be keeping a close eye on his little sister who was only six and up to all the mischief she could find. Betty had realised the situation and had taken overall charge of the three younger children. She made them all hold hands and said that, in no way were they to get into separate carriages. They had only a short time to wait before a man in a railway uniform stood on a box at the front of the queue and shouted above the puffing and blowing of all the engines,

"You are all to follow me on to the platform. Stay in the same line as you are now and I will count you into the doors of the carriages. Don't run, but I want you to walk as quickly as possible. You will be given a seat to sit in and you are to remain there until you have all been checked in. Do you understand?"

There was a mumble of acceptance from most of the children. The man then asked,

"Are there any questions"?

David was surprised to see Betty put up her hand and wave it at the man.

"Yes".

"What happens if we want to go to the toilet because we have been on a bus for about an hour."

"Don't worry, Luvvy, there are toilets on the train and the ladies will take you to them in turn". He waited for a moment longer, then got down from the box and began to walk onto one of the platforms past the most enormous steam engine with smoke billowing from its funnel and steam hissing from between its wheels. A very nice man, again in uniform, was standing on the footplate waving to them. Behind him was a red and yellow glow from what looked like a large oven into which another man was shovelling coal. David thought that he would never forget the scene and particularly the strange and distinctive smell of steam and smoke, mixed. They continued along the platform with carriages on either side and after passing about seven very long lines of windows were ushered into a door at the end of one of the brown, dirty carriages. A lady directed them along a very narrow corridor on one side of the carriage and another lady stood at the opening of one of the compartments. There were four seats on either side, but the arms had been removed and they managed to cram five into either side. Betty managed to push their bags on the overhead rack and they all sat down. Peter and David had both managed to get a seat by the window, but could only see the next platform and the rails next to them. As they sat and looked out of the window their view was blocked by another engine pulling into the station. It was followed by several carriages and as the train slowly passed their window they could see that the train was full of soldiers all in khaki uniforms. When the train finally stopped there was a lot of shouting on the platform and all the soldiers jumped up from their seats and climbed down from the train. There was another loud whistle from an engine and the children's train, amidst banging noises and shaking, started to move out of the station. It went very slowly and by the jolting and bumping they could tell that they were crossing some points. The train was packed with children with at least three ladies in the corridor of each compartment.

They were just about clear of the station and the train was picking up a little speed with the engine puffing and blowing louder than ever, when they were aware of the siren sounding outside. The train slammed on its brakes and slowly came to a halt. They could still hear the siren going outside and they all craned their necks to look at the sky and try to see what was coming over. Was it another bombing raid by the German bombers, or was it one of those deadly Doodle Bugs? The train began to reverse. The ladies came along the corridor and told them all to stay in their seats as they were going back into the station.

Above all the noise of the train, the steam and the shouting there came a low roaring noise, which grew louder and louder. They all knew what that was and they rushed to the window to see the black devil like plane heading towards them.

187

Chapter 23

David's thoughts were interrupted by the sound of high heels walking on the pavement on the other side of the small green. He could recognise the step immediately as Janet had a distinctive sound to her walking . There was a sharp click as the heel hit the ground followed by a slight tap as the heel just caught the pavement before being taken through to the next stride.   He felt the same thrill and increased rate of his heart as they gradually grew louder. He experienced a warm glow throughout the whole of his body and he just couldn't wait those last few minutes until she turned the corner by the green, walked around the top section and came to his gate.   This was not the same feeling he had had when he was in the shelter with Polly, helping her to lift down the crates of Tizer.   He knew that was based on sexual desire and he felt quite ashamed of himself for allowing that situation to develop.   Polly seemed to exude desire and sex appeal whereas Janet was all love and avoidance of becoming too intimate.   Mind you, on the way home from the youth club, visiting a friend or an evening dancing at a local dance hall, they would find their way into a dark spot somewhere and kiss and cuddle.   Occasionally David remembered that he would slip his hand up onto her young, but very well developed breast and gently fondle the wonderful rounded swelling sometimes loosing a little control and squeezing a little too hard. Sometimes she would push his hand away and on some occasions she would open her coat or blouse and let him slip his hand into her bra.   But on some occasions he couldn't avoid pressing his groins and his erect penis up against her crutch.   He wasn't sure, but now and again he felt that she didn't pull away quite as quickly as he had anticipated and seemed to get some of the thrill out of the encounter that he was experiencing.   He remembered that he had had the very same desires with a beautiful young art student that he had met at the Art School about a year earlier. This again reminded him of his first encounter with the Art School when he was only fifteen.

He had gone to the Sutton School of Art and Craft as an evening student. He had shown some leaning towards painting and drawing when he was at the Wallington Grammar School and the art teacher, spotting his gift for colour and design, thought that he would do well to improve his drawing and appreciation of line and shape if he signed on at the Art School. He said that he thought David should request to visit the Life Class and spend a couple of terms having real tuition from teachers that had become experts in that field. Peter had continued his schooling at a local boy's secondary school, and co-incidentally he also had developed a desire to paint and draw. When he heard of David's intention of signing on for evening classes, he asked if he could join him. They had taken the bus to Sutton early in the summer holidays and had walked up past the Granada cinema and down past the fire station to the Art School. It was a very strange, but somehow attractive building. It had a front door much like a house set in a column that jutted out at the front of the building. This was extended up through the first floor to a pointed roof giving the appearance of a tower. On either side was one large window made up of enormous panes of glass, the sort one would find in the front of a large shop. The first floor had a similar lay out and the roof seemed to be made up of tiled turrets. They had seen the back of the school earlier when they had been to Sutton swimming baths which lay directly behind the school. From the back it looked more like a glass house with the whole of the upper floor made up of these massive windows which extended onto the roof up as far as the ridge at the top.

They hesitated as they opened the door not knowing if they should have told them that they were coming or perhaps just pressing a bell, but as there was none in sight they went in. The first thing that they both noticed was the smell. It was thick and oily with a slight sharpness similar to a vinegarish touch. Unknown to them at the time, it was of course mainly the smell of linseed oil and turpentine. They thought it must be something that had been poured on the floor as the wooden boards were dark, wet looking and springy. There was a notice at the bottom of the old wooden stairs saying "Office" and an arrow pointing upwards. At the top of the first flight they found that they were above the entrance and had a good view out of the window to the road outside. At the top of the second flight a corridor turned to the right and on the wall opposite was another notice "Office". They walked gingerly towards the door at the end of the corridor and found, through a door which was open on the right, a room with two ladies sitting at desks. They were both using a large typewriter which half hid them from view. The boys paused, not sure whether to go in or turn and run back down the stairs and outside. The older lady looked up from her task and said,

"Yes, can I help you?"

She had dark, short, curly hair and wore horn-rimmed glasses which were on the end of her nose. She was wearing a dark cardigan buttoned up to the neck which showed off the top part of her body as being thin and wiry. Peter turned to David and whispered,

"I don't like this, let's make a dash for it".

David grabbed Peter's arm and stood his ground. He suddenly felt short of words and just stood looking.

The older lady stood up and beckoned to them.

"Come in then boys if you are going to".

They moved gingerly into the room which was surrounded by bookshelves all full of books and files. There was a nasty smell of stale smoke mixed with a sweet smell of perfume. Both desks were strewn with paper and files and on the end of the larger desk was a pile of, what looked like, magazines.

"How can I help you?"

David half spluttered and half mumbled.

"Please Miss, we would like to join the art evening classes".

"Had you any particular one in mind?"

Not knowing quite what it meant, or what he was letting himself in for David answered.

"Life drawing".

This, he felt, must be O.K as that was what his art teacher at his grammar school had advised.

"How old are you?" asked the older lady.

"Fifteen"

"And how do you know that it is life drawing that you want to do, have you had any advice or persuasion from anyone?"

"Yes, my art teacher said that I was good at painting, but he thought that I should learn to draw and study form and perspective".

David didn't know exactly what that meant, but that was what Mr. Wood had said and he was just repeating it.   The ladies' attitude changed completely and she beckoned them to two chairs that were placed in front of the younger lady's desk.

"Yes, of course you can join our Life Drawing class, in fact you will be very welcome. You are a little young, but we have full time students that are about your age and they all do Life Drawing as a part of their Diploma Course. Now what about your friend, is he wanting to do the same class as yourself? Is he artistic or does he want to follow more the design track?" Peter had said nothing until now, but felt that he should make some contribution to the conversation.

"Yes, I would like to study design".

"Any particular class, technical drawing or calligraphy?"

David was surprised to hear Peter's immediate answer. "Calligraphy please Miss".

The lady with the dark curly hair opened up one of the drawers of her desk and began to fish inside through a mass of papers. "That is good; we don't have many students for that class so I am sure that the teacher will be pleased". She handed them a sheet of paper and a biro pen and asked them to fill in a form. The younger lady moved some of the papers on her desk to one side and said,

"Pull your chairs over and rest on my desk to fill in your forms".

David had filled in a lot of forms in the past at his grammar school so he had very little difficulty in answering all the usual questions. When it came to "Country of Origin", he did wonder if he should put English or British, but in the end decided on British because he thought that it sounded much more important. Peter, on the other hand, was finding the form a difficult problem. He seemed to be unsure of many of the answers such as "County" or "Status". When David had finished he leant over Pete's form and suggested some of the answers which Peter readily accepted. When David handed the two forms back to the older lady, he saw that the two of them were smiling to each other.   The younger lady came around the desk and said to Peter,   "Would you like a syllabus?"

Peter stood with his mouth open.   He obviously had never heard of the word and was unsure what he was being offered.   Not wanting to accept something which might cost money and as they only had just enough for their bus fare home, he said,   "No thanks, I've already got one".

David quickly jumped in, saying,   "I would like one please, and could I have one spare in case our other friend would like to join?"

Smiling, the young lady handed him two small booklets and a list of instructions of what they needed to bring with them on their first evening class.   "The classes start in two weeks time.   Life Drawing is on every night in the large room at the end of this corridor to the right and Calligraphy is on twice a week, Tuesdays and Thursdays.   All classes start at 6 o'clock and end between half past eight and 9 o'clock.

They left the school wondering what they had let themselves in for. It was as they passed the fire-station, which lay by the side of the Art School that David asked Peter what calligraphy was.

"I don't know" Peter admitted, "I just chose the last of her suggestions as it was the one I could remember.   Anyway, what was that she was offering me at the end, I had never heard of that word before".

David began to laugh, "It was one of these books, stupid.   That is why I asked for a spare so that I could give you one when we left". With that he handed Peter the second syllabus.   When they reached the bus stop they searched through the document to see if they could find out what Peter had chosen to study, but all they could find was the name of the class with its times and class room.   On arrival home David took out the dictionary which he had won in the secondary modern school he had attended for about six months. There they found, to Peter's delight, that he was going to study lettering. He was not so happy, however, when they read his sheet of instructions and found that he would need to have a set of calligraphy pens. David was even more worried when he read that he needed to take with him a set of HB, B, and BB pencils plus a drawing board at least 3 feet by 2 feet.

Two weeks later they arrived at the Art School ready for a new adventure. David's dad had produced for him a large piece of three ply wood of the correct measurements and he had scraped together the correct pencils, some from around the house and some he had 'borrowed' from school. With the money he had earned for jobs done, Peter had managed to buy a cheap set of pens from the local newsagent. One of the items on David's sheet had said that cartridge paper could be bought at the school for tuppence a sheet. He wasn't sure what cartridge paper was but he was equipped with a spare fourpence for the purchase of two sheets. They had arrived right on time although they had arranged to get there early so that they could become acquainted with the lay out of the school. The downstairs corridor which led behind the stairs opened up into a wider corridor running to the right. There were lots of people rushing here and there and the wide double doors straight in front of them were open, revealing stairs leading down to a very large room, taking up the whole of the back of the school. Inside they could see, what looked like, weaving machines and shop window dressers models, some with clothes on and some without.

An older man with grey wavy hair and dressed in a dirty brown overall came along the corridor from the right and asked if he could help them. David explained that they had come to join the evening classes and this was their first visit. The man had a pleasant warm face which seemed to hold a permanent smile. He asked them what classes they were booked in for. He proceeded to direct Peter into a smaller room on their right and then led David upstairs pointing him to a shiny, blue door ahead of him. He said, "Go straight in, you are a little late but Mr. Peterson will be expecting you".

David turned the large brass handle of the door and pushed it open as quietly as he could. He slipped through the small gap he had made and turned to face to the left and the middle of the room. In a circle was a ring of men and women, some sitting and resting their boards on a chair back in front of them and some, standing with their boards on a wooden easel. All were looking towards a platform up against the wall behind the door which had on its centre a large settee bathed in bright lights. Then David had one of the greatest shocks of his life. His mouth dropped open and his face flushed with blood. His heart seemed to race so fast that he thought he could hear it beating aloud. He had great difficulty holding onto his board and pencils. Lying on the settee, clearly so everybody could see was a woman. She was completely nude and was holding a most provocative pose with her left arm draped across the back of the settee, her right arm bent with her hand behind her head which was covered with long blonde hair. Her left leg was bent so that her foot was resting on the far arm of the seat and her right leg was draped over the front so that her foot was resting on the floor. Nothing was covered, in fact it looked as if the pose was designed to show all the parts of the body David had never seen but always imagined. Added to this, two large balloon-like breasts hung down from her chest with the big brown nipple of the right resting on the cushion and the other lying over the top of it. He didn't notice what her face was like but he got the impression that she must have been quite old to have breasts as big as that, perhaps she was in her late thirties. He turned his eyes towards the large windows lying directly in front of him, but then wondered where else he could look without looking as if he was ogling the naked lady.

"Are you joining us in the life class?"

A tallish man with black hair surrounding a bald patch and wearing thick horn rimmed spectacles approached him from the left from between the circle of students.   He wore a shabby brown, corduroy sports jacket which covered a dark brown shirt.   His tie looked as if it had been only half tied with a knot spreading at least two inches and the front looking as if it had seen more of his breakfast than had entered his mouth that morning.   He was wearing bottle green corduroy trousers and extremely large suede shoes with crepe soles. David was so amazed at this man's dress that his thoughts of the naked woman eased slightly.

"Are you joining us in the life class?" the man repeated.

"Yes, my name is David Fellows and I registered in your office about two weeks ago.   It is my first evening and I wasn't sure I was in the right room".

"Yes, you are correct, we were expecting you. I'll just pull up a chair and get another one so that you can rest your board against it. Do a pencil drawing of the model and show us how you are getting on. My name is Mr Peterson and I will be your tutor for this academic year".

He then turned towards the windows, grabbed a couple of chairs and walked to the ring of men and women who were quietly carrying on their sketching.   He placed the two chairs in position for David and beckoned for him to sit down.

"I will leave you to get on for about half an hour when we will have a break, then I can take a look at what you have drawn and perhaps give you a few pointers.   Is that alright David?"

David sat down and positioned himself so that he could rest his board on the chair in front of him. "Yes that's fine, sir, but I haven't got any paper".

"We'll soon remedy that". Mr. Peterson rushed out of the door and in less than a minute emerged with a large sheet of paper. David had spent the whole time with his eyes on his feet not knowing where to look. He was a little surprised that Mr. Peterson called him David as all the teachers at his school called him "Fellows" or more often than not "Boy". David spread the paper on his board but found that it slipped around over the surface. Then a man on his right, noticing his predicament, handed him four drawing pins.

"Thank you", David whispered and began to push them into the corners of the paper and then into the board. Another embarrassing minute was spent trying to push the drawing pins into the hard ply wood. He took out his pencils and started to draw what he could remember of the lady on the settee without looking up too much. He was sure that she was watching him and may think that he was looking at the forbidden parts too much. After about ten embarrassing minutes with his face getting hotter and hotter, Mr. Peterson came round the back of him and looked at his first effort. He was obviously not impressed as David's drawing showed no resemblance to the model. He quietly crept up to the side of him and, in a low voice, said,

"I think your drawing would be a lot better if you looked at the model before you started to draw. Now turn the paper over and take a careful look at the model before you put pencil to paper. She has such beautiful shape and form, try to bring that out in your drawing and by varying the darkness of the strokes you will be able to get a degree of perspective".

At the break, the drawing pin man, who looked as if he had come straight from the City and was still wearing a waistcoat and a white shirt with long sleeves with cuff links, came over to David and just chatted about where he came from and what he wanted to do in the future. He, apparently, only came because he liked the drawing and the company.

The two boys met in the hallway at the end of the session and made their way to the bus stop so that they could catch the 80, 80a or 88 bus back home.   David had the drawing he had completed rolled up and held under his arm.   Peter only had a pad on which David could see what looked to him like squiggles and circles.   When they alighted from the bus they had about a twenty minute walk home past an estate of newly built prefabs.

"Well let's see what you have drawn" said Peter.

"No", answered David, "I don't know what to do with it".

"Why?   Come on let's see.   I promise you I will not tell".

David unrolled the large piece of paper and showed his drawing to Peter.   He stood with his mouth wide open and his eyes popping.

"Crumbs! What made you draw something like that?   What did they say at the Art School?"

"That was the model we had to draw"

"Was it a real woman?" asked Peter.

"Or course it was, otherwise I wouldn't have drawn it, would I?"

"And did she have no clothes on?"

"Yes".

"What, none at all".

"She was completely naked, not a stitch of clothing on, not even the part between her legs or her breasts" explained David.

They stood for some time under the street light so that Peter could ogle over the parts of the body he had only ever dreamed of. Then David said,

"What am I going to do with it? I can't take it home as my mum will go mad and stop me going to the classes anymore and I can't leave it in the street, or throw it over someone's privet hedge because they may inform the police".

"I know", said Peter, "Do like they do in the detective books, tear it up into small pieces and we can scatter them in different people's gardens, then nobody will be able to piece them together".

"That's a good idea", said David, but as he was about the tear the drawing in half Peter stopped him and said.

Let's have one more look at those lovely breasts before you tear it up".

After gazing with desire at the drawing for a few minutes they did as Peter said and tore the drawing into small pieces scattering them along the gardens of the prefabs and other houses. They went through the same routine every evening that they went to the evening class. As his drawings became better and better he became more and more reluctant to tear them up, but he knew that if Mum or Dad saw them they would stop him going to the Art School. Strangely, he was becoming much more appreciative of the privilege he had in drawing the human body and the changing from female to male and fat to thin and beautiful to ugly was a challenge. He began to get much more depth into his drawings and with some of the techniques suggested to him by Mr. Peterson, his drawing ability was improving rapidly. In fact many of the other members of his class and other teachers would come round to view his attempts and he was very encouraged by many of their comments. On looking back on these times he felt very sad at all the drawings he had done and how he had ended up with none of his earlier works. In fact he had very few of his drawings, paintings of models mainly due to the speed and suddenness of his exit from the Art School.

There was a click at the gate and David was immediately brought back to the present and the imminence of Janet's arrival. He didn't jump up immediately because, firstly it could have been someone else coming in as he had not been aware of the clicking of the heels on the path leading to the gate, and secondly, if it were Janet, he always liked to make out that he had not really been waiting for her and was surprised to see her. She came up the pathway and David then stood up to face her. She was dressed in a light blue, taffeta dress which was sleeveless and having a "v" shaped front which revealed the upper part of the front of her chest. The skirt was quite short and stood away from her legs as if being held there by some stiffened undergarment. Around her waist she wore a broad white belt with three golden coloured vertical fasteners. This was tight around her waist which was very slim, and emphasized her beautifully shaped and ample bosom. Her very dark, curly hair was brushed back off of her face and swept over to one side. She looked an absolute beauty. She took his hand and climbed the two steps to enter the porch where David closed the front door quietly. He took her in his arms and they kissed. He could feel the warmth of her back through the silky material of her dress and he pulled her tight up against him. The contour of her front he could feel through this thin dress and he had a tremendous desire to go further than just kissing and cuddling. She immediately realised what was going on and reached out and turned the handle of the inner door so that it swung open and with that turned and walked into their front room.

Chapter 24

That evening had been one of the happiest David had experienced for a long time. The dancing was particularly pleasant as several of the girls in the club had made streamers out of old paper bags which they had painted and hung across the hall. Some of them had baked small cakes and some had brought biscuits to add to their cup of tea at the interval. It was only dancing to records, but a couple of the boys had brought along some twelve inch records of Doris Day, Guy Mitchell and Glen Miller, while David had brought his latest records of Frankie Lane and Johny Ray. None of them were that good for dancing; those records they had of Victor Silvester were still the best.

They had been a little late in getting to the club that evening as they had been delayed by David's family who all wanted to see and speak to Janet. She was very popular with them all. Directly she had opened the door Mum came over to greet her with a kiss on the cheek. Janet then went across to Dad who was in his favourite chair between the window and the radio. Janet's mother and father had just bought a television set and they were the envy of the whole neighbourhood. David had been round there several times and watched with amazement as live pictures came through on the screen. He couldn't make out how a radio signal could be changed into a picture and although there were lots of times when the reception was poor, everybody accepted this small inconvenience. Janet leaned over Dad and gave him a kiss on the cheek which pleased him no end and he even put down his book of cowboy stories to have a short chat. Both Bobby and Susy looked forward to giving Janet a hug and always hoped that she would come round when they were there.

David had entered the room, after Janet, being embarrassed by the bulge in his trousers. He had developed a sort of slight stoop forwards to try to cover this up, but he was sure that Mum would have noticed. She noticed everything. They were persuaded to stay for a quick cup of tea, a privilege that was only afforded to special guests, before they finally left the house. David was pleased to see that the games on the two greens had finished and he was fairly sure that Polly and her two children would have gone home.

All his friends at the youth club were particularly pleasant to him that evening and he appreciated their concern and care that they had afforded him over the past couple of weeks. The only slight fly in the ointment was a tall young man who had just joined the club. He, also, was obviously attracted by the beautiful Janet and had asked her several times if she would dance with him. Not wishing to offend a new member of the club she had obliged. The only thing that upset David was that she seemed to enjoy it and came back to him full of how nice he really was and how polite. On this particular evening he had again asked her to dance and David noticed that he had held her very close to him. He also held a clean, white handkerchief in the hand behind her back which she explained was very thoughtful as it prevented any dirt getting on the back of her dress. After the dance had ended, a group of them would walk down the main road together talking. In the group the new member, Phillip, walked on the other side to Janet and engaged her in conversation for much of the time. Realizing that David was not too happy with the situation he made his way to the group in front and started talking to Janet's sister. David took the initiative and suggested to Janet that they should turn right at the bottom of the hill and go up towards the hospital. Janet was not too happy about this change of plan, but as there seemed to be some big party going on in front of the hospital and as Wilfred and Doris, two other members of the club, were also going that way, she agreed.

"That was a smart move" Wilfred whispered to David, "That chap is beginning to become a bit of menace". David just smiled.

At the turning before the hospital David and Janet turned left towards the roads which led them down towards Janet's house. It was as they turned the corner that David remembered that the school on their left was the very school that they had arrived at on the morning of the evacuation during the war. The houses that had been bombed were now just cleared spaces and the council had erected a fence around the spaces to keep people out. They strolled down the road to Janet's corner and as it was now getting a little late she said that she would have to go in straight away. David was very disappointed as he was looking forward to a wonderful experience of holding her tight in his arms and feeling the desires that he had experienced earlier that evening. They did kiss and he did hold her close to him, but it wasn't quite the passion he had expected. After walking her to her gate, he gave her a final kiss goodnight and watched as she walked down her path, opened her front door with a key, and went in. What had started out as being such a wonderful evening seemed to have turned a little sour and he was feeling a little dejected. Perhaps he expected too much from this beautiful young woman that he had the privilege of escorting and kissing. After all she was still only fifteen and must feel quite tied down by having a single boyfriend. He knew that he was the only boy she had ever been out with and he wasn't altogether the best company or the best prospects at this moment in time. He had built up a wonderful relationship with her parents and they treated him almost as a son. He was always made very welcome and although her father was a construction worker on the railways, he always commented that he thought education was very important and hoped that both his daughters would hold down good jobs with good prospects.

David decided that it was a little too early to return home; his parents were sure to be up and would ask questions why he had come home so early and without Janet. He strolled back down the way they had walked trying to recapture the wonderful feeling of walking along with his arm around Janet and where they had stopped for a kiss. He wandered past the school he had attended for about six months and up to the main road.   There were parties going on in many of the houses and occasionally a group of revellers would be in the garden with a record player or an old piano.   He could hear the sound of Frankie Lane singing "Your Cheatin' Heart", which only made him feel worse as it was on the back of the record he had taken to the youth club that evening.   He spotted a group of people about his mother and father's age doing the "Palais Glide" up and down the main road and he wondered what would happen if a car or lorry came along .   This was quite unlikely as it was now getting late and the road wasn't that busy anyway.   Everybody was celebrating the Coronation of the Queen, except for him.

He made his way up the road leading to the hospital and retraced his steps around to the right passing the bomb sites and ending up on the corner by the school. He crossed the road to the large green opposite and found that the council had placed a park bench facing the school. This had been part of the development they had carried out in front of the hospital since the shelters had been removed. He sat down deep in thought and realised that he had walked past this very spot, with Mum, when he had been discharged from the hospital following his football accident when Mike had kicked him under the chin when he was about to head the ball, biting almost completely through his tongue. He also recalled quite vividly that the bus they had boarded on the day of the evacuation had stood no more that twenty feet in front of him on the road outside the school gate. How clearly he could remember the joy they all felt at going to the country and perhaps living on a farm and the tears he could see in Mum's eyes as the bus pulled away.   He remembered the singing on the bus and him stupidly thinking that they were being evacuated to a Cathedral. He erroneously thought that Hitler would not bomb a place of worship. He found out later that it was actually St. Pancras Station.   After the train was loaded to capacity with many of the children from the estate and had left the station, it had to pull back because of the air raid sirens sounding.   Before that time, planes used to make a point of bombing moving targets, but no one had really realised that the

Doodle Bug had no pilot, so the chance of hitting a moving train would be about a million to one.

They had waited in the station for about fifteen minutes, until the "all clear" was sounded and the train began, for a second time, to pull out of the station. It crossed the points and gradually began to pick up speed. All the children in the carriage peered out of the window to try to see if there was any smoke rising from around the line. They had heard the "Doodle Bug's" engine stop followed by a very loud explosion and they knew that it must have been near. As the train picked up speed they could see that the office buildings and factories were gradually being replaced by rows and rows of houses. They in turn gradually were replaced with open fields, trees and bushes. The engine was making a loud puffing sound and they could see clouds of smoke and steam flying past the window. It was quite peculiar to the boys as the train appeared to be at the middle of two very large turn tables. All the trees, bushes and occasional houses were racing past the windows at high speed and yet the fields seemed to be passing much slower. They could even see the horses and ploughs being manned by, what looked like ladies in brown uniforms. Then, strangely, at a distance, the trees and hills were hardly moving and it took a long time before the passing of a distant church steeple or a high chimney. David was surprised to see so much green countryside and in amongst the green were many fields golden with the growing wheat and corn. He thought how more convenient it would have been if the Germans could be persuaded to bomb the open countryside. This would avoid all the damage to the cities and buildings as well as avoiding all the people that were being killed for no real reason.

The train was now running along at a high speed and every now and again the whistle would sound making them all think that the small stations that they were passing through would realise what an important cargo this train was carrying. The ladies, who were in charge, came along the corridor and opened up each of the sliding doors in turn and told the children to now open their lunch boxes and start their picnic. David looked sadly into his box and saw that all that was left was his apple and half a bottle of drink. Peter and his sister were even worse off, for, although they had kept their boxes, there was nothing in them. Betty handed one of her sandwiches to David and one of the boys, who didn't like fish paste, gave Peter and Rita one each. A little later one of the ladies came around with a spare box that had lots of sandwiches in and they all took one more. The wheels of the train were making a fast clickerty clack on the rails and every now and again there would be all hell let loose as they crossed points. During that first hour Betty made it her task to keep the entire compartment amused. She made each child in turn stand in the middle of the floor and either sing a song or recite a poem or a nursery rhyme. She then began to teach all of them a very funny little poem about a "snapdragon". It went:-

Mr. Snapdragon sat up in his bed,
"I don't feel the dragon I aught to", he said.
"Pray call Dr. Bee in and say I'm not well",
So Dr. Bee came and he rang at the bell.
"Mr. Snap-dragon, I've knocked and I've rung,
So now I will come in and look at your tongue.
It's a very fine tongue, long, curly and yellow,
I'm sure I can make you a fine healthy fellow.
Just swallow this pollen I'm leaving behind,
It will do you a great deal of good you will find".
"Will you call in tomorrow?"
"If possible, yes".
"Good day Dr. Bee, then".
"Good day Mr. S.

This took a lot of Betty's time and patience, but kept everyone amused. It wasn't until they had all made a good attempt at learning the poem that they noticed that the train had slowed to almost walking pace. They looked out of the windows but all they could see were masses and masses of railway lines and railway trucks which seemed to be full of coal. The excitement of the journey seemed to have disappeared and some of the children had dropped off to sleep and others were looking very mournful and sad. Some had even cried and still showed tears in their eyes. David thought of home and what he would be doing if he were back there. He knew that he would be a lot happier if he was with Mum and Dad, but he also knew that Betty would look after him. The train seemed to wander on through a maze of rails and points and occasionally they were passed by a very fast train going the other way or a steam engine going slowly the same way. After about two hours the train again picked up speed and raced over the lines making the familiar noises. Suddenly, without warning everything went dark and the noise from the slightly open window at the top was deafening. Small lights came on above the seats and a man in uniform raced in to the compartment and closed the window, but not before a mixture of steam, smoke and ash came rushing in. They spent a little time coughing and spluttering and more time brushing the ash from their clothes, as the train emerged from the tunnel.

After what seemed like hours and hours and after they had all visited the toilets at least three times, the train slowed and they pulled into a station with lots of people standing on the platform. The train jolted to a halt and the ladies came along to each of the compartments and told the children to collect their bags from the netting shelf above their heads and to wait for her to come back and give them more instructions. She left the door open and David could see lots of activity on the platform. By the time they were herded off the train it was getting dark and all the children were very quiet. They were led to a line of strange looking buses. Some were dark green, some brown. Many of them were only one deck and others had the opening at the front. They were nothing like those they were familiar with, red double-deckers. Betty took David's hand and told Peter to hold on to Rita and stay right behind her at all times and make sure that they got on to the same bus. Ladies ushered them along like sheep and told them all to sit down and be quiet. This was quite unnecessary, as the only noise they were making was a sobbing sound mainly coming from the younger children. It was strange, David thought, he was only eight at the time and yet he was helping to look after the "younger children".

Their bus drove firstly through a fairly large town and although there were no lights, he could make out some large buildings and what looked like a cinema. The small shop windows soon gave way to rather grubby looking houses, similar to his auntie's in Battersea, with the front doors coming directly on to the road and only a step in front of the door. Nobody was sitting on their top steps or even chatting at their front doors. They had no idea where they were as all the street names and place names had been removed, even the station where they had arrived, had no sign of where it was. They soon left the town and made their way down a hill, which had trees on either side and a large pipe running down the side of the road. At the bottom of the hill they entered another town made up of more modern looking houses, but all very close together. There were even a few shops, which were closed, of course. The bus then laboured up a long hill and on arrival at the top, turned into a gravelled area in front of a school. Schools were the same where ever you go and nobody could mistake them. They alighted from the bus and were herded into the front door of the school and along a corridor into a large hall. All round the walls were benches and one of the walls was covered with bars similar to their gym at home. They were all feeling very tired by now and were pleased to sit on the benches around the walls. Kind ladies with funny accents came round handing out beakers of diluted lemon squash and some home made biscuits. By this time they were very hungry and thirsty and were very grateful for the food and drink. A man came round with sheets of paper which he tore up into slips on which he wrote the Christian name of each child. A lady then pinned it to front of each child's jumper or shirt. After all of them had been labelled, the man opened the double doors of the hall and a mass of men and women, all dressed in very shabby clothes came rushing into the hall. After quickly glancing around they rushed up to one or possibly two children and pointing to them announced in a very strange accent.

"We'll take them, or her,"

With that the lady who was with them would pull out the cringing child or children and after writing their names on a piece of paper, passed them on to the couple or woman who had done the selecting. David noticed that very few picked the boys so that by the time half of the children had been led out of the hall, there were very few girls and mostly boys left. One attractive looking lady came over to Rita and said,

"I will take the girl".

At which Rita bust into tears and Peter said that she was his sister and he must go with her.   After a little bit of argument and persuasion from the lady in charge, Peter and Rita left the hall holding the hands of the lady.   They didn't even have time to say goodbye.

Chapter 25

David and Betty sat for a long time on those hard benches while the people in the centre of the hall continued to choose the children to take away with them.   Several couples had been over to Betty and said that they would be willing to take the girl, but not the boy.   There was always some excuse or other such as they only had one bedroom or only one bed.   One lady said that she would like to have Betty, but she only had girls and if she took the boy, David, he would have to sleep in the same room and they couldn't allow that.   Each time Betty was offered a place she gave the same reply,

"My mum said that we must not be parted.   I am to look after my little brother".

Time passed and now very few people remained in the hall.   The ladies in charge had nearly all gone home leaving just a few to get rid of the last of the evacuees.   David was becoming a bit of a problem and the fact that they were both very tired and a little tearful didn't help matters.   They were the only two left at the end and the group of helpers were getting together in a little huddle to sort out what they should do with the difficult couple of children.   David was a little upset as he hadn't done anything wrong. In fact he hadn't even spoken to most of the prospective guardians, and yet he had been rejected by all. As things were looking unsolvable, the lady with the daughters came back into the hall with two of her children.   They came over to Betty and David and the lady said to him that the lady next door said that she would be willing to take a small boy, if we took the girl.   She then addressed David by name, which made all the difference, and told him that the lady and man were very nice people and they had two boys, a little older than David, who would be willing to share their room with him.   They left the hall, to the relief of the helpers, and made their way down the corridor. David told the lady, Mrs. Mount, that his best friend had left the hall earlier and he thought that he may not see him again. When they reached the front of the school Mrs. Mount had to fill in some forms, which she did for Betty and David. She was then given a sheet of paper with instructions which included where they were to report the next day. Mrs. Mount then asked the officer if she could be told where David's friend had gone and where he was to report to the next day. "He and his sister are being put up by Mrs. Tanner, who lives in a road opposite the school. He had got to report to St. Paul's School tomorrow afternoon". He then gave David a slip of paper with the address of Mrs. Tanner.

They left the school and began to walk down the hill while Mrs. Mount filled them in on some of the information they had been unable to attain so far. This school apparently was named Ravensdale School and it was on the Ravensdale estate, which was just outside Mansfield in Nottingham.
David was none the wiser as he had never heard of any of these places and he was pretty sure that his sister Betty knew as much as him. They also found out that he was to report to the River Trent School the next afternoon. They were to be given the morning off to recover from the long journey and late night.

As they walked down the hill it started to rain and added to the fact that there were no street lights or light from the windows of the houses, the place looked more and more miserable. Oh how David wished that he was still at home with his Mum and Dad. He would quite willingly put up with the Doodle Bugs and the bombing raids just to be in his own shelter. Even the big black spiders would be tolerable compared with this miserable town in the middle of nowhere. After about a quarter of an hour they came to a row of about six shops all closed and with no lights. A couple looked as if they had been closed for a long time and one even had its windows broken. They turned left into a small road at the end of which was a "T" junction. They turned left again and began to climb the hill.

Mrs. Mount then turned into a small gate and walked down a couple of steps to the front door of a house about the same size as theirs at home. She tapped gently on the door and almost immediately it was answered by a rather plump lady with her hair tied up in small bunches and what looked like chicken wire tied round each bunch. She wasn't much taller than Betty and she was wrapped in a brown and grey blanket. Behind her, and to her left stood a man just a little taller. He was wearing a flat black cap, a black waist coat with an open neck, long sleeved dark blue shirt. He had a chain running from one of the front pockets to a button on the front of the waistcoat. Directly behind them were the stairs of the house and on them David could see two boys, both obviously older than him and the one nearest the bottom seemed to be much taller than their mum and dad. None of them smiled, or gave any sign of welcome, in fact they all looked stunned as if they had agreed to something that they were now regretting.

Mrs. Mount introduced David and explained that both children had been travelling all day and were most probably very tired and hungry. She then turned to David and said, "This is Mr. and Mrs. Baron, David. They will be taking care of you for the time being until we can find somewhere else for you to go". She then pushed David forward and Betty reluctantly let go of his hand and David mounted the two steps to enter the narrow passage. He looked back to see Betty, but the tears in his eyes blurred his vision. Mr. Baron said something to Mrs. Mount and quietly closed the door while Mrs. Baron put her arm around his back and ushered him past the stairs to the kitchen at the back of the house.

"We've made you some soup, do you feel like eating anything?"

Little did they know that David was ravenous and had not eaten since the sandwiches that he and Peter had devoured so early on the bus. Mrs. Baron produced a couple of slices of bread which seemed to be very heavy and puddingy, but in his state tasted absolutely wonderful.

He ate rapidly and only when he had reached the bottom of the bowl did he look up to see all four of the occupants of the house gazing at him in wonder. After David had consumed another bowl of the unidentifiable soup kindly produced by Mrs. Baron, Mr. Baron said that he thought that it was time they all made their way to bed. Mr. Baron had already taken David's gas mask case and his kit bag upstairs and had put them in the front bedroom under the window. There was only one bed in the room, but a mattress had been laid on the floor along one wall which was covered with blankets. Albert, the younger of the two boys slipped into the bed and after David had put on his pyjamas he quickly lay on the mattress and pulled the blankets over him. He didn't want anyone to see that his pyjamas had a patch of white material sewn, by Mum into the bottom where they had been torn. Mr. Baron turned off the light and David felt the tears running down his cheeks as he suppressed the sobs below the blankets.

He must have slept very soundly because when he woke it was a bright morning and through the closed curtains he could see the sun shining. Albert's bed was empty and the bed was made. He could hear a lot of noise going on outside so he pulled back the blankets and went to the window. He parted the curtains just a little and could see lots of children in the street. They all seemed to be walking down the hill and David assumed that that must be the way to the school. He suddenly felt an urgent need for the toilet and after slipping on his short trousers went down the stairs. He hurried to the back door where he knew the toilet was which he had used before going to bed the night before. It was outside the house under a sort of cover. The door was like a shed door and had a gap at the top and bottom. Last night he had been frightened to go into the door as it had no light and he had to feel for the bowl of the toilet. This morning, things were a little different as light came in over and under the door and his need to pass urine overcame all his worries. He went back into the kitchen where he washed his hands in the sink. Mrs. Baron was still dressed in the blanket she had around her on the night before and her hair was still in the wire mesh. She told him to sit at the table and passed him a large bowl of porridge. It was a lot thicker than he had seen before; in fact it seemed to be one massive lump. It tasted absolutely dreadful obviously having no sugar in it but masses of salt. It was only then did she say anything to David.

"A lady came round this morning and said that you don't need to go to school this morning as you had a long journey yesterday, but they want you to report this afternoon to the Trent Valley School, the same school where Albert goes. It is about ten minutes walk away. Mrs. Mount will be taking Betty that way, but to the girl's school, so she said that she would drop you off. Mr. Baron had to go off to work very early this morning, as he works in the mines, but he will be back this afternoon. Be quiet when you come back as he will be asleep in bed and doesn't like being woken up by noise. Derek went to work later as he works in the offices of the pit".

David finished his plate of porridge and tried not to make a nasty face as he slid the plate across the table. "Thank you Mrs. Baron, that was very nice".

"Would you like some more, there's plenty in the pot. We always keep some in the saucepan in case the boys come in hungry".

"No thanks, I couldn't eat any more", David replied.

"Well, perhaps you could go upstairs now and make your bed, then it would be a good idea if you emptied your kit bag and put your things on the table by the window. I can then see what you've got to wear".

It was while David was unpacking that he heard a knock on the door and the sound of Betty's voice. He dropped what he was doing and rushed down stairs to the front door where Betty and another, elder girl, were talking to Mrs. Baron. She turned to David and said,

"Quickly, go and get dressed, your sister and Molly, from next door want to take you out for a walk to look around the streets and see where the schools are".

Quickly slipping on his outdoor clothes David rushed down the stairs and almost threw himself into Betty's arms. They walked down the street hand in hand and David at last thought that perhaps it wasn't so bad after all.

When they returned to number 31, Mrs Baron was at the door talking to Mrs. Mount. She said that a lady had been round with another boy and his sister and they would call on David in the afternoon to go to the school together. David knew immediately that this must have been Peter and his sister Rita and he felt how sad it was that he wasn't there when they came. When the two adults went in the three children sat on the top step and Molly explained to them some of the nice things that they did up there. She said firstly that she didn't understand why they had come there in the first place as they had had a bomb which fell in the main road and had burnt for at least ten minutes. David laughed and said that that was only an incendiary bomb and was nothing to worry about. She said that the town of Mansfield was a long way up the main road, but on Saturdays they were allowed to go there to see a special children's show and on Sundays they always went to the Salvation Army Hall, where they sung hymns and played in the band.   This all sounded great to David and he hoped that he would be included in the group when Saturday and Sunday came along.   Molly also said that in the winter the snow came right up to the windowsill and they had great fun making snow men and having snow ball fights.   This appealed to David, but he hoped that by that time he would be home and amongst his own friends.

That afternoon Peter and Rita came knocking on Mrs. Baron's door. David remembered that he rushed to the door and was delighted to see an old face and a friend from the past.   He had forgotten that it was only yesterday that they had been with each other all day.   It seemed like a life time to an eight year old. They walked off down the road with their arms around each others shoulders and laughed and joked at all the events that had occurred in only twenty four hours. It wasn't until Peter said that he was going to St. Paul's school that David became a little alarmed. It appeared that they were to go to different schools and the two pals must be parted whilst they were in Mansfield.

The next morning, David decided to take the matter into his own hands. He accompanied Peter and Rita to St. Paul's and entered, with many other children, through the main gate. David could see that it was an old school built of grey stones and the windows were tall and thin, similar to those of a church. It even had a tower with a clock over the main door. They went inside and made their way to the hall which was packed with children from their estate. There was lots of shouting and even some crying, but above all the noise a short man with a black beard and dark hair was shouting. He was wearing a grey suit with a waistcoat and a pair of round wire rimmed spectacles on the end of his nose. He was making the children form lines of about twenty and into one of these the two boys and Rita slipped. Almost immediately a fat lady with a scarf around her head and dressed in a sort of overall came over and pulled Rita out of the line and took her over to the other side of the hall. Rita was not too upset as she was going to join a group of girls of all ages who were already in a line. Anyway, Rita had a mind of her own and was always into some sort of mischief. She was not the easiest child to handle and even Peter was pleased that someone else had taken over some of the responsibility. The man in the grey suit was shouting out boys surnames and was herding them into lines on the opposite side of the hall to the girls. As he was nearing the end of a long list Peter heard his name and, after a quick glance at David, went to the side of the hall. When, only about eight boys were left, the man called out,

"Browning",

There was no response. He repeated the name and when David saw that none of the boys was called Browning, he stepped forward and said,

"Yes sir".

"Wake up boy, didn't you hear me call you name before? Are the boys from the south deaf or something? Come over here and get on one of the lines".

David immediately joined the line with Peter. After a few more minutes the lines left the hall and headed down a dark corridor to a small room which looked like a prison having an old wooden floor and bars at the windows. At the front of the room, sitting at a high desk with large ink wells perched on the front, was a younger lady with long black hair tied back in a pony tail. She was wearing a grey sweater and if it wasn't for the awful round, wire rimmed glasses, reminded David of his favourite teacher at home. The first thing she did was to read through all of their names. David automatically answered to the name of Browning, which made Peter burst into laughter. The teacher stopped and stood up from her chair. She was a little taller than David imagined and she came striding down the room towards them.

"So, what is so funny", she said, addressing Peter in a strange sort of accent.

"Nothing miss, it's just that he forgot his name outside in the hall and I was surprised to hear him answer so quickly".

Strangely, she smiled and ruffled Peter's hair. She then walked back to the front of the class and continued calling through the list. She then closed the book and called for silence.

"I am Miss Tapsfield and I will be acting as your teacher all the time you are here, at St. Paul's. I am a general teacher and will cover all the subjects including sport, which we will do on Wednesday afternoons. We will start tomorrow at nine o'clock and you will go home at four o'clock. You will be given a sandwich and a drink at lunch time and you will eat and drink it in this room. Do you understand?"

There was a chorus of "Yes miss". She continued,

"I will not stand any misbehaviour or too much noise. Anyone misbehaving will be sent to the headmaster and he will punish them in an appropriate manner".

"Does that mean the stick?" whispered Peter to David.

"Stop that talking" she said, standing up again.

"I have not taught a class of boys before so I expect you all to cooperate and make your stay here as pleasant as possible. If any of you have any problems either at school or in your homes that you have been allotted to, you must tell me immediately and I will do something about it. Do you all understand?"

"Yes miss".

It wasn't until two days later that David's change of name was found out. It was after they had returned home from school and were playing in the street that Mrs Baron shouted out from the front door step. David dropped what he was doing and ran down the path to the front door. He was surprised to see the lady he had seen up at Ravensdale School on the first night that they had arrived. She had a board in her hand and was looking very severe. Mrs. Baron asked David,

"Why haven't you been going to school, David?"

"I have been going to school"

"No you haven't", said the stern lady.

"I have, you ask Peter". Peter was called over and confirmed that David was in the same class as himself.

"But I have been to St. Paul's and they say that they haven't any boy named Fellows in the school.

"That is funny" said David, "because they call me Browning which I thought was a nick name, my teacher, Miss Tapsfield will tell you that I am telling the truth".

On hearing the name, the lady marked her sheet and said her goodbyes to Mrs. Baron saying as she left the gate, "I will check on this tomorrow, but in the meantime don't worry, just carry on".

On Saturday morning Betty and Molly came early to Mrs. Baron's door ready to take David to Mansfield and the Saturday morning film show. David always laughed when Molly said film as she pronounced it fillem. It was only one of the funny ways they spoke up north. They had arranged to meet Peter and Rita at the end of the street and all go along together. This was the first time that they realised that they were not very popular in that area. David didn't know why, but the other children started shouting names at them and some even threw rolled up tickets and bits of cardboard at them. Even when the film started David felt little pellets hitting his head, but this was soon forgotten as the very exciting film of rock men and space ships hit the screen. On the way back to the Ravensdale Estate they balanced along a large pipe that ran down the side of the road, but were still followed by a group of older boys shouting rude words to them.

During the second week Peter and David left school and as they walked down the road a group of very rough boys started pushing and hitting them. They started to run and the boys chased after them. At the bottom of the road was a large area of waste land with piles of what looked like coke. They raced between the piles dashing in and out to try to avoid being caught, but unfortunately, Peter tripped and the boys piled on top of him. David ran back and with screams and shouts dived into the group. They were a little taken by surprise and pulled back. Then one boy came forward with his fists up. He must have been about ten and stood a good twelve inches taller than David. Remembering the fights he had at home in the woods and the training Jack had given him, he rushed at the boy throwing punches to his face and his body. He felt several punches find their target before the boys turned and pushed back into their group. They all started shouting and were about to rush David when three boys came up behind them.

"So what's going on here" said a voice in an accent sounding more like home.

"These boys have been chasing us" said Peter, who was still sprawled on the ground.

"Is that so" said the boy with the black curly hair, "Now, who wants to have a real fight with three tigers from the south then" So saying, the three boys walked towards the group who turned and ran as fast as they could. The boy with the curly hair pulled up Peter from the ground and said,

"I'm Doug and this is Pete and Red. We come from Wallington and have been evacuated up here. You had better come with us and we will see you to your road. We heard the shouting from the railway line and thought someone was in trouble".

"What were you doing on the railway line?" asked David innocently.

"We were laying coins on the rails and when the trains ran over them they spread out and become larger", said Doug. "If you have any more trouble from those boys you let us know and we will deal with them".

They met up several times with, "the three tigers from the south" as they liked to call themselves, and each time they were greeted as old friends. In fact one day they took David and Peter over to the railway line, which was not guarded by any wire or fence, and showed them how they could make a halfpenny the size of a penny, only much thinner. David thought that they were very tough boys and often took chances in crossing the lines when the train was approaching. Both David and Peter would shout when the train was near, but the boys always managed to jump clear at the last moment. They were never close friends, but David and Peter knew that they could be called on if that group of thugs approached them.

All the Baron family treated David with some suspicion and spent quite a bit of time just watching him. They looked as if they didn't quite know what they had let themselves in for and although they were kind and generous with what little they had, he never seemed to be included in the group. Albert lent him some of his cowboy books and David remembered that it was the first time he had read about Jessie James and Wyatt Earp. He would read them just before he went to bed which made him a little less homesick. It was always in the evenings when he felt that he would like to be at home with his mum and dad and his little brother and sister. He missed Jack a lot and was still hoping that he would also be evacuated up there to Mansfield. Little did he know that Jack was nearly fourteen and at that age he was considered to be a working man and too old to be evacuated. Derek, Albert's elder brother was a little older than Jack and was already talking about going into the army as soon as he was old enough. He would give David paper and pencils which must have come from the place he worked. He never said too much to David, but, nevertheless, was always kind and helpful. In the evenings, when David came in from playing with Betty and Molly, he would join the family group, but they said very little. The men usually sat and read and Mrs. Baron would be darning the socks and jumpers of the boys. Sometimes Mr. Baron was at work, occasionally at the local pub or most times at home with the family.

On one of these evenings about two weeks after David had arrived, Mr. Baron broke the silence and said,

"David, I have something to tell you which might make you understand why we are not making you feel quite as at home as you would like. You see, when we agreed to have you to live with us we said that it would only be as long as it takes them to find you somewhere more permanent. They said that you had nowhere to go on that evening and we said that we could put you up for just a few weeks. You see, we are going away on holiday to Scarborough for two weeks the week after next and we can't take you with us. We did tell Mrs. Mount right at the beginning, but she seems to have forgotten".

"Where will I go then, do you think that they will have to send me back home cause I would like that".

"No", answered Mrs. Baron, "they will soon find you somewhere else, as long as we let them know in time. I'll have a word with Mrs. Mount and see if she has any ideas. I am sure Betty would want to know where you are going".

David had forgotten all about Betty and how she would react to the news. All the time David was next door she felt she could keep as eye on him, but she would be very upset if he was to be moved any distance away. On the way to school the next day David was about to tell Peter of the bad news when Peter said to him,

"I've got some bad news. The lady who looks after us has got sick and tired of Rita's shouting and screaming and said that she can't put up with us any longer. She has put in for us to be moved somewhere else. I don't know where we will go; we may even have to change schools".

David told them what had happened to him and they spent the rest of the day worrying about where they may end up. It wasn't until school had finished that their young teacher came up to David and said.

"Is there something wrong, you haven't been your usual cheeky self today"?

David remembered that she had said that they were to come to her if they had any problems either at school or at the homes that they were in, so he told her of the bad news that both Peter and he had had the day before. She listened very carefully and put her arms around Peter and David's shoulders. It was wonderful to feel the comfort of the warm arms and the kind voice of the teacher. She said,

"Now you both go home and don't worry. I will have to go to the headmaster and explain what the situation is and I will then let you know what I can do to help you. I don't dare do anything straight away as I may get into trouble, but believe me; I will give you some news tomorrow".

The boys collected Rita from her class and made their way home feeling much better because they knew that teachers were very important people and she had acted a little like their teacher at home and shown them concern. At lunch time the next day she asked them lots of questions about where they were staying, how they were treated, what they were given to eat, where they slept and so on. At the end she looked a lot happier and said,

"So you really have been treated quite well by the families that look after you".

The boys nodded their heads.

"The only problem is that they can't continue to accommodate you in their houses".

The boys nodded again.

"I have been given permission to come home with both of you this evening and have a word with your families and see if we can sort things out. Are you happy for me to come with you?"

Both boys nodded.

True to her word, when school closed that evening she put on her attractive dark blue tight fitting coat and a funny round large beret and walked out of the school gates with them. David noticed that the headmaster was standing a little way away and seemed to nod to her as she proudly followed the two boys down the road. When they arrived at 31, David knocked on the door, which was opened by Mrs. Baron. Poor Mrs. Baron, she looked shocked and frightened. When Miss Tapsfield explained who she was, they were all invited into the front room. Mrs. Baron explained that her husband was upstairs in bed as he had been on a night shift at the pit and usually slept until about five o'clock. When she heard what the problem was she went up stairs to wake Mr. Baron and after about ten minutes they came down the stairs. Mr. Baron looked very tired and was, at first, a little grumpy, but explained their situation and how they were going on holiday in a weeks time and must find somewhere for David to go. Miss Tapsfield then went next door to Mrs. Mount's house and after about twenty minutes came back to No 31. She looked pleased with herself and explained that Mrs. Mount had agreed to put David up for as long as it takes to find another home for him. She said that David would have to sleep in the living room, but as his sister was in the house she was sure David would be happy. Mr. and Mrs. Baron looked very relieved and thanked Miss Tapsfield for her help.

"Now", she said, "Lets see if we can sort Peter's problem out". With that she said her goodbyes and went off down the road with Peter and Rita, who they had picked up on the way home. As they walked up the road towards Ravensdale School they passed a group of boys who they knew and with whom they had played football in the road. One of the boys, Colin, was in the same class and came over to say hello to his teacher. He asked why she was going along with Peter and Miss Tapsfield explained that Peter and Rita needed somewhere else to live. Colin said that they had a spare room and his mum would be pleased to have an evacuee as she had heard that they would be given some money to look after them. She didn't know that when they first arrived.

"If you come along to my house, Miss, at the top of the road I will talk to my mum."

Colin introduced his teacher to his mum and Miss Tapsfield explained again the problem they had. Colin's mum was a tall thin, wiry woman who looked a little like Peter and Rita's own mum. The two children were now looking tired and worn and a very sad sight. Warm hearted Mrs. Taylor, Colin's mum, solved the problem straight away and invited them all in to the house. It was not very well furnished although spotlessly clean and Miss Tapsfield seemed very satisfied that arrangements could be made for them to move. In two days they had made the move and kind Miss Tapsfield was as pleased as punch. When the Baron's went off on their holidays David moved in with the Mounts who were friendly and kind and although the last week with the Barons had been much more enjoyable with all the family doing all they could to make him feel at home, being in the same house as Betty, his sister, was a real joy. The Mounts were really quite religious and attended the Salvation Army Service on

Sundays. The first time they attended one of the services they were made extremely welcome with everybody trying to do as much as they could to make the evacuees feel at home. They sang songs accompanied by a brass band and all those taking part were dressed in smart red and black uniforms. The men wore peak caps on their heads like officers in the army and the ladies wore dark tight fitting suits and a rounded type of bonnet on their heads. After the singing one of the young ladies came over to David and asked if he wanted to join the band. He said that he couldn't play any instrument and she said,

"Well, that's easily remedied, I'll go over and get you a tambourine and you can start straight away"

Another lady came along with a plate full of home made cakes and all three children took one. Although they were a little stale, they were really tasty and after a cup of luke warm tea, which was poured from an enormous brown, metal teapot, larger than any David had ever seen, the pretty lady with the tambourine came back. She showed David how to hold the instrument and how to get it to shake in rhythm. After a few feeble attempts several of the onlookers clapped. She then said that if he turned up next week he could be part of the band. David didn't know what to say. He knew that his attempt was not very good, but thought that they were just trying to be nice.

During the next week he persuaded Peter and Rita that they would be treated to cakes and tea if they came along to the meeting on the Sunday. David also explained about the band and that he might be part of it if he could just keep the tambourine shaking in time with the music. Both Peter and his sister seemed very keen but David thought that this was most probably just he mentioned the word cakes. The next Sunday Mrs Mount proudly led her three girls, Betty, David, Peter and Rita along to the Salvation Army hall. They sang songs, as on the previous week, and the band played. David was given a tambourine which he managed to bang in time with the tune and was pleased to have the pretty Salvation Army girl at his side smiling at him and banging her own tambourine. All went well until they put on a special show, where one of the ladies, dressed up as Mary, came onto the middle of the floor riding a donkey. All the children were delighted and cheered and clapped. Suddenly, without any warning, the donkey started to pass urine on to the middle of the floor. David, Peter, Rita and many of the other children began to laugh. The Donkey, still passing water with a loud splashing noise, became frightened at the noise and turned suddenly. The lady on its back fell off into the large puddle. David and Peter were in hysterics and were quickly ushered out of the hall. Mrs. Mount decided that in the future she might take David along on a Sunday, but certainly not Peter and Rita as they seemed to make more noise than all the rest of the children put together.

Near the end of the two weeks living in Mrs. Mount's house, the only solution put forward by the lady in charge of the evacuees was that David should move to a house on the other side of Mansfield, which meant leaving Betty and all of his friends and even moving to another school. Betty was very upset at the prospect and every time they discussed it with Mrs. Mount they both burst into tears. David was feeling more home sick than he had ever felt before and it seemed that as soon as the other people had cleared out one of their rooms he would be moved over. To add to his sadness, Peter was now only just up the road and Colin had managed to include them in with his friends when they played in the street. He looked out of Mrs. Mount's window and saw Mr and Mrs Baron struggling up the road with two heavy cases and Derek and Albert following up behind. The last two weeks with the Barons and the two weeks in Mrs Mounts had made his stay in Mansfield tolerable, but now he could see no future.

Chapter 26

It was Sunday morning and David had, with the help of all the other
ladies in the house, packed his kitbag again and was ready for the
move to the other side of Mansfield into a house and home which was
new to him.   All he knew was that it was two old people who had
agreed to take him.   They had no children, as far as David could find
out, and they lived in a terrace house on a main road with no garden.
He had resigned himself to the fact that there was no alternative,
although he had asked to be sent home.   That, was apparently not
now possible as the letter Betty had received from their Dad during
that week, informed them that Mum, Bobby and Susy had also been
evacuated, by train, to a place even further north, called Oldham.
Jack was still at home because he was too old to be evacuated and he
was now working in London.   The Doodle Bugs were still pounding
the south of England and particularly London and the routes leading
into the City. David feared for the safety of his brother whom he had
always looked up to and relied upon for guidance.   How he wished
that he could be with him now and ask him for his advice.   The lady
in charge of the evacuees was coming over at twelve o'clock to collect
him and they were going to get on the bus, outside the fish and chip
shop, and travel into the centre of Mansfield where they would pick
up another bus to the place where the old people lived.   The lady had
pointed out to David, during the week, when she had come to see him,
that he could be of great help to the two old people and things might
not be as bad as he imagined.

David, Betty, Molly and Mrs. Mount sat in her front room waiting for
the knock at the door.   No one said anything except Betty who kept
mumbling that she didn't know what she would say to Mum when she
saw her for allowing David to be passed on to another family and out
of her control.   David kept thinking of the great times he had spent

228

with Peter and his new found friend Colin. They had played all sorts of games up and down the road and Colin, who was very athletic, taller than the others and very wiry, had taught them all sorts of jumps and tricks. He could do the amazing thing of leap-frogging over David when he had Peter on his back. He was obviously good at football, but they only had a tennis ball and had to play in the street.

At twenty past eleven there came the inevitable knock at the door and Mrs Mount went to open it. David picked up his kitbag and Betty put her arms around his neck and David felt the tears on her cheeks against his face. It was with some surprise that Mrs. Mount returned into the room followed by Mr. and Mrs. Baron. Mrs. Mount told them all to sit down and Mr. Baron, who was still in his working clothes and with coal dust over his face turned to David and said,

"David, as you know we have been on holiday for the last two weeks and while we were there we bought you a present". With that, Mrs. Baron handed David a long parcel wrapped in brown paper. David felt a little disappointed, but nevertheless quickly undid the wrappers and took out a long thin boat fitted with an elastic band connected to a propeller. It was one of the best presents he had had for some time as money was scarce and he immediately went over to Mrs. Baron and gave her a hug thanking her for the gift.

"There is something else we wanted to ask you and be honest with us. We wondered if you would like to stay with us for the rest of your time in Mansfield?" Before he could say any more David replied,

"Yes please".

"We thought about this a lot on holiday and decided that we didn't want you to go anywhere else and be with anyone else. We all felt, including Albert and Derek that we liked having you around the place and the house would be quite empty without you".

229

David went up to Mr. Baron who put his arm around his shoulder, which surprised David as he was quite a reserved type of man although he was obviously the master of the house.

"Now, are you sure that is what you would like as I believe we have got to make a pretty swift decision"

David already knew that that was what he wanted and that was what he thought they were going to say when they first entered the house. That was why he had felt so disappointed when he was given the boat as this meant much more to him. "Yes, I would like to stay with you, but I think that the evacuee lady is coming around soon to take me to the other house".

"You leave that to me", said Mr. Baron, "she will have to find some other youngster to take to the other side of town". They all started laughing and David felt a warmth that he had not experienced since he had left home in the South. Mrs. Mount, Molly and Betty all went into the kitchen and returned with tea and what looked like flat scones, which they called buns, for them all. It all seemed as if Christmas had come early to David until he heard the knock on the door. His heart sank and he wondered if the lady would insist on his leaving the Baron's and going to the new people. Mrs. Mount answered the door and David could hear a lady's voice saying that she had come to collect David. Mrs. Mount came back into the room and told Mr. Baron who went straight to the door. He heard the lady say that this had all now been set up and it was impossible to change the arrangements. She said that perhaps David could go along with her today and they would review the situation later, otherwise she would have to report to her superior and may get it in the neck.

"Now look here lass", said Mr. Baron in a very firm voice, "we have decided that the lad will stay with us. I know that we were unsure at first, that was because we were caught on the hop, late at night, but we have looked after him until now and although we have been away on holiday, we want him to stay with us.   He is more than welcome and it is what he wants".

There was silence for a while and then the lady said, "Let me take him with me to the other people and I will try to clear it with my boss tomorrow".

"No", replied Mr. Baron, "he is going to stay here with us and if you have any trouble with your boss, you tell him to come to see me tomorrow evening when I have had a rest, but tell him that I am not very tolerant at that time in the evening and he might   get a rough ride".

"Can I just see David on his own and ask him if he is happy with the situation as it is?"

Mr. Baron came back into the room and David went to the door. After being satisfied that this was what David wanted she got Mr. Baron to sign a form and left them to carry on with their tea.   She did, however, give David a little smile as she left and he knew that she was quite happy with the arrangement.

On arrival at the classroom the next day Miss Tapsfield seemed overjoyed to see David again although she did take him outside the class to ask him how he had managed to come back to that school. She had been informed that David was to move schools on that morning.   When David explained what had happened she took him by the hand and led him along to the headmaster's office.   There she checked that it was alright to carry on in her class and after receiving the all clear, took David back to the classroom.   David couldn't remember learning a lot while he was in that class, but he did know that he was very fond of the young teacher and would do anything to avoid upsetting her.   In fact he noted that when she took her glasses off and let down her hair she was very much like his favourite teacher at his own school. He was beginning to quite enjoy going to school as he met up with a lot of his friends and they would share their stories of what went on in each of their digs. Some were very funny and some were quite serious, but whatever the tale they all knew that it was better than facing the Doodle Bugs at home. The evenings were long as there was still double summer time which extended the daylight hours right up to nearly eleven o'clock, so there was lots of time after school to go exploring. They would often go into part of Sherwood Forest to race around the area frequented by Robin Hood and his Merry Men and if they went deep enough into the third wood, which was well away from the main road, they could enter the cave where Robin and his men were said to have lived.

It was on one of these expeditions that while they were in the cave pretending to hide from King John's men that they heard the sound of men shouting and cheering. They thought that it sounded like a football match and carefully made their way to a clearing in the forest. They crept along the ground and through the branches they could see a group of about 30 to 40 men gathered in a large circle. They all seemed to be throwing money into a blanket and two of the men stood by the side of the blanket writing something down on sheets of paper. The boys had no idea what was going on until they heard the low growls of dogs. They moved a little closer just as two, large, vicious, black dogs went racing at each other snarling and biting and snapping. The boys had seen dog fights at home, but never as vicious as this. The men were all shouting and screaming and the noise was deafening. They couldn't see too well due to all the men surrounding the dogs so they climbed up the first few branches of a nearby tree. That was their big mistake. The branch that Peter climbed onto gave way with a large "crack" and he fell to the ground. Some of the men turned and on seeing the boys came running towards them. David remembered that he was the highest in the tree, but jumped to the ground almost knocking all the breath out of him. All three of them turned and ran as fast of their legs would carry them, dodging in and out of the trees and bushes. They thought that they knew the woods well, but the men that were chasing them had obviously done this before and were gaining on them with every step. Perhaps it was due to the fact that they were only eight years old and their little legs covered less ground than the adults.

Colin led the field with David a close second. Peter was dropping back and David thought that he may have injured himself when he fell from the tree. A tall, tough looking man with a black beard and curly hair, dressed in black trousers and a black waistcoat with a coloured trim all round the edges and over the pockets, and a red scarf tied over his head leaped through the bushes in front of Peter who stopped in his tracks. At that moment they heard a whistle blow and they turned to see where it came from. Two policemen, dressed in the same uniform as Dad came through the bushes towards them. They were caught between the two sets of men and not knowing what to do, just stood still. As they looked back the pursuers had disappeared back into the woods. When Colin explained what had happened the policemen took their names and addresses and told them to go straight home and they would be in touch with their parents later that evening. The policemen then carried on their route into the Third Wood. The boys ran back to their street as quickly as they could. When they were outside No 31 they started to discuss what sort of story they should tell Colin's parents and Mrs. Baron.

"I think we should tell them the truth" said David, "if the police come round tonight they will know the truth anyway".

Peter was all for saying nothing and waiting to see if the police would bother with small boys who were just playing in the woods. After a long argument they agreed to tell. Mrs. Baron said that David should tell his story to Mr. Baron as he had more to do with that sort of thing and it would be best to tell him after he had woken up and had had some tea. Mr. Baron was not so nice when David told him the story.

"You shouldn't be in that part of the woods and I blame Colin for taking you there. I know what goes on with the dog fights. It is not only illegal but very cruel. The men are very rough and wouldn't hesitate to severely injure anyone who watches them and you were lucky that the two policemen arrived. God knows what would have happened if they had caught you. I don't know what your parents would say if they knew the danger you were in".

"I'm sorry Mr. Baron, we only went into the woods to play at Robin Hood and his merry men. We didn't know what was going on until we heard the cheering and shouting".

"Now you must promise not to go in there again and it would be best if you came straight home from school in the future. Do you understand?"

David felt like crying as he had never been reprimanded like that by Mr. Baron before. He just said, "Yes, Mr. Baron. I am sorry. Do you think the police will come round to see you?"

"No, I am sure they have better things to do. Now you go and get Mrs. Baron to give you some tea and I think an early night would be a good plan".

David remembered that he was in bed in his pyjamas, reading his cowboy book that Albert had given him. He was just at the part where Jessie James was shot in the back by one of the other cowboys, when there was a knock at the door. David could hear two men talking downstairs and then was horrified to hear footsteps coming up the stairs followed by his door being opened. It was Mr. Baron and he was looking very stern and serious.

"Come downstairs with me David, the two policemen want to talk to you". He turned and went downstairs. David jumped out of bed and went down the stairs very slowly. When he entered the room he saw the two large policemen, still in uniform, standing with Mr. Baron in the middle of the room. David was upset to see that Mrs. Baron,

Derek and Albert were all there sitting in the chairs.   One of the policemen addressed David and said,

"Come in lad and sit on a chair, we've got something to ask you and we want you to tell the truth".   David sat on the only free chair, which had been brought in from the kitchen.

"Did you know what was going on in the woods before you went in?"

"No sir".

"Did you see what was going on"?

David described the circle of men and the dog fight that seemed to be taking place in the middle of the circle.

"Did you recognise any of the men?"

"No sir".

"Can you describe how any of them were dressed and what they looked like?"

David gave the policeman a description of everything he remembered, how they were dressed, what they wore on their heads and he even remembered the colours of the blanket and the size and colour of the dogs and which of the men released the dogs.   When he had given all the descriptions he could remember, the policeman looked quite pleased and actually thanked David for his cooperation.   He then explained that they had set up a trap to catch the men red handed and the diversion caused by the boys only helped to alert the group of police coming in from the back of the woods and the men ran straight into their trap.   The policeman advised David not to go anywhere near that part of the woods again and as he had given such a good description, he would not have to call on the other boys.

When they had gone David was sure that the Baron's would ask him to leave their house and find somewhere else to live. He was almost in tears and thought to himself that he had only just begun to feel at home and accepted by the family. Trying to hold back the tears he said,

"I suppose you will want me to go to those people on the other side of Mansfield now I have caused all this trouble"

"Of course not", said Mr. Baron, "you didn't know what went on in those woods; I bet dog fighting and betting on the winner doesn't go on where you live. Anyway, we were quite proud of the way you helped the police and we were quite surprised that you were not frightened by their uniform. Now you go off up to bed, you'll have some stories to tell your pals tomorrow. I wouldn't tell your teacher too much as she might feel that she would have to report it to the head. Now off you go".

David did tell the whole story to a group of children, including Colin and Peter, the next day, but they didn't believe the bit about the visit of the police as they had not gone to their house.

Although they were attending St. Paul's School, they were taught in a class which was full of evacuees. They didn't mix very much with all the other children and even their play times and finishing times were different. David had the feeling that many of the local children were not too pleased to have them around. This was made very clear one day on the way home from school when a group of local lads grabbed David and Peter and twisted their arms up behind their backs. They forced them into a derelict air raid shelter which was set half way into the ground. They pushed the door closed on them and put something in front of the door to stop them opening it. At the back of the shelter was the escape hole, which had had the bricks broken away to leave an opening. David pointed this out to Peter and they decided that when the other boys had gone they would climb out. Little did they know the intentions of the local boys for in a couple of minutes, sand came pouring in through the hole. It was either being thrown in or kicked in because it was filling the air with dust. It got into their hair, eyes, nose, mouth and lungs and they began to choke. David grabbed Peter and pulled him under the escape hole where the sand was going over their heads and towards the front of the shelter. It became darker and darker with the dust and they couldn't open their eyes as they filled with grit. It seemed to go on for hours and they were both coughing but in between the coughs shouting for help. David remembered that he lost all sense of time and place and only vaguely remembered the door being pulled open and two men dragging them out into the open. David didn't recognise the men. Colin had seen the boys throwing sand into the hole at the back of the shelter and heard the cries. He saw two miners returning from their shift and begged them to come and help him. Immediately the local boys saw the miners they ran off. The men shook Peter and David free of some of the sand and with Colin took them to their homes. David didn't have time to thank them as he couldn't stop coughing.

When Mrs. Baron saw the state of David, his hair and his clothes, she was shocked, but after the men explained what had happened, she quickly took him indoors and stripped him of all his clothes. She then got the tin bath from the back yard and stood him in it and proceeded to wash him down with saucepans full of cold water. David just stood and coughed and coughed and coughed. After drying him down and getting him some clean clothes, she made him a tasty bowl of hot soup. When Mr. Baron came down from his sleep she told him what had happened. They were both very concerned and after a short discussion, it was agreed that Mr. Baron would go up the road to Colin's mother and see what they should do about it. Colin's mother was very, very angry and they both agreed that they should go to the school and have a word with the headmaster. So, the next morning, all four of them, Mr. Baron, Colin's mother, Peter and David went off to the school together.   David and Peter went to their classroom and the other two went to the headmaster's office.

About half an hour later the school secretary came to the classroom and had a quiet word with Miss Tapsfield.   She asked Peter and David if they would go with the secretary to the headmaster's office. They were surprised to find that Mr. Baron and Colin's mother had gone and there was just the headmaster and another lady who they didn't recognise.   The headmaster asked them lots of questions about the boys who had attacked them, where they were pushed into the shelter and whether they would be able to recognise the boys again. He spent a lot of time writing it all down in a large book and finally ended up by assuring the boys that he would do something about this and they were not to be worried about being bullied again as he was sure it would be stopped .

He was quite right, they were left well alone except for one small incident when David was pushed into the deep end of the swimming baths and had to be rescued by the attendant. It seemed to have its benefits too.   The Baron's were particularly kind and treated him as one of the family.   They found him a real bed which they put in Albert's room and he was kept well supplied with cowboy comics and books to read.   Miss Tapsfield was particularly helpful at the school and always asked if they were being well looked after.   She was also extra kind and supplied them with pencils and paper so that they could continue with their hobby of drawing and Colin's mother even invited David to their house for tea on a couple of occasions.   Colin had quite a large garden and they could play football using the fence as the goal. Colin was extremely good at football and could do all sorts of tricks with the ball such as kicking it up with one foot many times and then hitting it on his knee and then catching it on the back of his neck.   He would then throw it up into the air and head the ball about ten times before trapping it on the ground with his foot.

It was during that week that David was treated to a very special visit to the cinema. He had, of course, been there with Betty, Molly, Peter and Rita to the Saturday morning children's cinema, but he had never been in the evening, when all the adults were present. It was while they were having tea that Mrs. Baron asked David if he would like to come with them to see a new film, which had only just been released. Of course, David jumped at the offer as he hadn't seen a proper film since right at the beginning of the war, before all the air raids started. She said that directly Mr. Baron woke up and had had a cup of tea they would all get on the bus and make their way to Mansfield. When they arrived outside the cinema David noticed that Mr. Baron was looking very nervous. He got his money out, but didn't know where to go to get the tickets. Mrs. Baron wasn't very much help, she just stood silently waiting. It was lucky that Derek and Albert were with them because they immediately took the money from Mr. Baron and went to the ticket office for the tickets. David suddenly realised that Mr. and Mrs. Baron had not been to the cinema before and this was as much an adventure for them as it was a treat for himself. He took Mr. Baron's hand and led him into the already darkened cinema to their usual seats in the stalls. The film was entitled, "Rose-Marie", but all David could remember of the film was the mounted policeman and a beautiful woman standing on a wooden balcony overlooking a snow covered mountain and singing the title song, "Oh Rose-Marie, I love you". During the interval Mrs. Baron produced some cakes and a bottle of fizzy water. As they walked back to the bus Mr. and Mrs. Baron looked quite amazed but very happy. They had all enjoyed the film and even though it made Mrs. Baron cry she had now recovered. David thanked them for the wonderful evening and said how much he had enjoyed the film.

Betty had settled down very well with the Mounts. She and Molly had become great friends and would go all over the place together. Many times they would take David with them, the only problem was that they always met up with lots of other girls and David felt quite out of place. Betty would write to Mum on one week and would write to

Dad on the other. Mum always replied straight away, but Dad may leave it two weeks or even get Jack to write for him. One week Betty came into David and said that she had to read the letter she had received from Jack. It told of how Mum was very unhappy where she was billeted. She and the two young children had gone to a house where there was only one old man. The house was attached to other houses on three sides so that it had no back door. She said that the toilet was just a board with a hole in the top and underneath there seemed to be a stream running. The house was filthy dirty and by the smell she was sure that the man didn't always visit the toilet when he wanted to pass water. Jack wrote,

"Dad is so worried that he is taking time off from the police and is spending his savings on going up to see them. I have also decided to take a week off and go with him as I don't think that Dad has been on many train journeys and may want a little company".

Within a week Betty received another letter from Jack. "Dear Betty, Dad suggested that if you can arrange for us to stay the night we will try to come in to see you on the way back home. Could you have a word with Mrs. Mount and see if this is possible, if so write immediately so that we can make arrangements. Lots of love, Jack and Dad. David and Betty couldn't believe their eyes, they read the letter again and then went to see Mrs. Mount. She said that she would be delighted to see them and would make room in some way to put them up for a couple of days, or as long as they could stay.

It was all fixed up and about three weeks to the day saw Betty, David, Molly and Mrs. Mount all standing on Mansfield Railway Station platform after purchasing a penny platform ticket. They seemed to wait for hours before the train from Nottingham came puffing into the station. They watched as the windows were lowered on the leather straps and people stuck their heads out. As the train came to a blowing and steaming stop they spotted Jack climbing down from the carriage followed by Dad and to their great joy and amazement, little Bobby and Mum carrying Susy.   They ran down the platform and threw themselves into the arms of Dad and Jack and when Mum had put down Susy, they both gave her a special hug.   It was some time before they got round to introducing them to Mrs. Mount and Molly. Mum and Dad couldn't thank them enough for looking after their two children and after another round of kisses and cuddles they made their way back to the bus and to Mrs. Mount's house.   It seemed very little with the two families in it.   Mrs. Mount first of all made them all some tea and then said that she should have to go next door to the Baron's to make some arrangements about sleeping.   It was agreed that Dad would sleep in Derek's bed and Derek would sleep on the floor.   Jack would sleep on the floor in Albert and David's room, while Mum would sleep with Susy in Betty's bed with Bobby on the floor and Betty would sleep downstairs.

The Baron's were also delighted to meet the Fellow's family and invited them into their house for the first evening. Mr. Baron, Dad, Jack and David went off to the local fish a chip shop and bought fish, chips and mushy peas for all the family and Mr. Baron even found a bottle of beer for Dad, who still liked his pint. After their meal, which was better than anything David had ever tasted, Mum, Dad and Jack relayed to them the events of the past few weeks. Mum said,

"After we had seen you off the Buzz Bombs seemed to get worse. We had three fall quite near our street and one hit the school.   Luckily it was at night and there were no children there.   Anyway they decided, and Dad agreed, that it was time for us to be evacuated.   It was decided by the authorities that all remaining children and their mothers should leave the estate and head for safer areas of the country".

"This time", came in Dad, "there were no buses and we had to take the tube up to London to Euston Station and we would be met there. When we arrived in the front doors of the station we saw that it was packed.   I was worried that if a bomb came over at that time it would be a disaster. Anyway, we got Mum and the two kids on the train to Manchester and that was the last we saw of them".

"When we arrived in Manchester", Mum continued, "we were transferred to a train to Oldham and there we were just allocated billets. Ours was terrible; I think Jack has told you about it. I spent most of my time cleaning up the place and making sure that I was not around when the old man came back from the pub at night. Anyway, after a week or so I asked for a transfer and ended up in a nice house rented by a younger couple. That was much better and when Dad and Jack came up we were beginning to settle in. Dad said that the bombing had become a little less now, so I decided there and then to go back home with them. So here we are on our way home".

"Can we come home too?" asked David.

"Not yet", replied Dad, "you are obviously well looked after here and I think it would be wise to stay on a little longer".

"How long?" asked Betty.

"Give it about one more month then I think it may be safer and you could come home then".

There followed a period of moaning and groaning and then a reluctant acceptance of the decision. They stayed for three days and David remembered going to the station with them and as the train left the station he could see tears in both Mum and Dad's eyes. It had been a wonderful three days, but David remembered sitting on the back steps on many evenings with tears flowing down his cheeks and feeling more home sick than ever. One time Mrs. Baron called him into the front room and said,

"What's wrong with your eyes David, they look all red and wet?"

"I think I have got something in one of them and it has made me rub them."

He realised later that they knew what he was going through and why his eyes were red, but they said nothing and just gave him a little hug from time to time. He had gradually grown to love the Baron family, they were a little strange in the things they ate and the times they had their meals, but David accepted this as being up here in the north of England, or as he thought. He found the accent a little difficult to understand at times, but as his favourite teacher, Miss Tapsfield spoke in the same way, and it must be alright.

True to Dad's word, a letter came about a month later enclosing a postal order for their fares home. Mum had looked up the times of the trains and where they should change. She wrote,

"Dad will meet you at this end at St. Pancras Station and if either Mrs. Mount or Mr. Baron could see you on to the train at your end and had a word with the guard to keep an eye on you, I am sure all will go well. We are all looking forward to seeing you soon, All our love, Mum and Dad".

It was strange to find out how much David had grown to love the people of Mansfield who had taken so much care of them when they were in need. One of the saddest goodbyes was when David left the school. His favourite teacher had tears in her eyes and David put his arms around her neck and kissed her cheek. Kissing was not done too much in those days and that was a sign of deep affection. The headmaster even came and shook him by the hand, something David couldn't remember doing before, and wished him all the best. The ladies at the Salvation Army said "au revoir" as they said one should not say goodbye because it was too final. David had a lump in his throat when he said goodbye to Derek, Albert and Mr. and Mrs. Baron. They had been so kind to him and he knew that he would never be able to repay them for their kindness. He said he would write to them when he got home. Mrs. Mount and Molly took them to the station and Peter was allowed a morning off from school to say goodbye. He was a little bit upset that David was going home and yet he hadn't heard from his mum and dad when he could return. David couldn't remember the journey home. He could remember Dad meeting them at the station and the bus that took them from the underground at Morden, but the next he could remember was sitting on the top step at his front door exchanging stories with Danny, who had come home, with his mum and dad just a fortnight before.

Danny had been at a wonderful farm, overlooking the sea in Devon. He said that they could eat meat, butter and eggs whenever they liked and he could ride on the farmer's tractor whenever he wished. David didn't know how much he should believe and did wonder if things were so good down there, why had he come home?

First of all it looked as if everybody was right and the Doodle Bugs were getting less, in fact he hardly heard or saw another one. Apparently, the launching pads for the bombs had been overrun by the allied troops and any that were now launched came from mobile lorries further back from the coast. They all thought that the German barrage was now over, but how wrong they were.

Chapter 27

David got up slowly from the bench and made his way down the hill towards his house. It was just about the time Mum would expect him back after taking Janet home and saying goodnight to her. This had grown later and later according to the route they took and recently they had made their way via the park where they would spend some time kissing and cuddling. This evening, however, she didn't act in quite the same way. The route home had been fairly direct and there had been little stopping for a kiss. She seemed intent on getting to her gate and then went in without more than just a peck on the cheek. David blamed it all on this new chap in the club who seemed to enjoy chatting up the girls and was always full of jokes and smiles. All the girls seemed to laugh at his very poor jokes and it was difficult for the others to say anything that would even bring about a smile.

David remembered that this wasn't the first time this had happened. Some months before they had been invited, with many other couples in the club, to one of the members birthday parties. Don, the lad who was throwing the party lived in quite a small house and most of the guests were standing. Nearly everybody had a drink in their hand, most of the boys a light ale, or lager and lime, whilst the girls had a fizzy drink in a flat glass with a cherry on the top. It may have been a Babycham. As the party started to swing, some of the lads who were sitting down got up to offer their seats to the girls. One of Don's friends, who didn't get up from the arm chair he had acquired before most of them had arrived, said that Janet could sit on his lap if she wanted a seat. David was shocked and dismayed when she took up the offer and sat down. David tried to pretend that he didn't care too much, but his heart was racing and he couldn't take his eyes off the two of them. Janet had her beautiful light blue taffeta dress on and David knew that if you put your arm around her you could feel the smoothness of her skin below. The Don Juan was tall and had long thighs and it wasn't long before he had pulled Janet right up to the top so that she rested on the lower part of his hips. She leant back on him and they seemed to enjoy having a private conversation which was obviously very funny. He had his arms right around her waist and every now and again moved his hand up and down as if caressing her. David was livid and partly because of the beer he had been drinking and partly due to his anger, he made it an excuse to visit the toilet. He couldn't believe his eyes, when he returned the chair was empty and there was no sign of either of them. He walked quickly around the house and asked Don if he had seen them.

"Yes, they both got their coats and said that they were going to go out for a little walk, I shouldn't worry, he is quite a decent bloke and I am sure that Janet won't come to any harm".

That was exactly what David did not want to hear. He hoped that Janet would be upset and that Don's friend would try to be too familiar with her. He couldn't take part in any of the games or chat that was taking place, his mind was completely taken up by his thoughts of what they were doing and why Janet had allowed such a thing to take place. He decided to go home early and went upstairs to the bedroom to get his coat which had been thrown onto one of the beds at the front of the house. He was even more shocked to see, underneath the coats, the darkened form of a boy and girl making passionate love to each other. They were making so much noise that they didn't notice David come into the room and just carried on bumping up and down on the bed. David quickly moved towards the window and pretended that he hadn't noticed anything wrong. As he pulled aside the curtains he spotted Janet and the tall fellow walking up the road towards the house. They had their arms around each other and were obviously enjoying a good joke. David rushed downstairs to the party and with a light ale in his hand joined one of the groups. He wanted to give Janet the impression that he hadn't noticed that she had gone out. He waited for at least ten minutes with no sign of either of them, so he rushed up the stairs again and looked out of the front window. At first he could see no sign of the couple, but he became aware of someone below the window and almost out of sight at the front door. His heart nearly burst when he realised that they were kissing and embracing at the front door. David again went downstairs with his coat in his hand. He had taken it off the top of two figures that were obviously deeply asleep.

When David reached the front room of the house Janet was already in and taking off her coat. He had already put his on and when she saw him she said.

"Where are you going the party's not over?"

"It is for me, I have had enough. I saw you at the front door kissing and cuddling so I suppose old lover boy will get the honour of walking you home. I am not going to be a gooseberry, so I am leaving now".

He went to the front door and, leaving it open, walked down the path to the gate. He was half way down the road when he heard the sound of Janet running up behind him. He didn't stop and it wasn't until they reached the end of the road that she arrived at his side.

"Don't be silly David, there is nothing in it. We weren't kissing, as you put it, he was just telling me funny jokes".

"I saw you walking along towards the house with your arms around each other".

"Oh, so you have been spying on me. If this is how you are going to behave when we go to parties then I think we should see less of each other".

David felt his heart pounding like a train and was unable to speak. In fact neither of them spoke all the way home and at Janet's gate there was no goodbye, she just went straight in without even looking around. It was weeks before they even spoke to each other again. David would walk slowly down from the church hoping that he would bump into her either going to the church or coming home, but it was only rarely that he spotted her and even then she would be in the company of a group of club members. She was obviously doing all she could to avoid them meeting and David knew that even if they did she would ignore him, or make some cutting remark. It wasn't until the dancing classes started again that the two of them came into close contact. David was thrilled by the reunion, but it was quite difficult to dance together and learn new steps when they were not speaking to one another. All the club knew of the problem, as most of them were at the party in the first place. All the girls seemed to support Janet and thought that she had good reason to behave as she did, After all, she was only fourteen and why should she be tied down to just one partner. The boys, on the other hand, said that she was making herself too available and that they would not put up with their girl eyeing up other men. David feared, however, that Janet had lost all feelings for him and just wanted a change.

The dancing instructor noticed the problems immediately as the dancing had lost all of its rhythm and togetherness. She suggested that David should find another partner if he wanted to carry on improving his dancing. The only available girl at the time was a very young sister of one of the members. She was a pretty little girl with long blonde hair and deep blue eyes. Unfortunately she had no figure, being as thin as a pole, and was a little shorter than David. Luckily, she had always liked him and was delighted to be asked to be his partner. She had done little dancing before and therefore kept catching her feet on his, or turning the wrong way. Nevertheless, as the weeks went by she became quite a good dancer and they began to click as a couple. Janet had the same sort of experience except that she was matched with an older lad than David who danced as if he was wearing diving boots. He spent most of his time looking down at his feet and had the bad habit of sniffing every ten seconds or so. This didn't match Janet's image at all and David could see from a distance that she was spending most of her time trying to lead him instead of him leading her.

One evening, before the dancing instructor arrived, David was surprised to see Janet approaching him with two cups of tea in her hand. Imagine his amazement when she offered him a cup and asked if she could sit on the seat by the side of him. She still looked as attractive as ever and David felt his heartbeat increase in speed and his face begin to flush. Trying to be noncommittal he said,

"It's up to you, you can sit where you like. It's a free world".

"If that's how you are going to behave then perhaps I will find somewhere else to sit. I did want to have a word with you, but it seems that you are going to be as stupid as ever".

She turned to walk away when David quickly replied, "No, I am sorry. That was rude of me and no matter how things have gone in the past there is no reason for being rude. Please sit down and we can just talk, if that is what you want".

Janet turned and came back. "Now I don't want us to go back to what we were, but I do think that dancing has suffered with our new partners and we would do well to begin to dance together again. I am not looking for a boyfriend again but just a good dancing partner".
David didn't know whether he felt pleased or devastated. She was obviously not very happy with her new dancing partner and David would love to hold her in his arms again and twirl her around the dance floor, but that remark about not wanting to have a boyfriend again after all they had enjoyed in the past hurt him deeply. He had the feeling that he was being used and without thinking he said,

"Well, I am getting on quite well with Jenny and we are, just about, getting around the floor without too many mistakes. At least we talk to one another and she seems to enjoy dancing with me".

"If that's what you want, to just get around the floor, then forget it". With that, she stood up, with her tea in her hand, and walked off to the other side of the floor. How could he have been such a fool? It was just what he wanted and here he was throwing it all away again just to get one up, and for what? He sat for just a moment and then, looking up, he saw that she was sitting on her own looking either very sad or very angry. He immediately got up and went over to her.

"I am sorry. I get so nervous when you are around that I say the wrong things. I didn't mean that I wouldn't love to dance with you again as I used to enjoy it so much and if you agree, I will not expect anything more".

Janet looked up and smiled and said,

"I hoped you would say that. Shall we begin this evening when the dancing starts and give everybody a surprise". And so the relationship began again, not quite the same as before, but nevertheless it was a start.

Chapter 28

It was so good to be home again. He had only been away a few months, but to a boy, who had now turned nine, it seemed like years. So much seemed to have changed in that short time, the grass looked greener, the trees looked taller, the local kids were so much friendlier and his bed seemed so much more comfortable. Mum and Dad were as overjoyed that he and Betty were home as they were to be home themselves and although there were still all the remains of the devastation around the estate the actual bombing appeared to have stopped. He and Danny were now allowed to roam as they wished, visiting the park and the river at any time and playing cricket with the rest of the lads went on till quite late at night, just as it did before, at the beginning of the war.

It was during one of these trips to the park that they had their first experience of the German V 2. It was getting late in the evening and they were considering whether they should pull up the stumps and head for home, when there was an almighty explosion, which seemed to come from the Croydon area. They first saw a bright flash followed a little later by a very loud bang. Looking across the fields they could see a tall column of smoke. Stumps were soon drawn and a race back to their own street was on. Many neighbours had gathered around the small green and Mr. Stamp, who always heard of news way in advance of the B.B.C., was telling the surrounding group that Hitler had developed another weapon which travelled so fast no one could see it and it was packed with high explosive. He said that no one could tell when they were coming; there was no sound from their engines and the first thing you knew was an almighty explosion much worse than any Doodle Bug. Of course, this frightened the life out of all the ladies and the children, while most of the men took his stories with a pinch of salt. The unfortunate part was that he was correct in most of his information. Danny, in his usual confident way said,

"Well, if one of those rockets falls on us then we wouldn't know anything about it as we wouldn't hear it coming and by the time it arrived we would be dead".

This didn't seem to cheer anyone up, but they knew that it was most probably true. In actual fact most of the V.2's fell on London and only one or two fell short. This meant that life went on fairly normally. There was as much chance of being caught by a V 2 if you were in the park, down by the river or safely tucked up in your house. There was little point in going to the shelters because there was no warning of them coming. Once, at night, when he was out in the front of the house with Dad, they saw one of the V 2s scudding across the sky. It looked a little like a shooting star except that it appeared to have a flaming tail. Sadly, there was no point of, or no excuse for, missing school. This was carried on as normally as possible in the circumstances. There were only about half as many teachers as there had been when they left for evacuation, which wasn't too much of a problem, as there was less than half the number of pupils. They still held most of the lessons in the air raid shelters at the back of the school as they said that it was safer if a rocket fell close.

During that winter and the next spring they listened to all the news broadcasts they could from the B.B.C. and studied closely the Allied advances into Europe. Mr. Churchill made many speeches and broadcasts telling of the victories the Allies had achieved and when the different countries were liberated from German occupation. It all sounded so good to all of them at home, but very few realised the suffering and the death that was occurring in the war zones. They saw wave after wave of bombers heading south towards the coast, but never knew how many didn't return. It was with great joy that all the family and neighbours greeted the news that the Allies had entered Germany and they were all en route for Berlin, the capital. They knew now that the war was coming to an end and preparations were made to celebrate the victory.

David couldn't remember when he heard the wonderful news for the first time. He remembered running into the street and joined in with the hundreds of local people that had gathered on the large green. He and Danny had been joined at home by Peter about two months before, and they raced around the green jumping and cheering and wrapping their arms around people they had never seen before. They made their way to the far end of the green, where Jack and many of his friends, plus a group of older men, were deep in discussion of how they should celebrate the victory in Europe. Many of them had suggested a large party on the big green with a bonfire, others were making arrangements to travel up to London and see the victory in style. David remembered that he had no idea of the size of the bonfire the men were suggesting. He and the two others went back to their houses to find things to go on the bonfire. Between them they had gathered one bag of branches, about five newspapers, three pairs of old boots, a piece of carpet and three old combs. They put their collection on a growing heap in the middle of the green, but were amazed when some of the men turned up with large logs and then tree trunks. By the next day the small heap had turned into a pyramid about fifteen feet high. Tables had been gathered from many of the houses and placed at a safe distance from the fire and people were bringing chairs out from all of the surrounding houses. All the ladies were gathering together what food they could find or spare, and someone had even dragged out a piano, on which, to the owner's disapproval,   the children were banging the keys and making a terrible noise. Dad organized a collection so that some of the men could go round to the Off Licence and buy as much beer as they could afford and after he had visited nearly all the houses surrounding the two greens he and a couple of others went off towards the St Anthony's Arms. They returned about an hour later with two wheel barrows, one containing an enormous barrel of mild and the other full of crates of bottled beers. Many of the neighbours had covered the fronts of their houses with bunting and some men were stringing flags from tree to tree. By the time early evening came the whole area on and around the green looked a 'right' picture.

Children and adults, mainly women, sat at the tables and handed out cakes, sandwiches and tea and all of them were serenaded by the owner of the piano and a group of about twenty friends singing all the old songs. Just before it started to get dark two of the men poured paraffin over the base of the bonfire and after getting everybody to stand well away, set fire to a cloth on the end of a long stick and lit the bonfire. It was soon a blazing pile with flames licking high into the sky. Many of the onlookers formed a large circle around the blaze and danced about singing and laughing. What a night it turned out to be! No one left the party till the early hours of the morning with the fire still burning brightly. The only sad part David felt was that Jack had gone with some of his friends up to London to stand in the Mall and see the King and Queen with the two Princesses standing on the balcony of Buckingham Palace, accompanied by the man who had inspired the whole country during those dreadful years of bombing, Winston Churchill.

There was a similar celebration in the middle of August, when the Japanese surrendered and the war was finally over. Danny had told him and Peter that he had heard that the Allies had collected up all the bombs they had left over from the war against the Germans and put them all together in one bomb and dropped it on the Japanese. David had made the comment to Danny that there couldn't have been a plane big enough to carry such a bomb as the Flying Fortress was the biggest bomber we had. Danny was so sure that he said that they must have built a plane bigger than anything we could imagine. They were happy to accept Danny's stories now as what mattered most was that the war was really over and they could return to a normal life and freedom to wander anywhere they liked without fear of being killed.

All three boys moved up into the top class of the junior school, this was mainly due to their age and not as a result of intelligence. They were a little taken aback one day when the teacher handed everybody a large printed document having about ten pages of questions. This had come completely out of the blue and had to be finished before they went to dinner break. David took the situation a little more seriously than the other two and tried to answer as many questions as he could, but by the time the bell rang he still had a couple of pages to go. They felt that it didn't matter anyway as they were going to move to the senior school after the summer holidays. A few minor celebrations were held but they were so pleased to think of the long summer holiday with no school, anything else was forgotten.

In actual fact, the boys spent most of their time being fairly bored although the tall pyramids of telegraph poles were removed from the park which made the playing of cricket and football a lot easier. Many of the shelters had been removed, especially the Anderson shelters with the corrugated metal panels. He and Jack had helped Dad remove the shelter before the men came round and they filled in the concrete base and sides with earth making the garden look a little as it did pre-war. It wasn't until nearly six months later they found that the concrete box had filled with stinking water and they had the smelly task of digging down and banging a hole in the base with a hammer and chisel, that is after they had drained out most of the foul smelling fluid.

The warden's shelter on the corner of the street had been abandoned immediately after the end of the war and all the equipment and telegraph pole was removed. The three boys managed to force the padlock on the door and get inside. A little light did get in through a large grill and the boys adopted it as a magnificent camp. They played war games where they pretended that one of them was the warden and the other two were high ranking policemen. They managed to get some boxes from the local shops and made them into rudimentary furniture. By keeping the padlock on the door it kept others out and they would only enter the shelter if they knew they were not being overlooked. It wasn't until several weeks had passed that they discovered that the thick cable that emerged from the floor on the far side of the shelter was carrying electricity. They had seen the cable before but sensibly had never been anywhere near it just in case. Then Danny had a good idea, he said that if he threw some water on it from a distance it should spark. They got an old milk bottle and filled it with urine, then Danny threw some of it on the cable and to their surprise an enormous spark shot out. From then on, if they wanted to visit the toilet they would stand on one side of the shelter and squirt their urine up into the air so that it fell on the cable with a loud bang and a shower of sparks. It was only later that they were told that if the urine had formed a complete unbroken line one of them could have been electrocuted. Later on that year a crane turned up with a big metal ball on a chain and smashed the shelter to pieces. The debris was removed and the green was returned to its original state with bushes and trees.

After the summer holidays they attended their new senior school. There seemed to be many more children as they were drawn from all of the surrounding area. They were all in the same class under the control of an older teacher called Mrs. Barfit. She was round and cuddly and wore round brown rimmed spectacles and her hair was always the same, tied into buns on either side just above her ears. She always wore an off white overall which came down to her mid calf. She looked an easy target for ridicule, but not at all, she took control of the class as a sergeant major would his troop of soldiers. No one would dare speak out of turn and no one would speak when she was speaking. On the other hand, she was held by the class with great respect and could always get the best out of those that wanted to learn. David enjoyed being taught by her so much that he would not miss school at any cost and remembered that he actually won points at the end of the term for not missing one day. He also received for being top of the class, a new, blue dictionary. He enjoyed the football, which was taken by the senior teacher and the boxing taken by the gym teacher. He actually joined the boxing club and after some early tuition he and two other boys were included in the school boxing team taking part in several tournaments against other schools. He was always well equipped to defend himself thanks to the training that Jack and Dad had given him earlier.

During that term they were again presented with an official looking document about ten pages long. This time he romped through the questions and even had time to spare at the end. Strangely he had no idea what it was in aid of and no one had told him about the scholarship examination, or if they had he didn't put two and two together. What a surprise it was when he received a letter telling him that he had passed the examination and would he please list the grammar schools he would like to attend in the order of his preference. Mum and Dad were completely taken back by the letter and thought that he should stay where he was as they knew it was a good school and he could easily get a job in a factory afterwards. On the other hand, Jack, who now had left school, and had worked in the jewellery business in London for the past three years, persuaded them that this was a great opportunity for David to get a more academic education and this sort of opportunity only came once in a life time. Dad was very much opposed to the move and Mum, who usually listened to the advice of Jack, could not make her mind up one way or the other.

When David went to school the next day Mrs. Barfit had obviously heard the news because she was delighted. Three of her boys had achieved passes, this was more than any other year. When she heard that David was unsure as to whether he would be able to take up the place she was devastated. She spent a long time talking to him and asking him questions and as they left the class to go home, at the end of the day, she handed him a letter addressed to Mr. and Mrs. Fellows. David didn't know what she had said in the letter, but the atmosphere at home changed a little and Mum reluctantly joined Jack in the argument. Finally, it was decided that he would choose Sutton

Grammar School as his first choice and Wallington as second. About a week later Betty and he went off by bus to see both the schools and give him an idea of which one he would like to attend. They both turned out to be completely unexpected. All the boys were in uniform one in red and one in navy blue and they all seemed very respectful of visitors to their schools. The teachers, or masters as they called them, were wearing funny gowns and he even saw one in the school hall wearing a flat hat on his head. He now felt very unsure himself as to whether he wanted to leave the school he had begun to love and the friends he knew so well and go off to, what a appeared to be, such an impersonal place. His mind was made up however, when he found out that the other two boys from his class had applied for Wallington.

Now arose another problem. About a month later all three boys heard that they had been accepted for the school of their choice. With the acceptance letter was a list of all the uniform and equipment that they would need before their attendance late in September. Mum and Dad were shocked as they had very little money and Dad, since he left the police was only working as a council worker relaying all the shrubs in the greens at the corners of the roads. David realised the situation and immediately told them that he would stay at his senior school and not take up the offer. At the end of the week, however, Mum suddenly said to David that they were going to Sutton and Wallington shopping for his uniform. Jack was obviously pleased with the decision, but Dad said nothing.

Chapter 29

Wallington was a whole new ball game. It wasn't somewhere in the day that you attended for lessons, it didn't just start at nine and finish at four; it seemed to be a new life. There were lessons, of course, but all the teachers and all the pupils seemed to be keen to do everything they were asked to the best of their ability. Most of the boys spoke with a la-di-dah accent and most of them came from the local area of large and detached houses. They were all so pleased to be at the school and wear the uniform with the cap and badge but David found it hard at first, to mix with them. He and the two other boys from Mrs. Barfit's class, Jamie Porter and Jimmy Stanford, stuck together for the first few days for company.

Although they all went to the main school for the first day and were addressed by the Head and several of the masters, they were all led across Beddington Park to a large, old house, which they were informed was called Carew House and dated from the time of Henry VIII. Part of the main school had received a direct hit by one of Hitler's bombs and was out of action so there weren't enough classrooms for the new intake. It was a wonderful old building with lots of back stairs and hidden rooms. The classrooms were large reception rooms which were painted in a dull, dirty green colour and all the windows gave the appearance of being part of a church. They only used the north wing of the building and were forbidden to venture into the main section. Their recreational area was an old medieval courtyard surrounded by what looked like cloisters. Just behind this wing was a beautiful garden surrounded by a high wall which they called the Orangery, and behind this was a small swimming pool filled with clear, but freezing cold water. On the south side of Carew House stood the beautiful old Beddington Church, parts of which dated from the eighth century.

Much to everybody's dismay, they were split into three groups and were all given another examination paper to complete. David, at that time, read very slowly but understood what he was reading. He found the questions all straight forward and really just a matter of general knowledge or common sense. His only worry was that he may not complete all the questions in the time allotted. When they collected the papers he had still two left to answer, but instead of having a quick guess at the answers, he just left them blank. The next day they were allocated the class they would attend. The first thirty were to be labelled Two Special, the other two classes were labelled Two Alfa and Two A. The special group were considered to be the high flyers, but as in a football league table, it was explained that at the end of the year the four bottom boys would be replaced by two from each of the other classes. David was pleased to find that he had achieved a place in the Special class and was extremely pleased to see that Jamie and Jimmy had also made the Special class.

That first year was a very informative year. All three boys came on the same bus to school after a twenty minute walk to the bus stop. They would get off the bus at the entrance to another park, Grange Park, and walk along the small streams that begun as springs issuing from the ground. The water was clear, clean and icy cold, even on a hot summer's day and they regularly either drank from the springs or filled a bottle to keep in their satchels. They would make their bus tickets into boats and race them along the small streams under the wooden bridges to a previously agreed winning post. This became a regular game and they would list the wins and seconds ending up with an overall winner for the week. They had, many times, to race across the park to reach Carew House in time for the bell. You had to be in the quadrangle by nine o'clock and when the first bell sounded you had to stand still. The masters and the prefects would walk around between the boys inspecting their shoes, trousers, blazers and caps and on the sound of a whistle they would all form up into three lines to be led into their respective classrooms.

David still retained his spirit of adventure and inquisitiveness. One day, he and a couple of the other boys crept off down one of the corridors towards the central part of the house. They came across a magnificent stairway which was lit by a very large stained glass window. They quietly made their way up the broad stairs and at the top entered a large hall beautifully decorated in red, green and gold, but unfortunately filled with large bales of what looked like strips of plastic. It was while they were trying to open the side of one of the bales that a man caught them. He was very angry and escorted them back to the school area. He said he would report them to the master in charge, but luckily, they didn't hear any more! Another time they were all standing in the quadrangle under the covering that went all around the roof. Although they had been sent out at break time, it was raining heavily and the water was pouring off the gutter just above their heads. One of the boys, David couldn't remember who it was, had a great idea. He said that if he climbed on David's shoulders he could reach the gutter. He could then shake it and all the water would pour down over those who were sheltering underneath. Obligingly, David let him climb on his shoulders and he took hold of the gutter. As he started to shake the gutter the water poured all down David's neck and he automatically ducked and stepped away. The boy was left hanging from the gutter which was made of cast iron. But alas, before anyone could come to his rescue the gutter came away from the fascia board pulling with it long lengths of gutter on either side. Not only were all the boys covered with water but the gutters were full of a muddy slime which covered them from head to foot. That was not all, the gutters, on hitting the cobbles, smashed to pieces. Luckily, no boys received any injuries from being hit by the gutter, but it was a near thing. No one saw what happened, or so they said, and no one knew who was to blame. It must have been just the weight of the water they said. Mr. Massing, their master, said that he was pleased that no one was hurt, but couldn't imagine how a gutter that had been there and carrying water for nearly five hundred years could suddenly become unsafe. He said it with a sarcastic look on his face so they were a little unsure what he believed had happened.

If the boys got off the bus one stop earlier, they could enter the far side of Beddington Park and this way they could follow the river Wandle up towards the Beddington Cricket Ground. As they neared Carew House, they would have to cross over the river by a small bridge. Just below the bridge was a weir, only about four feet high, which held the water back in the upper part of the park. David and the other two thought it would be a great idea to create their own tributary and dug a shallow trough that led from the upper part, round the weir and joined the river at the bottom section. When the trough was complete they took away the barrier they had made at the top section and a little trickle of water gradually made its way down to the bottom section. This they thought was extremely clever and named the new river the Welbeck. Each day they would inspect the flow and were pleased to see that it grew bigger day by day. After a week there was quite a rapid flow of water. After the weekend they came back to find that the Welbeck had become quite a torrent. They were so proud of their river that they visited it every morning. It wasn't until just after a weeks half term holiday, did they suddenly get cold feet. They saw that the weir was now dry and so was the upper part of the river. There was just a stream that ran down the middle and straight into the Welbeck. They walked along the upper part of the original river and found many dead fish lying on top of the mud. From then on they avoided going that way, but later on that term Mr. Massing addressed the whole of the ninety boys and explained what had happened to the river and how many of the fish had died. He said that a great deal of money must now be spent to put in concrete sides to the river, above and below the weir and the land filled in. The council thought that the original stream had been dug by boys, either local or from this school and wanted everybody to know the cost involved in putting it right. No more was said, but the boys never went that way again.

The school was proud of its sporting achievements. There were four main sections, in the winter there was rugby and cross country running and in the summer there was cricket and athletics. David hated cross country running and would avoid it at all costs. He was not too keen on athletics either, but he loved rugby and cricket. In rugby he was always a little small and reluctant to dive at the attacking three quarters. Although he enjoyed playing, there were many more boys better than him and he never made the school team. On the other hand he loved cricket and was particularly good at bowling. He had had a lot of practice when he was younger when they invented a game of putting one stump at the end of the pavement and placing a large can where the batsman would stand. The aim was to hit the stump without hitting the tin can. This paid off well when he went for his trial one evening after school. Some of the better batsmen were completely flummoxed by a ball which he would bring in from either the off or the leg side at medium pace. When the colt's team was announced for the first match against Beckenham County, he found his name on the probable list. Their first match was at home and David was brought on to bowl after the opening pair of fast bowlers. They had been quite wild; some bowling was short, some full tosses and many wides. The captain, a brilliant batsman and someone David admired from the first time he met him, put David on from the school end. He was a little nervous as he had never been included in a team like this before and had never worn white trousers, a white shirt and white cricket shoes. The trousers Mum had adapted from an old pair that Dad had kept from his youth and the shoes he had borrowed from Mike, who still lived about five doors away from them. The batsmen found it hard to play David's bowling and it wasn't long before wickets started to tumble. Each time a batsman was out the next came in a little more apprehensive. He knew that the first thing the last batsmen would say to the incoming batsman was,

"He swings it in from the off side so cover your off stump". David therefore brought the next ball in from the leg side and usually got him L.B.W. If it were a right handed batsman he and the captain Edward, packed the slips and David would bowl an off break and if the batsman was left handed they would reverse the procedure. David ended up, in his first match, with nine wickets for only five runs and they won the game by seven wickets. In assembly, in the school hall, that Monday the headmaster announced the results of the weekends games and made a special mention of David's nine wickets for five runs. Although he didn't bowl quite as well as that again, it kept him in the school team for several years, being one of the main bowlers.

There was one serious drawback to going to Wallington and that was that a slight gap appeared in the close friendship that he had built up over many years with Danny and Peter. He was given homework every evening and although he tried to get it done on the way home or on the way to school, it was often needing time spent sitting at a table and thinking. The only room in the house he could use was their bedroom and as this was fairly full with a double bed and a single, plus a large sewing machine and a dressing table, he not only found little room to work but little time to join his friends out on the green. They did get together in the holiday periods, but as the years went by even these were spent with friends from his new school. He would be invited to join one of the Wallington boys at his home to play in their garden or watch the cricket at Beddington Park and sometimes he would be invited by the boy's mother to have tea with them. David's closest friend became Jamie, one of the boys that had gone up with him from Mrs. Barfit's class. He lived in a very comfortable flat above one of the local shops. In fact his dad owned the shop and was considered to be one of the up and coming members of the area. Jamie's mother was very attractive and very hospitable. She would always invite David to join Jamie and his two younger brothers for tea, which always included cakes and buns. Jamie was a little wild; in fact all three of them were a little wild and got up to all sorts of mischief. Nevertheless, they were all very friendly and would do anything to help anyone. Another draw back of going to Wallington was that they were expected to wear their uniform as much as possible and they became the target for the local boys who would chase them in gangs and try to pinch their hats or tear their blazers. They thought that the boys were snobs because they were polite to people and touched their caps on passing a senior member of the community.

A very nice group of boys from Wallington mainly made up of the cricket and rugby teams would go to watch the pupils from the girl's grammar school play hockey. Some of them were sisters of the boys and welcomed the support they gave. On one or two occasions David would accompany them and, although he knew little about hockey, enjoyed the camaraderie of the encounter. He had little to do with girls up until now and always thought of them as those to be avoided, except for sisters and friends. He had met one girl on the bus going home from school, Lucy, who lived close to him, just by the park, to whom he used to chat as they went up the hill, or crossed the park. He and she did quite a lot together and even on one occasion visited the cinema at Morden. That was the time when there was terrible smog all over the London area and it was impossible to see any further than two yards ahead. They waited at the bus stop to catch the bus home, but every bus went by with the conductor walking in front with a flaming torch. After a while Lucy stopped one of the buses and asked if they would take them on board. Unfortunately, they had all had instructions to return to their garage and carry no passengers. Lucy pleaded with the conductor and said that they were completely lost and had no way of getting home. It was the first time that David had seen her behave as a woman. There were tears in her eyes as she asked the conductor just to take them part of the way. In the end he took them up to the back of the bus and told them to keep their heads down. As they passed another bus stop a man and a woman asked where they were going. Lucy immediately piped up,

"We are going towards Sutton, jump on, I'm sure the conductor won't mind".

When they arrived half way up St. Anthony's Avenue the conductor stopped the bus for them to get off. Lucy then turned on the charm again and persuaded the driver to turn left to Bishopsford Road, from where they would know their way home. David gradually grew to admire this little ball of fire, but he thought that the main attraction to her was that her brother had a snooker table in their front room and he was often invited to join him and his father for a game.

The Wallington boys thought that it was time David was introduced to a girl as they all seemed to have girlfriends at the time. They persuaded him to go with them to the cinema in Wallington High Street and said that they knew a girl that would be pleased to accompany him. That Wednesday afternoon, when the grammar schools were still on holiday and the rest of the schools had begun their term, David put on a clean shirt and some Brylcream on his hair and was about to leave the house when Bobby, who was off school, decided that he wanted to go with him. There was a terrible row, David knowing about meeting the girl and Mum not. In the end David was made to take Bobby with him. You can imagine the look on everybody's faces when he arrived at the cinema. The girl was already a young lady; she had long dark hair, a very attractive face, touched up with a little make up, and the figure of an eighteen year old. To add to David's embarrassment, she was a good three inches taller than him. He was even more embarrassed when they decided to go into the circle, which was an extra three pence. David not having the extra money didn't know what to do until, Jenny, the beautiful brunette paid the extra. On the next Monday, when they were all back at school, the captain of the cricket team, quietly took David aside and very pleasantly said that Jenny thought that he was a little young for her and didn't want to go out with him again.

It was about that time that David, Jamie and another boy, Alan started going to school on their bicycles. David had built his himself using an old frame with handlebars and one wheel he had found on a dump and many other parts that he had found either in the shed or been given by other boys. The most expensive parts of his machine were the tyres and the brakes which he had to buy from the local cycle shop. He changed all the ball bearings and lined the cones with thick grease. He had stripped the frame right down to the metal and then applied the paint, first a sealing coat, then an undercoat and finally a glossy top coat. The only disadvantage was that he had only one gear, but to a boy that originally had no bike, this machine was tops. Jamie had a new bike, bought by his mum and dad for one of his birthdays, a Claude Butler. This was considered to be one of the best of its time and was equipped with cantilever brakes and a three speed gear. They became quite proficient on their bikes and would spend the weekend visiting places like Windsor, Hampton Court or Box Hill. As they grew fitter they would spend a day cycling to Brighton up and down such hills as Reigate and Cockshot. They used to take it in turns to be at the front and when the leader was beginning to get tired the one at the back took over the pace. The hills were always a problem to David as he had only the one gear, but he soon caught Jamie up on the downhill stretch.

They joined the Youth Hostel Association somewhere up in London and were impressed at all the hostels there were all over the country. They proudly sewed the triangular, green badge on their shorts and bought, at very little cost, maps of England. They would spend hours sitting on David's front step pouring over the wonderful red and white roads and the hundreds of unknown towns and cities spread all over the country. It was on one of these occasions that Jamie suggested that during that summer holiday they could do a cycle tour of Devon and Cornwall. They had heard a lot about Land's End and thought that this would be the time that they could see the place for themselves. They had been cycling down to Brighton and back in one day with no stop. They would just cycle around the island by the Pier, see the sea and then head for home. This they worked out to be close to one hundred miles, so they planned to do about that distance each day. This was their big mistake. They decided to make Littlehampton their first stop as they had been there before, then on to

Winchester, Bridport etc. paying visits to Weymouth, Plymouth, Falmouth and then to Land's End. Here they decided to have a two day break to look around the area. The homeward journey would be via Newquay, Clovelley, Barnstable, Minehead, Glastonbury, Newbury, Windsor and then finally Carshalton. David thought that he must have been stupid to think that they could cover such a distance in the time. They had allowed themselves only three weeks. With their minds made up they approached their parents who, not really taking much note of the distances involved, both agreed. They booked up all the hostels in advance sending them the deposit for each night and prepared for the trip by racing to Brighton on every occasion they could spare.

They set off in the middle of August, David being just fourteen and Jamie coming up to his fourteenth birthday that week. Jamie knew that for the first three or four hostels he was breaking the rules by being a little too young, but he made himself a little older on the membership forms. Each of them had a saddle bag filled with a sheet sleeping bag, a change of clothes, a pack of sandwiches, two tins of baked beans and a small metholated-spirit burner and a billy can. The first part of the journey went well. They were used to the roads down to Littlehampton and stayed at a hostel about two miles inland. They even took a break on the way down, something they had not done before, but they thought that as this was the first day of their holiday, they would make an exception. They even took a quick ride down to the sea and had a look around Littlehampton itself. The next day was an easy ride as it was only along the coast to Winchester. They arrived too early for the hostel to open so they walked around the town, wheeling their bicycles. They were intrigued to find that the hostel was built over the mill race of a stream and was actually an old mill house. The men's dormitory was over the mill race and to wash in the morning meant gathering some water in a bucket from the racing water and pouring it into a bowl. Someone in the past had left a board with ropes attached to a bar over the mill race and a group of young Germans were doing some surf riding on the raging torrent of water. One of them, who had been washing naked, took his turn on the board, but, alas, he suddenly lost his balance and fell into the stream. He just disappeared in the water. The rest of his friends ran upstairs, slipped on some clothes quickly, and accompanied by David and Jamie raced out of the front door, up the small road to the main road and over the bridge to the park beyond. As they entered the park they saw the surfer walking towards them completely naked. Everybody in the park was standing and looking, many with their mouths open. One of the German boys ran over to his adventuresome friend, slipped off his shirt and tied it around the naked man's waist. That breakfast was one of the best David and Jamie had ever had, it was full of laughter and joking.

The next two or three days as they made their way past Bridport and Weymouth the roads were fairly straight forward although more hilly than they had anticipated. It wasn't till they reached Devon that they realised that they had overestimated the number of miles that they could travel in a day. They had booked to stay at a hostel called Pool Mill. It was set deep in the country somewhere in Devon. It started to rain heavily and they had the Dickens of a job finding the small hut that was their next stay. When the hostel was opened they found it was just one hut with a screen between the men and the women. All their clothes were soaking wet and it took them some time to light a fire in the open grate. By this time David was feeling quite home sick and very hungry; he just lay on his bunk and said nothing. Jamie had no problem. He went out to the table in the middle of the hut and began to talk to the other travellers who were all in the same boat. After about half an hour a young lady who was obviously several years older than David came over to him with a bowl of soup and some bread. She was tandem riding with her brother and was heading in the same direction as the two boys. She spent a long time talking to him about home and then without any embarrassment asked him to take his clothes off.

"Give them to me and I will dry them by the fire".

David slipped off his shorts, socks and shirt. She took them in her hands and then said,

"What about your pants, they must be soaking. Come on, don't be shy, I must be old enough to be your mother".

David slipped them off, carefully wrapping the blanket from the bed around his waist.

"Now come on over by the fire and get warm. We are all having a chat about tomorrow and where we are going".

It turned out to be one of the best evenings of the tour so far, but they were all a little worried when they heard that the boys were heading for Falmouth the next day, a distance of about one hundred miles.

They were the last to leave the next morning as they had the wood collection duty to do. They had to replace all the wood that they had burnt the night before for the next visitors. The weather had improved and the sun was shining and they set off with renewed vigour. Jamie took up the lead and they raced along the quiet empty roads. They would wave at any car they saw going in the opposite direction and if they saw a cyclist they would shout, "Tuggo" at the top of their voices as this seemed to be the thing to do. After a while they could see in the distance what looked like their two new friends on their tandem, but what they gained on them up the steep hills they lost on the way down the other side where the tandem could pick up tremendous speed in high gear. Nevertheless, they gradually gained on them and there were shouts of delight as they passed them. After that the journey seemed to drag and they began to feel tired and hungry. They knew that they had a long way to go so they just opened a tin of beans and ate them out of the tin. They were surprised that they were not overtaken by the tandem again although they looked out for it.

They looked at the map and Jamie noticed that if they took a ferry across one of the inlets it would take about ten miles off of the total journey. They therefore decided to take one of the minor roads and cross the inlet by the ferry. They cycled for miles before they came to the inlet and then had a great deal of difficulty finding the ferry. Once on board they had a rest and felt very pleased with themselves. It wasn't until they reached the other side that they realised that that wasn't the ferry they should have boarded and they were now on roads that they couldn't find on the map. They arrived at the hostel in Falmouth at about half past nine at night and were lucky that the warden spotted their plight and let them in. They were exhausted and fell straight into their bunks without any food. The next morning they were woken up by some lads who had brought them up plates of bread and jam and a mug of tea each which they polished off with relish. The warden tried to make them stay for a day to recover, but Jamie, who was ready to go, said that they would have a days rest when they reached Land's End.

There were a lot of people staying in the hostel at Land's End and it was lucky that they had booked ahead. Although they arrived quite late again they were made very welcome and a group of young hostellers were playing the piano and singing. They had bought some Cornish pasties on the way and found that they were a good filling meal. As it got nearer the time to turn in, one of the more local lads told them all the story of a young woman called Liddy who used to live in the hostel. She had a boyfriend who lost his footing on the cliffs at the end of the valley and fell into the sea hundreds of feet below. Liddy was so upset by the loss of her lover that she left the house one evening in the mist and walked to the cliff and threw herself over. It was said that when the mist came down over the valley she could be seen leaving the house and walking to the cliff. They all thought that this was quite an interesting story until the warden told them that the men's dormitory was some way away from the house down the valley. As they walked across the field they

271

could see the mist rolling in from the sea and David was terrified, and was more than relieved to reach the dormitory and his bed.   They were all in their beds when one of the boys said that he thought that he would lock the door.   David was pleased as his bed was nearest to the entrance.   He had a great deal of difficulty going off to sleep that night and was woken up suddenly and with a great fright by the door crashing open and swinging backwards and forwards.

One of the boys shouted out, "Who's playing the fool, has someone gone outside?"   He lit the hurricane lamp that was on the table and went around the dormitory to check who was missing, but to their horror they were all there.   He left the hurricane lamp burning and David spent the rest of the night under the covers, but fully awake until the light of morning began to come through the window.   They looked out of the window and saw that a thick fog had come down and they couldn't see more than a couple of yards in front of them. To add to their misery not only could they not see Land's End or the sea, but they had another two nights to spend in that hut in the middle of a mist filled valley with the ghost of a woman likely to walk in at any time.

Chapter 30

David, still thinking of how his relationship with Janet had gone through ups and downs, crossed the main road by the bottom of the woods and entered the far end of his road. Even though it was getting quite late he could hear festivities still continuing on many of the greens and he could see that many of the people had decorated the fronts of their houses with lights. He could hear pianos being played and groups of revellers singing. He didn't know why he had gone this way home. Perhaps it was because it took him past Polly's house and he would get a little of the feeling of desire that he had experienced that afternoon or perhaps it was just that he wanted a little more time to think whether it was him that was at fault and that he expected too much of a fifteen year old girl. He never actually thought of her as a girl, to him she was a young and beautiful woman with hidden beauty and depth. Things had certainly been a lot better over the past few months although he suspected there may be an element of being needed. He only hoped there was no underlying feeling of caring for someone or, he hated to think of that word, 'pity'.

He was still deep in thought as he came to the small green where Polly lived and he could see that there were some people sitting around a table drinking. He walked slowly by subconsciously hoping that he might hear her voice. He walked on past the house where Polly's friend lived and heard some voices from people sitting on the front step. He had just about reached the corner of his group of houses when he heard the sound of running feet behind him and a voice calling out, "David, is that you?"

The voice was undoubtedly Polly's. He turned and saw her coming up to him. She was obviously wearing high heels by the sound of her footsteps and her height. She was wearing a gabardine raincoat over her shoulders and only buttoned up at the neck giving the appearance of a cloak. Her hair had been let down and was long enough to fall on her shoulders and made her look very young. She put out both hands and took his,

"This is a nice surprise; I thought that you would have passed here long ago. It is a bit late for the youth club to finish, isn't it?"

David was unsure as to what to say, he and Janet had not come home that way that evening, so he had not passed her door before, but he could not think of a good excuse why he was now coming this way home without Janet.

"Oh, we packed up early and as I could hear all the festivities going on I didn't want to go straight home so I went for a little stroll".

"I wish I had known", said Polly, "I would have come with you. Why don't you come back with me to Julie's house? We are just having a chat on the doorstep before turning in for the night".

"No, I don't think I had better. It's getting a bit late and I want to be up early in the morning".

"Oh, come on, don't be such a spoil sport, you can spare another half an hour surely, or will your mother be waiting for you to come home?"

This made David mad. Did she think he was under the thumb of his mother? Did she also think that he was the type whose mother sat up and waited for him? He imagined Mum would be fast asleep by now.

"No, of course not".

"Well come on then, just for ten minutes. Anyway you look as if you have lost a sixpence and found a penny". With that she put her arm through his and they turned to walk back to her friend's house. As they came level with the gate she said,

"Oh dear, she must have gone in. Never mind we can sit on my front doorstep and chat. They came to the next gate and walked up to the door which was slightly ajar. Polly pushed it open and stood inside the porch.

"Come in then, don't be frightened, I won't eat you".

David stepped up into the porch and to his surprise Polly gently pushed the door to. Suddenly the only light coming in was from the six small windows in the door. David felt Polly come up against him and her mouth came into contact with his lips. He felt her lips parting and her tongue thrusting into his mouth. He could just notice the trace of gin on her breath, but by now his mind was in a complete whirl. He slipped his hands through the opening of her raincoat and around her waist and almost immediately she took one of his hands and drew it up to her full and well shaped breast. He began to fondle her and she exploded with a writhing and twisting movement. He felt her crutch thrusting against his firm and erect penis and although his mind kept saying, "stop, this is all wrong", he felt compelled to go on. She undid the front of her blouse and released the strap at the back of her bra. David brought both hands up onto her breasts which, now released from her bra, seemed to be twice the size. The zinging in his head and the whole of his body became quite uncontrollable as he felt Polly undo the belt of his trousers and slowly slip each button out through its hole. She pulled down his pants and lifted up her skirt.

"Is that you David?" David heard Mum's voice shouting from the front bedroom as he very quietly closed the front door.

"Yes", replied David in a loud whisper.

275

"You're a bit late tonight; don't forget you've got to be up early tomorrow"

"O.K. Mum".

As David gently slipped into bed trying not to disturb Jack, he wondered what the hell he had been up to. He knew that it was wrong before he started and he shouldn't have gone back to Polly's porch, in fact he shouldn't have gone that way home at all. If only he had come straight back home after seeing Janet to her door, this would never have happened. He lay for some time wide awake. His mind kept going over the events of the evening and he could only excuse his behaviour by thinking that if Janet had not behaved the way she had he would not have been tempted to go that way home and by now he would have been tucked up in bed fast asleep. He had a terrible feeling of guilt and wondered how the future would pan out if Polly met Janet. Another thing that terrified him even more was that he didn't know just how far he had gone with Polly, his mind had been so much in a whirl and his body had been so uncontrollable, which, what with his lack of general knowledge of this sort of thing, may have led to her becoming pregnant.

"That's a strong perfume that Janet was wearing tonight, I think I prefer her, what was it? Evening in Paris you bought for her. Now don't you think it is time you laid still and got some sleep? I expect Mum will be shouting to you to get up in a few hours".

"Sorry Jack, I just can't get to sleep. I'll lie still from now on".

As Jack had forecast, Mum not only gave him a loud call in the morning, but also accompanied it with a banging on the wall. David immediately slipped out of bed and washed and dressed as quickly as he could. He wasn't sure that Janet would come round for him to go to church that morning after her coolness on the evening before, but David was going to make sure that he went to church that morning to check to see if "old lover boy" turned up and how she would approach him. Instead of waiting on his front step, he decided to walk to the alleyway to meet Janet. This would kill two birds with one stone. It would save him losing face if she decided not to come and it would also avoid them walking past Polly's house. Not that she would be up at that time in the morning, but it would save David reminding himself of what had happened the night before.

As he was walking down the alleyway, he heard the familiar steps of Janet coming up the main road. As he turned the corner he saw her, dressed in her new green coat with matching beret, coming towards him. She put out her hand and took his and after a quick peck on the cheek, they resumed the walk up to the church. Most of the youth club were there, they had all agreed to meet up the night before and they all took their regular places in the church. David and Janet moved up the centre isle and after genuflecting knelt down for the private prayer that always preceded the service. David prayed that he could be forgiven for his behaviour the night before and also prayed that no one found out about it. The service was the same as at all the communion services he had attended since his confirmation, until it came to the prayers for the sick and suffering. He was overwhelmed to hear his name on the list including a little of his history since he left the Art School. It was during this that Janet slipped her hand into his and gave it an affectionate squeeze. He heard little more of the service as he knew that she still cared for him and last night was just a blip in their romance.

After the service, when all the congregation was invited to join the regulars with tea and biscuits in the hall at the back of the church, Father Kingswood came up to David and asked him if he would like to come with him the next weekend to his ordination, which was going to be held in the Cathedral at Chichester, where he had been at theological college. David knew that he had just bought a new Sunbeam, shaft driven motorbike and assumed that he would make the journey on it. He was quite surprised to be asked to attend such a

277

special occasion and immediately said he would. Father Kingswood said that he would pick him up at his house on the next Saturday morning about eight o'clock and told him to put on some warm clothes as although it was approaching summer, it was always cold on the back of a motorbike. He then said in his usual joking fashion,

"I bet it will turn a few heads when a new man of the cloth turns up on a motorbike. I'm just dying to see their faces".

He then went on around all the members of the youth club and the members of the congregation chatting and joking. He was that sort of person; he could talk to anyone on any level, from the Bishop, when he visited the church, to the local doctor and the youngsters working in the local garage. David didn't realise that he wasn't ordained because he was held in such high regard by the vicar. His invitation pleased Janet no end as she was very fond of him and in an indirect sort of way, thought that it raised their status as a couple. Janet seemed to show no interest in the wanderings of "Lover Boy", who seemed to pass from group to group trying to chat up the girls. He wasn't sure whether this was because she had no interest, or that she felt that what had happened the night before could put her in bad favour with all the boys in the youth club. As they walked home from the church that morning, she tentatively took David's hand. Forgetting his anger and heartbreak of the night before he immediately responded with a squeeze which was quickly followed by them slipping their arms around each others waist. David again felt that tingle of excitement that came on even by just seeing Janet and he could feel pleasurable warmth flowing through him. As they reached the corner where they normally parted Janet turned to David and said,

"There is a good film at the Odeon, Morden this week. It is a musical and my mum and dad have already been to see it. They say it is full of wonderful music and singing and well worth seeing. Do you think we could go one night this week?"

David couldn't believe his ears. Up until that time it had always been him that had made the running and Janet was always the one that either agreed or opposed the suggestions. Here she was now asking him if he would take her out.

"Of course I would like to go. What night would be best for you?"

"Well, I am washing my hair on Tuesday, what about Wednesday?"

"I could make it tomorrow night if that would be better for you", said David, knowing that the wait till Wednesday would seem endless.

"No, tomorrow is too close, Wednesday or Thursday would be best for me".

"We'll make it Wednesday then" replied David, "What time will I see you?"

"I will come round to your house at half past six and we will then be in time to catch the seven thirty house". With that, she gave David a quick peck on the lips and turned for home.

Although "Lover boy" did come to the youth club during the next few weeks he received a cold shoulder approach from all of the girls and his interest in Christianity soon began to waver and he moved on.

Chapter 31

Land's End had been a bit of a let down for the boys. Not only had David been unable to sleep for the first two nights because of his fear of the ghost of Liddy coming into the dormitory again but because what was originally just a mist had now turned into a thick and impenetrable fog. They were not only suffering from lack of sleep, but they were also given the task of pumping all the water up from the well to the tank, which stood above the roof of the hut. Most of the day was spent in a small coffee shop, called the Copper Kettle, where they bought one cup of tea and a cake and made it last for most of the morning or afternoon. The owner was very kind and unless he had an influx of customers, which was highly unlikely in that sort of weather, let them sit and talk. David quite enjoyed these sessions as many of the visitors to the youth hostel joined them and the stories that were told were interesting and helpful. David thought that they learnt more about the goings on in the world and the relationships between people in those meetings than he had ever learnt at school. He and Jamie did walk down to the point at Land's End a couple of times as cycling was out of the question. They both realised the value of their bicycles and knew that if they had any break down or damage to the machine, except for punctures, they would be stuck and getting home would be a real problem.

On the third night they slept like logs. All fears of a visit from the ghost of Liddy had been overcome by the desire to sleep. They woke on the morning they were leaving to clear warm sunny skies. After packing their saddle bags and pumping the water up from the well for the next visitors, they mounted their bikes and headed for Newquay, but before they got onto the road they paid a final visit to the point at Land's End. They were absolutely amazed at the sight before their eyes. The rocks ran out to sea from where they stood and the sea was crashing over them. Seagulls were diving and swooping over head and making a terrible cawing noise and on one of the rocks set well out to sea was a lighthouse which looked small from where they stood, but was obviously set well above the crashing waves. They had little time to waste standing there on the cliffs as they had a long journey in front of them. By this time they had both become very strong cyclists and had no need to dismount either up or down any hills. Jamie took a great delight in racing down the hills as fast as he could and many times took terrible risks taking corners at speeds likely to throw him off the road. David was much more cautious, as he was still a little unsure of his bicycle's safety, especially his brakes. When he applied the back break he could skid for a long distance, but if he applied the front brake it sometimes gripped and sometimes missed, so that it felt as if he could be thrown over the handlebars if he didn't exert some care. Up the hills they would race to see who could reach the top first. It was always Jamie. He was not only a better cyclist but he also had a much better and lighter bike with a three speed gear.

They stayed at a hostel just outside Clovelly and were amused to find that the high street was completely cobbled and had steps running all the way down to the sea. In fact the last part of the road was just a dirt track and they had to climb down some rocks to reach the shore. This was just a cove full of rocks with large waves breaking over them. They spent some time looking into all the little shops that lined the high street. Jamie would have ridden down the high street if he had had his way, but he didn't think that it would do his wheels that much good. They had found this place completely by accident and had only booked the hostel because of the distance they had to cycle.

They had got into the habit of cycling apart now. They had said all there was to say to each other and were getting a little on each others nerves. Jamie would cycle sometimes a mile or so in front of David and only when they came to a crossroads or a fork in the road which needed an examination of the map, did Jamie wait at the roadside. As

David pulled up, usually puffing, Jamie had made up his mind as to the direction and set off immediately. It was like the hare and the tortoise, the fast one would race ahead with a break every now and then and the slow one would come up the rear, but never get a proper break. By now they were on short rations. They carried no food with them and money was scarce. They would, most times, skip breakfast and around twelve o'clock look for a town with a Woolworths in it. They would buy a Cornish pasty, which was the cheapest and most filling meal they could find, and eat it in the store. This would avoid carrying it in their saddle bags, which by now were not that clean, and give them the nourishment to continue.

Just before they got to Barnstable they came across a house that had a notice in its front garden,

"Main course, sweet, cheese, biscuits and coffee, 9d."

They could not believe their eyes. Although nine pence was going to cut down the money saved for the rest of the journey, this sounded too good to be true. They placed their bikes up against the inside of the front fence and went in to the open front door. They turned right into a living room and found a man sitting reading the paper in a large arm chair.

"Can I help you?" he asked.

"We wondered if the notice in your front garden was correct, would we get a full meal including cheese for nine pence?"

"That is nine pence each you understand, have you got that sort of money?"

Jamie was a little put out by this last comment and replied, "Of course we have, we wouldn't be asking if we hadn't".

"Well then", said the man, "I will get you seated in our dining room and then go and have a word with my wife." He led them into a room opposite that had just two tables in it, each surrounded by four chairs. The room was very clean and smelt of polish and the walls were covered with ornaments such as copper bed pans, china jugs, large plates and pictures of country scenes. He told them to sit in the seats by the window so that they could keep an eye on their bikes and went off to see his wife in the kitchen at the back of the house. He seemed to be a very nice man, warm and homely. He wore a cardigan over a clean white shirt with what looked like a college tie neatly tied around his neck. He had been smoking a long pipe when they saw him in the first room, but put it out before he went into the dining room. He was very well spoken and the boys immediately liked him. They sat for a while, then the door at the back of the room opened and a very attractive lady looked in. She was wearing an apron and the boys imagined that she must be the cook. She didn't say anything, but quickly drew back and closed the door. The man came back in and said that the meal would not be too long; it was steak and kidney pudding and vegetables, was that alright. Both boys nodded approval. He then drew up a chair and came to sit by them,

"Where did you come from today?"

"Clovelly", answered David.

"Where do you live?"

"Carshalton, Surrey".

"You haven't cycled all the way, have you?"

"Yes, why?" asked Jamie.

The Man didn't reply but asked another question. "How old are you?"

David had a horrible feeling that he may have been a policeman and they knew that Jamie had started out when he was too young to use the hostels without an adult.

"We are both fourteen", answered David.

"Where have you visited on your journey?" asked the man.

David went through all the towns and cities they had visited and the names of the hostels where they had stayed. The man listened with amazement and then got up and went out of the back room. He returned in about ten minutes with a plate piled high with steak and kidney pudding, mainly pudding, and all sorts of vegetables. As he placed the plates in front of them two boys of about six or seven years old and a lady came to the door and stared at them. They were absolutely starving, so they took no notice and just piled into the plate of food. It was during the pudding of apple pie and custard that another group of people came into the house. The man showed them to the other table and began to talk to them. Within a couple of minutes another older couple arrived and he took them into the living room. He then came up to David and Jamie and said would they like to go into the backroom for their cheese and coffee as they now had more people for dinner. He said that they would be made comfortable and because of the inconvenience he would reduce the cost to eight pence. The boys thought that this was a great deal so they accepted readily and were shown through into a back room which was quite cluttered with furniture, all of it looking as if it had seen better days. The two small boys were sitting on the old settee and although they had books on their laps didn't look as if they were reading them. They seemed more interested in the two visitors entering the room. The man took them to a small table by the window, which overlooked, what looked like quite a large garden, and pulled up two wooden chairs. He left the room, but almost immediately returned with a plate full of water biscuits and two small pieces of cheese. David asked the boys what they were reading and realised that their first impressions were correct when one of them replied,

"Oh we are not reading, we are just looking at the pictures".

Jamie went over to them and looked at the book. He loved books and was an extremely good reader and liked to show off his talent.

"Would you like me to read the story to you?"

The elder of the two boys replied,

"Yes please", and moved along the settee so that Jamie could sit between them. David couldn't remember the actual story, but he did remember that it was about animals and included some sad sections. Jamie did his usual act that he had performed in David's front room when reading a story to Bobby and Susy, of reading in a sad voice and then he started to actually cry. Tears were rolling down his cheeks when the door opened and in came the lady, who was obviously the boy's mother, with two cups of tea. When she saw Jamie she immediately put down the tea on the table and went over to him and put her arms around his shoulders.

"What is the matter, tell me, can we be of any help? Are you homesick or something?"

Jamie had become so involved in the story that he now found it difficult to stop crying and amongst his tears, he tried to tell her that he was alright. She gave him a great hug and after a while got up and left the room. Jamie finished the story, but reduced the emotion and the play acting. The two small boys asked if he could read it again, but put in the crying parts at the end as he had in the beginning. Jamie got up and went over to the table and ate his cheese and biscuits and drank his cup of tea. He said,

"If you can find another story you like, I will read it to you before I go".

The two small boys rushed out of the room and up some stairs. The door opened again and the man came in to the room. He stood for a while looking at the boys and then came over to pick up the plates and cups. As he stacked them he enquired,

"Are you boys in some sort of trouble. Do you need money?"

"No", answered David "we are fine. We have budgeted for the next week and have already paid for the hostels we are staying at". Although this was true, they were more or less at the end of their funds and would have to spend very carefully in order to last the many miles until they reached home.

"My wife tells me that when she came in with the tea one of you was crying and we have had quite a discussion in the kitchen as to what could be the problem and how we can help."

David and Jamie began to laugh and David explained about the stories that Jamie told and how he tried to introduce as much feeling into them as he could. He said,

"Jamie was just reading a sad story to the two boys when your wife came in".

They all began to laugh as the door was thrown open and the two small boys and the lady re-entered the room. The two boys looked excited and the lady looked surprised. After Jamie had read the extra story to the small boys they collected up their things and made for the dining room. All the other guests had now gone and the couple were clearing up the tables. They were surprised and delighted when they went over to pay the bill as the man asked them if they would accept the meal as a gift. He thought that they had earned it by amusing the boys while they were busy in the café. David and Jamie didn't try to force the payment on to him; he was a commanding sort of man and would have been offended by the offer. They thanked him very much and were about to make their way to the door when he said,

"My wife and I wondered if you would like to stay here for the night. We have a spare room and as no one is using it, it will be empty. You have a think about it and if it doesn't put your schedule out too much we would like you to stay. If you like, sit down a minute and let me know your decision". With that, he left the room and went into the back of the house. They didn't take long to make up their minds. The hostels were always a bit cold and dull and this seemed to be a nice family who would make them very welcome. They didn't know what the room or the bed would be like, but it would certainly be better than the bunks that they had endured for the last two weeks. They went to the door at the back of the dining room and found all four of the family sitting and drinking tea.

"Well", said the man, "have you made up your minds?"

"Yes sir", answered David, "if it is not going to be a bother to you we would like to stay. The only problem is we can't afford to pay for the room and we ought to let the hostel warden know that we will not be there tonight".

"That is no problem. I will phone the hostel and explain to the warden about you staying here the night, and as for paying for the room, you will be staying as our guests and we will see you safely on your journey before we open tomorrow. Now go and get your bikes and bring them around the back of the house into my shed. Then get your things and I will show you the room". That evening turned out to be one of the most homely and pleasant they had encountered during their first two weeks. They had masses of stories to tell the family of their homes, their school and their journey so far, including the ghost of Liddy that haunted the Land's End hostel. Mr. and Mrs. Swift, as the couple were called, seemed very impressed with the attitude of the cyclists and when it came time for the small boys to go to bed there were tears as they wanted to listen to more of the adventures. This was overcome, however, by Jamie offering to read them a story. He returned to the living room about half an hour later having been persuaded to read three or four stories including the emotion and the acting. When they left the next morning Mr. Swift gave each of the boys two packs of what looked like raisins. He also slipped a sixpenny piece into each of their hands and asked them to write to him when they got home to assure them that they were safe. Mrs. Swift and the two small boys kissed them goodbye and they set off on the long journey home.

They got a little lost on the first day. Jamie had heard of a place called Porlock Hill, which was supposed to be one of the steepest in the country. He thought that he would like to try to ride down this hill to get the thrill of going at a fast speed. They seemed to go out of their way to find the hill and were a little disappointed to find that from where they had come they were at the bottom of the hill and had to climb it and not race down. They were determined not to get off of their bikes and as they were just about as fit as they had ever been, they certainly didn't want to be beaten. They struggled up the hill very slowly, zigzagging as they went to reduce the incline. It took them some time to get to the top where they got off of the bikes exhausted. Jamie then had the mad idea of now turning and going down the hill. He explained, quite sensibly, that they would be going in the right direction for home and would get a good start. David remembered that many of the turns were hair-pin bends and there were several areas, laid out with sand, for cars or lorries to run off if they got into difficulties. Nevertheless, they mounted their bikes and set off on the winding descent. Jamie went ahead and was lost to David's vision as he went racing around each of the bends at high speed. David kept his brakes on nearly all of the time. When he arrived at the bottom, after a hazardous descent, he looked around for Jamie. He was nowhere to be seen. David had a terrible feeling that perhaps he had come off the road on the way down and was now lying in some ditch. He was about to make his way up the hill again when he saw Jamie's bike propped up against one of the small houses. He went over and looked through the window, which was more or less abutting the road. To his amusement he spotted Jamie sitting at the table with a pot of tea in front of him. He entered the front door of the house, which served teas as a side line and joined his friend. So much for the race towards home!

They arrived home one day early due to the fact that their last stop was at a place called Hannington. After leaving there they were heading east and were supposed to stop next at Windsor, but as the wind was behind them and they were covering the miles at some speed, they just continued through Windsor, Staines, where they had often been to swim at Runnymede, past Sunbury, down the Kingston by pass, through Morden to home. Their families were delighted to see them and they were equally delighted to be home. Everyone wanted to know about the adventures they had had on the way, although noone of their friends seemed that interested in the details. When they went back to Wallington the English teacher, a strange fellow who was a bit effeminate, heard of their journey and asked them to write it up as a diary. It was only then, that anyone showed any real enthusiasm for their story. After reading their report, and obviously passing it on to the rest of the staff, they were asked to give a talk on their trip at a reading club that met after school. This was a great success and they became quite well known for their cycling prowess.

It was at this time that David thought that he ought to find some way of earning a little money. Although he was now able to take the whole of his bike apart, repaint the frame and reassemble it putting in new ball bearings, new cones, and align the wheels using a spoke key, he needed money to buy the grease and paint he required for the jobs. He also needed to buy quite a few extras that the school suggested

289

might help in maths and science, which his parents could ill afford. Danny had taken on an evening paper round at a newsagents close to Mitcham Common and recommended David for a round when one of the boys left. David had done a morning paper round when he was thirteen, but it involved quite a long ride into Mitcham and a delivery which included some large factories next to the Wandle, which he didn't like very much. He had help on occasions when his cousin Pam came to stay. He would give her a ride on his cross bar to the shop and she would go around helping him with the delivery. This new round was much more convenient being after school and around the estate where he lived. It paid four shillings a week and at Christmas there was the opportunity of picking up a little extra cash as tips. It did interfere with his homework, a little, and if the school knew of his new venture they would have certainly disapproved. He now had a little money in his pocket for all the necessities of life and the fact that he rode his bike to school meant that he didn't have to ask his parents for his fares. At Christmas he collected nearly ten shillings in tips and moved that straight into his post office account ready for any emergencies that might arise. Danny took a break over the Christmas holiday and went with his mum and dad to his auntie's. One evening when David was marking up the papers, Bob, the owner of the shop, gave David an envelope to pass on to Danny when he saw him. David thought that it must be a letter terminating his evening paper round and at the end of the week, when Danny returned home, he gave him the package. Danny immediately tore it open and found inside a £1 note and a two bob piece. Danny could not hold on to money for very long and said,

"Go and knock on Peter's door and see if he is able to go out this evening. I would like to take you both to the cinema and we can follow that up with a slap up meal".

David rushed over to Peter's and explained what had happened. Peter got permission from his mum to go out and David checked with his parents whether it was O.K. Mum said the usual sort of thing,

"What about your homework? When will you do that?"

"Oh, I haven't got much to do and I can easily do it tomorrow".

They each slipped on a thick coat, Danny put on his newly acquired cap, and they took a bus down to Morden, to the Odeon Cinema. Danny bought the tickets and David was surprised when the very attractive usherette in a smart uniform led them up the stairs to the balcony. David had never been to the balcony before and, although you could see all the cigarette smoke floating up through the beam of the camera, it gave you a much better view of the screen. David couldn't remember what the film was, but after about five minutes Danny produced a packet of Woodbines and handed one to each of the others. He pulled out a box of matches and they all lit up their cigarettes. Danny was fine, but Peter and David had not smoked before and felt sick and dizzy. After only seeing the supporting film they made their way down to the foyer and out into the open air. They walked over the bridge where the underground trains travelled to their sidings and to a line of shops, one of which was a fish restaurant. After sitting at a table, they were served with a large piece of battered cod and masses of chips and as an extra Danny ordered two pickled onions each. They arrived home a little later than they expected, but feeling that they had now grown up and were ready to enjoy life. David remembered that Danny still had 1s. 6d left from his tips which he said he would save for another time.

When David had been doing the evening round for about nine months Bob Levey, the owner of the shop told him that a morning round was becoming available at the end of that week, would he like to take it? David jumped at the offer as it meant more money and he could do it before going to school in the morning. For a couple of weeks he was landed with doing both rounds and found that very difficult, but the money was good. He received four shillings for the evening round and ten shillings for the morning round. This round was much longer and he had to carry many more papers than before.   Some houses even had two papers.   There was also much more of a mixture.   He could remember the Reynold's News, The Chronicle, The Herald, The Express as well as The Mirror and The Times.   Luckily no one had The Times as it had no pictures and was twice the size of any of the other papers and had to be folded in four.

Later he took on a Sunday round as well, which pushed the income up to £1 a week, giving him enough money to keep up with all the activities of the boys at the grammar school and not being left out. They were all very helpful from that point of view and often either paid for him or lent him the money needed.   If, after he had completed the Sunday delivery he went round to collect the money for the papers from each of the customers he could earn another three shillings and sixpence.   This was hard work, but it taught him to add up difficult sums, avoid being cheated and even pick up a few pence in tips.   He had over a hundred customers to visit and it would take him right up to dinner time, but he could save time in the shop by adding all the small amounts up as he cycled down the hill to the shop and he was so accurate and honest that Bob would allow him just to drop off the money and book and go straight home.   He was sure that Bob did a quick check when he had gone, but never found any mistakes.   Sundays were certainly hard work with papers such as the News of the World and Pictorial, which weighed much more than the weekday papers.   In compensation he could listen to the records being played on Two Way Family Favourites with Cliff Mitchelmore and Jean Metcalfe, linking up with the forces stationed in Germany.   He could also read through most of the papers as he went along and especially the front page of the News of the World which carried all sorts of sexual misdemeanours.   Bob, trying to promote his shop to the whole estate, would produce an almanac which the boys delivered, with the papers, a few days before Christmas.   David decided that he would forfeit one of his evenings, usually the one before Christmas Eve, to make a special delivery of the almanac.   Nearly all the customers would reward him with a generous Christmas box, which, as they got to know him grew bigger and bigger. He would often end up on Christmas Day with quite a large sum of money to be deposited in the post office account.

Chapter 32

David remembered that school gradually became more enjoyable. The boys were always full of ideas of what to do and where to go and the masters, although being quite strict, made most of the subjects as interesting as they could. He found languages some of the most difficult classes. French was taught by a master who played cricket for the team, Beddington, and unfortunately although David would like to have pleased him with his knowledge, he always fell short of what was expected. The master would sometimes stand aghast at some of the answers that David produced to the simplest of questions and would make jokes to the rest of the class in French, which they all seemed to understand. They learnt several poems and songs in French which had put David in good stead for learning more in the future, but at the time, meant very little. If only he had listened and learned a little more when he had the opportunity. Latin was taught by a weedy little man with little teaching ability, but who was a brilliant Latin scholar. David did pick up the basics of the language and the strict adherence to the rules of grammar, but David's best performance in the subject was to ask questions which would make the master go off on a tangent and tell the class all about life in ancient Rome, which was far more interesting.

When it came to Mathematics, Science, English and sport, David did well, not extremely well, but just well. Both Maths and Science were taught by excellent teachers. The Maths master was not only brilliant at his subject, but could also draw. He would always begin his class with a drawing on the side of the board in chalk. He would start from an unlikely part of the drawing and gradually expand it with the class making guesses as to what it was. This caused about five minutes of amusement which was followed by everybody being ready to work. The Chemistry master was very young and the brother of one of the boys in David's class. He would explain how and why things worked and would do all sorts of experiments in front of the class, some being quite dangerous. One of his experiments almost led to David burning his house down. He was demonstrating the updraught caused in a vertical tube if a flame was lit at the bottom. The master did it in the laboratory with a large glass tube and a candle and made all sorts of light objects fly up the tube and out at the top. David thought that he would do the same experiment in front of Danny and Peter to show this phenomenon. He took a couple of sheets of news paper and rolled them up into balls. He then placed them at the bottom of the down pipe of the water drainage system at the front of his house, which allowed the rainwater to drain from the gutters down into a drain. He lit the paper and at first all went well. The paper blazed and the flames ran up the drainpipe. The pipe made a tuneful roaring sound and the boys were very impressed. Suddenly, the flaming paper was sucked up into the pipe. Strangely, the roaring continued and they saw flames at the top of the down pipe. The flames gradually made their way along the gutter. The leaves that were in the gutter had caught light and smoke and flames were issuing from the gutter. Luckily, firstly due to the prompt action of Mr. Stamp, who was standing by his gate, rushing out with a ladder and a bucket of water and partly due to the fact that there was still quite a lot of water in the gutter, the flames were quelled and the danger was over. When David reported his exploits to the Science class the master nearly collapsed with horror whilst the rest of the class spent a good ten minutes laughing.

David managed to stay in the special group for three years. At the end of this period five of the boys were asked to visit the headmaster's office. They spent some time trying to guess what misdemeanour they had performed that would warrant such an interview. It was very rare that anyone was summoned to this higher sanctuary, except for something very serious. Only once before had David been there and that was when he broke a large window by throwing his shoe at another boy who stupidly ducked. He was made to pay two shillings and nine pence for that inaccurate throw.   This time all five of the boys were given chairs and the headmaster greeted them with a smile. Was this a smile of kindness or power they all wondered?   He explained that the examination system in the next year was going to change and instead of doing the normal matriculation they would be doing a new examination called "O" Levels.

"The only problem with you five boys is that your birthdays fall earlier than the final date for the exam.   It means that you will be required to take the examination a year earlier than was planned. Some of the subjects you have been studying are not those covered by the examination and in some, such as maths, science and English you will not have covered the full syllabus.   To compensate for some of the problems, we have decided to move all five of you up a year and into the alpha group.   You will have to drop Latin and will have to try to catch up on the syllabus that this group has already covered.   There are however two advantages, one is that you will have a sight of the type of examination a year early, and two, you have the option to stay on the next year to take it again.   I want you all to go home, explain the situation to your parents and make up your mind how you wish to progress.   Of course some of you may want to leave after the examination; that is entirely up to you.   The decision does not need to be made immediately and I will arrange for you to be counselled by one of the masters".

David did not confront his parent's with the problem immediately. He thought that it would be better to wait until he had been counselled by one of the masters and find out just where he stood.   The move to the alpha group was a little sad as he was moving away from a class of friends he had got to know very well ,although the group he was now about to join consisted of many boys he knew well through the sport and other activities, such as the scouts and the cycling club. Although he knew that his parents wouldn't really know or care too much about this change of class, he knew that Jack would soon smell a rat and he mustn't leave it too long to let him in to the changes that were taking place.

His best subject, by far, was his art work. He had got to know the art master quite well and had built up quite a rapport with him. He remembered that he spent many happy hours sitting in the Grange park drawing and painting the old house or the boats on the lake and would even stay on some evenings to complete a painting or drawing that Mr. Wood thought showed signs of a gift that he may need to develop. Much of his other school work benefited by his ability to draw and he was tempted to move towards some sort of draughtsman qualification. His English had improved dramatically ever since his brother Jack took to writing his composition for the week and he copied it out on Sunday evening after being out all day. On the first occasion he spent some time making a neat job of the essay, laying it out carefully and writing in his best hand writing, of which he was particularly proud. He remembered that the master was very impressed with this latest composition, which was entitled, "The Value of a Penny". It was about all the things one could buy with a penny, which in those days were numerous. The master read the essay out to the rest of the class with great feeling and warmth. David felt as pleased as punch until at the end he said,

"David Fellows. I find it hard to believe that you not only would have such an original idea, but to have expressed it in such a clear and precise manner, and knowing of the feeble attempts you have made in the past, leads me to believe that this has either been copied from another's work, or you had some sort of assistance in its production. Nevertheless, I will give you the benefit of the doubt and award this work an "A" plus. I hope that this standard is the beginning of something revolutionary and I will monitor your performance very carefully in the future".

From then on David would spend hours on his English homework only seeking the help of his brother Jack when he was really stumped for either ideas or composition. This did a lot to improve his English and although he was not treated to the embarrassment of it being read to the class with the master's sarcastic comments, his marks increased dramatically and his ability to write improved.

To his pleasure, the master that had been chosen to be his counsellor was Mr. Wood. David didn't know how these choices were made, but it did seem that the master who taught the subject, at which the pupil was best, was chosen. It was at this time that Mr. Wood suggested that David should sign on for evening classes at the local Art School. Unfortunately this was in Sutton, but from where David lived this was an easy town to access. He suggested that he should study "Life Drawing" as this was the area which was essential for good drawing but was not available at Wallington. David's drawing improved enormously and Mr. Wood was pleased to see that it was showing up in the work he was producing in the art class. His personal credibility was also improved with all the boys when he told them about his first visit to the "Life Drawing". Each time he had an evening class he had to give a report to all of the boys before their class started. His marked improvement most probably made Mr. Wood's views very biased and although they approached the difficult subject of David's future by looking at all the alternatives, he suggested that, at the end of the year, David should approach the Art School for a permanent place and study for the National Diploma in Design. David didn't know how to approach his mother and father about this recommendation as this would mean another two more years of study with no money coming in. Although the fees for the Art School would be covered by the local authority and his bus fares and materials could be covered basically by the money he earned on his paper round, there would be no wages out of which he could pay something towards his upkeep. In addition, there was still conscription where all boys at the age of eighteen were compelled to serve for two years in the Forces, again removing him from the ability to contribute towards the finances of the family. Conscription would mean that David would leave the Art School and immediately be called up into the forces.

Jack had already served in the Air Force and, although he had been full of the tales of hardship that they had to endure, appeared to enjoy that sort of life. When he first joined up David was only twelve years old and in his second year at the grammar school. It was quite a blow to David as the boost that he had received from Jack with his essays etc. almost disappeared except for when he was home on leave. He had joined up in the Air Force with his very close friend who lived opposite. Roger and Jack must have been almost exactly the same age as, not only did they join up together, but they did their "Square Bashing" at the same camp somewhere up in the north of England. They would get home as many times as possible on what they called a forty-eight hour pass and would amuse all the children with their tales of their sergeant major, the battles they waged with the mud and rain and the endless cleaning of their uniforms. Roger was a happy-go-lucky type of person, always having a smile on his face and full of jokes and funny stories. After they had served about a year Jack arrived home unexpectedly and in a terrible state. It took a long time before Mum and Dad could calm him down and get from him the reason for this unexpected leave. Apparently, his friend Roger had been killed in an aircraft accident. From what they could gather from Jack's stuttering and mumbling, was that Roger had been hit by an aircraft propeller when the engines were starting up and had been killed instantly. Immediately Mum and Dad went with Jack to the family friends on the other side of the green to offer their sympathy. They, of course, were in a terrible state. Mr. and Mrs. Rose could not be consoled and his younger sister, a close friend of Betty, was sobbing her heart out. David didn't remember the funeral, but the loss of such a fine young man for no apparent reason left the whole neighbourhood in a state of grief for a long time.

By the time David had reached the age for the decision concerning his future at Wallington or Sutton Art School, Jack had left the Air Force

299

and was now involved in working on the aircraft at Heathrow. He had acquired a post which involved him in the production of instruments for aircraft and was doing very well in that field. David knew that Jack would be of great help to him in making his choice and held a senior enough position in the family, now being around twenty one, to approach his parents for their permission for David to continue with his education. As the year progressed he began to build up a portfolio of all of his drawings and paintings so that if he was interviewed at the Art School, he would have something to show them. This concentration on the art work led him to scale down his extra studies needed on his other subjects and some of them, which he knew he was unable to catch up on the work done, such as history, geography and French he was allowed to drop.

In that same year, his close friend Jamie had been told by his parents that he was to stay on and do the second year of the examination so that he could achieve sufficient subjects to take his "A" levels. Jamie, however, was confronted with another problem. His father had had to sell up the hardware store that was his own creation and move into another occupation which involved him in travelling all over the country. Jamie's family moved to a flat close to Clapham South underground station. Jamie had thought at first that he would have to leave Wallington and move to a grammar school nearer his home, but it was agreed by him and his parents that as he was now a proficient cyclist he could travel to school by bicycle. As he and David spent many of their weekends and evenings together, either doing homework or improving their cycling, they would cover the ten miles or so many times. If Jamie came to David's house Mum would provide him with his tea and if they went to Jamie's house his mum would do the same. Tea at Mrs. Porter's was always worth staying for as she would provide jars of fish paste and cakes. His two younger brothers would enjoy them travelling up to Balham as they would always have great fun together. The only thing David had to be careful of was that he was not seen by his aunties or his cousins as his Gran and one of the aunties lived in a road exactly opposite the block of flats where the Porters now lived and his other uncle and aunt lived across the main road with his two cousins.

Jamie had acquired some very peculiar friends since he had been living up in the outskirts of London. One particular boy, Daniel Dexter, was full of adventure and performed daring acts that to David and Jamie were outrageous. He had been given the nickname of "Dare-Devil-Dexter" and was an expert in balancing, climbing, throwing and exploring. On one Saturday, when David had decided to spend most of the day with the Porters, they were playing cricket in the middle of the side road, between the flats when Dare-Devil-Dexter decided to demonstrate his balancing skills along one of the scaffolding poles that had been erected around the bombed out skeleton of the Balham Hippodrome. David had seen the remains of this building when he travelled up to London by bus at the time they were being evacuated. Nothing had been done to the ruins since that time. Dare-Devil balanced on the poles around the back of the building and shouted to the rest of them that he could see an opening in the brickwork that would allow them access to the interior. He actually shouted,

"Hey, I can see a bloody great hole in the back wall. Get yourselves up these sodding poles and we will get a butchers at the inside". He was renowned for his swearing,

To not follow Dare-Devil in his exploits would have been cowardly in the extreme, so all of them, including his and Jamie's younger brothers, crawled along the scaffolding poles to the gap in the wall which was obviously the results of the bomb. Once inside and when they had grown accustomed to the dark they started to make their way, very carefully, towards what looked like a very large sheet of steel. Part of it had been buckled backwards and had become partially parted from the rest. Dare-Devil climbed up the sharp edge of the sheet until he reached a wooden platform hung with many ropes. Some of them had been burnt by the fire that had gutted the building following the direct hit by a bomb and many of the others looked as though they would not bear a persons weight. Nevertheless, Dare-Devil took hold of two of the ropes and swung himself onto the front of one of the boxes. After climbing over the front he swung the ropes back to the others and one by one each swung across the gap to be hauled, by Dare-Devil, into the box. They went through the opening, which was once the door, and made their way towards the front of the building along a narrow corridor where areas of the floor were missing giving them a view of the corridor below. Near the front they came across a stairway where all the steps had been either removed or burnt. The cast iron hand rail and decorative support were all intact and it was not difficult to climb to the next floor. Here they found a spiral staircase and although, again, some of the stairs were missing, they made their way to the top. They were amazed to find that they were in the top of the tower at the front of the theatre and they could see all the trams and buses passing along the main road way below them. David felt quite frightened being up at that height as there were no windows in the frames which came right down to floor level and in addition, he didn't feel that the floor was that safe. Dare-Devil, on the other hand, was standing on the edge of the window and waving to the people in the high street below. They all pleaded with him to come back in, but he was enjoying his achievement and meant to take advantage of it.

As they watched the traffic down below they could see and hear the bell of a police car and down the high street from the direction of Balham they could see this car weaving in and out of all the traffic. They were all enjoying the sight and wondering what the police car was chasing, when the bell stopped and the car drew up in front of the Theatre. They suddenly realised that someone had seen them up in the tower and phoned the police. They quickly made their way down the stairs and corridors taking all sorts of risks until they reached the box at the front. Alas, the ropes had all swung back into place above the stage. To jump from there would have been suicidal. They retraced their steps to the corridor and Dave-Devil climbed through the hole in the floor and dropped to the corridor below.   He then lowered each of them to the floor after they had climbed through the hole.   They climbed over a pit in front of the stage and then through a hole that ran underneath .   At the back they made their way up on to the stage and to the hole in the back of the building.   They could hear the voices of the policemen outside the barriers, so Dave-Devil led them over a wall at the back of a yard.   They found themselves in someone's garden.   They raced to the gate at the side of the house and out into the street.   The owner of the house came rushing out of his front door and began to chase them so they turned up the road, past Gran's house towards Clapham South station and Clapham Common. After about half an hour it was agreed that they would go back to Jamie's block of flats in ones or twos which would look less conspicuous.   The amusing part was, as Dare-Devil and Jamie's younger brother approached their street a policeman came over to them and asked if they had seen a gang of boys running away from that area.   David decided that he was not too keen on that sort of escapade.   He told Jamie that he would not go on any more of Dare-Devil's adventures as he thought that it would not be long until they got themselves into serious trouble.

Chapter 33

David, with a fair bit of persuasion from Mr. Wood, decided that he would approach his parents about leaving Wallington and trying to get a place at Sutton Art School. This was, in some ways one of the best, but in other ways one of the most disastrous decisions he had made in his life. First of all he had a word with Jack who knew already that something was going on and it wouldn't be long before he would put two and two together. Jack had been selected to play for the local St. Anthony's Cricket team and had become one of their opening batsmen. When David wasn't playing for the school team he would go with Jack to wherever they were playing and support them. Sometimes he was even allowed to take the scores and record them in the special book they had for that purpose. He enjoyed doing this as the very dedicated man who usually came recorded all the names and scores in such beautiful copperplate handwriting. David could copy his style, producing a work of art each weekend. On a couple of occasions he had even been asked to play for the team. The first time he hadn't even reached his fifteenth birthday when the team was reduced in number by one of the bowlers hurting his back whilst trying to bowl too fast. David was brought on as a fielder, but was not allowed to bat or bowl. Trouble arose when he fielded the ball near the boundary and threw it in to the wicket keepers end. He scored a direct hit on the stumps with the batsman well short of the crease. The batsman refused to leave the field and complained that David was too young to be in the team and shouldn't have been brought on. On another occasion, later in the year, St. Anthony's team were one man short at the beginning of the match. They approached the other team who agreed to allow David to be included. The other team went into bat first and David was sent to field on the boundary at square leg. The bowlers were being thrashed all over the field and the opposition score was mounting rapidly. The captain had used all the bowlers he had and things were becoming a little desperate. It was at that time that Jack went to the captain and mentioned that his brother could bowl quite well and even bowled for the school. David was put on from the main road end and in his first over managed to pick up a wicket. In his second over two more wickets fell, and although they were still getting more runs than David wished, the taking of the wickets was imperative. When their innings was complete he had bowling figures of seven wickets for forty nine runs.

It was during one of these matches that David explained the situation to Jack. He had already batted and had made a decent score, so he was feeling in good humour. After hearing all the pros and the cons he said to David,

"What would you like to do? You can stay at Wallington and continue with your education and perhaps get better results in your "O" levels which would give you a good start in life and may lead to you continuing into "A" levels. You can apply for a place at the Art School and continue in the one subject which you already enjoy, or you could leave and get yourself a job. I would certainly cut out the last option as you may throw away all the advantages you have gained already at Wallington. That, therefore, only gives you two choices and if the Art School is where you would like to try, I will certainly support you".

"I really feel that I would like to further my art career if it were possible, but what do you think Mum and Dad will say?", asked David.

"Leave that to me, I will come with you when you talk to them and I will explain to them that you have just asked me for some advice".

That evening, when they were all sitting in the front room, Jack brought the conversation around to David's problem. He explained to his parents why David had been moved into the alpha group, which had upset Mum when she first heard, and then he went on to clarify the decision that had to be made. Mum and Dad listened very intently and although David knew that Mum would easily be influenced by Jack's opinion, he knew that Dad would think all around the problems and may be difficult to persuade. As this would most probably put some pressure on the finances of the household he may be very reluctant for David to continue at school.

"You are already going to the Art School for evening classes; won't that be enough to get you a job of some sort in design?" asked Dad.

"No", answered Jack, "there are so many subjects that David can't cover in just one or two evenings a week and he will have to prepare for examinations at the end, which will need him to be full time and with the backing of top class teachers".

"What will he do for money?" Dad asked, addressing Jack. David quickly answered, feeling that he had been left on the side lines for a while. "All my tuition fees will be paid by the local authority as I am continuing with my education and my fares and food at lunch time I can cover from the money I make on my paper round".

"All we have to cover" said Jack knowing that Dad was the main wage earner and would have to foot the bills, "is the cost of David's living here, and as it will not be any different than it is at the moment, I can't see any problem". David realised that Jack and Betty contributed to the cost of their food and he was a little upset to think they were all willing to support him. Of course the main burden would fall on Dad and Dad had a hard job raising enough money to make ends meet and Mum had to struggle hard to make the wages last the week.

"So what do you think David, would you like to go on into the Art School or what?" Dad asked.

"I would like to try to get into the Art School if possible. I know the place well now and I like the way they approach life. I think I could do well given the chance. No matter what Jack has said, I know that it will make it more difficult for you and if you think it is too much, or you think that I am taking advantage, I will drop the whole idea"

There was a pause for a long time and then out of the blue Dad smiled at David and said, "O.K. son you go for it and good luck. Don't you worry about the rest of us, we will go on as normal and perhaps it won't be long before you are earning vast sums of money designing cars or aircraft".

With more encouragement from Mr. Wood, David put together a fairly general portfolio of his work including paintings, mainly watercolours, drawings and lettering and when it was more or less complete Mr. Wood made a phone call to the Principal of the Art School, a Mr. Bailey. They had known each other when they were at The Chelsea Art School and had kept in touch. Mr. Bailey already knew of David's work as he was attending evening classes and suggested that they should have an official interview, when he could look at David's work and discuss the opportunities an art training would provide for him. The date of the interview was duly arranged which fell just before the major "O" level examinations took place. David, now relieved of the burden of decision making, put all the effort he could into the subjects and sport he enjoyed, but spent much of his time visiting the two parks painting and drawing. There were, of course, some subjects which he knew it would be impossible to pass and he hadn't covered the work required to complete the syllabus, so he spent most of that time looking interested and thinking of other things. If only he had listened and tried a little harder! This was just about the best year he had spent at Wallington; he had built up a wonderful group of friends who were hard working, keen and sporting. He was included in many of the birthday parties all over the area and although he found it difficult on his small income to buy presents, they always made him welcome.

Just before the examinations started David went off for his interview with Mr. Bailey at the Sutton School of Art. As he entered the front door of the school in his school blazer, grey flannels, white shirt and school tie, with his portfolio under his arm, he felt on top of the world. He had arrived at the student break time and they had all left their study rooms and were out in the corridor talking and laughing. As he made his way to the stairs which led up to Mr. Bailey's office the chatter began to subside and all heads turned towards him. It was only then that he realised that he was over dressed for the part. He was surprised to see that many of the men had long, straggly hair, some even having beards. Most were dressed in dirty looking, but very colourful shirts and corduroy trousers. Many of the girls were wearing trousers and tight sweaters and some even had overalls on top of their clothes. By the time he had reached the top corridor the hall had become silent and there was a passage left down the middle. One of the students, nearest the door marked "Mr. Bailey," knocked as if he knew where David was going and as David approached it was opened from the inside. Framed in the door was an extremely elegant, tall man with flattened, long, black hair and supporting a beard and moustache. He wore round horn-rimmed spectacles which were perched on the end of his nose. He was wearing a maroon jacket with a bright yellow waistcoat and his red and white striped shirt was open at the top button. Around his neck he wore a dark blue, spotted cravat held together at the front by a large, jewelled tie pin. His long legs were clad in vertically striped trousers and his shoes were highly polished, reminding David of the boots that Jack had to wear in the Air Force. On seeing David he first gave a gasp of surprise which was quickly followed by a beaming smile of recognition. He rushed forward with his hand outstretched to shake David's hand which was still holding his portfolio. David tried quickly to change the portfolio over to his left hand, but in doing so dropped it on to the floor. He left it where it had fallen and took the outstretched hand which gripped his tightly and shook it violently. By this time a couple of the students had dropped to their knees and were beginning to pick up the scattered paintings and drawings. They began to replace them in the folder but at the same time glancing at each and making comments such as,

"Oh, very pretty" or "What beautiful colours".

Ignoring the sarcastic comments, Mr. Bailey picked up the folder and putting his hand on David's back pushed him into his office.

He settled David into a very comfortable chair set at the front of his dark mahogany desk and with the folder in hand, went round to his large leather, swivel chair. He then called out to the ladies in the next office and asked them to bring in some tea. Opening the folder he proceeded to go through each of David's pieces of art giving each one of them no more than a quick glance. When he came to one of the paintings of the sea, which David had quickly composed the evening before, his idea of what a rough sea breaking on to the shore, would look like, he paused and raised his eyebrows.

"I can see that you handle a brush and pencil well. Your drawings show good progress and Mr. Peterson tells me that you are keen and quite successful at life drawing. However, most of your work lacks imagination and the colours you use are appalling. Your lay out, composition and presentation leave a lot to be desired and......" He was suddenly interrupted in his criticism of the work by the younger of the two ladies in the outer office coming in with a tray of tea.

"Put it down on my desk, Penelope, I will finish those letters in about ten minutes when David and I have finished looking at his work".

There were two cups of tea on the tray, one of which he brought round to David. They sat and drank their tea as Mr. Bailey stroked his beard and gradually replaced the drawings and paintings back into the folder. He then turned to David and looked straight into his eyes. Without removing his piercing blue eyes from David's, he began to ask questions, such as, why do you want to move from a good school with high academic standards to an Art School, and, what do you see as your future career? David answered all the questions as best he could, but he was quite uncertain of some of his answers and wasn't too sure that Mr. Bailey agreed with his forecasts. After finishing the questioning he began to write on a pad in front of him. He then tore off the top sheet, slipped it into an envelope, which he sealed, and together with the folder, handed it back across the desk. David felt very upset that all the hopes he had had and all the work he had put in over the past six months had come to nothing. Mr. Bailey stood up and leaned across the desk to shake David's hand and said,

"I have written a note to my good friend Mr. Wood. Will you give it to him when you return to your school tomorrow? There is nothing secret in there. I have written a short note letting him know my opinion of your work and thanked him for sending you over to me".

David thanked him for the advice and for the interview and turned to walk towards the door.

"If you would pop into the office on your way out and fill in a few forms, you will be able to claim your fares back for coming here and sign on for the new term starting in September".

David stopped in his tracks and turned back to face Mr. Bailey, "But I thought that you weren't impressed by my work and I had the feeling that you had turned by application down!"

"What gave you that impression? I must admit that the work you have produced will only just about get you through the preliminary examination, but we will be pleased to teach you a thing or two about drawing, composition and painting, that is what we are here for. I have explained to Mr. Wood that I will submit this work for your preliminary exam and I am sure, with my recommendation, it will pass. I have also said that you will have to take the intermediate

310

examination one year early and your National Diploma the following year. Now you go off and enjoy your examinations at your own school and we will expect to see you in the middle of September".

David was so pleased with the success of his interview he hardly remembered how he got home. All the family were delighted with his news and he spent no time in telling Peter, who was still attending evening classes with him. At school the next day he proudly presented Mr. Wood with the note, knowing of its contents and was pleased to receive another shake of the hand in congratulations. Mr. Wood replaced the letter in the envelope and told David to go round to the headmaster's office and ask the secretary if she would pass it on to the head. The secretary made him sit outside, but within a couple of minutes the Head came out and also shook David by the hand and congratulated him. David knew that the Head really wanted his boys to succeed in academic work and move on to their "A" levels, but he was obviously impressed by what Mr. Bailey had written in his note and showed marked approval of the chosen future.

The next week started the "O" level examinations and all the boys spent every spare minute revising the next subject on the diary. It was a time of feverish study and each morning they would assemble in the school hall, faces grey and eyes looking hollow. They were allowed, for the examination period only, to wear open neck shirts with short sleeves, but most of the boys still wore their school shirts with rolled up sleeves. The stress of each examination was increased by the rules that were all laid down before they entered the school hall. Each boy made his way to a numbered desk and any talking after the papers were handed out would warrant being expelled from the hall. To add to this, one of the masters, clad in his black gown, would pace up and down the central isle, looking from side to side as he went. As the exam neared its end the master would call out the amount of time left before the end of the examination, which was always met with groans of agony.

311

"Stop writing now and close your examination papers. Do not talk until all the papers have been collected up".

Directly this was done all hell was let loose, each boy checking what his surrounding examinees had put for a particular question and sometimes realising that he had missed the point completely. There followed a period of several weeks before the results were published and that was one of the best times spent at the school. They were free to do any subject they wanted, including sport and even sitting in the library, just reading. David spent most of his time in the park, sometimes painting and drawing, but many times rowing a boat up and down the lake racing other oarsmen.

In that particular year the results were due in the week following the end of the term, so all the boys had said their goodbyes on the Friday, but they were all meeting up again on the following Wednesday. The results were posted up on the outside notice board of the school and there were so many boys trying to see how they had performed that it took David and Jamie some time to get to the front. David did not expect too much as he knew he had eased up considerably over the past couple of months knowing that his future was already planned. He was more than surprised to see that he had passed in four subjects, Maths, Physics, English and Art. Jamie, who had decided to stay on at school to retake the next year, the year they should have taken the examinations, had done very well with six subjects. In addition to those in which David had passed, he also passed in French and History. He, of course, was delighted and knew that his parents would certainly reward him for his achievement.

It was during that summer holiday that David began to get to know the members of the youth club a little better and spent many hours going on hikes or visiting other youth clubs with these new found friends. Box Hill was a favourite spot to visit closely followed by Leith Hill and the tow path along the Thames Valley. It was also, during that holiday, that one of the club and his girl friend, who were extremely

312

good tennis players, persuaded David to visit the Sutton Tennis Club and learn the rudiments of the game.   Nearer the end of the holidays he was persuaded by the Curate to spend a week with the club at a large house in the New Forest. It was there that he first set his eyes on a young lady that was going to influence his life for many years to come, sometimes in a very loving way and other times, causing him heartache.

Chapter 34

Wednesday evening saw David, clad in his best dark brown suit, clean white shirt with a yellow tie and shoes that had been spit and polished for a couple of hours, sitting on the top step at the front door of his house. He had money in his pocket and he was ready for a wonderful evening at the cinema with Janet. He hadn't been able to concentrate on anything over the last couple of days and spent most of his time either listening to the radio or to some of his latest records which he played on the old record player that Jack had converted from an old phonograph. They had just moved on to high tech needles now which were made of fibre and could be sharpened to improve the quality of the sound. The scratchiness had been reduced considerably and the wear on the grooves of the record was reduced. He had always been keen on music and was particularly fond of the latest singers, Frankie Lane, Guy Mitchell, Nat King Cole, Eddie Fisher etc., but he was not so sure of Dad's recommendations of Bing Crosby and Frank Sinatra. He thought that these two were the tops, but to David they were old fashioned and sung the wrong songs. David would like to have enjoyed more serious music and when he had mentioned it to Father Kingswood, he lent him four twelve inch records of the New World Symphony. He had listened to them several times, but the family would ask him to turn off that awful dirge, which didn't help David to appreciate its quality, although he was beginning to enjoy the themes that ran through the composition.

At six thirty precisely, David heard the familiar step of Janet's high heels and was overjoyed to see her come through his front gate. As she came up to the front door he could see that she was dressed in a green and white flowered dress, her shoes were white and her hand bag, slung over her shoulder, was also white. Her hair, as always, was neatly groomed and brushed back off of her forehead, just reaching the collar of her dress at the back. David could see why he loved her so much, even her voice was music to his ears. He stood up and after a very short embrace they went into the house. Janet did not like showing her feelings too much in the open during day light. She was, perhaps, a little shy. The family were always pleased to see her and David would have been frowned on if he had not taken her indoors to say "hello". Mum and Dad thought the world of her and were delighted that David was so keen. Mum always said that she would make someone a good wife.

The film was all that Janet's mum and dad had said. It was full of beautiful music and singing and as they managed to get seats in the front row it felt as if the sound was surrounding them. David would really like to have been in the rear of the cinema as it was a little more private, but this didn't stop him from slipping his arm around Janet's shoulders and pulling her over towards him. He did hold back, however, from letting his hands wander onto forbidden parts, although he was sorely tempted. He didn't follow the story of the film too much, his mind was on the wonderful feeling he was getting from his right arm and the pressure of her left shoulder against his chest. He had experienced this amazing feeling once before at the same cinema, when he had persuaded her to accompany him to see the film, "High Noon" starring Gary Cooper. That story he had followed very closely as it was a love story mixed with cowboys and gunplay. Although Janet was a little cooler at that time she did allow him to touch her for the first time and didn't push his hand away. He remembered that they also walked all the way home with their arms around each other.

At the interval between the two films and before the news came on, David went off and bought two choc ices. Having seats in the front row did give him a quick entry to the side and he was the first in the queue which was forming in front of the young lady with the tray of goodies hanging by a loop around her neck. The usherette's mode of dress had not changed for all the years he had been going to that cinema. The whole uniform was made of a type of silk material.

The trousers and the cloak were of a royal blue and the blouse of the same material was cream. The whole ensemble was finished off with a pillar box hat in the same colours. Choc ices were quite a novelty as up to that time only tubs of ice cream had been available and usually, to David, they had been too expensive to buy.

It was still fairly light when they left the cinema so they decided to walk part of the way home. Janet was particularly loving and kept stopping for a kiss and cuddle. They walked with their arms around each other and Janet's slim waist always amazed David that he could rest his hand on the wide hip bone which gave her figure such a beautiful shape. They strolled through the streets of Morden, along a familiar route which took them past a hall where they assembled before they walked through the streets as a procession of witness at Easter time. When they reached St. Anthony's Avenue, it had become quite dark and they decided that they should catch the bus for the last part of the journey. On arrival at Janet's door, she asked him if he would like to come in for a short time and have a cup of tea. David readily accepted and was shown into the living room. He was a little sad to find that Janet's mother and father were still up watching the final programme on the new television. They, as always, made him very much at home asking him about the film and whether he enjoyed the music. Soon they were joined by Janet and the tea which included cups for her parents. All David could think was that they would obviously stay up all the time they were there and there would be no kisses and cuddles in their front room. How wrong he was! They quickly drank their tea and Janet's dad got up and said,

"Well, we've got work to go to tomorrow, so we will make our way to bed. Now Janet, don't keep David too long, drink your tea and say goodnight".

With that the two of them went out of the door and upstairs. Janet immediately came over and sat on David's lap and they began to kiss. David had his arms tightly around Janet's waist and back and pulled her close to him.   She released one of her arms from around his neck and taking his hand placed it on one of her breasts.   David was in a complete trance and the room seemed to be swinging around his head. He had no idea how all this had come about, only last week he thought that the love affair was all over, but now it seemed to be even better than before.   The joy of Janet in his arms and them kissing each other passionately was suddenly interrupted by a heavy knocking on the ceiling and Janet's dad calling out that it was time David went home. They kissed again at the door and then Janet said,

"Can I see you on Saturday evening?"

David felt a sudden regret as he had taken up the kind offer of Father Kingswood to go to his ordination ceremony at Chichester Cathedral. "I would love to see you then, but you remember that I said that I would go to Father Kingswood's ordination.   I don't think that it would be very nice to let him down at this late stage".

"Oh no, I didn't mean you missing that trip, I thought that if I came round to your house about eight o'clock, I could wait for you, that is if your mum and dad won't mind"

David was delighted by this answer as he wanted to see her more than anything and to feel that she would be waiting for him would be marvellous.   "No, of course my mum and dad would be pleased to have you visit for the evening and anyway I am sure that Susy will be there".

David left Janet's front gate feeling on top of the world.   This was the best evening out they had had.   It certainly put the dreadful events of the past couple of weeks out of his head, although he knew there were problems ahead of him which he had no idea how to solve and even his relationship with Janet would be badly effected by his decisions. Could it be only one month ago that he was riding on the crest of a wave enjoying every minute of his study at the Art School, knowing that his future career was more or less assured and being surrounded by good, talented friends? How suddenly things had changed! He could see no future as the situation stood at the moment and many of his friendships would end through no fault of his own. He hoped that this new loving relationship between him and Janet would survive, but even this was very doubtful. If only he knew.

Chapter 35

Life and study at the Art School compared to Wallington was different as chalk is from cheese. First of all, there was no rigid timetable as there was at Wallington. Students were expected to be in one of the studios and ready to start work by ten o'clock. There was an official lunch break from about twelve 'til one, although most students went on working while they were eating their sandwiches. The main classes would end at four thirty, but again many of the teachers and the students seemed to ignore these times and on most occasions left well after the end of the session. Breaks during the morning or afternoon would vary according to the subject. In Life Drawing there was a break every three quarters of an hour to give the model time to move and have a stretch. In these breaks many of the students would go outside for a cigarette or a chat, although both were allowed during the class. In fact, sometimes the room would be filled with smoke which made it quite hard to breathe. At the end of the daytime sessions there would be an evening class, which normally started at about seven o'clock, but this was usually preceded by the day students commencing the class on their own. It was a very carefree atmosphere mostly created by the desire of the students to just perform at their own speed and in the direction they wished to go. Every student seemed to be a completely different individual and their views were not only sought by the teachers, but were listened to and acted on.

Much against Mum's wishes, David dressed down on the first morning, wearing an older pair of trousers, a check shirt and a sweater. Again he carried his portfolio under his arm and an old wooden case, which used to house Dad's tools, in his hand. Inside he had packed brushes, pencils, several pots of poster colour and a Stanley knife. Much against Dad's recommendation he had let his hair grow long over the summer holidays and as it was thick anyway it had now become a mop. He arrived at the school at half past nine and was surprised to be met by the caretaker, a Mr. Clarke, who met him at the door and showed him to a locker, in the main corridor, where he could store his possessions. Mr. Clarke then took him along to the secretary's office, which was adjacent to Mr. Bailey's room. Here he was introduced to the two secretaries, whom he had met before and new quite well. They greeted him as if he was an old friend and asked him to fill in a couple of forms including one which allowed him to claim his bus fares to the school. This was an unexpected benefit of which he was quite unaware, except it had been mentioned at his interview but he had forgotten. Next, Mr. Clarke took him along to the Life Class to introduce him to Mr. Peterson, whom, again, he knew well from his evening classes. He introduced him to all the other students in the class and he immediately felt a friendly warmth between them. As the class filled with students Mr. Peterson took the trouble to introduce each in turn, eight male and three female, each being quite different in character and dress.

At ten o'clock precisely, a green curtained cubicle opened at the far end of the room and a large woman in a dressing gown stepped up onto the dais and stripping off her dressing gown took hold of a vertical bar and stood in a slightly provocative pose. She was completely naked and not nearly as sexually attractive as the models that attended the evening classes. She was really obese and had large rolls of flesh around her waist. Her breasts hung low and her bottom was immense. David noticed that not one of the students batted an eye-lid, but just seemed to accept the subject as normal. Mr. Peterson stood by the platform and described the type of pose he would like her to hold and when he was absolutely sure it was correct he walked away. All the students, without saying a word, took up a position either on a chair or with an easel and spreading a large sheet of cartridge paper on their drawing boards, began to draw. David spent a little time trying to absorb the new atmosphere in the room and observe some of its characters. To his left, sitting with his board propped up on another chair was Ray Chattem, a more serious type of student who seemed to draw with great precision. He wore a black, thick shirt with the sleeves rolled up just to the forearms and thick, dungaree looking trousers held up by a white belt. He seemed to smoke most of the time, but never let his eyes stray from either the model or his drawing. On David's right side stood a well built young man with long hair reaching down as far as his shoulders and what looked like two weeks growth of beard and moustache. He was dressed in an open necked shirt which was a muddy green colour and a pair of black, paint splashed corduroy trousers which looked as if they had never been taken off. Two strange things David noted about Patrick Dealth was firstly he wore sandals without socks and secondly he was using a paint brush and black paint with which he seemed to attack his board, mounted on an easel.

David thought that perhaps he should stop observing the students around him and get on with drawing the enormous woman that stood in front of them. He still found that drawing the more personal parts of a woman a little off putting, perhaps it was because he didn't like to let his eyes dwell on the vulnerable parts for too long. Mr. Peterson made his way around the students spending a little time with each advising them on their technique. With David he spent some time in explaining how he could produce more depth to his drawing and the art of producing a "3d" image on a flat piece of paper. It was quite strange to hear the other students just chatting about what they had been doing during the holidays and even making jokes or telling of funny experiences they had encountered. After three quarters of an hour Mr. Peterson called for a break. The model immediately went back into the cubicle and pulled the curtains around her. Nearly all the male students went out of the door and down to the toilets and all three girls stayed in the room but went over to the large windows that overlooked the swimming baths.

David went around the room looking at the work of the other students and was surprised to see the differences in technique and interpretation of the subject. Ray's drawing so far was clearly going to be a work of art. It actually looked like the model and was fashioned with such precision and care that it actually stood out from the paper. Patrick's, on the other hand looked slap happy. It had lines and shading all over the paper and amongst the chaos of brush strokes there was the feeling of a woman in complete torment. It seemed to be less picture and nearly all feeling, something which David had never experienced before. The ladies had produced drawings which were obviously a reproduction of what they saw. David went over to the window and stood close to the women students. Two of them were very ordinary as far as looks were concerned, one being very petite with long flattened blonde hair and a figure more like a broom stick than a woman and the other dressed in a dark, thick jumper and long skirt and having her hair pulled back in a bun. The third, however, was very attractive, she had large brown smiling eyes and her hair was dark, short and curly. She wore a tight, pink sweater and a short silky skirt, which showed off her long, shapely legs. The only thing that seemed to spoil the image was that she wore white leather boots with low heels. Neither of them spoke to David or even looked at him. He could have been invisible to them for all he knew. After about fifteen minutes the class reassembled, Mr. Peterson reappeared and the model took up her original pose on the platform. All the students except Patrick continued to add to or improve their drawings, but he pulled off the first sheet of paper and after mounting a second sheet, began to attack it again with his loaded brush.

The syllabus was varied and David was surprised to find that so many subjects were covered by this particular section of the course. Some he found to be very interesting and others a little boring. History of Architecture was taken by Mr. Bailey himself and although the subject was interesting he was so involved with the information that he didn't notice that he had a class of students with him. Much of the class was conducted using the epidiascope with all the blinds closed. It wasn't long before many of the students had their heads on the desks finding it impossible to stay awake. On one occasion, the good looking girl and her friend sat in front of the projector and about half way through the lecture the picture on the screen bounced up and down violently. A few minutes passed and the same thing occurred. After it happened several more times Mr. Bailey exclaimed in an angry voice,

"Drat this dammed machine, it seems to have developed a fault".

He played with the focusing and the brightness, but still the jumping continued. The rest of the students had all woken up and were trying to stifle their laughter as they could see that the fault was due to the fact that the attractive girl's head was dropping backwards as she dozed and was hitting the front of the stand. Mr. Bailey could see very little in the room as he was looking into the light of the machine.

The holiday work that was set for this subject was extremely interesting as it involved visiting the ancient churches all around that area and drawing examples of architectural interest such as buildings and arches etc. of different ages. This not only filled David's sketch book, but improved his drawing ability enormously.

One of the subjects David had never heard of before. It was called Lino Cutting. After fixing a piece of thick, dark brown lino to a backing board, a tracing of a design, first made on paper, was transferred to the surface. It would then be grooved by sharp tools leaving the design in relief. The printed sheet was transferred onto another block and cutting was carried out to match the first block. Sometimes even three or four blocks would be sculptured and the final print would be a combination of all three designs and all three colours and their mixtures. David enjoyed this class and became quite proficient at the art of cutting the blocks. The teacher of this subject was a motherly sort of woman. She wore her brown hair in a sort of ring on the top of her head which reminded David of a halo. She was comfortably built with a round, very pleasant face. She always wore the same green, wrap around overall and flat shoes. She would encourage David, approving of his designs and his cutting skills making the class so enjoyable that David would stay on for evening classes in that subject.

After the first week of getting to know most of the students and teachers, he was beginning to find his feet and enjoy the freedom of doing his own thing and being encouraged to do so. He never went down to the toilets and showers for the first break but usually had to pay a visit after the second session. Andy Keen, one of those in the Life Drawing class explained to him that this was not just a toilet break but a time when they would meet in the toilets for a chat and a joke away from prying ears. Andy persuaded him to join the rest at the first break, but was a little surprised to see them all rush out when the break was called. He made his way downstairs but found that although all the door of the cubicles was closed, the main section was empty. He thought that he had made a mistake, but just looked into the shower room to check. It was quite old fashioned and had a central area with a pipe running all round the corner of the ceiling with the walls. Unexpectedly the door behind him slammed shut and almost immediately cold water came gushing out of the pipe around the ceiling. He tried hammering on the door and shouting, but to no avail. After about five minutes the water was turned off and the door was opened. Mr. Clarke, the caretaker, had heard the noise and realised what was going on. He guided David along the corridor to his small room through a mass of students, men and women, all laughing. He felt so embarrassed. Mr. Clarke made him take off all his dripping clothes and produced a pair of trousers and sweater for him to wear while he took David's clothes off to the boiler room to dry. After about half an hour he returned to the Life Drawing class feeling really dejected. Had they hated him so much, to make such a fool of him? He thought that he was getting on well with all of them and they all seemed so friendly, but he was obviously mistaken. He entered the strangely silent room and sat at his drawing board. There was five minutes of absolute silence and David had a lump in his throat and was close to tears, when there was a sudden uproar of laughter. Many of the students from other classes came rushing into the room to enjoy the scene. At that point Andy came and put his arms around David's shoulders and said,

"Don't be upset. It is all part of the initiation ceremony. It happens to all newcomers that join an already formed set. You were lucky, it was a little warmer outside when I came and my initiation was in the park pond".

Then Ray, Patrick and Andy picked David up and carried him around the room on their shoulders to the cheers of all the onlookers, including Mr. Peterson and Mr. Bailey, who stood and smiled at the proceedings. David, with a smile on his face, waved to all the cheering onlookers and immediately felt that he was one of them and accepted by all.

David's days settled into a routine which, whilst being heavy going, seemed to suit him well. He still had his paper round to do in the mornings and although this was the part of the day he liked least, he knew that it was an essential part of his existence. Mum would give him a call at seven o'clock in the morning and he could be dressed, on his bike and down at the paper shop by half past. He did not need to mark up his papers as he knew what paper each of the customers took and he could put them in order in about five minutes. He would race up the hill and complete all the deliveries by eight forty five. He would then race home, change into his dark green corduroy trousers and maroon shirt and consume the breakfast, usually of spam fritters or fried bread and tomatoes, collect his jacket, case and folder and race to the bus. Sometimes he would need to race up the main road to the stop outside the church as the cheaper fare started from there. He would arrive at the Art School at just before ten and proceed to the first class of the day. At lunch time he would usually go into the lecture room with many of the other students and eat the sandwiches which Mum had provided and drink the milk which was delivered to the school and given to the students free of charge. Mr. Clarke made

325

a very large pot of tea which was distributed to all the students at three thirty and at about five o'clock a small group from his set would go over to the Lyons Corner House at the end of the street, where David would normally have a crispy, new roll and butter accompanied by another cup of very strong tea. The other lads would often have a Lyons apple, or cherry pie and sometimes Ray would say that he couldn't finish his and would give it to David. David always thought that he did this purposely as he, David, was a little short of money.

This small group, which usually consisted of Ray, Patrick, Alec, Andy and himself, the group that visited the historic churches in the area, always seemed to be testing traditional rules and how far people would go before they would break. One evening whilst sitting in the front window seats upstairs, Patrick noted that no one seemed to take much notice of situations if they were carried out with confidence. They decided to put this to the test. Andy, who would always push ideas to the extreme, suggested that they should pick up their table and see how far they could take it, through the shop to the stairs at the back and then past the whole length of the counter and out at the door which lay just below where they were sitting. He suggested that Patrick should go in front, as he was taller than the rest and looked more mature, calling out in an authoritative manner,

"Mind your backs please, mind your backs please".

Two of them, Ray and Alec, would carry the table, but when they got to the stairs, which were quite narrow, David would help to turn the table on its side and hold on to the legs to make sure that no one would be hurt. Andy would stay at the rear and make sure that no one overtook them. They moved the chairs back and picked up the table, Ray in the lead. They walked all the way to the back of the tea rooms between the secondary counter and the tables until they reached the stairs. Patrick went ahead calling out,

"Mind your backs please".

At which command the customers with trays of food and tea about to come up stepped back and left the passage free. They turned the table sideways and proceeded down the stairs and along to the front door. Patrick held the door open and they walked out on to the street. This being accomplished without any enquiry, Alec suggested that they should continue up to the Fire Station to see if anyone would be worried about the removal of one of the tables. It wasn't 'til they reached the Fire Station and put the table down that a little man in a suit came running up the road and said,

"Where the devil are you going with one of our tables?"

Ray explained that they were just testing their security, at which the little man nearly burst a blood vessel and swore violently at them. He said that he would report them to their Principal and he was sure that heads would roll, at which Ray said that he could also write to his head office and point out that they had not been challenged by anyone in the shop. It was agreed that if the table was returned to the original place, no more would be said. They replaced the table in the same manner as they had extracted it, receiving a ripple of applause and laughter from the customers who now realised what had been happening.

One of the evening classes that David chose to join was Lettering. He had always been keen on the subject and had developed quite a pleasing script that he liked to show off whenever possible. He was keen on this particular class as, firstly, he wanted to be able to produce the type of lettering such as that at the top of the Telegraph Newspaper and different types of script, and secondly, because the lettering teacher was new to the school and was a beautiful young woman of about twenty. All the students were impressed by her looks and although she gave no encouragement to anyone, all were striving to get into her good books. She was called Miss Saleen, and assured everyone that she had a fiancé and was not interested in other men. Half jokingly, the boys would vie for permission to carry her portfolio to the station, an offer which she always declined with a very sweet smile. During the class she would often take the pen off a student and leaning over them from the back, in very close contact, produce the type of letter she was seeking. David's lettering came on rapidly and he would write a whole letter to Peter, who had now left school and evening classes and joined the navy. Miss Saleen would always ask if David minded her reading the letter before she commented on it, often giving him advice not only on the lettering but also on the English he was using. Even Mr. Peterson was taken by this radiant young woman and would find all sorts of excuses for coming into the lettering class, some of which were so obviously fake that all the students would jeer.

After evening classes had finished, David would walk down the Sutton High Street with one of the students from the year below. It was, again, a strange phenomenon that all the students, no matter which year they were in, judged each other by the quality and originality of their work, therefore there was no sense of superiority due to age or year of study. Graham Langley was a very talented artist with a leaning more to the commercial side of art. He used lots of orange and blue in his compositions and he was very precise in his drawing and lettering. He knew of ex-students who had taken up the profession of window display and in which shops they were employed. That was the time when the windows would be redressed and the ex-student would be rearranging the models and the clothes. The two lads would walk on the opposite side of the road and guide the positioning of the exhibits to get the proportions and colours correct. The window dresser would look out for them as this advice from the opposite side of the road was invaluable. On Thursday evenings, however, David always made a quick exit from the evening class and made his way to the youth club, which was behind the church and exactly opposite the bus stop. There he would spend a very pleasant evening playing snooker or table tennis and dance to all the latest records. If there was a dancing class he would take the opportunity to improve his technique or even learn some new steps. It also gave him the opportunity to admire the young lady he had met in the summer, but never really approached her as he knew he would get the cold shoulder.

He normally finished off the day by strolling home with the rest of the club and then consuming the meal that Mum had left from their dinner, which was always on a plate over a saucepan of boiling water. He would then take out his brushes and pencils and spend some time in developing the piece of work which had been set for them by one of the teachers. The work he enjoyed most was when they were given a map of a town or village with an arrow drawn in a particular direction. All the students were given the same map with the same arrow. They were asked to imagine that they were standing on the arrow and looking in the direction it was pointing. They were then asked to draw what they would see in front of them. David was always keen on maps and contours and knew all the signs that occurred on an Ordnance Survey map. Sometimes there would be bridges and churches and the artist had to decide if the bridge was for the railway or for a road, and did the church have a tower, or a steeple. Sometimes there was a river and one had to decide whether it might have trees lining it and was there a field that might be fenced off? At the end of the week all the students would display their work on the board at the front of the class and each would be given a crit in turn. It was amazing how each of them differed although still having the basic layout. After all of them had been inspected the teacher would put up a photograph of the actual scene for them all to see. Some of the works were very similar to the photo, but most had missed out on either age or architecture.

This was a wonderful part of his life and although the work was hard, he never looked on it as a problem. Everything was a challenge and it didn't seem to matter if you got it wrong, as long as you had tried. It seemed to be the beginning of the term "lateral thinking" and he was developing the skill of searching around the problem and finding another way of doing it. David also knew that many of the students worked even harder than himself and were producing original works in all types of media. If it hadn't been for the Christmas Ball he may have developed all sorts of skills and techniques. It was his introduction to the opposite sex and the complete adoration of forbidden fruits.

Chapter 36

At the end of the Autumn term all the students were involved in putting on the Christmas Ball. David was surprised to find that they all took this function very seriously and was one of the ways in which they could put all their skills and techniques to the test and produce something practical. There was a meeting about a month before the end of the term of the whole student section of the school to put forward ideas for a theme. Each idea was discussed taking into account the cost of production, the amount of time allocated and the feasibility of the design. The views of all the students were sought and even the caretaker was brought in to make sure that materials and rooms could be available. It was like working in a large business, especially as a Board was formed to overlook the proceedings and check on the development of all the different sections that were involved.

This particular year many themes had been submitted but the one which became favourite and was finally adopted was that submitted by Patrick Dealth, entitled, "The Insect Carnival". All design students were given the task of drawing up a picture and plan of their interpretation of the theme. It had been suggested that the Board would choose the best from all of the original designs, and any part of any other design which would fit into the original theme. Each submission had to include the ways of producing the structures, the materials used and the cost involved. Immediately they could all visualise the scene and went off to do all the provisional drawings. David imagined large spiders sitting on webs in the corners of the room and some hanging from the shaded lights. He felt if the lights could be placed in the correct position it would give eerie shadows across the central dance floor. All the ideas were examined by the

Board, no matter whether it came from a senior or junior student, and a final plan was drawn up.

The large room used for dress design, millinery and weaving was chosen as the venue for the Ball and different groups were set to work on creating a section of the room or something which was common throughout the design. David was included as part of a team to make the insects. This they did by making the framework of chicken wire and then covering the frame with paper maché. They then painted the whole spider or scorpion in black giving them a sinister appearance. In some of them they left holes where the eyes would be, they then made provision for a small light to go inside making the model even more frightening. All their spare time was spent making these models although much of the diploma work had to be covered at the same time.

Included in David's team were two young ladies from the Fashion Design course. One of them he had seen many times at the tea break and even, on some days, he sat chatting with her at lunch time. She was very confident in her manner and was quick to suggest ideas and solve problems, added to that she was very attractive having short curly auburn hair and a very pleasing figure. They worked together on many of the models and David was surprised to see how talented she was at putting the final touches to any piece of work they made. On occasions when more materials needed to be bought she would ask David to accompany her to the shops, a task which, strangely, he enjoyed enormously. She knew exactly what she wanted and would drive a hard bargain to get it at the right price; perhaps that was his downfall. One lunch break, she admitted to David that she could not dance and knew that when they came to the evening of the Ball she would have to sit out and refuse any invitations. David had begun to dance quite well at the youth club and could not only lead, but knew many of the ladies steps, so naturally he volunteered to teach her the basics in the lunch period. He was quite surprised to find that several others from the Dress Design course came along to watch and even take part, although he concentrated on teaching Donna the basic steps of the waltz, quickstep and foxtrot. To take control of her steps he would, as is correct, place his hand on the base of her spine and pull her into him so that he could ease her legs in the correct direction. He did, however, notice that on these occasions she would forget her steps and gaze lovingly into his eyes. She would also push her pelvis tightly up against him causing him to react uncontrollably and become quite embarrassed.

The night of the Ball was fantastic. The dance hall looked like a scene from a witch's den and the insects and the lighting, added to by the cobwebs trailing from the lights to the corners of the room, gave an air of witchcraft. There were very few alcoholic drinks as most of the students could ill afford to eat let alone drink beer and spirits. This did not detract from the pleasure of the evening, in fact, it most probably increased the pleasure as they were all enjoying their own creation. David had supplied some of the records which would provide the music for the dancing and at first found that he was left to put on and take off most of the tunes. Just before the interval one of the students, who was always out for a bit of a laugh, suggested that they should take all the toilet rolls from Mr. Clarke's room and place them on the bumpers of all the cars parked outside the school. Tommy, David and one other student, whom David could not remember, took armfuls of the rolls and crept outside to the street. There they placed a toilet roll on the back bumper of each of the cars and tied the loose end to the bumper itself. They then slipped back inside the school and continued where they had left off.

When the buffet, provided by the Catering College students, was served, David found himself sitting by the side of Donna. She immediately complained to him that, although she had been asked to dance, she had not been asked to dance by him. They danced the whole of the second part of the Ball and even won a spot prize, which she boasted was the first prize she had ever won for dancing. After the prizes were presented and before the last waltz was played the lights were turned on and two men, one short and stout, clad in a light tan raincoat and a tall man who was much younger and dressed in a black raincoat with a belt, came into the room. They were both wearing trilby hats which gave them an appearance of plain clothed policemen, which of course, they were. There was absolute silence in the room and the shorter of the two men began to address the inquisitive students.

"As we were driving up Sutton High Street earlier this evening, we were confronted with a storm of toilet paper blowing across the road and pavements. What was obviously meant as a prank had turned into a highly dangerous situation. We were obliged to contact the emergency waste disposal team of the council, who I might say, were not amused. As all of the cars had left the vicinity before we arrived we had no way of tracing the culprits, if we do, prosecution will take place. I am not suggesting that it was anyone from this school, but as you were having a ball we thought that a word of caution should be given. A joke is a joke, but this was taking it too far".

With that, the two men turned around and walked out of the front door of the school. Of course nobody there except David, Tommy and the other student, knew anything about it and obviously looked and sounded innocent. David on the other hand was thankful that no more was said as he knew that it would mean being brought up in front of the Principal with, perhaps, dire consequences. He also knew that if the police wanted to trace the paper or the culprits it would have been very easy. They obviously, "turned a blind eye" as the force would say.

When the evening drew to a close there was a general clear up of all the plates, cups, glasses etc., but many of the students agreed to come back the next morning to take down all the decoration and put back some of the furniture so that the room could be used for its original purpose. As they left through the front door David noticed that Donna was standing on the other side of the road. She was looking absolutely stunning in a long chocolate brown coat tightly fitting around her waist and a very full ochre coloured scarf wrapped around her neck. He imagined that she was waiting for someone to pick her up in a car and take her home. He crossed the road,

"I thought that you had gone home long ago. If you are waiting for a lift, I will be pleased to wait with you".

"No, don't be silly", she replied, "I have been waiting for you. I thought you might like to walk me up to the bus stop in front of the cinema".

David was utterly amazed. He hadn't really had any girl friends, as such. There was the beautiful young girl at the youth club, but she seemed to spend most of the time trying to avoid him and when she did speak, she was really rather abrupt. Here was this very attractive young lady actually asking him to walk to the bus stop with her and obviously keen on sharing his company.

"Of course I will, in fact I would be delighted to see you to your carriage".

She laughed, "It's only a number 44 bus actually, but it is a little different from the rest: it's green".

David started to walk down the hill towards the Lyon's Corner House when she took his hand and said,

"We don't need to go right down to the main road, there is a shortcut by the side of the cinema, which brings us out by the main entrance".

David had walked through there many times before, but felt that it wouldn't be polite to take her up a fairly dark passageway. She turned into the gap between the two buildings and keeping hold of his hand pulled him with her. They passed one of the emergency exits from the cinema which was lit ready for the filmgoers to exit at the end of the performance. The next exit had no light and as they reached it Donna gently pulled David into the darkened opening. She immediately threw her arms around his neck and pushed herself against him. They began to kiss and he felt her mouth open and her tongue was thrust into his mouth. He had never done anything like that before, but to him it aroused a violent passion. He put his arms around her waist and pulled her to him as tightly as he could. They kissed for some time before she heaved herself away and undid the front of her coat. He slipped his hand inside and around her waist which she immediately pushed down 'til they were around her buttocks. He could feel her slipping up and down against his pelvis and her whole body seemed to go into convulsions. She pulled her mouth away from his and let her head drop backward making a moaning kind of sound. Her eyes were closed but her mouth was open. After a period of time at which David could not even guess, she dropped her head onto his shoulder and went quite limp in his arms. They stood like that for a short time and then after a few more kisses, not quite as passionate as before she said,

"I think that we had better make our way to the bus or I will never get home". Doing up the front of her coat and tucking in her scarf, they walked towards the front of the cinema and to the bus stop just beyond. They began to look up the times of the buses and noted that the last bus was at 12. 25. Donna glanced at her watch and gasped,

"God, do you know what the time is? It's twenty to one and the last bus has already gone. We must have taken an hour and forty minutes to get here from the School. Well there's nothing for it, I will have to walk home".

"Where do you live?'" asked David.

"Wallington" came the reply.

"That must be a good hour's walk from here surely you can't walk all that way?"

"There is no alternative unless you've got a bike" she said with a laugh.

"If that's the case", said David "I will walk with you".

"No, it's too far for you to walk all the way to Wallington and then to your home. I will be alright, don't worry".

She gave him a quick peck on the lips and turned and walked away down the road. David watched for a couple of minutes and then ran after her. When he reached Donna he grabbed her hand and they ran together for a good ten minutes until they reached the hill leading up to the beginning of Carshalton. They then stopped and throwing their arms around each other had a quick kiss and cuddle. They completed the journey to Wallington and David noticed that Donna lived in a road close to his old school. Donna was a little hesitant when David volunteered to see her to her door, as if she did not want to be seen by anyone who might know her, so they had a very loving good night kiss and parted. David knew that it was now very late and he began to run home. He didn't stop until he reached the back of the old mill at the far end of Wrythe Green. He then walked as fast as he could as he reminisced to himself about the wonderful evening he had spent with Donna. He knew, as he made his way home, that he was absolutely smitten by her beauty and personality and every time he recalled the stroll to the bus stop his heart would leap with excitement. How could he wait until tomorrow to see her again? Although he crept into the house, removing his shoes and most of his clothes downstairs, he was still greeted by Mum's familiar call of,

"Is that you David?" As he went to enter the back bedroom her door opened and she demanded, in a harsh whisper,

337

"What sort of time do you call this? Do you remember that you have got to be up at seven o'clock to do your paper round?"

"Sorry Mum", David replied, "I'll be up tomorrow morning O.K., don't worry"

"It is tomorrow" snapped Mum, and slammed the door.

David only drifted in and out of sleep for those four hours. He was still going over the events of that evening and the anticipation of seeing Donna again the next morning.

Chapter 37

David arrived at the Art School early the next morning, even before the caretaker had opened the building. They got down to the job of clearing all the models, tables and lights and made sure that all the paper decoration was put in the dustbins. At around eleven o'clock Mr. Clarke arrived with a tray of teas and handed one mug out to each of the workers. David couldn't help keep looking towards the door, every time it opened, to see if Donna had arrived, but there was no sign of her. At twelve o'clock, when they were just about finished, he was beginning to feel desperate. The students who would catch the same bus home as David, decided to go to Lyon's Corner House for a cup of tea and a roll and invited David to join them. He had decided that he would wait for a while outside the School and made the excuse that he was meeting someone to go shopping. At one o'clock and freezing cold he made his way to the bus to go home and embarrassingly, joined those who had left earlier.

That was one of the most miserable Christmases David had known. It was one of the times that he wished that the Art School only had the same length of holiday as all the other schools. The month seemed to drag although he made several bike trips over to Wallington and starting at the place where he had left Donna on that memorable evening, he would cycle slowly up and down the local roads just hoping that he might see her walking along the road. He had some work to do for the holiday and he spent some time at the Oaks, by Carshalton Beeches, drawing the old Manor. And over the far side of Beddington Park, drawing Carew House, where he had spent the first year at the grammar school, and Beddington Parish Church, which had parts dating back to the eighth century. Producing his sketches at the end of the trip gave him an excuse to be out all day, but his sad countenance must have arounsed some suspicion amongst his family, that all was not well.   Christmas itself eased his sorrows, as he attended church with many of the youth club and visited the local St. Anthony's Arms on several evenings, including Christmas Eve, before he went to Midnight Mass.   During one of the trips to the pub, just before Christmas, David met his brother-in-law's brother-in –law, a chap called Don, David couldn't remember his other name.   This Don seemed to be an expert in everything to do with building and landscape gardening;   after a few drinks, you can believe anything. Anyway, he said he could use another pair of hands to help him out doing a job which would drain the water off of a tennis court in Gander Green Lane, the other side of Sutton.   David agreed to give the last week of his holiday to helping Don.

David met Don at the tennis courts on the first Monday morning in January.   David could see from the start that this was going to turn out to be a disaster.   First of all, Don only had one spade. Undeterred, they climbed over the fence into Sutton Football Ground and finding a shed, Don lifted off the roof and withdrew two forks and another spade.   His idea was to dig a trench all the way around three sides of the court getting deeper and deeper finally ending up in a soakaway.   To add to their problems, it was bitterly cold and the ground was hard.   Don said that after they had dug through the upper crust, the subsoil would be softer.   This did not turn out to be the case and by the time they had reached two feet down it was decided that a pick axe was needed.   Don went over the the football ground and in the same manner as before, removed two picks.   At lunch time Don drove them round to his house, which was only about half a mile away, where his wife supplied them with bacon sandwiches, with thick slices of new bread and tender bacon oozing with fat.   The strange thing was that when they arrived she was dressed in a thin silk dressing gown and very little beneath and she didn't bother to dress while they were there.

At about three in the afternoon, on the first day, the secretary of the club turned up on a new motorbike.   It was one of the latest models and had a very quiet engine. It was one of the first "Silver Ghost" machines made by Vellocette. Don, who was an expert on motorbikes, showed the man how to clean it and how to tune the engine to get the best fuel consumption. Neither David nor the secretary knew whether this information was correct and they were amazed at the end that the machine still worked. The secretary was so grateful that he left the keys to the club with Don and said,

"Whenever you want a cup of tea, just open up the front and let yourselves in. There is some bread in a bin and a toaster in the kitchen if you feel a little hungry, but just make sure that you lock up when you leave".

This was a big mistake. Directly the man had gone off on his motorbike, Don opened up the front of the clubhouse and they went in to make some more tea. They made themselves some toasted jam sandwiches and after they had finished, they had several games of table tennis on the table that had been set up. By this time it was getting late and they decided to call it a day, locked up and went home. They had dug no more than fifteen feet to a depth of no more than two feet. It took them the whole week to do two sides of the tennis court, which Don said would be easily enough to drain the water and rapidly filled it in with ash, which Don had collected from the local gasworks. Don said that he would return the tools to the shed, but David believed that his tool shed at home had improved by the addition of two forks, two spades and two picks. He did pay David for the hours he had spent there, but deducted some for the time spent playing table tennis; he also said that he would contact him if he needed any more help at any time.

David arrived back at the school, for the beginning of the term. He had not covered the work that should have been done although he tried to do a rush job on some of the sketches needed for his diploma work. He had lost the zest he had had at the beginning and was wondering a little if he should carry on with this career or try something different. He seemed unable to settle to anything and his original idea seemed to have faded. On the first day, he was not inspired by anything he attempted and didn't bother to leave the Life Drawing class, even at lunch time. As he was leaving the front door of the school to go home he heard his name called out from the Fashion Design room,

"David, David, are you not even going to bother to say hello?"

David turned to see Donna still in her working gear, obviously ready for evening classes. He walked back towards her,

"I am sorry, I didn't see you there. Did you have a good Christmas?"

"Wonderful." she replied, "We had my sister and her family over with her two children, so we hardly sat down. What about you?"

"Oh, O.K. It could have been a lot better", David was remembering the miserable days he had spent just thinking and longing just to see her. Then he came straight out with it,

"What happened to you on that Saturday?"

"What Saturday?"

"The Saturday we arranged to meet".

"I don't remember making any arrangements to meet?"

"Yes we did. You said that we would meet up on the morning after the Ball and help to clear up the school", snapped David.

"Well, I don't remember making such an arrangement. Anyway, I had promised my mother that I would go shopping with her, so I am sure you must have imagined it".

David was livid. He said,

"Well if that is all you thought of our evening together at the Ball I am bitterly disappointed", with that he turned on his heels and walked rapidly along the corridor and through the front door. He did hear Donna shout his name out once, but he didn't respond and left the school. As he sat on the bus he went over their conversation time and time again, knowing that he was right. The only nagging thought he had was whether she had said that she would go in on that Saturday or not. Throughout that week he went to the Art School, but did very little work. He spent a lot of his time sitting and looking at a blank piece of cartridge paper, finally covering it with a poor drawing, more like a scrawl. On the next Monday he spent a lot of the day deciding whether to go to the Principal and tell him that he was thinking of giving up the course. He had had a miserable weekend and had not covered any of the work that should have been done. He decided to give it one more day and left for school. As he was walking down the hill towards the bus he was suddenly confronted by Donna standing directly in front of him.

"Have you got time for a cup of tea", she asked, "I wanted to have a word with you".

"I don't think there is much to talk about", replied David. "Anyway, shouldn't you be going to evening classes?"

"Yes, but I thought that this was more important. Now I am going for a cup of tea and I would like you to join me, but if not, that's up to you. Well! What do you say?"

"O.K., but I can't see what good it will do".

They sat about half way along the upstairs section, avoiding the front tables where other students may sit. After they had drunk about half of the cup of tea in silence, Donna said,

"I don't know what the problem is. You didn't come near me all last week and you have been moping around the school avoiding me. I just don't understand".

"Well, I will tell you the truth", replied David. "I have had a miserable holiday because you didn't turn up to the one date we had made. I had no way of getting in contact with you as the school was closed and I didn't know your address".

"I'll be quite honest, said Donna, "you will remember we were very late that night and I got a real telling off by my mum and dad. When I woke up late that morning, my mum was ready to go shopping with me. You see I had forgotten all about it. I couldn't let her down after the telling off I had had the night before, so I went along. It was far too late to get to the school after that, you must have all gone home, so now you can see what a spot I was in".

David leaned over the table and took her hand. "I am sorry he said, I got completely the wrong end of the stick". David felt her squeeze his hand and suddenly all the gloom and doom seemed to disappear although he thought that he should be very careful how he approached their future friendship. He said, "I'll walk you up to your bus stop and let's hope the last one hasn't gone this time". Tuesday evening David and Donna stayed to evening classes and as he walked out of the school he spotted her standing on the other side of the road dressed in that beautiful long, brown coat. They made their way to her bus stop through the alley at the side of the cinema and although they had a kiss and a cuddle in the exit doorway, it wasn't quite as wild as the night of the Ball. Over the next few weeks they made a habit of waiting for each other after evening classes and each walk through the alleyway became more and more passionate. During the breaks at the school they would sit together and hold hands or even put their arms around each other. One time they were sitting on the lower stairs away from most of the students and they went into a long, drawn out kiss, which was suddenly interrupted by a loud, exaggerated cough from behind. They were aghast to see that it was Mr. Bailey waiting to go down the stairs. Nothing was said, but the look on his face made them feel that they should be much more careful in the future.

David was quite unaware that Donna's course at the Art School came to a conclusion at the end of the Easter term. She was then allocated to certain fashion houses for a year of practical work followed by her final examination. She would not return to the school after Easter and David would have little or no time to see her. He was devastated by this news and felt that they must make as much of the remaining time together as possible and who knows what might happen after that. They would meet up as often as possible, David even skipped parts of the classes to meet Donna in the corridor outside, but they had to be very careful as all of the students and most of the staff knew what was going on. Mr. Clarke, the caretaker, had taken a liking to David ever since he joined the school and one day surreptitiously approached David in the entrance to his room, which was situated down a few steps at the end of the corridor. He told David that he would leave his door unlocked at break times and if he and Donna could keep it quite secret, they could go in there to get a little privacy. David thought that this was a fantastic gesture and thanked him for giving them this opportunity to be together. Donna thought that it was a brilliant idea and so, nearly every break and lunch time they would sneak away and let themselves into Mr. Clarke's room. Donna was extremely passionate and although they never actually had sex together they must have come very close to it. David was absolutely head over heels in love with Donna and the way she reacted, he thought that she must feel the same.

It was during one of their more passionate lunch breaks when the door was suddenly opened and a voice, well known to them both, called out

"Mr. Clarke, are you there?"

They were both horrified. It was the voice of Mr. Bailey. They both scrambled to make themselves decent and stood up to face the Principal who stood there with his mouth open and his eyes standing out like organ stops. He stood for a while and then in a familiar manner, stroked his hand down his moustache and beard. He seemed at a loss what as to say, but after a few moments, which seemed like hours to the two, he said,

"Fellows, you come to my office immediately and, Donna", (he always called the ladies by their Christian names), I will get someone to speak to you in half an hour in my office".

With that he turned and quickly walked along the corridor, his steel heels crashing down on the floor boards so that the whole school could hear.

David was not asked to sit down on the chair on the opposite side of the desk. He stood, head bowed and looking as if he had been drawn through a hedge backwards. He had made his way along the corridor which had all the doors open and silent eyes straining to see what was happening. David had never experienced such quietness and as he made his way up the stairs he had seen shadowy figures coming out of the doors behind him and creep silently up the stairs behind him. On knocking quietly on the Principal's door he had heard one word shouted out clearly,

"Come".

There was silence for a while as Mr. Bailey sat at his desk looking through some papers that he had open in front of him. He looked up slowly and said,

"I was stunned and shocked by what I just witnessed downstairs. I have never seen such bad behaviour in this school before. Did you know that not only were you behaving in an unacceptable manner, in public, but you were also trespassing in part of the school in which you are not entitled to be"?

As David tried to get out the words, no, or sorry, he was stopped by Mr. Bailey saying,

"You don't need to answer, but I would like to know if you had sought the permission of Mr. Clarke before using his room".

Immediately David realised that if he said that Mr. Clarke did know he would lose his job. On the other hand if he said that he didn't know David would most probably be for the high jump. He considered quickly and said,

"No sir, Mr. Clarke did not know we had been using his room, we just found the door unlocked and thought that it would be a private place to meet".

"I am not going to make a very serious decision on the spot and intend to sleep on it tonight. I will expect you to be outside my office at nine thirty tomorrow morning, at which time I will let you know what I have decided. Now pack up your things and go home".

David didn't see Donna. He packed away his paints, paper and easel in silence with all the class looking on, and he left the front door without looking round. He wondered how he could explain all this to his parents and his friends, who all thought that he was making such a success at the Art School. Mum and Dad knew something was up as they avoided asking David any questions about how the day had gone and why he was home so early that day when he usually appeared as they went to bed. Luckily Jack, and Betty were out that evening and

347

David made sure that he was in bed before they arrived home. They surely would smell a rat.

David was surprised to find Donna sitting outside Mr. Bailey's room when he arrived at nine o'clock the next day. She had obviously been crying and looked as if the world was coming to an end. David took her hand and sat beside her. She immediately began to weep and through her sobs said that she didn't know what she would tell her mother. Her parents had been so pleased with her progress at the school and they would be devastated if she was expelled. David knew that he was in the same position, but felt that he shouldn't say anything as it would not make things easier for Donna. They moved a little apart as they heard the familiar steps of the principal entering the front door and coming up the stairs. They both stood up as he approached but he showed no sign of recognition and went straight into his room closing the door behind him. After about five minutes, which seemed like an hour, the door opened and he beckoned them into the room. He told Donna to take a seat, but he left David standing.

"You may be surprised that I am seeing you both at the same time. This is such a serious affair that I believe that you should both know how I view the situation and you should both know how I intend to deal with it. I have not consulted any of my staff on this occasion as I believe it would be best for us all if as little were known about this misdemeanour as possible. You, Donna, have progressed well in this school and your work has been well above standard, it is hard to accept that you would put all of this in jeopardy. On the other hand, Fellows, although you showed great potential when you first came to the school and we could all see a great future for you, alas, your work has dwindled to nothing more than work put out by a novice and instead of progressing you have regressed to a point where you stand very little chance of catching up on the other students. You will remember that I took you on knowing that you would have to make up a year. This you have failed to do. I have decided that you, Donna, will leave the school immediately instead of waiting till Easter and I will try to settle you in a fashion house where you will continue to study and prepare yourself for the examinations at the end of next year. You will only return to take the examinations. As for you Fellows, I can see no reason for you to continue with your art career. I do not feel that you have it in you to pull yourself up enough to pass any examinations and I wonder if you have the aptitude for a future in the art world. I therefore suggest that you leave the school and try to find a job which will keep you occupied until you are called up for national service".

David felt as if he had been hit by a bomb. Although he had expected something of the sort, nothing could have prepared him for this dreadful feeling that he had let everybody down and was about to leave a life that he had known was meant for him. He felt as if he was falling through the floor.

"Have you anything to say, either of you?"

David could only shake his head and try with all his might to hold back the tears that were welling up in his eyes. He knew that he couldn't speak even if he tried and he could find no evidence that he could use in his defence.

Chapter 38

David was suddenly aware of Donna addressing the Principal in a very confident manner. It reminded him of their visits to the shops when they were buying goods for the Christmas Ball. She spoke clearly and without any signs of inferiority.

"I would like to ask a question Mr. Bailey, but first of all I would like to thank you for allowing me to go on with my study, in fact I am sure that I am ready to go to a fashion house and I can assure you, you will be pleased with my progress and development. In fact, I think that I have gained through my misdemeanour, whereas, poor David has lost everything. David has always been looked up to by all the students as having a gift for design and it is only because we did the simple thing of falling in love with each other that has sent us both a little crazy. I wonder if you would consider David's reinstatement if he makes a promise to devote all of his time to his studies and prove you wrong about his ability to catch up and reach the standard required to pass his finals?"

Both men were struck silent by the very profound and pleading question. David expected a thunderous response to such a mature young lady who was probably putting her future on the line with such a direct approach. David lifted his head to see the reaction of Mr. Bailey, who was obviously deep in thought and with his head slightly bent towards the desk. After a few moments he lifted his head and they were both surprised to see a slight smile showing through his beard and moustache.

"I see that my impression of you and your future, Donna, was correct. I have no doubts that you will make a success of your fashion design, that is, if you devote more time to work and less to boys. You have a very mature outlook on life, far in advance of your years, but I do take note of your observations and plea for the future of David.   I also thought that he had a gift for the design course, but that is not enough. The ability to succeed in art and design depends on hard work.   In fact it has been said that success is based on one tenth gift and nine tenths hard work.

If David will give me the assurance that from now on he will put all of his mind to study and practice and if he reaches the required standard by the intermediate examination, I will give him this one more chance. I must, however, lay down some strict rules which you may not agree with.   I insist that you do not meet up in this school or in the vicinity of the school until you are both qualified. I will also require a report on your progress and examples of your work throughout this period. Is that agreed?"

David found that he was unable to speak.   He was absolutely taken-aback by the commanding way that Donna had pleaded for his reinstatement and felt a tremendous relief at being given another chance.   He just nodded his approval.   Donna, on the other hand said,

"We can't thank you enough Mr. Bailey for your kindness and understanding in such a serious matter.   Of course David and I will abide by your rules and I am sure we will both work so hard that we will make you proud of the fact that you made such a correct decision".

"Now", concluded Mr. Bailey, "I suggest that you both go straight home this morning and try to forget all that has happened over the past twenty four hours.   Tomorrow, I will expect David to return to his normal studies and, Donna, I want you to come to my office at eleven o'clock to discuss what I have fixed up for you.   No one need know what has gone on here and I think it would be advisable if you treated our interview with a certain amount of secrecy.   I will, of course, have to let the rest of the staff know an outline of what has happened and will tell them of my decision. Now go off both of you and let this be a lesson to you".

As they went down the stairs David was unaware of anyone seeing them. There were no doors open and no one was standing in the corridor. David went a little ahead of Donna and as they reached the entrance to the ladies cloakroom David turned his head and tried to thank Donna for her support, but the words were stuck in his throat and he felt very tearful. She saw his predicament and just said quietly but clearly,

"Take your bus down to the Grapes pub and walk along to the bus station. I will see you there". She then disappeared into the cloakroom. David waited for nearly half an hour at the bus station and was finally rewarded by the sight of this beautiful young lady dressed again in that shapely dark brown coat and carrying a large portfolio and leather case. David took the case from her and they started to walk towards Wallington and towards her home. Nothing was said for a long time and when David managed to retrieve his voice, he said,

"I don't know how to thank you for the way you supported me when I was sure that my art education was finished. I was amazed at your confidence and I think it was only due to that which made Mr. Bailey keep me on".

"Don't be silly", said Donna, "I saved him from a difficult situation. We all know that you have the ability and education to reach the required standards and he was only too pleased to let me lead him into a "get out" situation. It was such an unfair solution he proposed. After all I was getting the very thing that I have been working for and you were getting nothing. I wouldn't be surprised if the crafty, old art lover hadn't planned the conclusion right from the start. He's a Wiley Old Bird and knows more than one way to skin a rabbit".

They walked on for sometime in silence and occasionally making remarks about the interview, but they never put their arms around each other or even held hands. When they reached Grange Park, they entered by the pathway behind the ponds, which was lined by thick pine trees in sight of neither the ponds nor the road. The sun was streaming down and there was an air of tranquillity with the warm fragrance of pine filling the air. It was a wonderful place for lovers to meet and David's passion was rising fast. The morning had been absolutely terrible, but here they were now as if nothing had happened. Perhaps Donna would suggest some way in which they could meet and their love affair could blossom in the secrecy of being away from the school. She may even invite him to her home and meet her family, of which, David knew very little. It was only then that they stopped to face one another. David asked if he could see her to her house and was given a definite "No".

"There is something I must tell you David. I don't think we should meet again. The school and even the whole of Sutton is really out of bounds and Wallington is very difficult for me. You see, I didn't tell you before as I thought it would hurt you, but I have a permanent boyfriend who is in the army. That was actually the reason I could not come on that Saturday after the Ball. He had come home on a forty eight hour pass and I couldn't walk out on him".

David was absolutely dumbfounded and hurt. He could feel his heart racing and banging against his chest and he could feel rising in him an anger far beyond anything he had ever felt before. He had loved her without question and had even put his future on the line for something which was only an extra love affair to her. He was about to burst when she put out both arms and put them around his neck. She kissed him passionately for at least five minutes and then she bent down, picked up her case and portfolio, turned and ran away around the pond. David moved past the trees and just caught a glimpse of Donna running up the avenue of lime trees to the gate leading to the main road. She had her head down and never even glanced back.

David never saw or heard of Donna again.

Chapter 39

David decided to walk home. He had done it many times before when he was at school in Wallington. He walked past many of the scenes that he had painted in those early years and remembered the satisfaction he had felt at capturing some of the beauty of both Grange and Beddington Parks. He crossed the small wooden bridge between the two parks and headed up the broad avenue of chestnut trees that had been such a joy to him and his pals when the conkers fell, or were felled from the branches by a well aimed stick. Some of the Wallington boys were playing hand tennis along the avenue and he remembered that it was his group that had started the playing of this newly invented game. He made his way through the trees and came to the River Wandle and stood on the concrete sides that had had to be built to prevent their river, the Welbeck, from draining all the water from the upper section to the lower reaches. They had placed a seat close to the new banks and close to the bridge which bore an inscription. He wondered whether it may be in memory of all the poor fish that had died due to their diversion of the river. It had, "In memory of Peter Cotes, Member of the Beddington Cricket Club for twenty three years". David remembered that he was one of the teachers from Wallington. He wondered how he had died as he was only a relatively young man.

He sat on the seat and tried to work out all the happenings of the day. He was heart broken about his parting from the one and only girl he would ever love, but couldn't understand how she could have been "two timing" him for so long. This young lady had grown enormously in his eyes when she had pleaded for his reinstatement and had obviously wanted to see him on the way home. How could she have been the girlfriend of a soldier when she gave him such encouragement? Her kisses at the back of the cinema and in the caretaker's room were warm and exciting and she had used her body as if she wanted more from him. She was obviously very experienced and knew exactly what would turn a man on. Perhaps she had gained this knowledge from her soldier boyfriend! That final kiss was not put on. She had opened her mouth and thrust her tongue between his teeth and almost to the back of his throat. How could she have done that if she had another boyfriend? Another thing, wouldn't she have glanced back when she left him by the boating lake if she thought that it would be the last time they would meet? David's mind was in a complete whirl and his heart was aching so much he thought that it would break. Perhaps they would find him sitting on this seat, slumped forward, having died of a broken heart.

After about half an hour, when nothing had happened, he decided to wander on towards home, but not going too fast as it would cause Mum to ask why he was home so early. He made his way up to the top of the railway bridge at Hackbridge and stood for some time looking at the trains racing along towards Victoria and Sutton. He remembered the time that he stood there when his beloved "Blackie", their pet dog, had been run over by a milk cart and how he had rushed him down to the Hackbridge Dog Kennels in an old wheel barrow only to be told when they arrived that his well beloved "Blackie" had died on the way. He remembered with sadness the way he pulled the barrow up hill all the way home to have him buried in his garden. This pain he now experienced seemed to be far worse than for the death of his dog although he knew he would never see either of them again.

On the way up the main road, which led to the alleyway and his home, he spotted the young girl from the youth club, to whom he had been so attracted when they were on holiday in the New Forest. She was on her bicycle, most probably coming home from school. She waved at him, but didn't stop. Perhaps that was a good thing as he was in no mood for talking to anyone. He remembered that he was quite taken by her on the holiday and had even tried to walk her home, but she obviously had a heart of stone and hardly even smiled at him. If she had been a little more friendly perhaps he may not have fallen head over heels in love with Donna and this situation may never have arisen.

At the Art School, the next day, everything seemed to be back to normal. The place looked dull and uninviting knowing that he would not see Donna and she would not be coming there again. The building had lost a great deal of its charm and none of the students seemed to be as colourful as they were in the past. It was strange how a building or location is at one time a joy to be in and everything is pink and rosy and the sun always seems to shine, but when just one person who one loves is not there, the whole place seems dull and uninteresting. He joined the students in the Life Drawing class, but seemed to have lost all interest in capturing the image on paper. The model was an extremely obese woman who was well over the age of fifty and obviously had not taken any care of herself, or her figure since she was a teenager. The only saving grace was that she had with her a large black Alsatian dog, which she tied to the post in the middle of the platform. Normally, Mr. Peterson would climb up on the platform and adjust the pose of the model exposing different parts of the human anatomy for the students to capture. This morning, however, every time he approached the dais the dog would face him and growl showing its teeth. He was obviously quite scared of the beast and when on the occasion that he placed one foot on the platform the dog went for him and grabbed his trousers. There was a complete uproar of laughter from the students as he tried to drag his trousers away from the dog's mouth. From then on he did all his instruction from a distance and was obviously shaken by the incident. To the amusement of all, some of the students did a beautiful drawing of the dog with Mr. Petersen's trousers and leg in its mouth.

As the week went on David struggled through each of the lectures doing the best he could, but all the time he hoped that the door would open and there would stand Donna, as he had seen her last, in that beautiful dark brown coat.   He just could not clear his mind of her and several times went down to the Fashion Design area to look at the table where she used to sit.   He would wander back to his own class and make out that he had visited the toilet or gone to get a drink of water.   Most of the students seemed to be avoiding him and the staff would only pop along to see how he was doing, but offered no real criticism of his work.   Somehow his world seemed to have crashed and he could see no light along the passage or hope for the future.   He had no vision of what he wanted to do or where he wanted to go and he couldn't even make up his mind whether he wanted to go on with his art career or find something less stressful and away from anyone who knew him.   The one thought that kept nagging at the back of his mind was, had Donna been two timing him and had she put on all the loving and affectionate times they had had together.   Could she really have had another boyfriend to whom she showed the same feelings, or was that last day a partial lie and in her maturity she had decided that there must be a clean break for both of their sakes and their futures?

One evening, later on that week, in the break between the afternoon and evening sessions, David made his way over to the Lyons Corner House to get a cup of tea and a roll and butter.   He had not really been eating all that well and anyway he thought that he could capture a little of the feeling that he and Donna had had on their visit after the Christmas Ball.   He bought a cup of tea and a roll and butter and went to the table where they had sat earlier.   Luckily there were no other students over there at the time, which quite surprised him.   He was gazing at the people passing on the road outside when he spotted Mr. Petersen walking down the road and entering the front door of the café.   Even more surprisingly he suddenly saw him approaching the table carrying a cup of tea.   He was still dressed in the corduroy coat and trousers and he seemed to walk with more of a stoop than usual. Strangely, David had never seen him, in all the times he had been coming over there, visit Lyons for a cup of tea. He would normally jump into his little "matchbox on wheels", Austin Seven car, which had seen better days, and race, or rather chug, home to see his wife.

"Would you mind if I join you". This was unusual; he never, normally, joined anyone for a cup of tea. In the breaks, he would find a quiet spot to be away from all the noise and have a short dose.

"If you like", replied David, "although I'm afraid I am not very good company at the moment".

"That doesn't matter", he said, "A quiet break is all I need". He sat down opposite and for a while they sat in silence drinking their tea and looking at the people walking up and down the road. At one time the fire station bell started to ring and they saw the fire engine come racing out of the station. A policeman who was conveniently walking down the High Street, just outside the front door of Lyons, raced into the main road and threw his hands up to stop all the traffic. He stood there with his arms spread and his chest blown out with pride at his prompt initiative. The fire engine turned up the hill instead of down towards the High Street and the poor policeman walked from the centre of the road with his head down in embarrassment. Many of the customers in the café noticed the incident and it was met with a roar of laughter. This seemed to break the ice for Mr. Petersen, who was normally a quiet, reserved man. He said,

"I hope you don't mind, but I wanted a word with you. If you think I am speaking out of turn, please just tell me to shut up and I will leave you in peace. You see, I was one of the first teachers to meet you when you came for evening classes, so I feel I know you a little more than the others. I have seen you develop and move on from a school boy drawing what he could see to an artist who paints and draws what he feels. I have also been through the same situation as you and know a little of what you are going through. When I was at Art School I fell in love with a wonderful young lady to whom I devoted nearly all my time. It is a long story, but I eventually found out that she was already married and my hopes for the future were completely dashed. I found that the only way out of the situation was to put all my effort into my second love, that is, art. I worked so hard that I began to feel less for my first love and more for my second love and gradually I became really quite accomplished in the art world".

"I am sorry Mr. Petersen, but I can't get this young lady out of my mind. All the beauty in life seems to have gone and I can't see any way in which I could retrieve it".

"There is something which I don't think you have yet grasped in our study of the History of Art. Have you not noticed that all the great artists and musicians as well, have produced their best pieces of work when they are experiencing some form of deep emotion? The famous painters, on the whole, produced their masterpieces when they were either madly in love, had just been jilted or were experiencing deep sorrow at the death of a loved one. Can't you see, this is the time you should be trying to turn these unbearable emotions into works of art".

David gave a disbelieving laugh and said, "Do you honestly think that someone like me could produce a work of art?"

"Not at the moment, and perhaps not in a few years, but who knows, many of our old masters were produced by students or young men and women no older than yourself. Anyway, I have said what I wanted to. If you think that I have overstepped the mark please excuse me, I feel that we have a bond which I would like to continue. If you need any help at any time, or even someone to talk to just let me know". With that, he stood up and turned towards the stairs and the front door. David sat for ages looking blindly into the street and thinking of what Mr. Petersen had said and how difficult it must have been for him to open up his past and give him advice.

Monday morning always began with life drawing with Mr. Petersen giving advice and criticism. David did not feel that much happier about the situation and still hoped that Donna may come back, just for the day, for a visit to see him, but this hope was to no avail. He took up a good position in the room with the light coming in from behind his head giving the model a kind of flat, marble appearance. All the students said hello to him and seem to greet him with some sort of care. He sat for a while looking at the model and thought to himself that from where he was sitting she could be made up of just a pile of beautiful shaped pieces of marble. He thought I will shock them; I will express what I see as a sculpture which has been smashed down by hammers with each part falling into a pattern on the ground, but holding the same form as the pose of the actual model. He drew quickly so that it could be finished before the first break and before anyone could see what he was doing.

At the end of forty five minutes there was a break and a time when students would walk around the room talking and looking at other work. Two of the young ladies came towards David to try to include him in the group again, but when they saw what he had drawn they looked aghast.

"What in the hell have you drawn, it looks like the ruins of an old Greek Temple"

Hearing their remarks, Patrick Dealth came over and looked at the drawing. He was one of the more forward looking students who dressed, acted, painted and drew like a forward thinking artist. "Hey, this is fantastic, you've captured the scene in one go. You've got the form and the shapes, but not in the same order".

At these comments nearly all the students gathered round and some seemed to like what had been drawn and some seemed to think that David was just drawing any old rubbish. David knew that many of them were trying to use the situation to draw him back into their community and hoped that they were not saying these nice things just to please him. This was the first time he had let his emotions go on to a piece of cartridge paper and felt he had at least achieved something. When Mr. Petersen re-entered the room he did his usual round to

361

check on the progress of each of the students. David removed his drawing from the board and replaced it with another clean piece of paper. He put the first drawing on a seat behind him, and then moved to a new position in the room which gave him a completely different aspect of the model. After about five minutes Mr. Petersen called out,

"Patrick, is this your first drawing of the session?"

Patrick walked over to the chair on which David had placed his drawing. Looking down at the page he said,

"No, this is the one that David did. I think that he is trying to disown it, but I think that it warrants more than a few minutes to study it. I told him that in my opinion it was great, but that wasn't the view of everyone".

Mr. Petersen picked up the drawing and walked round to David, studying the sketch as he went.

"Is this yours David?"

"Yes sir, I just thought that I would let my imagination run away with me and draw what I imagined the model could have been if she were made of marble and all the separate parts had become detached and fallen in a heap on the floor. I am sorry, I will draw something decent now".

Mr. Petersen lowered his voice so that no one else could hear. This was, of course, impossible as the class was absolutely silent, something that was very unusual. "This drawing is nothing like the model, in fact it would be quite difficult to label it as a life drawing. On the other hand it shows a mind in torment and deep sorrow. The feeling you have captured is quite frightening and it is the first time I have seen anything in your drawings which has been more than shape and form. Your drawing technique is good as you have moved quickly and without hesitation, so you have lost none of the artistic value. All I can say is", and he lowered his voice at this point almost to a whisper, "you must keep control of these feelings and use them to your advantage. Do not let them get out of hand".

Over the next couple of weeks leading up to the Easter break David remembered that he allowed himself the freedom to see and to imagine, not caring what the result was and not worrying about the criticism from tutors or students. He knew that many of his fellow would-be artists, had already achieved this ability to think on paper, something which he had always admired, but wasn't able to carry out. Three in particular he knew had broken through the barrier and he would spend a great deal of time studying their work. They all worked non-stop only having short breaks for tea, food and sleep, but the works they produced were amazing. One of the younger lads, Tony Scott, who seemed to move from year to year worked so hard and so long that his mother came to the college and asked the staff and his friends if they would ask him to take a break from his work as he was becoming ill. He was a good looking young man with long, wavy hair and deep blue smiling eyes set in his round tanned face. He dressed in the typical artist robes of dark shirt and corduroy trousers. Although he was a little short, he was very popular with the ladies of the school, but, sadly, he was never attracted to any one of them. As far as asking him to ease down on the work load , there was little anyone could do as he was a law unto himself and just carried on as before. His paintings were brilliant, full of colour, depth and character and each of the finished works told a story about the people he had captured. David remembered that he was a year younger than himself, but had been offered a place at Slade School of Art which he could take up as soon as he reached the required age.

David was invited by some of the students who lived in Mitcham to join them over the Easter holiday and spend some time visiting some of the old churches around the area, where they would sit in the graveyard and sketch or visit the Common and either paint and draw. On occasions, which he found quite strange, they would involve him in a game of tennis on the local tennis court although they didn't dress in tennis gear but stayed in their arty clothes. He began to feel the old comradeship back again and would look forward to their meetings. His sketch book, which he carried everywhere, was becoming full of sketches of local trains, trees, houses, churches, people, etc., which pleased him no end, as this must be submitted for his intermediate examination. To add to this, his relations with the young girl in the youth club seemed to improve. This may have been because he wasn't trying so hard and was happy to have a relationship which was more on the friendly side with little emotion. He would go to the youth club and church at regular intervals where his friends knew nothing of his heart problems and where he could play table tennis and snooker as often as the tables were free. His dancing was also improving and now that Janet had become his main partner he began to enjoy himself again. He still hoped, however, that Donna would suddenly appear and their relationship could continue as it had in the past. There was still that ache which never seemed to go away and he still dreamed of her regularly, waking to that emptiness and loneliness that only parted lovers feel.

Chapter 40

That summer term David worked harder than he had ever done in the past. He remembered what Mr. Petersen had said and knew that by working hard he could lose himself in painting, drawing, lettering, History of Art, and all the other subjects. He had also become quite talented at clay modelling and converting the model into a plaster cast. He allowed himself the freedom of trying to express his feelings in his work and would receive quite fervent criticism at times. The strange thing was that at this time all of his paintings seemed to move into the same tones and colour and no matter how hard he tried he could not break the mould. The purples, browns, smoky blues and yellow ochre always seemed to dominate the scene and the subjects always leaned to scenes of broken ships and boats and derelict buildings. The one thing which he was striving for was the ability to look at a piece of blank canvas or paper and see, in his minds eye, the finished work. He knew that many of the students had achieved this and he was quite envious of this gift. He could now do quite fine lettering with few guide lines and could judge the distance of the line and how the letters would fit. The very beautiful lettering tutor, whom he had met in his evening classes, would give him great encouragement and to his enormous pleasure would spend a good deal of time leaning over him.

He began to show keen interest in all the other student's work and would always give encouragement. Some of the young girls would even ask him for advice at times and this gave him a huge sense of achievement. The college was beginning to become home again and much of the colour which had been lost at the end of last term had returned. Although he was maturing fast he was still quite naive at times. At lunch times, some of the students would get out an old table tennis table and erect it in the middle of the room used for the Life Class. David had, of course, been playing quite a lot of the game at the youth club and would enjoy showing off his skill. The table would be surrounded by many of the students from all over the college, who sat and ate their sandwiches and drank their cups of tea, many times bought from Mr. Clarke. The girls from the Fashion Design Class would come along and chat and watch the game. They were a very attractive bunch and two of them in particular had faces and figures to match any models. When the ball left the sides of the table they would catch it and throw it back to the end of the server. One time, one of the attractive girls caught the ball and refused to hand it back. She raced off towards the door and quickly David grabbed her from the back. She held the ball in both hands in front of her whilst David held her from the back, with one arm around each side of her waist. They tussled for a while with her laughing and David getting annoyed. She then said,

"Open your hand then".

David opened one of his hands and she slowly scratched the middle of his palm with her index finger. She continued to do this as she turned to look into his face. David saw his chance and grabbed the ball in triumph. She continued to look into his eyes and still holding on to his hand said,

"You must be stupid".

At the end of the game, when the table was cleared away and the students were returning to their separate rooms, Ray, whom David had been playing at the time, said,

"What happened with that girl who took the ball"?

When David explained what had happened he said,

"You must be a bloody fool! Don't you know what that sign means. You've just turned down something which would make you hair curl. She was inviting you to make love to her, you thick head".

It was strange how that Life Drawing Class held more memories for David than any other part of the College. The models were never very inspiring to look at, although they were very interesting to draw. This was nearly always so except for one particular week in the middle of the term. Mr. Petersen would always hire the models from an agency and had no idea who would turn up. Some were fat and ugly, some would cry all the time they stood or lie there, some brought their pet animals and some reeked of garlic especially when the electric fire was put on for warmth. On this one week all the men met up, as was their custom, in the gent's toilets. As some were having a cigarette and others just stood and chatted, one of the younger students came rushing in and said,

"Hey lads, old Pete has done it this time, you ought to see the model he has hired for the week. She is an absolute peach".

There was a rush for the door and a race up the stairs. At the door they all slowed down and entered the room as if it was a normal day. It was the first time David had ever seen all the students sitting at their chairs and easels waiting to begin. It was also the first time he had seen Mr. Petersen, with hair combed, what there was of it, and ready to start the class on time. At ten o'clock precisely, the green curtain in the corner of the room opened and the most beautiful young lady of about eighteen years old, with long blonde hair, the deepest of blue eyes and the most shapely bronzed figure appeared for all to gasp at. Mr. Petersen took a long time setting her up in a delightful pose having to position her arms and legs by hand, which evoked all sorts of comments from around the room. She just sat and smiled at all of them showing a row of perfect, white teeth. There was no doubt, she was stunning. All the students drew ardently for the three quarters of an hour spending more time looking at the model and much less looking at their work of art.   Five minutes before the end of the session Mr. Petersen went hurriedly out of the room and returned in a matter of minutes with a cup of tea in his hand, which he presented to the model.   She took the tea and went into the corner with the curtain. Graham Langley, who had become quite a good pal of David's over the past few months, joined David at the large window overlooking the glass roof of the swimming pool next door and they drooled at what they had just seen.   Graham always had an eye for the girls, which tended to get him in a lot of trouble at times.   They were just commenting, as men do, on the shape of her figure and the pleasure she could give to some lucky fellow, when they were interrupted by a sweet voice with a kind of Swedish accent say,

"Would you mind if I joined you?"

She was clad in just a deep blue, silk dressing gown which was open all down the front revealing the inside of both breasts with a lovely deep cleavage.   She had an absolutely flat tummy and except for a line around her nipples and groin of white skin she was completely bronze.   It was very strange, thought David, that they had drawn naked women nearly every morning for months and at no time, except on the first or second occasion did they get inspired by the sexual innuendoes of these encounters.   Even when the models were young and attractive they were never turned on sexually, yet now, with the young lady wearing a silky dressing gown and the fact that most of her body was covered up, she oozed sex.   Graham was the first to recover his voice, which now sounded deep and dry.

"No, by all means. You are very welcome".

She came between them to look out of the window and they could smell the very light perfume that she wore. She said,

"You are all so clever. In my country most of the artists are much older than anyone here. They are all so serious. I was pleased to hear the jokes that were going on and the good humour".

David thought to himself that he hoped she hadn't heard all the comments and if she had he hoped that she perhaps didn't understand some of them.

"Where do you come from?" asked David.

"Sweden".

"You speak very good English".

"We all learn English at school".

"How long have you been here?" asked Graham.

"Just one week".

"Why are you doing a job like modelling?" asked David.

"Because I am trying to earn some money to study at college in London", she replied.

"Come on", said Mr. Petersen with a slight smile, "back to work, you can't spend all day goggling at this beautiful young lady".

That week saw the best attendance in that class for the whole year and strangely there were some male students from other courses that thought that they should improve their life drawing.

During that term David went off with Dad and Jack for a pint at the local pub. There they met David's brother in law, Ronald, and his sister and her husband Don. David knew them quite well as he had worked for Don during one of the holidays. After a few pints of mild and bitter they all became, as one does, extremely friendly, knowledgeable and vocal. Jack took Don's wife off for a dance on the small patch of floor which had been cleared of tables and chairs and Don sat with Dad, David and Ronald to discuss the problems of the world and to put them straight. Don explained to them all that he still had the gardening business, but had expanded his business more into the designing of gardens. He had moved into the laying of patios with York stone walls and wrought iron gates and fences. He said that he had a hard time trying to persuade potential customers how much their property would be improved and, more importantly, how much the value of their house would rise with his additions. David suggested that he should show them a drawing of what the final picture would look like if the improvements were made.

"Do you think that you could do a drawing or painting of the house with the York stone walls and the wrought iron gates for me to show them?" asked Don.

"Oh, that would be easy", said David. "If you could show me the type of wall you would like to build and the design of the wrought iron gate you would fit, I could produce a painting for you"

That started a long string of jobs that David managed to fit between his other studies. Don would go around an area looking for a house which looked well maintained, showing that the owner had a good income and needed the front wall and gate improving. He would then come round to David and give him the addresses. David would then get on his bike and visit the location taking with him his sketch book. He would then, either at home, or at college, draw up the house and enhance it with the type of walling and iron gates that Don had seen in a garden shop. When the painting was finished Don would turn up on the door of the house in the evening, when the man had come home from work, and show them the painting. Many times they would put in an order for the work to be done, but nearly every time they would

370

ask if they could buy the painting of their house.   Don, with reluctance, would let it go for thirty shillings and this he would pass on to David.   He was never quite sure whether that was the price Don asked, but David was extremely pleased to earn as much on one painting, which took him little more than two hours to complete and mount, as he did for the whole week on his paper round.   He even engaged some of the art students to help him when things became busy, but they tended to produce what they saw in their mind rather than a type of picture which everybody wanted.   He and Don built up quite a little industry and for the first time in his life he felt the pleasure of earning money and being able to treat himself and his friends to those delicious "Lyons Individual Fruit Pies".

Mr. Petersen was right, the harder he worked the more he overcame the deep heart break at his parting from Donna.   Now that some time had passed he was sure that that wonderful young lady had told a few white lies on that last day to make a clean break so that they could both get on with their studies.   His thoughts of her were wonderful, but did not give him quite the pain that they did earlier on.   To add to this, his relationship with the beautiful and young Janet had improved considerably.   They now danced well together and were often invited to take part in demonstrations in other youth clubs.   She had become much warmer and had even invited him to meet her parents.   He had taken her to the cinema on several occasions and been invited in to her house to chat with her mum and dad.   They were very generous and kind people and seemed to now approve of Janet having a boyfriend.   They knew that David thought very highly of Janet and would never take advantage of her.   He was not always pushing to take her out as he had so much to do with his paper round, studies at the art college and the small enterprise, which he and Don had entered into.   That summer Janet even asked him if he would go to the youth club holiday on the Isle of Wight and even though he had made up his mind not to go, this was easily changed.   They had had a wonderful and eventful time and any occasion he was not with Janet he would take his sketch book down onto the beach and enjoy just drawing some of the old craft that had been left on the sand. He had had his ups and downs with Janet at times but in the summer all was as near to heaven as he thought he could be.

He was particularly happy because, at the end of the summer term, the art college held its yearly prize giving. This was actually looked on by the students as a bit of a laugh, but to those who received prizes it seemed more important. David had nearly been expelled just before the Easter Holidays so he went along just to applaud the winners and congratulate them. He knew that he had dropped back a lot and the Principal had had doubts as to whether he would reach the required standard to continue with his studies. He knew that he had now proved his position in the college, but that was all. Nearly all the prizes had been presented and by now students normally would be leaving the room. This time, however, they were all still there and seemed to be waiting for something unusual. The only prize left on the table was a fully illustrated book by Stanley Spencer. David had, only two weeks before, paid a trip to his village of   Cookham Dean to study his work and the amazing museum dedicated to this intriguing painter.   Mr. Petersen, who normally took little part in these occasions stepped forward and took up the book.   He announced,

"A special prize is to be awarded this year and this is to be presented to the student voted by yourselves and the staff as the most improved student of the year. This year, for the first time, the student achieving this most important position is", and here he did a short pause, "David Fellows".

There was an enormous ovation of clapping, cheering and stamping of feet.   David stood up with his mouth wide open, he felt his legs go weak and he wasn't able to move forwards until he received a shove from behind. As he walked to the front he realised that the occasion warranted a few words from himself. No other students had responded verbally following their presentation, but this seemed to be something new and special. After being presented with the Stanley Spencer book by the Principal who beamed with pleasure and shook David warmly by the hand, David turned and faced the gathering. He paused for a while to let the noise calm down and then said,

"I am overjoyed at receiving this enormous honour and wonderful prize. I must say that I did wonder why Mr. Petersen asked me to name my favourite painter; I thought that it was some sort of quiz game. I must now admit that I have, in a way, deceived you all. You see, I had the furthest to go. Just before Easter I felt as low as anyone could and I know that my work was atrocious. Therefore, to be the most improved student of the year meant I went from rock bottom to get to your present standard. I thank you all for this honour and I can assure you I will not let you all down in the future." With that David made his way back to his seat amidst cheering and clapping. His only thought was that he wished that Donna had been there to witness what David was sure was a lot of her doing. He was now quite certain that she had made the break although it hurt her as much as it did him and it took a brave woman to lie just to make him get back to the work he needed to do.

During the autumn term he remembered that he had had a wonderful time being allowed to go more or less anywhere in the area drawing, sketching and even just observing. Their group of students paid trips to the Tate Gallery, The National Gallery and many other art galleries all around Piccadilly Circus. They would draw the inside of tube trains, men stoking the fires in the gas works, shoppers in the well known stores such as Selfridges and Harrods and they were even allowed to sketch the inside of many of the Cathedrals, such as Westminster and St. Paul's. They were all considered to be a little strange as they wore clothes with unusual colours, such as bottle green corduroy trousers and maroon shirts. Most of them had duffle coats and all of them, especially Patrick Dealth, let their hair grow longer than the norm. They had turned out to be the nicest and most friendly group David had had the pleasure of being a part and their kindness to all they came in contact with was unbelievable.

David's relationship with Janet became closer and closer and he would race from the evening classes to get to the youth club so that he could spend a couple of hours with her and dance to all the favourite music of the time. She became more and more religious and would spend a lot of her spare time either at the church or helping with the Sunday School. She had become very friendly with Miss Bowlinbrook and would help her arrange youth club events and church functions. She had left school that summer and had landed a plumb job in one of the publishing houses in Fleet Street and her organising skills were well thought of by the publishing staff. It was during this Autumn term that the publishing company put on its annual dinner at the Café Royal in Piccadilly and Janet asked David to accompany her. It was a wonderful reception and David met many of the cartoonists, illustrators and Directors of the company. They were very interested in his ideas and gave him great encouragement; in fact one of the Directors, who was well known at the time on radio and television, gave him his card and asked him to contact him when he had passed his final examinations.

The term ended with the traditional Christmas Ball and David took a full part in this adventure. The theme was the Witches Caldron which involved many of the dress designers and milliners producing most of the costumes. The room was filled with large steaming tubs and ugly looking cats and witches all over the walls. David invited Janet to accompany him this year and of course they had a wonderful time dancing nearly the whole of the evening. Nearly everybody there, except for Janet, knew of David's heart break at the same time the year before and were delighted to see that he was back to his old self and enjoying life again. Janet, who must have been the youngest person at the Ball enthralled everybody and enjoyed herself immensely. That Christmas turned out to be one of the best he ever remembered and the two of them divided their time between going to all the church services, having Christmas Dinner at David's house, tea at Janet's and some of the rest of the time up at the St Anthony's Arms enjoying the comradeship of all the local people.

At the end of the Spring term came the major examinations. Throughout the term all the students involved worked day and night to produce the required amount and quality of art needed to pass this very important landmark. Samples of oil paintings, pencil and pen drawings, linocuts, lithography plates, lettering samples and even clay models cast in plaster had to be available for inspection. The beloved sketch book had to be completed in advance and sent in near the end of the term. During this time the male students had to consider how they were going to approach their future. At the age of eighteen all males were required to serve in the armed forces. If they felt that they may go on to study at either the Royal College of Art or the Slade School of Art and had secured a scholarship, they could apply to be deferred for two years. If, however, they were going into some sort of employment they normally tried to find the niche they wanted and applied before they went into the forces knowing that they had a job when they came out. Two of the students had acquired a place at Slade, one at the Royal College of Art and nearly all the rest were going to seek employment in scenery design in films or the theatre. David thought that the future lay in television and imagined that there would be designers required to forward this new media. He applied to the BBC for an interview although he hadn't seen any advertisement that designers were required. He was delighted when he received a letter inviting him to come for an interview.

Although he delved hard into his memory he couldn't remember where he went for the interview. It was somewhere in the centre of London because he remembered travelling on the tube. It was a very impressive building and David felt like a million dollars walking up to the reception with a portfolio full of samples of his work under his arm. After a short wait during which he was given a cup of tea, he was led along a tiled corridor to a large dark wood door. The young lady that had accompanied him tapped on the door and then turning the brass handle opened it. He entered to be faced with the side of a long table with a lone chair on his side and three very large men and a lady on the other. The man at the centre beckoned for him to sit down on the chair and began by saying,

"Good morning Mr. Fellows", David hadn't been addressed like this before; "We were interested to get your letter and felt that it was only courteous to at least see you and get your reactions to our situation".

"Thank you", replied David, "It was kind of you to even consider seeing me especially as you had not advertised for a designer".

"Exactly", said the fat man on the left who was smoking a cigar.

"That is why we considered at least seeing you especially as we were quite impressed by your letter which made certain statements which were a bit far fetched. Tell me why you chose the BBC for your enquiries".

"Well, it is the only broadcasting company in England and I imagine will be for many years to come".

The questioning became more and more involved and difficult to answer, but David had done some important preparation before going to London and felt that he coped with the questions fairly well. Then came the body blow from the man with the cigar.

"I find it difficult to understand Mr. Fellows how you think your skills as an art designer, possibly for scenery, can be of any use to us when television needs very little imagination behind the presenters. In fact, a back cloth is usually all that is required and secondly, Mr. Fellows, all these samples you have submitted to us are full of colour. Have you not noticed that television is only black and white?

There was a shuffling of feet and bottoms on the other side of the table as the other interviewers were getting a little disturbed by the rudeness of the man with the cigar.

"Tell me, Mr. Fellows, what is your answer to that?"

David paused keeping his eyes on the table in front of him. He had not really been ready for this onslaught, but knew that there must be some division on their side of the table, and anyway, why had they bothered to interview him. He lifted his head slowly and brought his eyes to bear on the cigar man.

"I find it very surprising to hear a man who is in charge of such a great and well known enterprise express such negative views. I have, perhaps, made a mistake with my application. I hope I have not wasted too much of your valuable time".

He stood up and began to gather his drawings and paintings, of which he was very proud, into his folder. He was about to turn away from the table when the Chairman said,

"Don't be too hasty Mr. Fellows, we would like to hear you expand on your letter and tell us what you see the future being and how you feel that you may fit into it. Now sit down again and tell us of your thoughts".

David reluctantly sat down and faced them again.

"Take your time", said the Chairman, "We are not in any hurry".

"I have seen your programmes and I must say that I have felt that a lot more could be done with some of your productions. It is not true that you only need a backcloth behind your presenters. I have seen the attempts you have made to improve the scenery. A very close friend of mine has a television and across the screen he had stuck a sheet of three colours, blue at the top, red in the middle and green at the bottom. This is his attempt at putting colour into some of the programmes. When films first came out they were poor productions, black and white and silent. Now look at them, top class photography, brilliant acting, wonderful costumes and scenery, superb sound and brilliant colour. I cannot see a medium like television missing out on any of these improvements and I wanted to be in on the ground floor and take some part in its development. I see, alas, those in charge of this nationwide communication media do not seem to think the same as myself and all I can say is I am sorry".

The cigar man put down his cigar into a large glass ash tray half way between himself and David and rolling back into his large leather padded seat said,

"So Mr. Fellows, you think that you have chosen a profession which entitles you to predict the future, do you? There is no chance in a million that television will ever go into colour and if you had only done a little more research you would see that we are only broadcasting over a very limited area and even then the reception is usually only adequate".

David now turned to face the chairman, who seemed to be a very pleasant type of man who said very little but listened carefully. He had spent much of his time smiling at the confrontation, he said,

"During the war, when I was only five, I drew one of my first cars. It looked a little like the Jowett Javelin only for its propulsion. I drew a large air intake like an old fashioned megaphone, a bit like the bell at the front of a trumpet. At the back of this I drew a tube that ran down the back of the car and on to a fan inside a cylinder on the back axle. I drew a petrol tank just in front of the cylinder so that the explosion would force round the fan. It wasn't until just recently that the jet engine was produced and if you had looked at my car it used the same sort of technology".

The cigar man burst out laughing and said,

"What a pity you didn't speak up during the war, we may have had the jet engine earlier".

"Don't take too much notice of our Mr. Feathergill, he likes to push any applicants as far as he can", interposed the chairman, "We have been impressed by your ideas, Mr. Fellows, but I think it will be some time before we come up to your expectations. Nevertheless, we have all been pleased to meet you and wish you every success with your career in the future". With that, he stood up and shook David by the hand.

David spent the next few days being quite angry about the time he had wasted on such a group of numbskulls. He even spoke of his interview and feelings to some of the members of staff and students. His work took on a violet look, which some thought was an improvement. About four or five days after the London visit a very important looking envelope was delivered through the door with a BBC motif on the corner. He opened it without any enthusiasm as he felt that the interview was a waste of time and unsuccessful. He read it aloud as if in a mocking voice of the cigar man,

Dear Mr. Fellows,

Thank you for attending the BBC recruiting panel last week. We found your work and your ideas, although a little futuristic, very interesting. We considered that the response you gave to our questioning was excellent and showed a maturity we find quite refreshing in this day and age.

We should like to offer you a position in the BBC as Graphic Designer commencing after you have completed your National Service.   We would like you to contact us approximately three months before your demob when we can discuss your position and salary.

The decision was made by the whole of the interviewing panel.   I do hope that you were not put under too much stress.

We look forward to hearing from you in two years from now,

Yours, etc. etc.

Chapter 41

David remembered that the Spring term of that year, the year of the examinations, the Intermediate just before Easter and the Final in the Autumn, was one of the best periods of his life. He enjoyed everything there was to do with art and design and would spend much of his time studying the works of the great painters, designers, etc., although he found some of the more modern styles, such as Cubism hard to understand. He was allowed, as were all the students in that year, to work in any field and locations, within reason, as long as they produced the standard required. He made arrangements to visit two of the cartoonists he had met at the Café Royal and was warmly welcomed by the artists to their studios, one being in the main office just off Fleet Street. This gave him extra pleasure as he was able to meet Janet for lunch and take a stroll up to St. Paul's Cathedral. He was very encouraged by both men and found himself practicing the techniques used by them in some of his work. Most of the other students would laugh and jeer at the results of bright colour and cartoon characters, but the tutor realised that this was something that may be developed in the future. Yes! This was certainly a good period of his life.

The father of one of the boys in the youth club did a lot of voluntary work for the local hospital. He acted as a driver, taking children for appointments or even collecting money to buy toys and games for the children's ward. One Saturday, Janet and himself were invited to go to a party at this lad's house. During the party he was sitting in an arm chair with Janet sitting on his lap, when the father came and sat by him. He said that he had heard that David was an art student and was particularly good at cartoon characters. David was a little taken aback by this and pointed out that this was only something he had investigated, but not something that he thought he would follow up.

His main study was in design and he hoped that in the future he would be working for the BBC in their scenery department. In fact, it was common knowledge that David had been promised a position at the BBC as he had spread his good news all over the Art School, youth club and neighbourhood. Mr. Broad explained that what he would like to do was to put up a poster sized cartoon painting on some of the blank walls of the children's ward and did he think that he would be able to spare just a little time to do one or two for him. David found that he had fallen for this "hook, line and sinker". He was at the man's house enjoying his beer and Janet, not realising the time concerned said,

"David, that would be super, just imagine how much the children would love seeing cartoon characters on their walls. Those two you do of Mickey Mouse and Donald Duck would look wonderful up on the walls at the hospital".

What could he say? "I will be delighted to do some for you Mr. Broad. I haven't got a lot of time, but I will drop them in to you as soon as I am happy with the result. You see, I am not a cartoonist and it will take me much longer to produce anything that is worth of the hospital walls".

"Don't worry about that", replied Mr. Broad, "anytime will do". He then moved out into the kitchen to do his penance for the evening of pouring out the beer to all the thirsty men.

In addition to the cartoons, which David was obviously going to produce for no payment, he was still doing the paintings of people's houses with the wrought iron gates and the York stone walling at the front. He didn't know how much work Don was getting from this enterprise, but he regularly received his thirty shillings for each completed work. It was only the exception where Don had to let the painting go for a smaller sum. Strangely, no one sent them back, unwanted. Don was still very happy with the arrangement and would come around regularly to either suggest an area he would like to work in or collect another sample.   David was always a little unsure how far he could trust Don, remembering his performance at the tennis court, but as long as he had this income, he wouldn't rock the boat. His paper round still provided him with additional funds although it was hard work getting up so early in the morning, especially in the winter time.

His relationship with Janet was growing into a real love affair.   They would take advantage of any time they could have together and were treated by all as a couple.   Janet even came round to David's house on a Saturday evening and spent the night there, so that they could be early for church on the Sunday morning.   She would sleep in with Susy and would greet David with a nice cup of tea early in the morning, with an added kiss and cuddle.   Nothing could go on more than that as he slept in a bed with Jack and Bobby was in the single bed on the other side of the room.   They spent many evenings at dancing classes and at local dances such as Cheam Baths, Wimbledon Town Hall and Baths and sometimes they would even go as far as Purley to the Orchid Ballroom or Hammersmith to the Palais or the Town Hall.   They both learnt a step in the quickstep which was called the "dicky bird hop", which involved crossing over the legs and then swinging into a hop and a skip at speed down the floor, which they did regularly throughout the dance.   Janet was still only fifteen, but David knew that this was the girl that he would love all his life and he longed for the day when he could ask her to marry him.

It had been announced that the Queen's Coronation was to take part in June of that year.   All the shops and public buildings were getting ready for the big occasion by getting designs for the decorations to deck either their windows or the fronts of their buildings.   It was at that time that Mr. Bailey, the Principal called all the staff and students together for an announcement.   This was very unusual; it was only on rare occasions that he felt it necessary to address the whole of the college.   They gathered in the large weaving room, which held such pleasant memories for David.   Mr. Bailey carried a great deal of respect from all of the students and staff and as he entered the room there was complete silence.   He seemed to create everything he did into a momentous episode and this was no exception.   He walked, or one might say, marched to the front of the room, stepped up onto the platform and turned to face his audience.   For a few moments, which seemed like hours, he stood looking at the ceiling at the far end of the room, then he spoke in a clear and loud voice,

"You will all be aware of the fact that Her Majesty, the Queen is to be crowned in Westminster Abbey in June of this year.   The Council of the Borough of Sutton has decided that they will take charge of the decoration of the High Street and want to make a special feature of the Town Hall.   Mr. Storey, of the Surveyors Office, has contacted me to ask if our Art College would be willing to produce designs for the decoration of the front of the Town Hall and after the winning entry has been chosen, for the whole college to make and help set up the decorations.   This is, indeed, a great honour and I was happy, on your behalf, to accept the challenge.   This will mean a lot of extra work for you all, but I have sought permission for the designs and the manufacture of the display to be part of your submission for examination purposes.   I think we can all be congratulated on receiving such an honour and I will personally take charge of the organisation of this project.   I will meet each group separately to discuss their role, but in the meantime I would be most pleased if you would all start thinking of how we can make this a great success.   Thank you".

He stood for a moment looking straight ahead of him through his pebble glasses, then he stepped down from the platform and marched from the room with his steel tips on his heels resounding all the way back to his office.   For the next few weeks the college was a hive of industry.   Some of the more senior students were making designs, some with flags, some with banners, some of bright colours and some of warm and pleasant colours.   At the same time, work was going on for the very important exams to be held near the end of that term. Much of the work had been accumulating over the whole year, but there were sections that required students to sit in examination conditions and produce a master piece in a regulated period of time, such as lettering, life drawing, lino-cut, or lithography design and clay modelling, which had to be cast in plaster. The practice for all these exams plus the year's work in painting and drawing added to the work on the designs for the Town Hall on top of Don's paintings, the cartoons for Mr. Broad, at the hospital and David's paper round filled up nearly every minute of every day. The youth club, church and most important, Janet, had to be fitted into the evenings and weekends. This was indeed a very busy time, but David had never enjoyed himself as much in all of his life. Everything was looking extremely rosy.

The beginning of the exams came halfway through the term when they were all given a slab of clay and an area of the basement to work and presented with the examination request: To create a model which depicts, "Intimate Friendship". David sat for a while thinking what this would mean to him and of course his immediate thought was of himself and Janet. He also considered that this model must be cast in plaster at the end and the best and easiest way of doing this was to make the base as large as possible. He decided that if he could build a young boy and girl kissing, with their arms around each other in the kneeling position he would have the narrowest part at the top and the widest part at the bottom this being the ideal shape for casting. The subject lent itself to his technique and it was not long before he was shaping the arms, legs and faces. The finished product pleased him immensely and he left the basement pleased with his efforts. The next day he cast the model in plaster and left it in its mould, overnight to completely set. Many of the other students had not studied the art of casting in plaster and were struggling to complete the task. David, already satisfied with his work set to and began to help, as much as he could with the problems of the other students, partly due to the fact that they had standing models and the channel for pouring the plaster was too narrow to take the thickening fluid. It took several evenings before all were complete and the other students were delighted with the work that David had put in.

The lettering went well as most of his work he did free hand and without too much time being wasted on guidelines. He had begun in the traditional way, but found that the spacing was not pleasing on the eye, so in the end he abandoned the two hours he had spent on the original piece and went for the free style which gave him much more flowing lines and the freedom to whip the ends of lines round in broad sweeps. The requirement for the lino-cut design was a "Circus Scene". David placed a clown at the centre of the design which would be easy to cut and left all the detail of the crowd and animals to be shown only in outline. The final part was the Life Drawing to be completed under strict examination conditions the next day. He was quite happy with this as in art nobody can copy and his drawing had come on so well over the past two terms that he knew that he would produce several pieces of work out of which he could choose the best.

How good life was. He was going into a profession which he knew would be fulfilling, he knew that he could cope with all the requirements, he was pretty sure that his work was good enough to get him through any examination and he knew that he had a loving girlfriend whom he adored. The world, indeed, was a bed of roses!

Chapter 42

David rose earlier than usual the next morning. For some reason he had had a disturbed night and lay awake waiting for the light to come through the window and time to get up. He had never done this before, he could always sleep until either the alarm went off or when Mum would bang on the wall shouting his name. He staggered to the kitchen where he washed quickly and set about eating a couple of pieces of toast and drinking a cup of hot tea which Mum had prepared. He struggled to complete his paper round in a bit of a daze and after another cup of tea with the family, dressed in his college gear, corduroy trousers and a dark blue shirt and went off with his box of pencils, brushes, to catch the bus. This was the last of the examinations as such, and although it held a significant part in the overall checking of the student's ability, by this time most were quite aware of their capacity by this period in their training. David was quite looking forward to the challenge and knew that his drawing was considered to be above the average and, the most important of all, satisfying to himself.

As he entered the Life Drawing room he noticed a strange quietness and the whole room seemed to be tidy, which was quite unusual. All the students were busy preparing their paper and drawing materials some with easels, some with support chairs. Mr. Petersen was fussing around the room doing nothing really but just keeping himself occupied. At five minutes to ten the model, a rather well built woman with arms and legs giving the appearance that she had, at one time, been a builder emerged from the cubicle and stepped up onto the raised dais. Mr. Petersen took only a few moments arranging her pose and just checking with the surrounding group of students that they were satisfied with the position, then he pulled out a piece of paper from his inside pocket of his favourite corduroy jacket and read out the rules and regulations of the examination.   At the end he was greeted with a cheer and   a round of applause to which he did a Shakespearian low bow.   This was followed by a short period of silence, then the clicking and shuffling of pencils and brushes.   The exam had begun.

It was only after about ten minutes that David noticed a strange phenomenon.   Although he was able to see the model quite clearly, she appeared as if she was a flat picture on a piece of paper.   He tried to create some form to his drawing, but could not see any depth on the model.   He closed his left eye and saw the model as one would with one eye, but when he closed his right eye the model had disappeared. He looked towards the window and the model reappeared, but when he looked back towards the model she again disappeared.   He went on for some time struggling to produce some sort of drawing, but the form required was not there.   He sat for some time doing nothing, which is not unusual with art students when they are thinking, and pondered the situation.   He tried rubbing his left eye, but to no avail. He tried blinking rapidly hoping that the lid may clear the blockage, but again, with no improvement.   Finally he decided that he must report his problem,

"I can't see the model Mr. Petersen," announced David.

"Well move yourself into a position where you can, Fellows"

"I can see the model", replied David, "but I can't see any perspective".

"Do remember", said Mr. Petersen, "this is an examination and one of the rules is that there is no talking. So be quiet, Fellows, and get on with your work".

There was a round of subdued laughter from the rest of the students with mock jeering at Mr. Petersen for his authoritarianism. This soon settled down and tranquillity was restored, except in David's mind. Another ten minutes passed with no improvement and by now David was becoming extremely stressed. He shuffled with his paper and pencils and tried drawing with his left eye closed. The results were appalling, and he knew it. He spoke up again,

"I can't see the shape of the model, she appears flat to me".

There was a roar of laughter and nearly all the students put down their drawing materials and began to make comments about the model and how well she was endowed. Mr. Petersen told them all to be quiet and settle down he said,

"If there are any more comic remarks like that Fellows, I will have to ask you to leave the examination".

He was obviously becoming extremely angry and felt that someone was disrupting his exam and testing his authority.   This was quite untrue as David had a great respect for the tutor who had more of less saved him from expulsion and encouraged him in every aspect of study.   Perhaps he had expressed his problem in an unfortunate manner, but what he had said was true.   He waited another five minutes or so and then said,

"If I close my right eye the model disappears and if I close my left eye she reappears".

Again there was a roar of laughter.   All the students knew that David had been a bit of a wag all the way through his art education and pushed authority to its limits, but even they thought that this was testing the water too much and Mr. Petersen would have to do something about it.

"I can't accept these interruptions to a very important examination, so I must ask you, Fellows, to leave the room.   If you feel after a little thought that you wish to continue with the exam you may return, but no extra time can be given at the end".

There was a gasp from the rest of the class as David got up from his chair and with his head drooped forwards left the room. He closed the door quietly behind him and stood for a long time in the corridor. To his horror, he heard the steel tips of Mr. Bailey's shoes coming in through the front door, up the stairs and along the top corridor. He stopped about three yards from David and said,

"What are you doing out here, Fellows, shouldn't you be in the Life Drawing Examination?"

"Yes sir, but I am having some trouble seeing the model and Mr. Petersen, quite rightly, sent me out as I was interrupting the exam".

David expected a sharp response from Mr. Bailey, who was really quite strict when it came to discipline. Instead he said,

"Come along to my room, Fellows, and tell me what the problem is".

Instead of his usual practice of striding ahead and into his room he walked at the side of David and opening the door directed him to a chair. Instead of walking around his desk and sitting in his swivel armchair he sat in a chair just in front of David. At that moment the younger secretary came into the room and said that his first appointment was sitting in their office and could she bring him in.

"No, ask him to wait".

She left the room, but was almost immediately followed by the older secretary coming in and trying to gain Mr. Bailey's attention. Politely he said,
"Please leave the room and tell my appointment to wait. I do not want to be disturbed. I will let you know when I am free". She left

the room in a bit of a flap. "Now David", he said, he had never called him by his Christian name before, "what seems to be the problem?"

David tried to explain the strange thing that had happened to his sight. He said that he could see normally with his right eye, but there seemed to be a patch in the middle of his left eye which moved with the eye and stopped him looking at anything although before he looked at them they seemed visible. He knew that this sounded completely muddled and incomprehensible and expected Mr. Bailey to ask him to pull himself together and get on with his examination. He didn't. He sat and thought for a while, then placing his hand on David's he said,

"We must get this sorted out immediately".

He went over to his desk and sat in his favourite chair. His door opened again and glancing up he said,

"Go away".

He then started to write on the pad in front of him. After about ten minutes, which seemed like an hour to David, he carefully folded the paper and slipped it into a long beige envelope.

"I want you to take this letter to your doctor as soon as possible, on the way home would be advisable and don't leave his surgery until he does something about it".

"What about the examination?" asked David, "Can't I just go back for a short time and try to complete some sort of drawing which could be submitted. I don't think that an hour will make that much difference".

"Dear boy!", exclaimed Mr. Bailey, "You can come and take the examination whenever you like, even in a year if necessary, but your health comes first and my chief concern is to get you checked over by your doctor, by the way what is his name?"

"Doctor Barns", replied David.

As David left the office Mr. Bailey drew his attention,

"David, good luck".

David spent some time on the bus admiring the writing of Mr. Bailey. Everything he did seemed to be clear and precise and not unexpectedly, his writing was perfect. Dr. Barns, on the front of the envelope, looked as if it had been produced for the cover of a book and equally matched the beautiful hand of Miss Saleen, the calligraphy tutor. By alighting from the bus one stop earlier he could actually pass the surgery of his doctor and thought that it would be a good plan to drop it in. The surgery was full of sick people young and old so he decided to knock on the front door. Mrs. Barns, a rather stern figure of a woman, well dressed but very sharp in her manner, asked him what he wanted. He explained about the note from his Principal and handed it to her. She explained that Dr. Barns was busy with his surgery and could not be interrupted. David said,

"Mr. Bailey said that it was imperative that Dr. Barns saw the note immediately".

"Oh did he?" Replied Mrs. Barns sarcastically. "Then you will have to wait until after his surgery".

Luckily, at that moment the door of the hall opened and Dr. Barns, a young man who had just taken over the practice, came into the hall with some samples to hand to his wife.

"Is there a problem?" he asked.

Mrs. Barns explained the situation and the request of the Principal.

Dr. Barns took the letter and opened it on the spot.   He took some minutes to read through its contents and then said,

"Come through into the surgery, I want to have a look into your eye".

After a very brief examination and a few relevant questions, he sat down at his desk and wrote another letter, which he sealed into a brown envelope and handed to David.

"I want you to take this to The Charing Cross Hospital, which is just off the Strand, in London, as soon as possible.   In fact, if you could quickly go home and tell your parents, or even get one of them to go with you. That would be the best solution.   I will keep this letter from your Principal not only as a reference, but as something to frame and hang on a wall.   The lettering is beautiful and his knowledge of medicine is incredible.   Now go quickly and let me know how you get on".

David began to be a little more worried now.   This urgency by two people of whom he valued the opinion, was a little disconcerting.   As he walked up past the shops he thought it may be better that he didn't tell his mother quite yet.   They all thought that he was taking an exam and would not be worried if he was a little late home.   He saw the 151 bus coming up to the shopping centre which he boarded.   He knew that The Strand was on the Northern Line of the tube from Morden and he was sure it would be no problem to find the hospital.   He could even ask the way if necessary.   It actually turned out to be a little more difficult than he imagined.   It was up a side road almost opposite Charing Cross Station and what with his eye playing up, finding street signs was not easy.

Not knowing too much about hospitals, the only time he had been in one was during the war when he bit his tongue in half. He saw a sign which said 'Casualty'. He entered and went up to the desk. There were several people in front of him some with bandages around their head, arms or legs, some carrying large plaster casts and even one on wooden crutches. When he reached the desk he was greeted by a miserable looking lady who didn't look up.

"Yes, what can I do for you?"

David handed her the note from the doctor and waited for her to read it, then she said,

"You're in the wrong department, you must go to Outpatients".

She handed him back the letter and said,

"Next".

After wandering around the corridors for some time David came across the sign he was looking for. He went up to the desk and handed in the letter. Again, the lady behind the desk read the letter, put it on to a large pile and told him to go and sit on the chairs in the waiting area. He waited there for what seemed hours. He was beginning to think that he should have gone home first as nobody knew where he was and it was now getting a little late. It was when he was about to go up to the desk again to see if they had forgotten him, when a young lady in a white coat came out of one of the cubicles and called his name. She was very pleasant and asked him to go through the story of when he first noticed the problem and how it manifested itself. She then spent some time looking into his eye with a bright light and then told him to strip down to his underpants. Oh how he wished he had taken Mum's advice and put on a clean pair. She always said,

"Always change your underwear; you never know when you will have an accident".

The lady seemed to be too young to be a doctor and he was mildly embarrassed when she ran her hands up and down each of his legs and arms. She tested his muscles and balance and then started listening to his heart and lungs with her stethoscope. Finally she took a sample of his blood and urine and after telling him that she would return soon, disappeared behind the curtain. This seemed a very strange and old hospital, he could see through the windows a series of spiral metal stairs crossing the view which seemed to look out onto a central well made up of off white bricks. It was a good half an hour before the young lady doctor returned, but this time she had two men with her, both dressed in white coats. The older man, with greying hair, just nodded to David as he entered, he put the notes on a table by the wall and just read. The other younger man came over to David,

"We have been asked by Dr. Green to take a look at you and her findings, I hope you don't mind?

He then took out what looked like a truncheon with a light on the end and asked to look into David's eye. It was very strange having a man's face so close to his, he could even feel his breath on the side of his cheek. He then asked David if he had fallen and hit his head at any time in the past. Then he felt all over his head and his neck checking the pulse as he went. He moved back to the elder man who had not looked up from the notes and they were joined by the lady doctor. They talked for a long time before the elder doctor came over to the plinth where David was lying.

"Hello Mr. Fellows. My name is Mr. Edwards. I am the senior consultant for the Outpatients Department". He paused for a moment looking down to the notes in his hands. Then he said,

"We are not too happy about this blurring that you have in your left eye. We are not sure what could be causing it, but it certainly needs further investigation".

"But it's only a slight blurring on one eye, couldn't it be that I have got something in my eye, or perhaps I have been drawing too much and my eye is tired".

"That could be so", said Mr. Edwards, "but there are many other things that it could be and we feel that you must come into hospital to have it checked".

"When?" asked David, "you see I am in the middle of some important examinations".

"No, I don't think you understand, this could be something serious or it may be nothing, but we can't take the chance. I would like you to be admitted to one of our wards this evening as soon as a bed becomes free".

"Sorry, I can't do that", said David in a bit of a panic, "you see I haven't told anyone I am here and my home is at least an hour and a half's journey away".

"Oh well, I'll leave that to you", so saying, he turned and walked out of the cubicle.

The younger male doctor came over to David and the lady doctor stood just behind and to his side. He seemed very pleasant and sat on the side of the plinth.

"Mr. Fellows, it is rather important that we start our investigation as soon as possible. I beg you to think again about staying in here now. Don't worry about letting your parents know, we have your address and they can easily be informed. I see that they haven't got a phone, but do you know of any neighbours that may have one?"

David shook his head. The only person he could think of was the curate at the church and he certainly didn't want to worry him about a minor issue like this. What was he to do? They obviously wanted him to stay and it sounded as if they felt that it was quite important, but if he did stay they would either let his mum know by telegram or by a policeman coming to the door. He knew in either case his mum always said that a telegram is always bad news and a policeman coming to the door means there has been a death in the family.

Whichever they chose, he knew Mum would faint on the doorstep.

Chapter 43

With a little more persuasion from the two doctors, David realised that to stay in the hospital was the only choice he could make. He was moved to a trolley like bed and covered by a thin sheet and blanket. His clothes were folded up and slipped inside a large brown paper bag and what money he had and the contents of his trouser pockets were sealed in a thick brown envelope and placed under the trolley. After lying in a corridor for some time a large monster of a man, who must have been a wrestler at some time, came up to the side of the trolley.

"Meester Fallow?" he asked.

"That is correct", said David.

"To S 6, O.K?"

He then kicked the bottom of the trolley, which seemed to release the brake and away they went at hair raising speed. David was travelling backwards and only looking up at the ceiling so he had no idea where he was going. All above his head seemed to be lined with pipes of all sizes which, he was certain, had never seen a coat of paint or even a cleaning mop. They seemed to be travelling through a series of dungeons until finally arriving at a lift. The porter, for that was what David assumed the giant was, slammed the gates open with a crash and shoved the trolley in, managing to hit the head of the trolley against the back wall. After slamming the doors closed with another enormous crash, the lift struggled to lift its passengers out of the mire of the basement. When the gates were thrown open again, they were in an area between two sets of double doors. The porter swung the trolley to the right and pushed open the doors with the front of the trolley. They were met by a very official looking lady dressed in a dark blue uniform and a white hat. All her hair had been pushed up under the hat which gave her a very severe look. The porter handed her David's file, turned and left. He had said nothing through the whole of the journey which most probably was due to the fact that he was not English. The lady in dark blue, whom David assumed was the sister of the ward, also said nothing but disappeared into her office.

David lay there for a good half an hour before two young female nurses came up to the side of the trolley.

"David Fellows?"

"Yes", David answered suspiciously. He wondered whether this was some sort of test, to keep asking his name to see if he had changed it on the way. The two nurses pushed his trolley to the far end of the ward passing all sorts of frightening sights of patients lying with tubes going in and coming out of everywhere in their bodies. One patient was even half lying in a tent like affair and he was making some horrible gurgling sounds. The trolley finally came to rest alongside an empty bed beautifully laid out with crisp white sheets pulled back ready for him to get in. He was quite surprised when the nurses, who were quite young, helped him to transfer from the trolley to the bed as David was only wearing his underpants. They tucked him in and one said that she would return later to take down his history. Strange, thought David, I have given it to two people already and he was sure it must have been in his notes. The two nurses walked off down the ward. They were both very attractive in their nurse's uniform, but one of them had the clearest blue eyes he had ever seen. It was strange, also, how so few words were spoken either to him or to each other. He hoped that he hadn't entered some sort of convent where inmates were not allowed to speak to each other.

"What's your problem, chum", came a cheery voice from the next bed.

David turned his head to see that the occupant was leaning out on his side and resting on the locker between them.

"I don't know", David replied, "I seem to have something wrong with one of my eyes, it seems to have become a bit blurred, that's all"

"Oh, they will soon sort that out. Nowadays they can just take them out and scrape them and put them back. It's quite a simple job. I'm Ricky Walsh, but I'm known by all as Mac, because I own a wet fish shop up Brixton High Street. What's you name?"

"David Fellows", replied David.

"Well Dave, it's good to know you. I've been in here for ages now, about two weeks, and I know my way around and all the routines, if you want to know anything, just let me know. I have got a very rare disease which all the doctors are interested in which I think they called sycodosis. I think they are only keeping me here so that they can all have a look. If you looked into my eyes you could see, well not from there, knobs of something which they can't identify. I get all the top brass come to see me, I'm glad it's not something ordinary".

David listened intensely for a while, but after about half an hour of telling about his condition, Mac went on to telling him all about all the other patients in the ward. David could feel his eyes closing, but struggled to stay awake. He was quite relieved when the large doors opened at the end of the ward and masses of people came swarming in and rushing along to the bed their relative occupied. Mac had two visitors which David assumed were his wife and young daughter. Mac introduced them and they both shouted,

"Watcha", and smiled.

David waved back and smiled, then he turned on his side and decided to have a doze while the visiting hour was on. He knew he wouldn't get any visitors as he wasn't sure whether they knew, at home, where he was. He kept thinking of poor Mum either getting a telegram or having a policeman knock at the front door. If only he could tell her that it wasn't anything important, only a blurring of one eye, and as Mac had said, they could take them out and clean them if necessary. He wondered how he would let the Art College know what had happened and what would happen about his final entry not being complete. How thoughtful Mr. Bailey had been. David realised that he had not seen him in a true light all the time he had been there, Donna had seen the quality of the man and had shown how much more mature she was than himself in worldly affairs. Oh Lord! How would Janet take it and how would she get to know where he was? She had been particularly loving over the past few weeks, but because he had been so busy with the examinations etc., he had had little time to take advantage of this warm period. She had persuaded him to do some posters for a bazaar, which they were going to hold at the youth club. He had managed to do two of them but had run out of time. His real worry about being stuck up here in hospital was that he would miss the youth club meeting tomorrow and would also miss the very happy couple of hours with Janet and the most enjoyable walk back to her home.

He must have drifted off to sleep because when he opened his eyes he could see that it had become quite dark outside and all the visitors had left the ward. He also noticed that on his locker, at the side of his bed, was a big bowl of all types of fruit. He raised himself on one arm so that he could see Mac. He had an awful feeling that perhaps he had had some visitors and they had left because he was asleep. He leant over the side of the bed and attracted Mac's attention. He was reading a book and was obviously enjoying it.

"Mac", David whispered, trying not to disturb the other patients in the ward, many of whom where either snoring, groaning or calling out for the nurse. There was no response from Mac who was chuckling away at something in his book.

"Mac" and then louder, "Mac".

He put down his book and turned to David.

"Oh, so you've finally woken up. The nurse has been along to you several times but I told her to go away and let you sleep on. Can I help you?"

"Yes, I wondered if I had had any visitors while I was asleep and they had not wanted to wake me up?"

"No, I'm afraid not chum, I don't suppose they've had time to get up here this evening, I expect they will come tomorrow afternoon".

"Who brought the bowl of fruit then?" asked David.

"That's easy to answer. I went round to all the other patients who had been brought too much fruit and asked for contributions to the new young fellow at the end of the ward. Most of them were pleased to get rid of some of the grapes. I reckon that visitors think that grapes are a cure for every disease there is. The only thing they actually do is to make all the old boys that can't get to the lavatories make a mess in their beds and give the poor nurses more clearing up".

Mac passed David a magazine to read, but David found that it was a "girly" book full of young ladies in scanty clothes and in provocative poses. How different they were to the models in the Life Class at the Art College. Was it only this morning that he was sitting with all of his friends in an examination. How much had happened in such a short time and how his situation had now changed. He looked across the ward to where the toilets were and with his right eye could see the number 55 on an enamel disc on the door. When he closed his right eye and looked with his left the number and disc disappeared. In fact he could only see part of the door. He hoped it would only be a short job to clean off the blurred patch from his left eye and get him back to normal. At his last visit to the opticians before he went for his medical for the forces, the optician had said that he had extremely good vision and just the type that was needed for flying aircraft. This was something David had set his mind on doing. His thoughts were interrupted by the sister of the ward coming up to the bed and saying,

"You have two visitors. It is highly irregular for me to let anyone in to the ward at this time of night, but they said that they have travelled a long way. They can only stay for ten minutes, then I must insist that they leave and come in the official visiting time".

She walked back down the ward and the large doors were opened and Mum and Jack came rushing up the ward towards him. Mum immediately put her arms around his neck and started crying, Jack just stood back and watched. After a few moments Mum sat back into a chair at the side of the bed and said,

"The sister said that we have only got ten minutes. I have brought you some pyjamas and a tooth brush and paste. We didn't know what you needed but if there is anything let us know and we will bring it next time".

Jack came over and took David's hand, It wasn't a hand shake, he just held it with a firm grip.

"They haven't told us anything about what is wrong with you, have they said anything to you? Jack asked.

"No, all I know is that they were quite insistent that I stayed here rather than go home and come back later. How did you get to know that I was in here?

"A policeman came to the door and told us that you had been taken into the Charing Cross Hospital and we should get up there as soon as possible. Of course, Mum fainted and it took us some time to get her recovered enough to think of making the journey. Dad said that he would stay at home to keep an eye on Bobby and Susy and as I knew my way around London I should go with Mum".

The ten minutes passed very quickly and the sister returned to the bed side and said that they must go. She stood there to make sure that they began to move. Mum gave David a great hug and Jack let go of his hand. As they turned to walk away Mum suddenly came back and said,

"Oh, I forgot, we bought you a bunch of grapes", and with that she pulled out, from her bag, a large bunch of black grapes. As they walked down the ward Mac shouted out to them,

"Don't worry about Dave, I'll keep an eye on him".

David only hoped that Mum or Jack didn't see the magazine that Mac had lent him which was lying open at the bottom of the bed. The next morning David was shaken from his sleep by the pretty nurse, who presented him with an enamel bowl of hot water, a bar of soap and a towel.

"Now I want you to wash yourself all over, and I mean all over. Any parts you can't get to I will do for you. I will be back in a while to collect the bowl, O.K?"

David saw a slight smile in these lovely eyes and he wondered how a young lady like this had such a commanding way. She reminded him very much of Donna in her ways and her ability to command. David did as he was told and covered all the parts that he was sure he didn't want the nurse to inspect and after combing his hair with the comb which Mac had lent him, which he swore was clean, he felt able to face the world. Breakfast was served by the nurses under the sister's supervision, and he was offered extra helpings as some of the patients found it difficult to eat the quantity allocated. About ten o'clock a porter arrived to take David down to a clinic of some sorts. There he went through the embarrassment of having young men and women lying across him and looking into his eyes with the light on the end of a stick, blood being drained from his arm, a young man inspecting his genitalia and thighs, having tuning forks placed on his skull, a young lady sticking pins into his legs and arms and someone trying to beat him at arm and leg wrestling. All in all, at the end of the morning he was worn out and to add to it all, when he arrived back at the ward dinner had gone. When he told Mac of his ordeal he seriously thought that he should complain. He said,

"You did know, Dave, didn't you that this is a teaching hospital and we are really only here for the students to learn. They will keep you here as long as they are interested in what they think is wrong with you. After that, it's home you go whether you are better or not. There's another thing you've got to watch out for. You'll notice that at the sister's office end of the ward they keep all the very ill patients. Each morning we take note of any empty beds that were full the night before. Sometimes during the night they put the screens around a bed and next day the patient has disappeared. One night I went to the toilet down that end and saw two porters wheeling out a trolley with a patient on it but his head was covered with a sheet".

David listened with horror to the stories that Mac told. He was a very bright man and knew his way around in the world, it was, David supposed, due to the type of job he did.

"Watch out", said Mac, "that they don't go moving you down the ward. They tried to move me once but I was having none of it. I said if you think you are going to move me down to the dead area you've got another think coming. They put me back up here".

That afternoon the porter returned with his trolley. Mac gave him a bit of a hard time suggesting all the things that might happen to him if he was treated as badly as he was in the morning. David smiled to himself as he was driven through the basement at high speed, as this was the porter that brought him in the first place and he knew could speak no English. This time, however, he stayed in the basement and went into a room which seemed to be full of gadgets. There was only one person there, whom David assumed was a doctor. He asked David to lie on a table which felt more like a slab of marble. Under his head he placed a very hard pillow, which felt as if it were made of wood. The man stuck electrodes all over his head and connected them up to what looked like one of the largest refrigerators he had ever seen. He was then told to lay absolutely still and relax. A large headlight was then placed in front of his face. The operator, who didn't say who or what he was then said,

"I am going to switch on the light in front of your face, first of all slowly and then rapidly. I want you first of all to only open your right eye. I want you to lay perfectly still as I don't want any more brain activity than that coming from your eyes. Do you understand?"

Could the spies being interrogated in Germany have gone through anything like this? He was looking into a bright light with one eye which began to go on and off. This grew more rapid until David couldn't tell whether it was on or off. After what seemed like an eternity, the man gave him a minute to relax and then started the same routine with the left eye open. This didn't seem so bad, since if David looked straight at the light the centre of it disappeared. He didn't know how long he was there, but he left aching from top to toe. This time he arrived back at the ward too late for tea, but the pretty nurse said that they would send down to the kitchen for something for him to eat. He yearned for seven thirty to come when he may have some visitors. The doors opened bang on time and first through the door came Janet with Mum a good second. Janet threw her arms around his neck and gave him one of the warmest kisses ever. It was sometime before he recovered to say hello to Mum. Janet had been at work all day so she only had to come along Fleet Street and then the Strand to get to the hospital. Mum had come all the way up on her own and David was so proud of her, the shops at Tooting and Gran's was about as far as Mum would normally go solo. His pile of grapes grew larger and larger.

More and more tests were carried out and there seemed to be an endless queue of students and doctors coming to look into his eyes. David found it very embarrassing having the younger female doctors and students leaning over him and looking into his eyes. He wasn't confined to bed so they usually just asked him to sit up on his bed. Only wearing pyjamas and the closeness of their faces and their bodies as they were studying the inside of his eyes made him react as a young man of seventeen would and he spent most of his time trying to think of more mundane subjects.   It became even more embarrassing on that second afternoon when he arrived back from another eye clinic. Mac said because he was able to walk around the ward, the pretty nurse had asked if he could, on his return, help to fold some of the sheets and blankets that had been returned from the laundry. David went over to the laundry room and offered his help. They folded the sheets lengthwise in four and then walked together so that she could take both ends.   She finally folded the last section up against her bosom pulling David's hands up against her. This was, of course too much for David and he felt himself coming up against the crisp white apron. She did this several times and seemed to enjoy the close contact and the effect she was having on him. After the final sheet was folded she held herself tight against him for a full half minute and looking up into his blushing face, flashed her beautiful eyes and said,

"Naughty, naughty!"

She moved away quickly as if nothing had happened and he was left standing for a while not daring to walk back into the ward until his ardour had reduced.

The next week was spent going from one department to another. He went back to the torture chamber once more and had the same tests done that he had endured the week before. The man in charge was much more communicative this time and even showed him some of the results of the multi-graphic machine. He said that they were looking for interference in some of the pathways from the eyes to the brain and although they could not read it all at the moment, in years to come they may be able to read what he was thinking at the time. David hoped that that would be a long time in the future as some of his thoughts were not very nice and the man wasn't as bad as he thought he was when the light was flashing. Janet and Mum visited as often as they could and they were supported by other members of the family and even the curate from his church. On one of Mum's visits she gave him a small box of chocolates which had been handed to her by two art students that David had helped during the casting process of the clay models in the examination. They had apparently walked all the way from Sutton to his house, which must have been all of five miles as they didn't have enough money for the bus fare. Mum, of course, asked them in and gave them a cup of tea and when it was time to go she gave them enough money for their fares back to Sutton. David was quite touched by this gesture as he didn't know the girls that well and never really gave them a passing glance.

The one very serious occurrence during that week was that David found that the right eye had also developed a blurred patch in the middle, the part they all referred to as the centre of vision. This changed the situation immensely as he was not able to see anything he looked at. This meant that when people arrived at the bedside he would look at them and they would disappear. Only when he looked to the side was he aware that someone was there and when he looked to see who they were, they disappeared. He looked at the book that

Mac had lent him and found that he couldn't see anything on the pages, either pictures or print although if he looked above the book he could see that there was a book in his hands, but he could not recognise it. When his right eye could see normally he just felt that the blurring of the left eye was an inconvenience, but now with the centre of two eyes the same he was absolutely lost. When he reported this development to the sister, he was bombarded with doctors and students clambering to look inside both eyes and getting together in groups to discuss their findings

On the second Monday Mr. Edwards did his weekly ward round. The group following him was enormous. There was the sister, two registrars, a house man, a physiotherapist, about ten final year student doctors and two nurses.

At each bed they pulled the screens down either side and left the entrance to the centre of the ward open. All David's results and notes were laid out on the table over the end of the bed with the students lining either side of the bed. Mr. Edwards stood for a long time reading the notes and looking at the results of the torture chamber. He then began to ask questions of the two registrars, then all three and the sister and houseman got into a huddle and obviously discussed the results. Finally, Mr. Edwards came down the side of the bed to speak to David,

"I am very sorry to hear about your right eye becoming blurred, it was something we hoped would not occur. We have all looked at your results and are disturbed to find that this problem seems to be progressing quite fast. We feel that there is no option other than for us to take a look inside and see what is going on. I'll be quite honest, we think there is something growing larger in part of your brain and may be pressing on the optic nerve. As it is the centre of vision of both eyes, we have a good idea where it might be. It will involve taking you down to the operating theatre and taking out a small spy hole in you skull. This will give us a chance to look inside. You

409

will know nothing of all this as you will be fast asleep and when you wake up you will be back here in your bed. Will one of your parents be coming to see you this evening?

"Yes, my mother", replied David.

"Then if the sister would ring me I would like to have a word with her, if that is alright with you? I will only tell her what I have told you, but I would like one of your family to know what is going on".

"When are you thinking that you will be able to do this operation" asked David.

"Tomorrow morning, depending on what is already on the list. Is that O.K.?

David was taken by surprise by the lack of options he had. He had no idea what they were going to do, but to him cutting a hole in his skull seemed a bit drastic. "Well if there is no alternative, I suppose you must go ahead".

Chapter 44

That evening Mum and Janet came to visit him. Luckily, because of the distance that Mum had to travel, she always came quite early and waited outside the ward. The sister, seeing her sitting there, had phoned Mr. Edwards and he came up to the ward immediately. They went into the sister's office and he explained what had occurred and how he thought they should progress. He must have explained the situation a little more fully to her, because by the time she entered the ward, on the official visiting hour, she had obviously been crying quite a lot, for her eyes were watery and red and her voice was slightly muffled as if she was trying to hold her tears back. David said that he knew what was going to happen to him as Mr. Edwards had explained it all, but he wasn't too happy about the hole being drilled in his skull. It seemed to be a more prolonged goodbye that evening and both Mum and Janet hugged and kissed him more than usual, which was actually very pleasant.

About nine thirty the same evening a young male medical student came to his bed. He explained that he was very close to taking his final examinations and would be very pleased if he could spend just a few minutes talking about David's eye condition and take a detailed history. He thought that it would be of great interest and help to him, although it might be a bit of a waste of time for David as he had gone through all of the questions before. David was quite pleased to take part in this history taking as it took his mind off the operation which was going to be performed the next day. Although he gave everybody the impression that he wasn't really worried about the procedure, he was in actual fact really quite nervous about the whole venture. Michael Buchannan, as the student introduced himself, was an extremely pleasant young man with thick horn rimmed spectacles, thick curly black hair and a warm, well educated voice. He was

411

wearing a very smart looking suit with matching tie and shirt. He ran through a long list of questions that he had obviously planned in advance. Most of the questions were well known to David as he had answered them before many times, but on occasions he would interpose a new question that seemed to have nothing to do with the diagnosis. After a while he approached the history of David's family and asked many questions about uncles, aunts, cousins, grandparents and even great grandparents. David knew very little about his grandparents or great grandparents as he didn't get on with one group and the others were long gone. Michael must have spent a good hour with David going over the history time and time again, eventually summing up the facts in an understandable order. He seemed very interested in just one aspect and kept going over it again and again.

"You say that you think that an uncle of yours may have had bad sight at some time and you have some recollection of another uncle that may have had a similar problem?"

"Yes, the only problem is that I have no idea where they might be as the family had some sort of break up and we haven't been in touch for many years. I do remember that my uncle Barry and aunt Jane used to buy me a book at Christmas time, but they found it difficult reading it to me, but that must have been just after the war."

Michael wrote this all down and as he was about to leave, he said,

"I would like to have given this information to Mr. Edwards, but it is a bit late in the day to phone him, I will have to let him know on the ward round before he starts his operation list. You have been told, haven't you that you cannot have anything to eat until after your operation?"

"Yes", replied David.

412

Michael stood up, picked up all his notes, slipped them into a thin black briefcase that he carried under his arm and shook David by the hand. "Thank you for your time and your help. I will see you first thing tomorrow morning". He turned and walked down the ward with his head drooped slightly forward as if he were deep in thought.

The next morning, on the dot of seven thirty, the doors of the ward opened and a host of white coated men and women entered the ward. They were accompanied by the sister dressed in her stiffly starched, dark blue uniform, two nurses dressed in equally starched green and white striped uniforms, one of which was pushing a trolley laden with folders of notes. For the first quarter of an hour they stayed at the far end of the ward around the bed of a man who had only been brought in the night before. The consultant and his registrars stood away from the group for a while, obviously discussing the case. Then they walked the whole length of the ward up to David's bed. The nurses rushed to put the metal screens down either side of the bed and all the white coated entourage moved down both sides of the bed. Mr. Edwards did not look or speak to David; he opened up his notes and stood for about five minutes reading them. The rest of the group stood in absolute silence. He then looked up towards David and said,

"Good morning".

"Good morning", replied David.

Mr. Edwards then moved up the side of the bed with the onlookers slipping backwards just enough for him to pass.

"We have had a good look at all your tests and we feel sure that there is something pressing on your optic nerve. Unfortunately, there is no other way of approaching the area than to make a small hole in your skull. This will give us access to the vital area. As I told you before, you will know nothing of all this as you will be asleep and the next thing you will know is waking up in this bed in this ward. I explained the procedure to your mother last night and she will be here when you come round. Is there anything you want to know about what we are going to do?

"Will you have to shave my hair off?" asked David. He was really worried that Janet would be put off of him if she saw him with no hair.

"Only over the area we are going to operate on. It will soon grow again".

He then turned to the rest of the entourage and said,

"Have you all read through the notes and made yourselves quite familiar with the procedures?"

There were nods of approval as he quickly made his way to the centre of the ward to discuss something with the sister and the registrars. David saw Michael try to speak to him before he walked away, but Mr. Edwards just waved his arm at him and walked on. Michael made his way through the other students to the centre of the ward and stood by the side of the small group, trying to gain their attention. Mr. Edwards waved him away again and they started to walk down the ward with the group in tow. David couldn't see them anymore, but he was told by Mac in the next bet, that Michael tried several times to get to Mr. Edwards but was prevented by the registrars. Finally, Michael rushed ahead and turned to face Mr. Edwards face on. The team stopped and there was a lot of discussion. After a few minutes Mr. Edwards, his two registrars and Michael came back to the side of David's bed.

"This young doctor tells me that you have some relations that you think had bad sight. Is that correct?" asked Mr Edwards.

"Yes" replied David.

"Why did you not tell us this before?" demanded Mr. Edwards in a more hostile voice.

"No one had asked me those questions before and I had no idea that it had anything to do with my blurred vision. It was only when Michael asked me questions about my family that I remembered about my uncles".

Mr. Edwards turned to Michael and asked to see the notes Michael had written. He studied them for a while and then said to him,

"I see that you have made some conclusions based on your findings. Is this based on facts or guesswork?"

"I made a special study of the eye conditions last night after I left David and I would really like to find the uncles that David spoke about and take a look at their eyes".

"You realise the gravity of the situation if you are incorrect and we are delayed in tackling this tumour, How do you anticipate finding one of the uncles at such short notice?"

"I thought that we could put out an appeal on the BBC special announcements just before the news at one o'clock each day. If we phone this through as an emergency, it could go out today, at lunch time", answered Michael.

They all turned away for a while, but this time Michael was included in the discussion. Mr. Edwards then came back to the side of David's bed and said,

"I am going to delay your operation for two days. In the meantime, this young man", pointing to Michael, "will try to contact your uncle.

If he is successful we will proceed from there, otherwise we will go ahead as planned in two days time. Is that acceptable to you?"

"Yes, of course", said David.

Mr. Edwards then placed his hand on David's shoulder and, quite unexpectedly, gave it a squeeze. He then smiled, turned away and walked down the ward with registrars and beaming Michael in tow.

That lunch time, so David was told as they had no radio or earphones in the hospital at that time, an announcement was made just before the one o'clock news,

"Would Mr. Barry Appleby, last heard of in 1945 living in the southeast of London please contact the Charing Cross Hospital, The Strand, London as soon as possible, where his nephew is seriously ill".

At about four o'clock that afternoon David was amazed to be joined by his uncle, who, after shaking David's hand sat down at the side of the bed and explained to David that he had already seen Mr. Edwards and he confirmed that the eye condition is the same as his and therefore they will not be going ahead with the operation. Uncle said,

"We were lucky to hear that broadcast and get here on time as opening up your skull and looking inside is not quite as simple as they make out. I am going down, from here, to have my eyes examined more thoroughly and then they will come to you and explain what is to be done and how they will proceed".

As Uncle got up ready to go, Mum came to the bedside and David was very pleased to see them put their arms around each other and kiss on the cheek. David thought that although this had been quite a harrowing experience for him it looked as if it may have healed the rift in the family and they would most probably see a lot more of

Uncle in the future. Mum had been told the good news about the operation being cancelled and threw her arms around David and gave him an enormous hug even though she was crying at the time. Uncle then took Mum by the hand and they walked to the middle of the ward where they spent a long time chatting. David was not sure whether it was to do with him and the eye condition or about the family and what had happened to members of the family with whom they had lost contact. Eventually, Mum came back to the side of the bed, and although it was not visiting time, sat and talked about what had been going on at home. They were joined by Janet when the doors were opened for visiting time and David was overjoyed to get a very fond cuddle and kiss from this young lady who now meant so much to him. Strangely, he was more worried about losing her love and affection than anything else and it took the tragedy of the blurred vision down to an acceptable level.

The next day he spent hours and hours in the ophthalmic department. He was even seen by doctors from other hospitals, including Moorfield's, and they all shone lights in his eyes and tested him with dots on screens and letters on boards. Each time David looked at the dots or the letters they disappeared, but if he dropped his eyes he could see that something was there. He arrived back at the ward absolutely exhausted and continued to see flashing lights for some time.

That evening he was surprised to see Mr. Edwards at his bedside dressed in his suit and not in a white coat. He pulled up a chair after getting the nurses to wheel the screens up on either side of his bed. He had David's notes in his hand and sat for a few moments just looking through the masses of information that had been gathered. He then turned to David and said,

"The young doctor who came to visit you two evenings ago was absolutely correct with his diagnosis and because of him we decided not to go ahead with the operation. He had made a special study of inherited eye conditions and after taking your history felt that there was sufficient evidence to check on your uncle's eyesight. His suggestion of putting out an appeal on the radio was excellent and the rapid response of your uncle was admirable. We now have to consider your eye condition and your future. Unfortunately, this is a very rare disease and we have no idea of its cause. We know that it runs in families and is carried by the women and shows up in the males. Not all of the women in the family will carry the disease and not all the men will suffer with it. We know that it destroys the cones at the centre of the optic disc which receive the detailed information required for reading and recognising people and objects. The outer vision is normally fairly good and therefore getting around, with care, is possible. Do you understand what I am saying so far?"

David nodded although his mind was in a whirl. Did he mean that this blurring was going to be permanent and how was he going to be able to do his art work and even read the newspaper.

Mr. Edwards continued as if he had been reading David's thoughts. "This condition is permanent, we have never had anyone with the condition who has recovered their centre of vision and it will also prevent you from carrying on with your career in the art world. It will in fact prevent you from doing most jobs and therefore I have no hesitation in contacting your local authority and recommend that you be placed on the blind register. There are people at your local town hall who will contact you and suggest ways in which you can learn to deal with your sight loss and I am sure that they will put you in touch with the National Institute for the Blind who will give you all the help you may need. I am sorry to have to give you such devastating news, but I thought that it would come best from me and not one of my staff. You can arrange to go home tomorrow and I will see that all is set for your follow up.

I am sorry to bring you so much bad news David, but all I can do is to wish you good luck for the future. I will make arrangements to see you in six months time".

He then stood up, placed his hand on David's shoulder, to which he gave a friendly squeeze and then turned and walked out through the gap in the screens.

Chapter 45

The next two or three weeks were an absolute nightmare. He wasn't sure what was going on. He knew that Jack had written to the local authority in Kingston to find out what was the next move, but had had no reply. He wandered from the armchair in the front room to the top step of the front door to try to keep himself active, but spent most of the time thinking of the past, the present and his future. Janet would come around most evenings when she arrived home from work and they would either sit and talk, or head off to the youth club on Thursday and Sunday evenings. The members of the youth club were very supportive and would try to involve him in as many activities as possible, even arranging for him to go with them on a Wednesday evening to a Judo class, which was held at an adult college in Sutton. David had no money and the organisers of the Judo would allow him to borrow a jacket and take part in the evening's tournaments. He was never there when they arranged the progression from one belt to another, so he never moved off the red belt which was really for beginners although he could compete with most of the members of the club. The fact that one doesn't need good sight to take part in judo made David feel equal with the others and because of his acute sense of balance, his fitness and his ability to resist powerful forces, he became quite good at the sport and would enjoy his trips.

As the celebrations for the Coronation of Queen Elizabeth II were developing, he wondered how the art work for the Town Hall in Sutton was progressing and then, on the day, he wondered what it all looked like. He remembered the drawings that they had submitted to the Council and how pleased they all were when their particular design was accepted. They all knew that it would not provide them with any income. Nevertheless, all the materials were going to be provided and their freedom to come and go between the Art School and the Town Hall was very pleasant. David wondered if it had all been finished in time and whether the final result was anything like the plans they had submitted.

He had been very surprised at the very close friendship he had encountered with Polly, the young woman that lived up the road. He had thought that his chances with the opposite sex would have been badly hampered by not being able to see their faces, or make eye to eye contact with them, but it seemed to be quite the reverse. It was the first time he had been so directly approached by a slightly older and more experienced woman. Although his love for Janet was unquestionable and was on a higher plain than this affair, Polly did attract him enormously and the way in which she kissed and used her hands was quite overpowering. Although in his mind he knew that this relationship was wrong he felt very tempted to call on her when he passed her door. He even found himself going out of his way to walk down that part of the street. He knew that his powers of resistance were poor as far as that was concerned and he also wanted to be assured by her that on the last occasion he had not gone further than was safe. He had been so excited by the sheer pleasure she had awarded him that he was unaware of the physical contacts that had been made. Anyway, he put all those thoughts to the back of his mind and said to himself that he would be strong and would not allow himself to be tempted in that way again.

On Friday evening Father Kingswood came round to his house to advise him on the type of clothing he would need for the next day. He pointed out that travelling on the back of a motorbike was always cold even on the warmest of days, so he should put on his thickest coat and perhaps, even slip on a jumper underneath. He said that he had obtained tickets for David to attend the Ordination Ceremony and the dinner that was to follow, so he should be dressed in his suit, with a shirt and tie, which he could have on under the jumper and overcoat. Janet, who had come round for the evening, didn't seem too happy with the thought that David was going all the way to Chichester and back in one day, and showed some signs of apprehension, but as she had a high regard for Father Kingswood said nothing. Mum provided them all with a cup of tea and some homemade cakes and they all chatted about the next day's trip. Jack said that he was quite jealous as he would love to have a ride on this Sunbeam shaft driven motorcycle. He had only just bought an old Matchless which he kept on the pathway outside of the front garden. As the oil would not circulate properly, he had fitted a small tube at the bottom of the crank shaft casing so that the oil could drain out on to the road. Although he knew that it was compietely illegal, he called it his "total loss system" and proudly boasted about it to his friends.

Before David lost his sight Jack would allow him to take the motorbike off its stand, start up the engine and speed around the road which encircled the big green as many times as he could before Jack came out of the house clad in his appropriate gear. He became quite an expert in changing up and down the gears and often imagined that he was taking part in a motorbike rally. Only once did he lose a little control of the bike; that was when some children tried to race across the road in front of him and instead of slamming on the brakes, he turned the throttle up and increased his speed. He was suddenly hit by a panic and immediately slammed on the brakes, skidding to a standstill across the road. From that time on he took much more care and kept his speed down to that required for those small roads. He never told anyone about this near accident, but it remained in his mind for some weeks after.

When David went to the porch for a goodnight kiss and cuddle with Janet, she told him that she was unhappy about not seeing him all day Saturday, but would be round his house early the next evening to welcome him home. She stepped back up on to the top step which raised her just sufficient for David to feel himself slip into the gap at the top of her thighs and although they were obviously still fully clothed, he gained an extremely exciting feeling from the movement.

It was only when Mum rattled the handle of the door that they decided to ease down and let Janet make her way home.

The next morning David was up by six o'clock. Father Kingswood said that he would like to be away by six forty five, so David was sitting on the top step, clothed as required, by twenty to seven. It was a beautiful morning with the sun already shining across the greens and into their front porch. The two oak trees on the small green had just come into bright yellow leaves and the air was full of the singing of the birds. Many of the sparrows would make their way up the garden path quite unworried by David's presence, some even coming up to his feet and pecking at the pathway close to the step. Although David was looking forward to the trip down to Chichester he thought, how lovely it would be if Janet had been there and how much he would have enjoyed a kiss and a cuddle, even at that time in the morning. They had sat there on many occasions secretly slipping a hand or an arm into places that gave them great pleasure and had made secret suggestions to each other of how wonderful it would be if they could lie together with nothing on. This sort of talk would put David on edge and knowing this, Janet would allow her hand to drop on the front of his trousers sending his mind into a complete spin.

His pleasant dreaming was interrupted by the sound of a very powerful motorbike engine and in seconds the machine stopped by the kerb on the other side of the small green. In a couple of minutes David was on the pillion seat of the bike with Jack's glasses covering his eyes and his overcoat buttoned right up to the neck. He was amazed to hear shouts of goodbye emanating from the upstairs windows and he knew that Mum and Dad were at the door waving goodbye. Father Kingswood pulled back on his clutch handle and raised up the gear lever with his foot. With a slight increase in engine speed the Sunbeam pulled away and they slowly drifted down the fairly narrow road in the direction of his old infant school and the main road. David remembered very little of the journey down to Chichester as he spent most of his time holding on for his life and being buffeted by strong winds. He could see nothing of the road in front, but was aware of trees flashing past on either side. He was quite pleased when they passed through some small villages as Father Kingswood reduced his speed giving them time to breathe normally and adjust their bottoms on the seats. On arrival in Chichester they slowed right down and passing over the central crossing of roads came alongside the magnificent cathedral on the left. They pulled into a narrow drive just beyond the tower that stood on its own and the engine was stopped. They entered a gate leading on to a beautiful garden and then through some French doors into a large dining room.

The whole room was bustling with men in cassocks moving around from table to table and there was so much chatter going on that it sounded a little like a bee hive. They were immediately surrounded by masses of clergy all trying to shake Father Kingswood by the hand and bombarding him with questions. David felt completely lost for a while until Father Kingswood introduced him to some of his colleagues. He explained why he had brought David along to the Ordination Ceremony and seemed to be greeted by words of approval. They were taken to two spare seats at one of the bigger tables and a very large breakfast seemed to appear from nowhere. David was amazed by the good humour that seemed to be radiating from all the surrounding "dog-collared" onlookers. Jokes were flying up and down the table followed by roars of laughter.

Later that morning they were all to attend a meeting in the college hall and so Father Kingswood took David outside and took him up to the main road. He explained,

"I am afraid the meeting is only for those who are going to be ordained, so you are free to wander around the town for a few hours. We will then have a reunion lunch, but just across the road from here is a nice restaurant where you will be able to get lunch".

He then slipped two half crowns into David's hand and said,

"That should cover any meal you order.   Be back here at two thirty and make your way into the back of the cathedral.   Here is a ticket which you will need to get your seat.   You will be quite awestruck by the volume of sound when the hymns begin as we have the band of the Grenadier Guards up in the transepts.   Now take care of the roads and I will look out for you after the service.   O.K.?"

As Father Kingswood turned to head back to the college all David could do was nod his acceptance. He wondered whether Father Kingswood had done this purposely or whether he was unaware that he could not see any signs, traffic lights, names of streets or people's faces. What a situation! If he had known that he would be left like this he would never have come and oh how he longed to have Janet at his side to give him the confidence of dealing with several hours wandering around a city completely unknown to him. He remembered that when he was studying at the Art College, one of the subjects was, "The History of Architecture". It was a favourite subject of Mr.Bailey, the Principal. They had studied the architecture of Chichester Cathedral, so David thought that there would be no better place to start than by going back into the building and slowly looking around. First of all he wandered up the side aisles towards the east end.   He then cut across the centre and into the south aisle.   He walked very slowly pretending to look at the stone coffins and the inscriptions just trying to kill as much time as possible.   On arrival back at the west end he was met by a woman David imagined must have been in her forties, clad in a very simple white dress with no sleeves and a hooped neck line.   She had very short blonde hair and was carrying, what looked like, a folder in her hands.

"Good morning.   Can I interest you in becoming a friend of the cathedral?   We need all the support we can get as we've got a massive restoration programme we've embarked on".

Damn thought David, I would bump into someone who wants money or help with collecting money. "I am sorry", he said, "I have only just arrived and have only enough money on me to get lunch".

"Oh don't worry", said the blonde lady, "I was only asking if you would become a friend of the cathedral, it doesn't involve giving any money".

"What does it entail then", asked David.

"Well all you have to do is sign a form filling in your details, address and so on, and we will contact you by post in the next couple of weeks".

She then handed David a form and gave him a pen, showed him to a table and pulled him up a chair.

David sat for about ten minutes wondering what to do. He could see nothing on the piece of paper; he didn't even know which way up it was. He felt an absolute idiot, what had he got himself into? Why hadn't he just wandered down the High Street and pretended to look at the shop windows?

He was about to get up and try to mingle into the groups of people visiting the cathedral, when the lady came back to him and looking over his shoulder said,

"Is something wrong, can I help you?"

"I am sorry", said David, "I can't read your form".

There was a long pause and then the lady said,

"The top line says, name of applicant, so you just have to write your name in there".

"Sorry, I can't see the line and I find it difficult writing my name there".

There was again a long period of silence, and then she said,

"Perhaps it's not a good plan for us to enrol you. We must have people educated enough to at least write their names and addresses".

David suddenly realised that he had given the lady the wrong impression and quickly said,

"Oh, I can read and write O.K., my problem is that I am registered blind and can't see any print".

He stood up and turned to walk away from the table when he felt a sudden tight grip on his forearm.

In an almost pleading voice the lady said,

"I am so sorry. It must have sounded extremely rude saying what I did. I have made such a fool of myself. Please forgive me. My name is Mrs Chandler and my husband is one of the clergy who help with the services in the cathedral. Look, we are serving tea on the back lawn of the college for visitors who are coming to an ordination we are holding this afternoon. Would you like to meet some of the friends?"

"That would be nice", replied David. He thought he would at least have someone to talk to and it may fill in some of the hours he had to spare. Mrs. Chandler took him over to a small camping table nicely set out with a table cloth. He sat down on one of the heavy cast iron chairs which were placed around the table and waited while Mrs. Chandler went off to get him a cup of tea. He didn't like to tell her that he had already had a very substantial breakfast in the hall off the college. She returned after a few minutes with a tray which had two cups of tea and two plates with what looked like homemade scones on it. Now that she was close up and in the sunshine, David realised that she was a very attractive woman and her voice, which was obviously the result of an education at some private school, was soft, clear and very sexy.

"I thought that you would like something to eat with your tea, so I have brought a couple of scones. They are both for you as I am trying to cut down my waistline. I don't seem to be doing too well at the moment, but my intention is right. As David drank the tea and tried to look enthusiastic over the two large, dry scones, Mrs Chandler began to bombard him with questions.

"How long have you been registered blind?"

"Only about a month".

"I am sorry. I don't even know your name".

"David Fellows", replied David.

"It must have been an awful blow to you. How did it happen? Were you in some kind of accident?"

David went on to tell her the sequence of events that had led up to this terrible situation. He explained that he seemed to have lost all of his independence and was passed from one person or situation to another, a bit like a package. He also explained how much freedom he had experienced when he was an art student and gave her a glimpse of the wonderful life he had had prior to the eye condition coming on. While all this information was being exchanged several women of varying ages came up and spoke to Mrs. Chandler, who seemed to hold some important position in the group. To one of these ladies she explained that she would have to go down into the city to get something her husband had ordered from one of the large clothing stores and asked her if she could keep an eye on any visitors who may look lost. She then turned to David and said,

"Would you like to come with me? It will only be a short visit, but you will at least see some of the city".

"That would be nice", said David, knowing that this would kill another half hour of so of the time he had to lose.

When the tea and scones were finished they left the garden, at the back of the college, and headed for the centre of the city. David would have liked Mrs. Chandler to take his arm in the normal way, but she insisted on him holding on to her arm as if he was being guided.

"By the way, you must stop calling me Mrs. Chandler, my christian name is Georgina. Now tell me David, why have you come down to Chichester?"

David explained about his involvement with the church and how Father Kingswood had thought that this little trip would break the monotony of sitting at home. He explained that he had been give a ticket for the service that afternoon and was to be back and in the cathedral by two thirty. Georgina suddenly realised that David had been invited to the Ordination and a barrier that seemed to exist at the beginning had now been pulled down. She said that she knew Father Kingswood well and it was typical of the type of person he was to think of others at one of the most important times of his life.

They visited several shops and in each, Georgina was well known. She made the point of introducing David and would often put her arm around his waist and give him an affectionate hug. They moved from shop to shop until they came to the men's outfitters. Here, Georgina left David looking at some very soft cashmere sweaters while she made the purchase for her husband. David was just feeling the beautiful softness of the woollen garments when he heard Georgina cry out,

"Oh my God! I am supposed to be chairing a meeting of the Friends of the cathedral, I must make a dash"

With that, she turned on her heels and rushed out of the shop bag in hand. David stood for a moment astounded. Had she forgotten about him and getting him back to the cathedral? Had she forgotten that he was unable to see anything he looked at? He waited for a while still fingering the sweaters until one of the assistants came over to him and said,

"Can I be of any assistance sir"?

"No", said David, "I am just looking".

He turned and walked out of the shop with the assistant trailing him as far as the door and began to walk in the direction he thought that they had come. They had been in so many stores and come out of so many different doors that he was completely lost. He couldn't even see the watch that he had on his wrist so he had no idea of how much time he had to get something to eat and make his way back to the cathedral. He thought to himself, that scatty woman had forgotten that he had difficulty with his sight and could only remember that she was late for an appointment.

Chapter 46

Turning left, he slowly made his way along the pavement taking care
not to walk into any of those dreadful grey posts which are set by the
kerb to prevent motorists parking their cars on the sidewalk. He
remembered that most of the walking he had done with Georgina was
slightly down hill, so he thought that if he headed up hill he should be
getting to the area of the cathedral and the hotel opposite where he
was supposed to get a meal. This road was far too narrow to be the
main road so he assumed he must have come out of the back of one of
the larger stores. After a minute or two of heart stimulating
manoeuvres avoiding people and pushchairs heading in the opposite
direction he came to a crossroads. Now what? This was not the main
crossroads in the centre of the city and he had no idea which way to
proceed. He tried to approach some of the shoppers who were
rushing up and down the road and eventually stopped a youngish
couple who were walking more slowly with a small child.

"Excuse me", called David to the passing couple, "could you tell me
which way it is to the Cathedral?"

The young lady went by with the pushchair, but the man came back to
David and said,

"Can I help you mate?"

"I am trying to find my way to the cathedral", said David, "can you
help me?"

The young man pointed to the left and said,

"See that blue sign on the right hand side of the road, if you turn right there and after about two hundred yards you will come across the main road. Turn right again and the cathedral is over the crossing at the top".

He then turned and ran to catch up with the young lady pushing the pushchair and walking with the small child. That sounded quite easy, thought David. He couldn't see the blue sign, but he was sure that when he was close, he would spot it. Isn't it strange, he thought, something which is so clear to fully sighted people is so easily missed if one's sight is impaired. He must have missed the sign and after crossing several junctions assumed that he was again lost. The man had said, "turn right", so if he did this he should be going in the right direction, but he now found that he was in some small side streets and away from the traffic, and unfortunately, many people. He decided to stop the next passer by and ask the way again, this time, however, he would come clean and admit that he had poor sight. No one passed him for some time. Then a small girl walked by in the opposite direction.

"Excuse me, could you direct me to the cathedral" asked David. The girl looked very worried and tried to walk on the outside of the pavement. David suddenly realised that this was not quite the thing to do. He should have waited for a more adult person to come along, but time was running short and he said again,

"I am sorry to trouble you, but I need to get to the cathedral and I cannot see too well".

The little girl stood for a while looking at David and then quite suddenly came over and took his hand. She didn't say anything; she just turned him around and walked in the direction she was going initially. She very carefully guided him around lamp posts and those dreadful grey, two foot high concrete posts until they reached a busy road. She stopped and firmly gripping David's hand prevented him from stepping into the road. When a clearing came in the traffic she quickly took him across the road. When they reached the other side she turned to face him and for the first time spoke.

"If you head up the hill from here you will find the cross. Go over the lights at the crossing and you will be facing the cathedral".

"Thank you so much", said David. He was amazed at receiving such brilliant guidance and instructions from such a little girl. "You have been very kind; I am very surprised to find such guiding skills in someone so young"

"Oh, that's alright", she said, "my dad also has bad eyes and I have to take him into town when he wants to go to the pub". She then ran off down the road before David could ask her her name. He walked up the road as instructed and came to the crossroads. He joined the group of people waiting at the lights to cross the road and realised he was back on the road opposite the cathedral. As he couldn't see his watch and had no idea of the time and how long he had before the beginning of the service, he stopped a man rushing past him.

"Excuse me, could you tell me the time".

The man stopped, turned and said, "Are you being funny mate or are you blind? If you look on the other side of the road there's a bloody great clock".

Before David could explain, he ran on towards the lights. Luckily, at that moment the clock began to chime and David was relieved to hear it strike one o'clock. That meant that it would give him at least an hour and a quarter to get something to eat and if he wasn't mistaken, he was outside the White Lion, the place Father Kingswood said he could get a decent meal. He entered the low front door and nearly went a tumble down the two steps that led in to the reception area. After leaving the sunshine outside, he was now confronted with a very dark room, in fact so dark that he could see nothing. He stood for a short time hoping that his eyes would become accustomed to the dark, but unfortunately, when a young lady asked him if she could be of any assistant, there had been no improvement.

"I would like to have a meal, but I am not able to see too well. Am I in the right part of the hotel?"

"Yes, just follow me", said the young lady, and disappeared altogether. David was afraid to move in case he fell over something, so he just stood still. The lady returned.

"I am sorry", she said, "take my arm and I will take you to a table".

Seated at a table for two at the side of the stairway, she gave him the menu and again disappeared. After about five minutes she returned and said,

"Have you decided what you would like?"

"I am afraid I can't read a menu, you see I am registered blind".

"Oh, I am sorry", she said. She then put her arm around David's shoulders and read out the menu. When the meal of fish and chips arrived she even offered to cut it up for him, something which David declined. At the end of the meal the bill was left on the table and it took some time before the young waitress realised that not only had he not put any money on the plate, he hadn't even seen the bill. She kindly read out his choice of food and the value finally coming to the total. As David left the hotel, being led to the door by the waitress, his situation became more of a reality to him than ever; Was it only a few months ago that he was an art student free to go anywhere and draw or paint anything he liked? Was it only a few months ago that he would travel on any bus or train without any problem of seeing signs or reading the fronts of buses or trains? He used to be able to see people he knew coming towards him and recognise them immediately, now they could pass him in the street and he wouldn't know. As he looked as if he could see they would assume that he had suddenly wanted to ignore them and some who were close friends would not speak to him again. He had lost nearly all of his independence and now had to rely on the good will of others to get him from one place to another. He had in fact become a package to be passed from one to the other like the game "pass the parcel", where the parcel was passed on quickly in case the recipient was made to open it. He walked back towards the lights and waited for a group of people about to cross the road and joined them.

The ceremony was all that Father Kingswood said it would be. Luckily he had been taken to his seat which was next to the centre aisle and he was able to see, in his outer vision the parade of all the curates clad in their vestments heading towards the altar end of the cathedral. The singing of the hymns was glorious and when the band, set high above them came in loud and clear he had a wonderful feeling of the magnificence of God and the glory of heaven. Perhaps God would be kind enough to grant him a recovery of his sight and he could again return to his chosen profession and the freedom and independence, as before. At the end of the service the newly ordained priests paraded to the west end and out of the magnificent large doors. The congregation followed on with those from the front going first. This meant it was some time before David could join the slowly moving throng and join the hundreds of people on the back lawn of the college. It wasn't long before David was joined by Father Kingswood, still in his robes, and he proceeded to introduce him to many of the new priests and their families around them.

After quite a formal dinner in the large hall of the college followed by some very amusing speeches, Father Kingswood changed into his motorbike gear and packed his robes into the pannier bags on either side of the back of the Sunbean. After saying goodbye to all his colleagues and friends, they started for home. David was quite pleased to be on the back of the motorbike again and away from the embarrassment of having to explain to all and sundry about his loss of sight. He had not bumped into Georgina again although he knew she must have been at the reception and the dinner. Perhaps she was too embarrassed to talk to him after leaving him high and dry in the middle of the city. As he thought back on the day and some of the scrapes he had got himself into, he was aware of them racing through the towns and countryside with the sun going down and the trees flashing past, but the joy of knowing where they were and the thrill of overtaking just about everything on the road was lost to him. They arrived at David's house a little later than they had expected and were met at the door by Mum, Dad and Jack who seemed to be pleased to see him. With Janet, however, there was an air of disapproval. Father Kingswood declined the invitation by Mum for a cup of tea and was quickly on the motorbike and had soon disappeared around the corner.

As they went back into the front room David could feel a certain frostiness that he hadn't encountered before. Although Mum, Dad and Jack wanted to know a little of David's exploits during the day and how he had managed when he was left on his own, Janet showed very little interest. In fact, it wasn't very long before she stood up and said,

"Well I must go home now my mum and dad will wonder where I am".

"Your mum and dad know where you are and they won't expect you to come home this early. Anyway I will walk round with you to make sure that you are OK", said David.

"No, I think I will make a move now and you needn't bother to come with me, I am sure you are quite tired after spending such a full day in other people's company". She took her coat off of the stair post and slipping it quickly on, made her way to the front door. David rushed to the porch to say goodnight and after closing the door between the front room and the front door, he said,

"What is wrong with you? You are very off this evening. Have I done something to upset you?"

"No, I just feel that I have had enough for this evening and want to get home"

"But we have hardly had a chance to talk to one another, and anyway I was looking forward to seeing you".

"Well, perhaps", said Janet "you could have made some excuse to come home a little earlier. I have been waiting hours for you to come home and worried sick in case you have had an accident and all you can do when you come in is to tell everybody how much you have enjoyed the day and how well you had got on with getting around on your own, or, rather, with older women. If you enjoyed their company so much, it is a wonder you didn't stay there". She opened the door and made her way towards the gate before David could even reply.

"Well, what was the matter with Janet this evening?" asked Mum. "She was quite chatty before you arrived home, then suddenly she seemed to turn. Have you had some sort of tiff?"

"No" replied David, trying to make light of it, "she said that she felt very tired and had a headache".

The trip up to the church for communion the next morning was equally as frosty and he hadn't even been greeted with a warm good morning kiss. In fact most of the day was spoilt by Janet spending most of it talking to other members of the club and almost ignoring him. When they made their way home in the evening she spent most of her time in the middle of a group and it was only when most of the other couples had peeled off to go their own way that they were finally alone. David's heart was beating so hard that he thought it would burst. It seemed to hurt right up to his neck and he knew that he would find it hard to talk. When they reached Janet's gate, instead of inviting him to accompany her to her door step for a goodnight kiss and cuddle, she opened her gate and went inside, closing the gate behind her. She then turned to David and said,

"I think that we should have a break from each other. I feel that I am too young to be tied down to one boyfriend; I want to be friendly with all the boys in the club and not have just one boyfriend. Perhaps in a year or two I may feel different, but at the moment I want a break".

She turned, walked to her door, took out her key and disappeared inside leaving David speechless and heart broken. He stood for some time hoping that the door would open and she would come running out and say that it was all a joke, but nothing happened. As he slowly made his way back home he just couldn't put two and two together. Up until yesterday all seemed to be well, his feelings hadn't changed, in fact, they were deeper than before, but why had Janet, the girl he loved so deeply, suddenly treated him as if he was any other boy. Her parting had been so cold and so final. As he was feeling so bad, he decided to walk through the back streets, which were familiar to him. He couldn't face the family at the moment because they would know something was up and would question him about it, and to be quite honest he hadn't got any answers. He wandered from road to road passing close to the park where they had had such warm encounters. There was the post of the park gate where they had made such fervent love that he had had to spin some yarn to Mum about having his trousers cleaned. He wandered back towards the pub, which was now closed. There were just a few people outside talking and two men sitting up against the low wall which surrounded the forecourt, singing and laughing, obviously too drunk to get home. By the time he reached his front door all the lights were out and he knew

438

all the family were in bed. As he mounted the stairs he heard Mum call out,

"Is that you David?"

David tried to reply in a loud whisper, "Yes Mum".   This was obviously not heard because Mum shouted in a loud voice, enough to waken the whole house,

"David, is that you?"

David stood close up to their door and said,

"Yes Mum".

The door suddenly opened and Mum's head came projecting out. "Are you alright? Have you been round Janet's all this time?"

David nodded and then turned the handle quietly on the back bedroom door and went in. He slipped off his clothes, put on his pyjamas and slipped into his side of the bed. He lay there for some time with his heart hurting as it had never hurt before. He had lost his useful sight so that he couldn't do his art anymore. He had to wait for others to take him around, so he had lost most of his independence. He had very little prospects for the future, his job with the BBC had had to be turned down, his entry into the RAF was put on hold and now the only girl in the world that he wanted to live with for the rest of his life had discarded him as if she had never known him. He had no future, what was he to do?

Chapter 47

All David could remember of the next couple of weeks was that they were a nightmare. He would wake in the morning with a heavy heart and with the feeling that there was little point in getting up as he would just spend most of the day sitting in Dad's arm chair listening to the radio. When he did get out of bed and go down stairs Mum would fuss around him and try to get him to eat a good breakfast. As David had no appetite he would first of all refuse the cooked breakfast and then, because Mum insisted on cooking it, he would pick at the best parts and try to eat as much as possible. He would sit so long, either in the chair or on the top step of the front door that he was beginning to get a nasty pain in his neck. He was sure something else was wrong as he also was experiencing dizzy spells accompanied by feelings of being sick. Occasionally, he would wander off from the front door and slowly walk around the local streets, as although he had no centre of vision he could still use his outer vision to avoid lamp post, gates and other obstacles. He did have a little difficulty with some of the kerbs and crossing some of the roads, but he thought that if he didn't do something he would go mad. He would try to wander off on one of his walks at a time when he thought Janet may be coming home from work just so he could perhaps talk to her or at least be in her company, but he was never lucky. Either he had picked the wrong time or perhaps she just crossed to the other side of the road to avoid him. In fact, peculiarly, he very rarely bumped into anyone he knew, well, no one stopped to talk to him. He found himself yearning for the time when the youth club was opened and he again met many of his friends, but it was strange how he still felt so lonely even when he was in a group and every time he moved towards a group which included Janet, she moved away.

Jack tried as hard as he could to involve David in anything he did. He began reading books to David and they often headed for a park somewhere and Jack would complete a chapter or two of a novel. One such book was called "Kontiki" in which some Swedish adventurer built a raft of balsa wood and sailed it all the way across the pacific. The whole idea was, David thought, to prove that the people of South America had crossed to New Zealand at some time. David spent so much time asleep that he missed much of the story and was quite unsure of what was happening. All he knew was that Jack enjoyed the book and would spend some time discussing the story and the braveness of the participants. He was obviously getting quite worried about David and felt very strongly that someone should be doing something about the future and what openings were available for registered blind persons. He contacted Uncle Barry and Aunt Jane for their advice and they were invited over to the south east of London to have a chat and perhaps find something which David would be able to do. So, several nights Jack and David would mount Jack's motorcycle and race through the streets of south London and over snacks and coffee would get advice on the possibilities for David's future. Having both studied at a school for the blind they were both conversant with Braille and typing, so their first advice was to start learning both media as quickly as possible.

David's neck pain and headaches were getting worse by the day and it wasn't long before he had to return to his doctor for something to ease it down. Being unsure of the problem and thinking that there may be more to David's headaches than it appeared on the surface, he sent him up to the hospital to see a specialist. After some careful examining it was decided that most of the problem was due to the postural position he was adopting sitting for many hours in an armchair and reading Braille. He was prescribed a course of treatment which involved the use of an infra-red lamp and soothing massage. He was also given advice on the positioning of his back and the support of his arms whilst reading Braille. Well, it wasn't really reading Braille as he was finding it very difficult to even recognise the letters in the basic form of the text. He remembered that he could take up to two hours to read one small page of Braille and at the end he was quite unaware of the meaning of what he had read.

His treatment was quite pleasant and he enjoyed the company of the very attractive young female physiotherapist who was treating him; she was always dressed in a stiff white coat. On one occasion she was called up to one of the wards to treat an inpatient. David was utterly shocked to find that her place was taken by a tall, thin, blind man. David thought to himself, "How can a blind man be able to not only treat his neck, but take a full and active role in the running of the department?" David didn't find out the man's name, but he remembered that he spent a lot of time asking him about his blindness and how he had acquired such an important position in a hospital. As he walked down the road from the hospital with Mum, his mind was made up. He would have a word with Jack and they could explore the possibility of changing jobs completely and find out what was the path they should take to possibly training for a profession. The blind physiotherapist working at St. Anthony's Hospital had told David that there was a School of Physiotherapy for the Blind in London, but had not given him any of the details of where it was and how anyone would get in touch with it. Jack, who was now working for the G.P.O felt that a phone call could solve part of their problem. He found the number in the telephone directory and, taking the bull by the horns, phoned. He spoke to the secretary of the school who, after hearing of the difficulties they were in, put him straight through to the Principal, a Mr. Jeskinson. Jack was pleased to explain to him the reason for his phone call and the difficulties that they were experiencing trying to get advice. Mr. Jeskinson listened carefully to the story and then offered to see David and at the same time give him some information about the school and their requirements. A date was fixed for the next week and Jack promised David that he would make himself available for the meeting.

The two of them arrived at the entrance of the building in Great Portland Street far too early for their appointment. Jack suggested that they took a walk down the road towards Oxford Street just to kill a little time. David was amazed to think that a school like this should exist in such a busy part of London and wondered how lectures and study could take place with this continuous traffic noise. They arrived at the secretary's office about half an hour early for their meeting and were sat in a small office at the end of the corridor. Mr. Jeskinson had been lecturing at the time, but soon made them welcome and invited them into his office. He listened, again, to the story of David's art career and how his future had all been dashed by the loss of his sight. Jack explained that they had only recently come into contact with their uncle and aunt who had poor vision, so their knowledge of the blind world was very limited. Mr. Jeskinson asked David a lot of questions about the grammar school and the Art School and then asked him to do some strange manouveurs, such as standing on one leg and touching the tip of his nose with his eyes closed. He then explained to David the requirements of the school for entry; this included having five "O" levels, to be able to read Braille at sixty words a minute and to be able to type at forty words a minute. Jack asked if the National Diploma he had achieved in the art world could count instead of an "O" level, but was informed that having an art qualification was of little use in the blind world. Mr. Jeskinson also suggested that David should spend some time at a rehabilitation centre to become accustomed to his loss of vision and that he should take his extra "O" level at a college for the blind where he would meet other boys who were intending to take up physiotherapy.

"How much will this all cost?" asked Jack realising that the family had very little money.

"Well, it will cost thousands of pounds" replied Mr. Jeskinson, "but there are grants that are available. I will have to leave all that to you as it is done through your local authority. Anyway, if you still feel that you would like to go ahead with this new career reapply for a position after you have achieved the requirements and you will be interviewed by a selection board when a decision will be made".

As they left the school to board the underground train to go home David felt quite deflated. He was sure that he could get the educational requirements without difficulty, but the time span for all this to take place was daunting. Worse than that, where would he get the finance to cover all the different rehabilitation centres and colleges that Mr. Jeskinson had suggested he attended? They sat on the underground train in silence, both deep in thought. It wasn't until they reached Tooting Beck station that Jack spoke.

"You seem to be very depressed since our meeting with the Principal?" David explained how he could see no way out of this dilemma. He didn't want to go away for so long and he certainly had no idea how they could raise the funds for such a venture. "Let's face one problem at a time", said Jack, "if we can get in touch with the local authority perhaps they will go some way into supporting you. It may sound a long time to you, but don't forget, you are only seventeen and even if it took two years to get entry into the physiotherapy school you will be only nineteen and would have still been doing your National Service. Anyway, a little time away from home may do you the world of good and give you a little of the independence that you seem to have lost. Keep your chin up and we will contact Surrey County Council Head Quarters at Kingston and see what they say".

David wasn't all together convinced that what Jack was suggesting was what he wanted, but as he had no other options and could see no other way forward, he said nothing to spoil Jack's enthusiasm. After all, Jack was doing this all for his benefit and he felt he must accept what was being done. In his mind the thought of being miles away from the one woman that he loved and spend years studying completely different subjects to reach the standard required to enter a profession as different from the art world as it could be, seemed daunting. When they reached home and Jack explained the success that they had had up at the physiotherapy school David was a little surprised by the reaction of both Mum and Dad. Mum was obviously very worried about the financial side and could see them being bombarded with masses of bills which they could not afford to pay and in addition, she was not very happy to hear that David may have to go away for some time to achieve the required educational skills. Dad was even more displeased and quite openly said that he thought that he did not like the idea of one of his sons crossing the line and moving out of the working class family and getting above his station in life. After all the efforts Jack had made, he was a little upset, he told Dad that he was talking nonsense and after trying to reassure Mum that he was going to try to get a grant, he pulled David aside and suggested that they went over to the telephone box, which was by the shops, to phone Uncle Barry and Aunt Jane to get their opinions. They were again surprised to get the reaction they did. Uncle Barry thought that David would have been better taking up some sort of shorthand typing course as he thought that they were aiming a little high. Jack was again very disappointed with the response, but in some way it made them both more determined to go ahead and at least try to get to the physiotherapy school. Jack said,

"If we can just get you into the college that Mr. Jeskinson suggested, it sounds as if your future would be settled. He said that many of the boys from the college had chosen physiotherapy as their career and if you can just join them the rest should be plain sailing".

As they walked back from the phone box, David said that he would go up to the club and let his friends know of their progress. As they parted David could feel Jack's eyes on him walking up the road. Jack knew that the only way that David would become independent again was to give him his head, but he still worried in case anything happened. Just before David reached the main road he did a sharp turn right and headed down towards his old infant school. Although the club was meeting that night, he had told Jack a little white lie, as

445

he wanted a little time on his own to think things out and try and decide for himself where his future lay. He strolled slowly along the front of the school and down the road that ran by the side of the woods where all the fights had taken place so many years before. At the park he turned right near to where he had had so many exciting hours with Janet and after making himself more depressed than ever, he turned up the road where the "Doodle Bug" had dropped, past the gap in the houses and up the long road that led towards home. If only he could get Janet out of his mind he could perhaps make a decision, but the very thought of her and the loss he felt kept clouding the issue. As he walked up his own road, towards his house, he slowed down even more and was thrilled to hear a familiar voice call out from one of the doors,

"Well, this is a surprise. Hello stranger, I haven't seen you for a long time!" It was Polly, she was sitting on the top step of one of her neighbour's door way. "Hold on a minute, I will join you".

David heard her mumbling to someone and then, after bidding them goodnight, came out through the gate. She slipped her arm into David's and said,

"Come and tell me all that has been happening to you. My friends keep asking me and as I haven't seen you, I always have nothing to report".

Polly opened the front door of her house and told David to sit on the top step. She opened the door into the front room and shouted.

"I am back, but I have just met David and I want to have a little chat with him before I come in. Get yourselves a drink and a biscuit. I won't be long". She then turned back and sat on the step by the side of David.

"I don't think it is a good idea for you to come in as the children are still up and anyway I don't think I can trust myself!" Polly genuinely wanted to know all that had transpired since she had last seen him. She listened to the events of the day, and she was the first to show absolute delight at their progress. She took David's hand between her two hands and as he was explaining about his doubts and the doubts of others, she warmly caressed his hand which she had pulled across onto her lap.

"And how has Janet taken all this?" she asked.

David explained about the strange break up and how he had missed the warmth of her company and advice on his future.

"To be quite honest", said Polly, "I don't think that she is the one to give you advice on your future. You must remember that she is only very young and she may be going through as much heart ache as you. It is very hard for a young lady to take on what may seem to her an impossible situation and it will be very difficult to weigh up in her mind the pros and cons. When she hears that you are on the way to solving your dilemma she may change and become a friend again. Anyway, I think that you have found a future in which I am sure you will be successful and I am delighted for you. That brother of yours sounds a real genuine guy; I would like to meet him sometime".

David felt much better to hear Polly's reaction to his future and thanked her for her advice. He didn't say anything about the warm caresses that she was making with his hands and he said nothing about the fact that she had now moved his hand up against her firm breast.

"What are you doing tomorrow evening?" she asked, out of the blue.

"Nothing really" replied David without really thinking.

"Well the children are spending the night with my mother and I was going out with my friends, but I am sure they will understand if I say that I can't make it. Perhaps you could come around about nine o'clock and I can hear what has been going on and perhaps I can give you some more good advice". She dropped her hands, still holding David's onto his lap and as she found that he had reacted to all the previous fondling, slipped one of her hands down the front of his flies and gripped him tightly. As David tried to release his hand to return to her breast, she held his hand tightly and said,

"No, not here, anyone may come along and anyway the children are just next door".

She removed her hand from his crotch with an upward tug and said,

"Save that till tomorrow, but don't make him cry in the meantime".

As David walked home he felt life was a lot better and the encouragement he had received from Polly both career wise and sexually had boosted his ego. All he had to do now was to walk slowly enough for all traces of his encounter to disappear before he went indoors. What had she meant by, "but don't make him cry?" He had no idea what she was getting at.

Chapter 48

Jack took the next day off from work. He was allowed ten days a year that was in addition to his holiday, for doctor's or hospital appointments which everybody took as bonus days. When David came down from the bedroom Jack was already dressed and had had his breakfast.

"Come on", he said, "get yourself going, we are going over to the phone box to get in touch with the local authority to try to get an appointment to sort out this grant that seems to be available. I want you to be there as I feel that you should know all that is going on and can deal with it if they come back to you when I am not here. We will go over to the shops where there are now two phones then we won't be blocking it for anyone else wanting to make a phone call"

Jack explained to the lady on the council switchboard exactly why he was phoning and asked to speak to the person that was in charge of educational grants.   After being passed from department to department he was finally put through to a man who seemed to know something about the subject. Jack explained the situation and what progress they had made so far, but wanted to know how David could receive some sort of grant to continue his education.   The man, a Mr. Jackson, said that he would send them all the forms and if they were filled in correctly, he would put them in front of the Education Board and they would decide what could be done.   Jack became quite annoyed and said that he wanted to see and discuss the problem with someone in authority. After a lot of argument Jack persuaded Mr. Jackson to see them at ten o'clock the following morning, even though it was a Saturday, at County Hall, Kingston.   They arrived home feeling quite triumphant, so much so that Jack suggested that they jump on his motorbike and go down to the Grange Park where they could continue with the book "Kontiki".

That evening David told Mum another little white lie. He said that the night before he had met some of his friends from the youth club and they had all decided to visit another youth club on the way to Morden. He had meant to be at the youth club the night before and they had visited this club near Morden on several occasions, so it wasn't hard to pull the wool over Mum's eyes. He said that he may be a little late as they were doing some square dancing and he couldn't leave until the end.

"Is Janet going along as well", asked Mum.

David was a little taken back by this question, but quickly replied that he didn't think so as it was the night she usually washed her hair. "Anyway", he said being pushed into an enormous lie "I am not really interested".

He left the house at about half past eight and headed towards the alley way and the road towards the youth club. He knew that Mum would be looking out of the window and would have become very suspicious if he had gone straight down his own road. After walking up to the shops he took the turning towards his infant school and just hoped that no one would see him or perhaps talk to him. It was one of the problems he had now inherited that he could do nothing out of the ordinary or go anywhere secretly without the thought that someone, he couldn't see may be watching. He walked up the road slowly keeping on the side of Polly's house. He hoped beyond hope that he wouldn't have to knock on her door as he imagined many eyes may be watching from behind the half net curtains that all the houses had behind their front room windows. He slowed right down as he approached the gate of Polly's house and was relieved to hear her soft pleasant voice say,

"Oh, hello David. Come in and have a chat".

Polly was sitting on the top step of her front porch and as he came up to her he noticed that she was wearing her silky gabardine raincoat over her shoulders in a similar fashion to wearing a cape. She patted the step at the side of her and beckoned him to sit down. She seemed a little less seductive than the evening before and spent quite a bit of time asking him about the progress they had made with the education authorities and how Jack had handled the situation. David could feel his heart pounding at a high rate and he could feel his face burning and his mouth dry. After spending more time than David wanted to waste Polly turned to him and said,

"Well, would you like to come inside?"

David was hardly able to speak, but managed to get the words out,

"Is there anyone at home?"

"No, does that worry you. If you have any doubts just say so, I will understand. We could just sit here and talk if you like".

"No", said David, "I would like to come inside".

They got up from the step and Polly quietly closed the door. Instead of turning to David and putting her arms around his neck, as he hoped, she just opened the front room door and led him inside. It was a very comfortable looking room with pictures all round the walls, some of flowers and poor landscapes and some of photographs. David couldn't really see any of them very clearly and didn't want to show off his bad sight by putting his nose on the glass. She asked him to take a seat and said,

"Would you like a drink?"

David thought that he had perhaps made a mistake and all she wanted was a little company and someone to drink with. He asked if she had a beer and she quickly swept into the kitchen. David sat in one of the small leather covered arm chairs by the radio in the corner of the room and felt a little disappointed at his reception. Perhaps she had realised the seriousness of inviting a young man into her house when there was no one there, or perhaps she had just cooled off.

Polly came back into the room carrying a glass of beer and a smaller glass which David thought may have been half full of whiskey. She sat down on the settee which was covered in the same brown leather as the small chairs and passed David his drink. They sat for a while talking about David's time at the Art School and the loss of his sight. David had drunk almost all of his beer when she at last stood up and slipped off the raincoat which had only been buttoned at the neck. She threw it down on the back of the settee and then said,

"Why don't you come over and sit with me, you seem miles away over there".

David got up and moved to her side on the settee. Polly was wearing a deep blue, silky blouse which had a fairly low neckline and no sleeves. Her skirt was long and looked and sounded as if it were made of taffeta and just showing from below were her high heeled white shoes. She had tied her hair back in a pony tail, but had allowed the sides to bulge a little giving her a very "young girl" appearance. She leant back against the back of the seat and pulled him close to her. She had obviously put just a touch of perfume on as she smelt warm and madly attractive. As David leaned back he could feel her raincoat slipping over the leather back of the settee and he was getting a little embarrassed at the bulge which was quite evident in the front of his trousers. If only he could persuade Mum that he should now have tighter pants that would hold him in. Polly slipped her arm around his back and taking her raincoat wrapped it around David's shoulders pulling it across his front. She then leant against him and under the cover of the silky raincoat placed her hand very gently on the bulge in his trousers. David was unable to speak, his heart was racing and his ears were ringing. Just when he thought that he was about to lose control she removed her hand and taking his hand placed it on her breast. Although she always looked as if she had very adequate sized breasts, they now seemed enormous. He suddenly realised the she was not wearing a bra and through the silky blouse he could feel her nipple as hard as a rock sticking outwards and downwards. She pulled the blouse out of her skirt and slipped his hand up inside. He was dying to feel her hand go back onto the front of his trousers, but she just thrust her mouth onto his lips opening her lips as she did so and pushing her tongue hard into his throat.

She pulled him up against her, but he still managed to keep his hand on her firm breast gently fondling the large nipple. He tried to pull her hand down to his crutch again, but she pulled her hand away. He tried again, because he knew that he couldn't hold on much longer, but she again pulled her hand away. She lay back over one of the arms of the settee and pulling up the whole of the front of her blouse took his two hands and placed them on both of her breasts. David had never imagined such a mountain of flesh could be hidden behind her bra. He was just about to climb on top of her when she suddenly stopped, pushed him off and sat up. She pulled down her blouse and removed her raincoat from David's shoulders. He was on the edge of something very wonderful and he had suddenly been stopped. How could she have led him on so far and not continued. She pushed back her hair, which was now looking a little dishevelled and said,

"I think we should finish our drinks".

They sat for some time not saying a word and just sipping their drinks. Then she said,

"I think you had better go, I don't know what people would think if they knew what we had been up to".

David got up with difficulty from the slippery surface of the raincoat on the leather seat and went towards the door. Polly followed him and as he was about to open the front door she took his hand and turned him around.

"I don't think it is fair for me to take advantage of you just because I am lonely and haven't been with a man for such a long time. What do you think?"

"I don't know. I have never been close and that far before and I am sure that I would like to have gone the whole way".

Polly put her arms around David's neck and kissed him tenderly on the mouth. He put his arms around her waist and pulled her in close and they stood like that for a good couple of minutes. He could feel the stimulation coming back and he was sure that she felt the same as she began to press her crutch hard onto him. He again slipped his hand onto one of her breasts and was pleased to feel that the nipple was still hard. As he fondled it she kissed harder and harder. Then without warning she turned away from him and taking his hand pulled him back into the room. This time, however, she walked towards the kitchen door and then towards the staircase. Leading him by the hand she opened the front bedroom door and pulled him in. She turned and they resumed their kissing and fondling. The room was in darkness with just the light of the hall coming through the door.

"I won't put the light on", she said, "in case there are prying eyes around the neighbours". David again tried to pull one of her hands down towards the front of his trousers, but she pulled it away.

"That will spoil everything", she said

She did, however, take her two hands away from his neck and started undoing his belt and the buttons on his flies. His trousers slipped to

454

the floor and quickly he removed his shoes and kicked the trousers off. Oh Mum, he thought, if only I had had better pants my ardour would not be so obvious. Polly pulled away and like lightening pulled her blouse over her head and slipped her skirt down to the floor. When David put his arms around her again he was surprised to feel that she was not wearing any pants, but sexily, she was still wearing her high heeled shoes. She began to undo the buttons on his shirt and seemed to relish the slowness of the procedure. When she reached the bottom button she allowed her hand to very gently brush the top of his penis. She then slipped the shirt off of his shoulders and let it drop to the floor. Finally she slid her hands down the sides of his pants and very slowly lifted them over his very erect penis. David could feel his knees shaking involuntarily and he felt he was about to burst. He moved up against her and tried to push her back onto the bed which was just behind her. Polly again eased him away and whispered,

"Wait, don't rush or it will be all over too quickly. I know what you would like".

She turned to the pillows on the bed and from under the bottom one slipped out a thin, silky nightie. She slipped it over her head and let it drop down covering her upper torso. David again put his arms around her and was almost overwhelmed by the feeling of the silk over her skin. He ran his hands down her back and noticed that the nightie only came down as far as her buttocks and as he ran his hands round to the front he felt her fall back on the bed pulling him down on top of her.

David had very little recollection of what went on after that. He remembered feeling as if he was swimming in space and on some occasions he could see her sitting astride him and looking as if she was in some kind of trance, she had removed her nightie and her hair was now falling over her shoulders and the front of her chest. Time seemed endless and even his hearing seemed to be strange with the sounds coming from miles away. The next thing he knew, all was calm and quiet and he felt so relaxed that he couldn't even raise his head from the pillow. It was as if he was in a dream and although he needed to move he seemed to be completely paralysed. As he tried to move his limbs he felt someone moving at the side of him and then, with a sense of shock, realised where he was. He had been sleeping and forced himself to sit up.

"Oh God!" he exclaimed, "What is the time?"

Polly turned towards the bedside table and reached out for the alarm clock, which was ticking by the side of the bed.

"Five to two", she replied.

David leapt up from the bed and started to scramble for his clothes not knowing where he had discarded them.

"Do you have to go?" asked Polly, "Can't you say that you were so late that you decided to stay with a friend?"

"No." said David, "My mother would never believe me as I have never done that before."

Making his way out of the bedroom door and down the stairs he was followed by Polly, who had slipped her dressing gown around her shoulders. She made him stop in the porch way to tidy up his hair and his shirt collar. She would have put her arms around his neck for a final farewell kiss, but, strangely, David didn't feel the same attraction as he did before. She said,

"Don't be upset, it always feels a little down after the event. Anyway, open the door quietly and I will close it. Try not to slam the gate and don't start running down the street, it will only draw attention. Let me know how you get on tomorrow, won't you? Pop in one evening if you get the chance".

When David climbed the stairs silently, he was suddenly shocked by Mum calling out,

"Is that you David?"

"Of course it's me", he whispered.

Mum's door was violently pulled open and Mum in her flannelette nightie reaching down to the floor and her hair in tight curlers shouted,

"What the devil time do you call this? We've been worried out of our lives in case you had had an accident or something. I hope you haven't been up to any mischief".

"No, of course not. I told you I might be late, we stayed for a drink at one of the boys houses".

"Well you look as if you have had a rough time to me", she said, "Now get to bed, you know that Jack is taking you out to Kingston tomorrow, don't you?"

David lay for a long time on his side of the double bed, thinking of the events of the past few hours. He not only felt guilty, but wondered why the hell he had gone in to Polly, knowing that he wouldn't be able to resist her advances. What if her husband had returned unexpectedly while he had been in bed with her or what will happen if he had been seen leaving at two o'clock in the morning and, oh God! What will she do if she becomes pregnant? He had never experienced this amount of remorse before and while he was worrying about all the consequences he drifted of into a deep sleep.

457

They arrived in the front lobby of County Hall ten minutes early and the girl on the reception desk asked them to wait while she tried to contact Mr. Jackson. It had been a bit of a race on the motorbike through the streets of Morden and New Malden as David had had some difficulty in waking up that morning. His mind had still been on the events of the night before and even as he sat on the back of the bike he was worrying more about the consequences of his actions in Polly's bed than on the interview about to take place. Jack was not too happy either. He was quite annoyed with David as he had done so much to arrange this meeting on the Saturday morning, Mr. Jackson's day off, and he didn't want to fail in his attempt to prize money out of the Education Authorities. He had not spoken to David since breakfast and even as they sat in silence in the waiting area he gave off an air of annoyance. The phone on the desk rang and the young lady answered it.

"Mr. Jackson will see you now Mr. Fellows. If you go through the double doors and down the corridor, his office is at the end on the right. He said that he would leave his door open".

"Come in gentlemen", was the greeting as they reached the open door. They were a little taken back by the soft polite voice that greeted them. "Come in and take a seat. Would you like a cup of tea or coffee?"

He was nothing like the man they expected to see. From his voice on the phone he sounded very officious and superior. This man looked very ordinary with thin hair combed across his head to make it look more than it was. He wore brown, round rimmed glasses and was quite short and wearing a suit that looked as if he had slept in it. He had, however, a heavily striped shirt and, believe it or not, a spotted tie badly tied with a large Windsor knot. He put out a slightly wet limp hand for them to shake.

"That's nice of you", said Jack, "A cup of tea would be very acceptable".

They both sat down and Mr. Jackson picked up the phone and did the ordering.

"Now tell me the story again", said Mr. Jackson, "It is never easy to get the correct information on the phone and sometimes one can get the wrong impression of the people one is talking to. If you would start at the beginning and I will make notes as I go along".

Jack pulled back his chair a little indicating to David to go ahead and tell the story from his point of view. David began right from the performance in the examinations at the Art School finally ending up with his visit to the Physiotherapy School in London. He explained what the Principal of the school had indicated as being the best course of action to take and also pointed out the rough estimate of cost that was given to them. At that point there was a knock on the door and in came the receptionist with three cups of tea placing one in front of each of them. After she had left the room, closing the door behind her, Mr. Jackson sat for a few minutes sipping his tea and thinking. Finally, he put down his cup and raised his head. Jack was pleased to note that he had a very pleasant smile on his face which he thought may be the indicator of good news. Mr. Jackson explained, in some detail, the options that were available. Basically, one was for them to provide a tutor who would visit their home and take David through the necessary "O" level that was required. They could also arrange for a home visitor to teach him Braille although the typing was a little more of a problem, which he was sure could be overcome. The second option was to sign on at a local Adult College to do the "O" level and perhaps the typing tuition with the Braille still being taught at home. The third option was to go to a specialist school where he could do all three subjects at the same time. The only problem with the last option was, however, that it would mean up to a year and a half at the college, the only one being in Wallingcester and the cost would be something that would have to be considered by their Education Board.

"I think that the best option for both you and us would be to have the tuition at home and apply for the Physiotherapy School a year early. The cost of the education at the Physiotherapy School may be the responsibility of either the Education Authority or the Minister of Labour. This could be sorted out later if you are successful in the first part of the plan. What do you think you would prefer?"

David immediately chose the first option. He didn't want to go away for a year and a half to some strange part of the country. He would lose all of his friends and his chances of making it up with Janet would be zero. Anyway he would have to mix with a lot of blind people and may have to be forced into holding a white stick in front of him. He had never been away from home for that length of time; when he was evacuated it had only been three months and that was hell.

"I would like to try your first option as that sounds as if it would suit me best and would obviously cost the least. What do you think Jack?"

Jack sat for a while thinking and David was a little surprised that he didn't back him up immediately.

"I am not so sure. The examinations will not be easy to organize from home and we don't know what quality of teaching these home visitors may have. You remember, also, the Principal of the Physiotherapy School did say that he thought that you may need some time for rehabilitation and he thought that the college at Wallingcester was the best option, that is, if they will take you. The saving of money for the council should not be our criteria, it should be, what is best for you".

They sat for some time discussing the options with David and Mr. Jackson firmly on the side of the home education and Jack firmly on the side of going to Wallingcester College for the Blind and updating his education there. David was sure that Jack was opposed to the home tutoring as he was unsure of the quality of the teaching and Mr. Jackson was obviously trying to save the council as much money as possible. After a while Jack, reluctantly, gave way and agreed to give the first option a try.

"How soon can David start studying with the tutors at home as it is essential to cover the ground that is needed for his "O"level and his typing, and Braille must also be up to standard before they will accept him at the Physiotherapy School"?

"We will get someone on to this next week and by the following week all the subjects should be in place. Now leave this to me and I will personally start the ball rolling on Monday morning".

By Wednesday, of the following week, they had heard nothing. As they had no phone they assumed that wheels had been put into motion, but hearing nothing was very frustrating. When Jack arrived home from work he became very annoyed and said that if there was no letter or communication the next day he would phone Mr. Jackson and have a word with him. He knew that time was getting short and the application to take the examination would have to be submitted soon. David waited for the post next day, but again there was nothing. At about eleven o'clock there was a knock on the door. Mum spent ages at the door talking to someone and eventually she came back into the room followed by a strange looking figure.

"This is Mr. Benjamin", said Mum, "He has come all the way from Wallington on his bicycle to help you with your Braille".

The forlorn figure was dressed in a very long rain garment buttoned right up to the neck. He was wearing a cap with the peak facing backwards and what looked like motor bike goggles. It had been pouring with rain so the poor man was dripping wet. Mum didn't know whether to laugh or cry, she just looked at the spaceman with her mouth wide open. Mr. Benjamin began to disrobe taking off layer after layer, all dripping wet.

"You had better give those clothes to me and I will see if I can dry them off a little before you go home. How did you manage to get so wet on a bicycle?"

"Well you see", said Mr. Benjamin, "I have a motor that sits on the back wheel and it pushes me along. It can get me up to quite a speed, but of course in this weather the spray shoots up into your face and over your back".

After removing his cap and then his goggles David could see that this was really an old man and he was even more surprised to see that he was wearing thick pebble glasses under his goggles. Mum went off with his wet clothes and said that she would return with a cup of tea for them both. It was not long before David realised that Mr. Benjamin was little better at Braille than himself and had only learnt to read grade one Braille. This was only the basic letters and all the abbreviations needed to read at some speed were quite foreign to him. They spent some time talking about what David wanted to do when Mum came in with the tea. By the time they had drunk the tea and opened the small books he had removed from his saddle bag, it was time for him to go. It must have taken another quarter of an hour for him to put all his gear back on and after mounting his machine just outside the gate proceeded to ride straight across the little green. Half way across the motor came into action and threw the cycle from side to side nearly throwing him off. He bumped off of the pavement into the road and was last seen zigzagging down the road. David and Mum just roared with laughter and went indoors. When Jack heard them telling of the funny visitor, instead of laughing he was absolutely livid.

"I will get on to Mr. Jackson tomorrow and give him hell", he snapped, "the man is obviously not a teacher, they have just sent someone along to keep us quiet and anyway, what about the typing and the "O" level, how are they going to be covered in time?"

During the next week Mr. Benjamaen came twice, but little was achieved due to the amount of time it took for him to disrobe and then re-robe. Mum would provide him with tea and homemade cake and he would spend a very pleasant couple of hours trying to fathom out what all the Braille signs meant. The two of them were becoming quite fond of the old man who travelled all that way just to help David with his Braille and by his refined voice and his broad knowledge; they assumed that he may have been in some government post at some time. The Braille alphabet David knew by heart, it was the feeling of the little dots that needed to be practiced and this seemed to be taking an age. There was no word on the typing tuition and for a tutor for the "O" level, that seemed very distant. David was getting frustrated concerning the inability for him to get on with the study required and Jack was getting more and more angry with the way they were being treated.

It was on the following Wednesday that things came to a head. A letter arrived with the address of the Physiotherapy School on the outside, but addressed to David. Mum said that they should wait until Jack came home before they opened it and stuck it behind the clock on the mantelpiece. They should have opened the letter as they spent the whole day worrying about it contents, but not daring to open it just in case it was bad news. It could just be a letter giving them more information or it could be that after some discussion they had decided that David was not the right material for the school. Both Mum and David stood at the window that evening waiting for Jack to appear, but as it became later and later they began to worry as to whether he was alright or whether he had had an accident or something. He had never been this late before.

Chapter 49

It was getting quite late when they spotted Jack running through the alleyway on the other side of the big green. It had started to rain earlier on that evening and what had started as just a shower or two was now quite a downpour. Jack had buttoned his jacket up to the neck and his hair was all flattened down with the rain. He kept rubbing his hand across his glasses to remove the splashes of the raindrops and his other hand was holding the bottom of his jacket together. As he came to the gate, Mum went to the door to let him in and greeted him with a barrage of questions of where he had been and why was he so late and so on. Jack said nothing as he came into the front room and began to discard his wet clothes drying himself with the towel Mum had brought from the kitchen cupboard. He explained that he had phoned Mr. Jackson from work during the day and had made such a fuss that he said that he would stay on at County Hall until Jack could get there from his workplace in London. He told them that he had bombarded Mr. Jackson with questions about the service they had had so far. He said that Mr. Jackson had no real answers but kept repeating that it took time to put the wheels in motion and they must be more patient. After they had heard the whole story, they presented the letter to Jack who quickly opened it and read the contents. Mr. Jeskinson, the Principal of the Physiotherapy School wanted David to attend a Board Meeting at the School on the next Thursday afternoon where a decision could be made about his future application to the School.

"Well that puts everything on hold for a time, doesn't it?" said Jack, "I will try to get the time off to come with you and we should be advised on the best way forward. You carry on with Mr. Benjamin, for what it's worth, and I will leave any further visits to Kingston until after the interview. I will write back to Mr. Jeskinson and let him know that you will be happy to attend the Board Meeting and that you will explain your progress so far when you are there".

"What do you think, Jack" said Mum, "does this sound good news or bad?"

"I don't know, it does mean that things are moving forward and any movement is good."

David and Jack went off to London the next Thursday both dressed in their best suits with clean white shirts and polished shoes.   Jack's time in the RAF had taught him how to look smart and confident and the feeling had rubbed off a little on to David.   Mr. Benjamin had been three times during the last week and was really trying his best to help David with the Braille, but the poor old man had limited sight himself and was finding the subject hard.   They all appreciated the work he was trying to do and Mum continued to make him welcome with tea and cake.   As in the past, the two smart "men about town" arrived early at the School, but this time they were shown into a largish room with metal chairs backing on to the walls.   They were surprised to find quite a few other people there.   Three Scottish boys, all totally blind.   They were talking so loudly and rapidly to each other that they were quite unaware of others in the room.   There was no point in trying to hear what they were saying to one another as their accents were so broad they may have been speaking a different language.   On the other side of the room sat three other boys, one tall and thin and the other two short and fat.   They were much quieter and seemed to whisper comments to each other.   They were obviously from the same school as they were in the same coloured blazers with the same badge on the chest pocket.   There were also three girls, each accompanied by a woman, possibly their mother or perhaps their teacher.   They just sat quietly looking as if they may be sick at any moment.

As they sat down a strange looking lad, a little older than the rest with long straggly hair and clothes to match came in and sat down in the chair by the side of David. He looked quite dejected and sat slumped forward, with his head in his hands. David was unsure whether he was an applicant or a member of staff. Almost immediately he was followed in by a short woman dressed in a dark dress and wearing horn rimmed spectacles. She walked up to the scruffy lad and said,

"The Board does not want to see you again Mr. Telford, you can go now. We will write to you in a couple of days to tell you of our decision".

Mr. Telford said nothing; he just got up and went out of the door. David was unsure as to whether he had bad sight or not. He did seem to hang his head forward and squint a little. The secretary then turned to David and Jack and said,

"The interviews are taking about twenty minutes each so I imagine you will not be seen for at least another couple of hours. Would you like to go out for a break and perhaps get yourselves a cup of tea and come back in about two hours time?"

They walked up Great Portland Street to the station and crossed the main road. After turning a corner or two they arrived at Regents Park and after strolling for a short time they sat on a bench and Jack produced from his pocket a book that he read on his way to work. It was called "Far From the Madding Crowds", by Thomas Hardy. David had never heard of it before, but was willing to listen to Jack reading just to fill in the time. They managed to get a cup of tea at the station café and arrived back at the School in just under the two hours. There was much more noise now, obviously all three Scots boys and those in the blazers had all had their interviews. Two of the girls were looking a lot brighter and one was having her interview. They had been joined by two more older lads, one looked totally blind and the other David thought may have been his guide although they didn't speak to one another. In a short time the tall, quite attractive, girl came back into the room bubbling over with excitement. She had obviously had a good interview and couldn't stop talking to the other girls about it. The secretary came into the room again and told her that she could go when she was ready. The secretary then turned to David and said,

"The Board will see you now Mr. Fellows, if you would just follow me".

Jack put out his hand and said,

"Best of luck David, see you soon".

David followed the secretary along the corridor to the Board Room and was surprised to find it full of old looking gentlemen. Only two were wearing white coats and they sat at the far end. The others seemed to be flopped across their chairs as if they had had enough, and wanted to go home. They were all jabbering away ten to the dozen and the room stank of pipe and cigarette smoke and stale sweat. Mr. Jeskinson, one of those in the white coat, asked David to sit on the chair in the middle at the door end of the room, but it was some time before the group came to order and showed some sign that he was there. David stood up, turned round, pulled the chair forward about a foot and then turned and sat down again. The room became silent and they all looked at the newcomer. Mr. Jeskinson started the questions with all the usual old questions about why did he want to take up Physiotherapy and did he know anything about it. David told them of his visits to the local hospital and how many hours he had spent with the Physiotherapists, particularly the blind man. He avoided telling them that he was actually a patient, but gave them the impression that the visits had been arranged for him to study the work in a hospital. He was then questioned by every member of the Board each question obviously being a list that they had used for all the other candidates. Things didn't seem to be going too well until one of the

467

women got on to the subject of his Art School and the work he had been doing there. David was very pleased to talk about this as he still missed the freedom of his painting, drawing and sketching. A long haired man with strong glasses asked David if he was interested in reading. David realised that this was a leading question trying to find out whether he had the ability to study. He told him of the artists he had studied and the autobiographies he had read. Then he suddenly remembered the books that Jack had read to him and added the "Kontiki" not saying how much he had slept through, and "Far from the Madding Crowd" not mentioning that Jack had only read about four pages. The man tried to catch David out by asking him who was the author and David replied immediately that it was Thomas Hardy. The man seemed quite impressed.

Finally, a very large man who spread across the chair so that as much of his bottom that was on the chair stuck out on either side, asked him about any sports that he was interested in. Of course, David spoke of his rugby and cycling, but made the most of his cricket and when he had played against Surrey Ground Staff at Mitcham. Luckily, the man was a keen cricketer and knew many of the batsmen and bowlers that David had met. When David told him that he had obtained the signatures of Alec and Eric Bedser and MacIntyre, the fat man was very impressed. David left the interview feeling that he had achieved a great deal and perhaps would be offered a place at the school. He sat for a while with Jack waiting for the secretary to give them the all clear to go. She came back into the room and said,

"Mr. Fellows, the Board would like to see you again. Would you follow me"?

As David got up and followed the secretary he couldn't help wondering why they wanted him back, they hadn't done this with any of the others, why him? He sat down in the chair he had just left, but this time the room was silent. Mind you, the smell was no better, perhaps worse as many of them had lit up a cigarette or pipe. The fat man was smoking a cigar which was billowing smoke and smelling like a dustbin that had been set on fire. Mr. Jeskinson then spoke.

"Mr. Fellows, we have brought you back because we feel that you do not quite understand what may be required of you to enter this profession. We, that is, the whole Board, feel that I should point out to you what will be required before you have any chance of entering training at this School. Firstly, we feel that you should attend a rehabilitation centre for at least six weeks before begining your education so that you can become accustomed to your loss of sight. Secondly, we feel that you should go to Wallingcester College for the Blind, that is if the head and his staff think that you are suitable, to complete your educational requirements. This should be complete by the year after next. If all is satisfactory at the rehabilitation centre and you are accepted by Wallingcester and you achieve the requirements for the professional body, then we will make a place available for you. Now, that is a lot to take in all at once. Do you understand what is expected of you and will you be willing to go through the course that we suggest?"

David was taken completely by surprise. It sounded so complicated and the time span seemed endless. It sounded as if he would more or less leave his home and may be away for up to two years. In addition to that Mr. Jeskinson did not mention the three years at that school and the examinations that he would have to take and pass there. It all sounded too much and his heart sank. All he could do at that time was to say,

"Yes, I am willing to follow the wishes of the Board".

"Do you have any questions" asked Mr. Jeskinson.

David thought of the problems he was having with the Braille, typing and the Education Authority. He could see that there was no way through if he went along the track that Mr. Jackson and he had determined was the best for him. He decided that this was the time that he took the bull by the horns and poured out their problems so far. He explained about the visit to County Hall and the advice given by Mr. Jackson, he also explained that his parents could not afford the fees that were required for a rehabilitation centre or a college, let alone the fees for this school. He also told them of his Braille tutor and the lack of typing and tutoring, he said,

"Although I am willing to go through with your requirements, you can see that the cards seem loaded against me. I can't see how I can come up to your expectations".

There was a period of silence then several of them leaned over and whispered to each other. The large man got up and went up to the back of the Principal's chair and spoke quietly into his ear. Mr. Jeskinson then said,

"Go home now Mr. Fellows. Carry on with your study and I will write to you in a day or two to let you know the Boards decision".

A week passed before the dreaded letter was delivered from Mr. Jeskinson. Arriving in the morning post it was placed behind the clock on the mantelpiece to wait for the arrival home of Jack. David would have willingly opened the letter, but of course he could not read what it said and he knew that Mum was very reluctant to take on the responsibility of reading either good or bad news. The frustration David felt was enormous. This letter contained information relevant to his future and knowing that it was sitting behind the clock waiting for someone else to read made David feel like a second class citizen. In the meantime he had continued to entertain Mr. Benjamin who, not only enjoyed his visits to the Fellows abode, but was beginning to tell them a little of his very interesting life story. He apparently had spent many of his latter years serving in a Government post in India. He had held a position of authority and had all his own servants and a beautiful large house where he would entertain many important visitors from England. He was about to be promoted to an even higher office when he began to lose his sight. At first he thought that it was just a case of short-sightedness due to his increasing years. He managed to cover up this loss of vision by promoting one of his servants to being his reader and scribe. This all went well until he was being considered for higher office as many of the documents he was obliged to read were considered to be fairly secret. His wife, who was a lot younger than him was Indian and although he trusted her implicitly not to reveal any information to anyone else, he was obviously placed in a difficult position. Someone in authority solved the problem by ordering him back to England to have his eyes examined by a specialist at Moorfields Eye Hospital. The funny thing was, and this made him roar with laughter, the specialist that examined him and diagnosed his eye condition was Indian.

David opened the envelope just as Jack came into the front room and handed it to him. Mum, Dad and David stood, very apprehensively, waiting for the contents to be read out. Instead, Jack read it to himself and then turned to them and said,

"That's great news, isn't it?"

He looked up at their blank faces and then said,

"Haven't you read the letter?"

"No", said David, "we waited for you to come home. Mum wouldn't read the letter to me in case it was bad news although I would rather she had".

"Well, Mr. Jeskinson has more or less put down on paper what you told me on the way home. He says that if you spend six weeks at a rehabilitation centre at Torquay, which is run by the National Institute for the Blind, and if you then get accepted for the college at Wallingcester, where you can take the subjects you need, then a place will be available for you at the Physiotherapy School in London. That sounds great, doesn't it?"

There was silence for a moment. David knew that this was what was possible, but the time scale seemed intolerable. He had spent the past two years studying already and had achieved nothing. Now he was embarking on another two years study which would only get him to the starting gates again at the Physiotherapy School. It would also mean leaving home for at least a couple of years and what would this do to his chances of making it up with Janet. She still figured highly in his life and he thought life without her would be unbearable.

"Does he say anything about the money that would be needed to get me through all of this further education?"

"Well he does say that the rehabilitation centre costs would be borne by the National Institute for the Blind and this could be fixed up directly he receives confirmation from you that you are happy to continue. The cost of you going to Wallingcester, however, should be covered by the Local Education Authority and this, he says, must be arranged by us with Mr. Jackson at County Hall as soon as possible. If you are successful at Wallingcester, then, he implies that a Minister of Labour grant would most probably be available. But let's cross one bridge at a time. What do you think?"

"Well", said David, "I seem to have no alternative".

"Do you want to go ahead and get yourself a professional qualification or not?" snapped Jack. After all the work he had put into this he must have felt a little hurt that David was not jumping with joy.

"O.K. I will dictate a letter to you tonight, if that is alright with you, and thank him for his letter and ask him to set up the initial stay at the rehabilitation centre".

Mum looked very unhappy about the whole business, but must have also felt that David had no alternative. He must accept the fact that his future was now in other's hands and he must also accept the fact that he was now a blind person and will have to mix with that group of people in the future.

"Do you think that they will make David use a white stick?" asked Mum, as she obviously thought that that would be so hard to take, especially around that neighbourhood.

"Only if he needs it, I imagine" replied Jack.

Several weeks passed before David received a reply to his letter of thanks and acceptance of the plan by Mr. Jeskinson. It informed him that prior to going to Torquay he had approached the Headmaster of Wallingcester College for the Blind and was now writing to inform David that the Head would like to interview him. Although the visit to Torquay had already been arranged for the six weeks before Christmas, as that was the only time they could fit in, if Wallingcester was not an option then they could think about training him for some other job. He said that the College did not return until mid September, so the interview must be early in October. The Head, Mr. Bradshaw, would write and let him know nearer the time. Jack thought all was going swimmingly, the only fly he could see in the ointment was, would the Local Authority provide the grant for David to go to Wallingcester?

Jack said, "I will make an appointment with Mr. Jackson to see him at some time in his working hours, which may make him a little more cooperative". This being done and the interview arranged they went racing off on Jack's motorbike to County Hall to confront the pleasant little man who held the keys to the money box held by the Education Department of the Local Authority. The little man was not quite so pleasant this time and when he heard the plan which Mr. Jeskinson had proposed he became quite obstructive. He said that this sort of

473

decision must be made by the full Education Board and he would have to put it on the agenda for the next meeting if they insisted in going ahead with the Principal of the Physiotherapy School's suggestions. David was very proud of Jack and his insistence on putting the proposal to the Board; he even volunteered to attend the Board Meeting if necessary. When they left the office, Mr. Jackson was in no doubt of their intention and said he would put the proposal to the Board in the best way possible.

"Tell the Board, if necessary", said Jack, "that my brother has tried everything to get ahead in life, and if the Board feels that there are not enough funds for this important member of their community, I will write to my Member of Parliament and put the case to him".

They left County Hall feeling that Mr. Jackson was on their side and would do all he could to solve the situation with a minimum of fuss. It was only a couple of weeks before they received a letter from County Hall saying that, if David was successful with his rehabilitation and if the Headmaster of Wallingcester accepted him as a pupil, they would cover the cost of this additional part of his education. On receiving the letter Jack and David jumped up and down with joy knowing that, if the rehabilitation went well and the interview with the Headmaster was successful and if at the end of all of this he passed the necessary educational requirements, his place at the Physiotherapy School would be assured. David realised that there were a lot of unknowns in this plan, but if all went well he could qualify as a Physiotherapist in about five years, but what about the lovely Janet, the girl he thought he would like to live with and love for the rest of his life. What about his home, the place where everybody cared for him and he felt safe. What about leaving all the very close friends he had in his youth club and finally, would he be a fool to lose contact with the desirable Polly, who seemed to understand his sexual needs and appeared to enjoy their secret liaisons as much as himself.

What a decision he had to make!

Chapter 50

When David told all his friends at the youth club about his progress, they were highly delighted. They wanted to know more about the Rehabilitation Centre at Torquay and the College at Wallingcester, but of course, not having been to either David could give them little information. The only amazing coincidence was that Wallingcester College for the Blind was taking part in a radio programme, Top of the Form. On the evening of the broadcast, which was the night of the youth club meeting, David stayed at home to hear the programme and was impressed by the knowledge of both teams. Unfortunately, Wallingcester lost, but gave a good account of themselves. It was the popular topic of conversation at the youth club and all of them assumed that he would get a place there without any difficulty. David was not so sure. The one positive element to the evening was that Janet came up to David with a lovely smile on her face and said how pleased she was to hear of his plans and wished him the best of luck in the future. David was surprised when she said,

"If there is anything I can do to help you in the next few weeks please let me know".

David knew only too well what she could do which would make his life well worth living, but hesitated to say anything at the time as he didn't want to destroy the massive breakthrough of actually talking to her.

Although David could feel his legs shaking and his mouth was dry, he said, "Thanks a lot; I may take you up on that offer in the coming weeks".

As she turned and walked away, looking lovelier than ever, David thought to himself, what a stupid answer to give to the girl he loved and how indecisive she must have thought he was. Mind you, she was most probably only being polite and any further loving relationship with him was most probably out of the question.

Father Kingswood was really pleased to hear of his plans for the future. He seemed as if he wanted to help in any way he could and began to involve David in his work in the parish. If he knew David was sitting around doing nothing, he would arrange to pick him up and take him on a visit of some kind. It began by inviting him to lunch at the curate's house next to the church. Two of them lived there and they had a very pleasant, short and round lady who came in and "did" for them. That was to keep the house tidy and produce the occasional meal. On the visits he made for lunch she always produced the tastiest of meals and would spend much of the time joking with the curates. Father Kingswood was very keen on music and knew of David's liking for jazz and popular tunes and singers of the time. His preference was for classical music and knowing that Jack had built a record player at their home, offered to lend David an album of "The New World Symphony", by Dvořák, a composer David didn't know. Although he had listened to some popular classics before, he had never waded through an album of four, twelve inch, LP's. He spent many hours listening and gradually being excited by certain passages when he would turn up the volume and indulge himself in the sounds. His ecstasy would often be ruined by Mum shouting out,

"Do we have to put up with that dreadful noise, can't you put on that nice music of Frankie Lane singing "I Believe".

David never realised it at the time, but he was gradually being influenced by the niceties of music, culture, eating and general living by Father Kingswood and the closeness of their friendship grew rapidly. They went on visits to his sister and brother-in-law and would have tea with an old aunt of his who lived in Kent. Father

Kingswood insisted on David calling him by his Christian name, Charles, when they were out visiting and David would enjoy the freedom that he had suddenly acquired by this close friendship. During the summer Charles decided that he was going to do a tour of the Devon and Cornwall coastline driving his new Lanchester car. He asked David if he would like to come along. It would be camping in a tent, but David knew that this would be quite easy as Charles was a scout leader and new all about camping. Charles pointed out that there would be a minimum of cost and he would cover all the main expenses. It turned out to be a very exciting holiday visiting all the quaint villages on the coast of both of these lovely counties. Some David had visited on his cycle tour when he was only fourteen, but this was so much easier and they had even taken a change of clothes so that they could visit the local church services and social events in the village halls. Occasionally they would visit a village pub for a glass of their local brew of cider, Charles never giving away the fact that he was a priest. He mixed so well with all the locals that they would invite him back. At one of the small churches they sat amongst the congregation, but were unable to sing the responses as they didn't know the tunes. One old lady leant over to Charles and pointed out the page and the response that was expected. She even pointed out with her finger to keep Charles up with the proceedings. They both laughed about it afterwards and it went down well with the youth club when they got back home.

It was one of those hot sunny summers and of course camping was a joy. They swam for miles out to sea. On one occasion off the coast in Falmouth, where the sea was crystal clear but icy cold, Charles got cramp and David, being a good swimmer, had a tremendous fight to keep Charles's head above water while he shouted for help. Luckily a boat was not too far away and they managed to get Charles into the boat, with some difficulty, and get them back to shore. They never ventured out too far again. The holiday had done David the world of good and he was deeply tanned from head to toe and he was as fit as a fiddle not having an ounce of fat on his body.

On the way home they popped into visit the Parish holiday in the New Forest. Many of the parishioners David knew, and this turned out to be a couple of days of shear luxury compared with the camping they had been used to. It was one of those holidays where everybody had a job to do and unluckily David had to help peel the buckets of potatoes needed for the dinner each evening. Acting as helpers at the retreat were several girls, or rather, young ladies, from Sherbourne College. One was particularly beautiful and spoke with an extremely cultured voice. She always looked after David and made sure that he had a good plateful of food. He and she would chat for a little time after the meal had finished and David began to think there was some sort of attraction there. One evening she asked David if he would like to stroll through the grounds with her and of course he accepted immediately. They strolled and they talked, but she was the type of girl that one wouldn't approach, even to hold her hand. When they arrived back at the house they received very black looks from all those in charge and it wasn't long before Charles took David aside and explained to him that the Vicar, who was responsible for the girl's safety, did not approve of David taking this pretty one out into the grounds unaccompanied.

"Anyway", said Charles, "she comes from a very wealthy family and a very expensive school. Her father would be very angry if he knew what had happened".

David found this hard to understand as they seemed to be saying that this young lady was too good for him. He felt very annoyed as firstly he had not made even a remote pass at the girl and secondly she was the one who invited him to take the walk. He was surprised to find how narrow minded the church was on such matters and felt tempted to ask her to meet him the next evening. This could not happen, however, as the next morning Charles and he packed up and set back on the road. David never knew, and didn't dare ask, if their rapid departure was due to his pleasant walk through the countryside with a beautiful young lady of high rank. On arrival home David soon forgot about this possible source of enjoyment and dropped back into the usual routine of sitting and listening to music with a little Braille practice in the mornings and on three days a week suffering the Mr. Benjamin visit. It had become a bit of a farce as David spent most of the time trying to teach him the rudamentaries of third grade Braille. David had learnt a lot from his aunt and uncle and had studied many of the abbreviations from the books that Mr. Benjamin brought with him. Knowing the system and the type of short hand was not too difficult as it followed a logical pattern, but feeling it with the fingers and reading fast enough to understand what one was reading was another matter. Each visit normally ended up with tea and a piece of Mum's home made cake and a chat about his life in India. In the evenings David would listen to the radio with the family. They usually liked comedy shows starring someone like Tommy Handley in "ITMA" or Ted Ray in "Ray's a Laugh". David would like "Take it from Here" with Jimmy Edwards, Dick Bentley and June Whitfield, or the new exciting serial of "Dick Barton, Special Agent". On Thursdays and after church on Sundays he would go to the youth club and either play snooker, with difficulty, drink tea or dance, sometimes with the beautiful Janet.

One of the evenings, when there was nothing on the radio and he was wondering if he should put a little more time into the learning of his Braille, he began to think of Polly. She had asked him to let her know what had happened with all the interviews he was attending. He felt his hands go sweaty thinking about it and his mouth became a little dry. Since that time he had tried to rid his mind of the pleasures of that evening and night, well up until two o'clock, but now he had retrieved some of his interest and as he thought more about it his interest grew and grew. Had she been waiting for him to come back to see her and was she still as sexually attractive as she was on that evening. David sat for a while pondering the thoughts of just sitting up against her and how she would react to his closeness. Soon he was so on edge that he got up and started walking from door to door, a matter of only about four yards.

Seeing his restlessness Mum said, "Why don't you sit down and read a book or something".

Then, before David could respond, she said,

"Oh, I am sorry, I forgot. Would you like a drink or something"?

"No thanks" replied David, "I think I might go out for a short walk just to keep my legs going. Look, I might pop into one of my friends' houses and even go out for a drink with him, so don't get worried about me, I am quite safe and happy on my own".

"Would you like me to come with you?" asked Dad.

David knew that this was a grand gesture by Dad as he never went out in the evenings during the week and was quite happy either listening to the radio or reading his books.

"No thanks Dad, I am quite happy on my own and I want to spend a little time thinking of what I am going to do over the next few months".

Firstly David walked down the road in the opposite direction to Polly's house. He crossed the small road and made his way towards Janet's house. He hoped that he would see her walking along the road and she would perhaps stop and talk to him. This would prevent him from indulging himself in the forbidden fruits that he knew would do him no good. Having no luck seeing Janet he walked down her road until he came level with her house but on the other side of the road. He could, with this outer vision, see a light in the window, but was frustrated to think that she was most probably there, but he had, because of his lack of sight, no chance of seeing her. He walked on past and went up the next road coming to the back of the woods. At the next turning he headed up to the pylon next to his infant school and then down the familiar road that he seemed to have covered a thousand times when he was young and when the war was on. He entered the opposite end of his own road and began to very slowly stroll along the pavement. He could feel the excitement of a sexual encounter and again his heart raced and he felt hot in the face. Something kept saying to him,

"You are stupid, you shouldn't be doing this. It would be better for you to walk straight past her house and go home and listen to the radio".

Then another voice said, "You are only going to tell her how you are getting on, there is no harm in it. After all, she did ask you to pop in and let her know and that is all you are doing".

As he approached her gate he slowed down again hoping that she would be sitting on the top step of her front door, a place popular with many of the people on that estate and a good place to catch passers by. Alas, she was not there. He walked past avoiding the temptation and came to the next small road. He stopped for a minute or two kicking the edge of the curb. There was no one around and it was beginning to get a little darker. The little voice came again,

"You must be stupid. She could be in that silky dressing gown and ready for bed".

He could feel his sexual urge was rising rapidly and he was shaking like a leaf. He shut all other thoughts from his mind and walked back to Polly's gate. He paused just before the gate. Then, lifting the latch quietly, he opened the gate and crept up the pathway leading to her front door. He hadn't knocked on her door before and experienced the desire to turn and run, as if he were playing "knock down ginger" a game they used to play when they were young. He raised his hand and gently knocked on the door.   He waited for a short while but there was no answer.   He looked towards the window which had a light on but the curtains were drawn.   He stood for a while and then knocked again but a little harder.   There was a noise inside and then a light came on in the porch way as the door was opened from the front room.   He heard the slipping back of the bolt on the bottom of the front door.   His heart started to beat violently as he thought of Polly, most probably ready for bed on the other side of the door.   He heard the latch of the door turn and the door was pulled wide open.

He stood there aghast with his mouth gaping.   He was unable to speak or even think of what to say.   Why hadn't he listened to the first little voice and gone straight home?

Chapter 51

"What can I do for you lad?"

Framed in the door stood a very large man. The light behind him made him look even larger and although not all that tall he seemed to stretch from one side of the door to the other. He was dressed in dark trousers which appeared to widen as the legs came down to his bare feet. He had no hair, but supported a rough looking beard, his torso being clad in just an off white vest. He appeared to move forward onto the top step and bent his head down as if trying to get a better view of the visitor.

"Come on lad, have you lost your tongue, what do you want?"

David suddenly came to his senses and stepping backward more or less into the privet hedge behind him he said,

"Is John in please?"

"John who?" snapped the man.

"John Jones", stammered David.

"Never heard of him. Hang on" he said, then turning to the inside door, "Polly, have you heard of someone called John Jones?" he shouted through the door. There was a movement inside and Polly's head came into view. Her hair was all ruffled and David couldn't see what she was wearing, but on spotting him she answered.

"Yes, he lives further down the road, number eleven I believe".

"There we are", said the man, "Try a bit further down the road. It's not surprising that I don't know him as I haven't been around for some time".

With that he shut the door more or less in David's face and the light in the porch went out as the inside door was closed. David quickly made his way out of the gate and turned down the road as if he were going to find number 11. Although it was the opposite direction to his own house he thought that they may have been looking out of the front window and would have become suspicious. Who the devil could that have been, he thought. Was it some other member of the opposite sex that Polly had been helping? He was just beginning to feel not only very jealous and hurt when he suddenly realised that it was most probably Polly's husband who had arrived home unexpectedly, as she said that he sometimes did. How lucky he thought that it wasn't the night that he had been up in her bedroom with her. He made his way home the long way round by the pub and felt very relieved when he entered his front room and could hear the sound of the radio. He knew that from now on he would not go that way past Poll's house just in case he should bump into the two of them with the two children. It would be very hard to explain why the children knew him and he had pretended that he didn't know Polly.

That summer the youth club had decided to visit Shanklin, on the Isle of Wight again for their summer holiday. David had told them that he would not be going this year, as he said that he had too much to do before he went off to the rehabilitation centre in Torquay. This was quite untrue as he would have dearly loved to be with them all down on the Island, but firstly he had very little money as he was now not able to do a paper round and he had no other source of income. Added to that, he felt that he couldn't face two weeks of being in that wonderful part of the country knowing that Janet was also there and probably ignoring him all the time. He knew he would be thinking of the wonderful times they had spent together and would feel heartbroken. As they got nearer and nearer the time Father

484

Kingswood came to visit him at his house. Mum was always pleased to see him as she knew that he was a very kind man and worthy of his position in the church. He came to David to explain that an anonymous donor had given money to help cover his holiday with the youth club and wondered how David felt about it? Mum and Dad were opposed on principal and showed their disapproval, so David explained that he didn't really want to go. Charles did not argue, he just accepted the decision and said that it was a bit of a pity as many members of the club would be disappointed.

At the youth club that Thursday David tried to keep himself occupied with playing snooker, although even trying to hit the white ball was difficult and to direct it down the table in the correct position was virtually impossible. The rest of the club members were discussing the trip down to the Isle of Wight and what sort of activities they would set up. After a short time David was aware of Janet standing close to one end of the table. She was dressed in a white dress with a green leafy pattern which reached down to her knees and around her waist was the very attractive white belt which emphasised her figure and the broadness of her pelvis. David began to feel more and more embarrassed as he made a fool of himself either missing the white ball or putting it down into a pocket by mistake. She stood and said nothing until the end of the game which came much quicker than he would have liked. As he turned to put the cue into its rack by the side of the hall Janet came up to his side.

"I have been asked by the rest of the club to ask you if you would consider changing your mind over coming with us down to the Isle of Wight. We know that you are having a bad time at the moment and we all feel it would do you a lot of good to have a fortnight's holiday. What do you say?"

He just didn't know how to respond. He couldn't tell her that he was short of money and could not afford to go and secondly he knew that he would be heartbroken to have her so close to him and yet out of arms reach.

"I don't think that it would solve my problems" he said, "Anyway, I told Father Kingswood that I just didn't want to go this year and I thought that was the end of it".

"Well, if that's how you feel, I will let the rest of the club know. Mind you, I would like you to remember that this is a Christian Youth Club and we try to be thoughtful of others especially our own members. Perhaps you would do well to try to look on the shiny side of the coin and make the best of what you have".

"You tell me then what is the best of the situation as far as I am concerned. I have no job, I cannot see properly, I have no money and the thing I most desire in life has gone. My art career is finished, I have had to cancel my offer of a post at the BBC and I have been rejected by the Air Force for my national service. You tell me what the shiny side of the coin is".

She stood and looked at him blankly not knowing what to say, and then she moved a step nearer and took his hand. David felt a zing of excitement at the mere contact with her and although he was looking and sounding angry he experienced a flow of warmth coming from this young and beautiful woman.

"I am sorry for reacting the way I did", she said, "It was the group that are going to Shanklin that wanted me to approach you as they thought you would be easier persuaded by me. We are all very concerned about your future and how we can help".

"Thanks Janet, I'm also sorry about the way I reacted, but to tell the truth I thought that we were more than just good friends and imagined that you thought the same. I would be very grateful if you would tell the rest of them that my mind is made up, I'll skip the holiday this year".

As they wandered down the road on the way home, David noticed that nobody mentioned the vacation. They all seemed very cheerful and asked many questions about his visit to the rehabilitation centre and his eventual entry to Wallingcester College and then the Physiotherapy School. No one seemed to doubt his ability to get over all the hurdles on the way and they were even asking him questions about what physiotherapists do and where they fit into the Health Service. They had their usual chat on the corner and then broke up to make their way home. David was pleased to find Janet at his side walking the same way home as himself. They talked a little about the evening classes she had joined and David enquired about her Mum and Dad, of whom he was particularly fond as they had shown such kindness to him earlier on. When they reached the turning towards David's house Janet said,

"Would you have the time to walk down to my gate with me?"

David was utterly amazed. He never expected such a welcome invitation and although it would not mean a reconciliation, it would give him tremendous pleasure.

"Of course", he said, "I am not in a hurry".

She again brought up the subject of the holiday, but this time approached it in a different way.

"I am sorry that you have made up your mind about not going to Shanklin with us. Many of the club will miss you being there and I know Father Kingswood will be very disappointed. Please take a little time to reconsider your decision, we would all be pleased if you came, in fact some of us will particularly miss you".

487

David was very impressed with the thoughtful way in which Janet had approached the subject and wondered how such a mature head could be on such young shoulders. He felt that he must be honest with her and tell her the real reason for not going on the holiday.

"To be quite honest Janet there is only one reason I am turning down the trip and that is because I still have deep feelings for someone in the club and I can't bear the thought of seeing her every day and not be close to her".

"Is this someone I know", she said looking a little hurt.

"You know her very well" he said.

"Is it my sister?"

"No, you fool, it is you".

"I thought you had gone right off of me seeing that you didn't talk to me anymore and made no effort to dance or walk with me".

She took both of his hands and squeezed them. "I am still very fond of you David, but I think it will take a little time to iron out our difficulties. Meet me on the usual corner on Sunday morning and we will go to Communion together. She reached up and kissed him on the cheek and then turned around, opened the gate and went down the path to her door.

That summer at Shanklin turned out to be the best that David had ever experienced. It always boasted as having the greatest amount of sunshine of anywhere in the country, and that year was no exception. It had not taken long for Janet to change his mind about the holiday. She made it quite clear to him that she had missed him and their close friendship and it was her in particular that wanted David to go with them. They swam in the gently lapping, blue sea, walked all the way into the towns of Shanklin and Sandown and played hand ball and cricket on the lawn. Strangely, David took part in the cricket and although he was a disaster when it came to batting, when he was asked to bowl he achieved one of the best results he had ever had. He had always been able to swing the ball to the leg or the off and naturally bowled at a regular length, about six feet short of the batsman. He was also aware of the position of the batsman so he bowled at his legs. He ended up by taking seven wickets and left the pitch to a round of applause. They danced more or less every evening and Janet, his partner, allowed him to become closer and closer to her, not only physically but also affectionately. They would often walk along the cliff path in the evening with their arms around each other and when no one was insight, would stop for a lingering kiss or two. David found that he was growing in confidence and it seemed that this was all because of his reunification with Janet. By the time they had arrived home they were again a couple, going to the cinema, church or dances together. Mum and Dad were delighted to see Janet back on the scene; they had always thought very highly of her and hoped that in time they may, in Mum's words, "Make a go of it". They were also pleased to see the change in David and how he now looked forward to each day and his positive attitude to his future. Although David was again enjoying life, at the back of his mind he still realised that he would have to leave Janet soon and spend some time away from home. They did talk about it and Janet would say that it was only the same as if he were going into the forces for two years and anyway there would be long holidays when they could be together.

It was during September that a letter arrived from Wallingcester College for the Blind. The headmaster explained that the interview that he was to have with David must be postponed for a month as he was tied up with business which would keep him away from the College. He suggested another date in late November or early December when he could be available. He wrote that he also knew of David's visit to Torquay and would arrange for them to release David for a day for the trip up to Wallingcester. It all seemed fairly simple organization until another letter arrived a week later from the man in charge of Torquay, a Mr Duke, saying that because of this rearrangement he must insist on David coming a week early to cover the interruption. It was not a very pleasant letter, but Jack pointed out that it may have upset the room allocation.. Janet became almost one of the family, spending many evenings round David's house and on the odd occasion would stay overnight. Mum always kept a close watch on what went on and Janet spent the night in Susy's room, in fact in Susy's bed. She would creep in to give David a goodnight kiss but little more as Jack or Bobby were usually in the room. Still, it was nice to have her around all the time and David could feel the closeness of their love affair growing by the day.

The last few days before he was expected at Torquay were a mixture of enjoyment and anticipation. Janet and David made as much of the time as was possible and would meet early in the morning and part late at night. Although all the plans were set for his coming trip he viewed it with a great deal of worry and felt unsure that this was what he really wanted to do. The thought of leaving Janet for at least six weeks was almost unbearable and he hoped that he wouldn't get cold feet at the last minute and cry off. The day before he went he spent mainly packing his case with clean clothes, toilet bag and anything he may need. Father Kingswood said that he would drive David up to Paddington Station to catch the train. Mum and Janet both wanted to come to wave him off, so they were all assembled in the front room in plenty of time. They all piled into the car at half past eight giving them more than adequate time to get to Paddington for the ten o'clock train. What they hadn't bargained for was that Charles did not know exactly where Paddington Station was and they spent a good twenty minutes racing around the streets of west London trying to find the way. Mum and Janet, in the back of the car, were becoming very agitated and Charles, although saying nothing, was on tender hooks and driving like a madman.

At last they reached the station and Mum, Janet and David jumped out and rushed to the ticket office as quickly as they could. After purchasing the ticket the man said that they should hurry to the platform as the train was about to leave. By this time Charles had parked the car and joined them as they ran on to the platform. They had little time to say their goodbyes. Charles shook him by the hand and wished him luck, Mum threw her arms around him and gave him a hug and Janet just had time to give him a quick kiss on the lips before he opened the door and jumped into the carriage. He undid the leather strap that held the window up and allowed it to drop down. But before he could lean out the train began to move. They walked along the platform with the train until it started to gather speed and then they stopped and just waved. David felt his heart sink as the three figures grew smaller and smaller as the train pulled out of the station and he felt that he wanted to open the door and jump out. They were the people he loved the most who were disappearing from his life and he was now to face an unknown future in an institution with a lot of other blind people, far away from home and in a town way down on the Devon coast. He could feel the tears welling up in his eyes and he wished that he had never made that decision to go away from those he knew and loved.

Chapter 52

David closed the window by pulling the leather strap towards him and fixed it by slipping the small rounded pin on the door through the hole in the strap. He picked up his case and began to shuffle his way down the narrow corridor on the opposite side of the carriage. He looked through the window of the sliding door of the first compartment and could see people standing. They may have been getting settled to sit down, but it looked quite crowded. He passed several compartments that all appeared full so he continued along the corridor until he entered the next carriage. He passed two more compartments and then peering into the third he noticed plenty of room. He slid back the door and was surprised to see that there was only one occupant, a lady, sitting in the forward facing seat near the window. He lifted his case up onto the rack above the facing seat and sat down by the window, but facing backwards to where the train had been rather than where it was going. This was not his favourite position, but he was pleased to even find an unoccupied seat. He sat for some time looking out of the window as the train began to gather speed. He could hear the pounding of the wheels growing faster and faster and the bellowing noise of the engine. Every now and again he saw a cloud of steam and smoke pass the window and he sat back to try to enjoy the long train journey. It reminded him of his trip to Mansfield when he and Betty were evacuated and would have done anything to have her by his side again. As he dreamed on he was growing more and more aware of the lady opposite. She would turn her head and glance at him when she thought he was looking out of the window, but what she did not know was that David was beginning to use his outer vision much more than when he had normal sight. He could concentrate on a point out of the window, which of course he could not see, but hone in on something in his outer vision. It was not clear sight, but it gave him a clue as to what people were doing. After about ten minutes she leaned forward and said,

"Excuse me young man, I see that you are very interested in the towns and countryside we are passing through. I have a brochure which explains the route and all you can see on one's journey. I have done this trip so often that it is of little use to me, would you like to borrow it?"

David leaned a little forward. The lady had a lovely voice, very cultured and clear, good enough he thought to be on the radio as a news reader. She was dressed in a light grey suit with a jacket which was open at the upper part revealing a crisp, white blouse. The skirt seemed to be quite tight and came down to just above her knees. It looked as if she was wearing high heels and strangely, a large brimmed hat. It was quite uncommon for ladies to wear hats where David came from except when they were going to a wedding. She had long blonde hair that came down to her shoulders which, to David's imagination, seemed to be very tidy. He thought for a while and, not wanting to make the mistake he had before and saying that he could not read, said,

"That is kind of you, but I have a problem with my sight and I am now unable to read. It would have been nice to know about the countryside we are passing through, but unfortunately that is one of the pleasures I have to forgo at the present".

David thought that he was sounding very mature and educated and was pleased with his response. There was again a pause for about five minutes, then the lady said,

"Would you like me to read the brochure to you? It is a long journey and it would help to pass the time for us both".

"I would certainly like to hear about the journey, but I wouldn't like to impose on you", then pointing to the brief case and papers she had at the side of her he said, "You obviously have a lot of work to do".

"Oh, don't worry, that can wait. Would you like to hear a little of the information in the brochure?"

"Yes please".

She was about to begin when David had a dreadful thought and interrupted her immediately.

"This is not a ladies only compartment, is it?"

She gave a little chuckle and said,

"No, you are alright, as long as you do not want to smoke as this is a non smoking compartment".

"No, I hate the habit, it makes me feel quite sick".

She began again to read from the small folded paper, but checked where they were before doing so. Her reading was clear and precise and her voice was one to fall in love with. During the periods between the places of interest she began to ask David questions about himself and how he had come to this difficult situation in life. By her voice and manner David would have guessed that she was about in her late twenties or early thirties, obviously well educated and very kind. It wasn't long before he got around to telling her of his aspirations in the art world and the cruel blow that ended them. He avoided all the troubles he managed to get into at the school and gave her the impression that ice cream would not melt in his mouth. He was in the middle of telling her of his trip to the hospital and the BBC broadcast that had been heard by his uncle, when the door was slid open and the ticket inspector dressed in a dark blue uniform and a flat cap came into the compartment.

"Tickets please" he said.

The lady looked into her handbag and then produced what looked like a card. The inspector just glanced at it and said,

"Thank you".

He then turned to David and put out his hand to take the ticket which David offered him. He looked at it and then at David.

"This is a third class ticket, did you know that?" he said rather abruptly.

"Oh, that is alright inspector, he is with me and I will sort it out when we reach our destination" said the lady.

Strangely, the inspector touched the peak of his cap and said,

"That's fine Ma'am", turned and left the carriage closing the door behind him.

David was a little confused by this conversation and knew that something was not quite right, but he couldn't fathom out what it was.

"Is it OK me being in here?" he said.

"Yes, don't worry, I know the inspector quite well as I travel on this train regularly. Now, go on with your story, I find it quite fascinating".

By the time they were approaching Torquay they had become quite good friends. She had asked David his name and said that her's was

Anthea. She said that she lived in Torquay and would like David to visit her while he was there. She handed him a card and said,

"I know that you can't read it, but keep it in your wallet as it has my phone number on it. I know the Manor, where you are staying quite well, I live quite close. Try to remember the address, it is Riviera View, Lincoln Close and it is about half a mile down the hill from where you are staying. I have got a car waiting at the station, can I give you a lift?"

"No that's kind of you, but I am being picked up".

As they left the train she turned and said,

"Are you sure you are alright, I will wait until your lift turns up".

Almost immediately a youngish man in a sports coat and flannels came up to David.

"Are you Mr. Fellows?"

"Yes" said David.

The man then picked up David's case and turned to walk off the station platform.

Anthea took his hand and whilst shaking it kissed him on both cheeks.

"I look forward to seeing you soon", she said.

David was quite surprised to find that he was not welcomed at the door of the rehabilitation centre, but was taken straight up to his room at the back of the house. He noticed that it was a room for four persons although there was no one there at the time. The driver, Simon, placed his case at the side of the bed by the door and said,

"When you have unpacked come down to the dining room on the right of the front entrance and you will get some tea and cake".

David began to feel quite lonely. He would have to put up with at least six weeks of this and he would have done anything to have been at home and getting ready to go out with Janet to the youth club. He began to unpack his clothes which he placed in the single wardrobe which stood at the side of his bed. The Manor itself appeared to be a beautiful house with a Gothic style although David knew that it was only mock. It must have belonged to some wealthy family at some time as it was set in its own grounds with a winding drive running up from very impressive gates to an entrance worthy of a stately home. He also noticed that to reach the first floor they had to climb an impressive wooden stairway with a magnificent mock Gothic window on one side. After hanging most of his clothes in the wardrobe and putting his underwear in the set of draws at the side of the bed, he made his way down the stairway to the extensive hall. He could hear the noise of voices coming from the room straight ahead and guessed that that was the dining room. As he entered the door he was at last greeted by a very pleasant, rather large lady in a white overall.

"Hello", she said, "Are you David Fellows? We have been expecting you. Sit over here". She took him by the arm and guided him to a table in the corner where three of the four seats were already taken.

"This is our new member, David", she said, "Sit down and I will bring you some tea and cakes". He was immediately made welcome by the three occupants. One was quite a lot older than the rest and introduced himself as Syd. The second about ten years older than David and was introduced as Charlie and the third, a much younger man, or perhaps a boy, was called Danny. They all showed great interest in David's reason for coming to the Manor and would become close friends of David's during his stay. They spent some time in telling David all the things he should do and not do and all the things he should know about the staff.   Apparently, the man in charge, Mr. Duke, was not a very popular character and most of the administration was carried out by his wife, who was a powerful, dominating kind of person.   They sat at the same table for the meal that evening, which was excellent.   The cook was obviously a professional and knew how to keep her clientele happy.   A gong was sounded about eleven o'clock and everybody made their way up to their bedrooms.   David had never experienced this kind of routine before and found it a little off putting.   There was only one bathroom for the four occupants of the room, one of whom was the younger member of the tea group.   At about eleven thirty the lights were turned off by a member of staff and they all settled down to get some sleep.   David lay awake for hours listening to the snoring of three of the occupants and when he eventually did dose off he was awakened by a very loud, intermittent alarm.   It sounded a little like the dive alarm on a submarine.   It was followed by a voice welcoming them to another day and a list of instructions.   This was followed by the BBC news.

After washing and dressing they all made their way down to the dining room where they were provided with a superb breakfast. David had been told that his first job was to go to Mr. Duke's office to be instructed on his programme for the weeks to come.   He knocked on the door and was taken into a plush office by a tall, rather cold woman.   She told him to sit on the chair in front of the large wooden desk and then went round the desk to sit at the side of a smaller, slightly balding man.   He started the instructions in a rather insensitive manner.

"We do not like people to come here with predetermined ideas.   We like to assess the candidate and put them on the correct road for their rehabilitation.   We believe that you have already made approaches to Wallingcester College for the Blind and we think that this is jumping the gun.   Do you understand?"

"Yes", said David, "But..." he was interrupted by the little bald man again.

"We have many crafts that we feel that you should study including mat making, stool making, clay modelling, needlework etc. and we expect you to do at least one hours Braille each day. Twice a week a lady will come in to teach typing and you will be tested each week. You will be expected to go on the organized walk each morning before breakfast, at seven o'clock and you will be in your bedroom by eleven at night. All meal times must be adhered to rigidly and tests will be done on your mobility at the end of three weeks. Is that all clear?"

"Yes".

"Now, is there anything you want to ask or request?"

"Yes sir, I need to get my Braille and typing up to scratch as soon as possible so I would be pleased if I could double up on these subjects. I also have done clay modelling at the Art School and would welcome continuing with that craft".

"We will see what can be done", said the woman who David assumed was Mrs. Duke. "It's not always best for a newly blind person to do the things he did when he was fully sighted".

She then took David by the arm and led him to the door which she opened and thrust him through.

David was extremely disappointed to find that his timetable, which was given to him by the very pleasant lady in charge of stool making, did not follow any of his requests. He had only the hour per day at the Braille and twice a week typing. He was also put into the stool making and not into the clay modelling class. The teachers were very pleasant and he enjoyed each of the classes, but he doubled up on the

Braille and typing in the evenings when the others were listening to music or the "Goons" on the radio. On occasions, two young ladies, one about David's age and the other no more than sixteen, would join him in the craft room and seemed to enjoy just talking to him. They would often bring in mugs of tea and just sit and chat. David did complain to Mr. Duke that he was not getting enough Braille and typing tuition, but it was to no avail.

One morning, during stool making David heard his name being called out over the loud speaker system. He was asked to report to the office. Everybody was intrigued to find out what it was all about. He knew that he had done nothing wrong so he felt that it must be something pleasant. He was delighted to see, sitting in the office, Anthea, the lady from the train. He went straight up to her and said,

"How lovely to see you Anthea. I thought that you would have forgotten all about me".

"Of course I hadn't", she said, taking him by both of his hands and kissing him on both cheeks. "I have just come to ask this kind Mr. Duke if he would allow you to have the afternoon off and come to my house for tea".

"That would be marvellous", said David and turning to Mr. and Mrs. Duke said,

"Is that alright, I am sure that I can find my way there and back without any difficulty".

"That will be quite unnecessary" said Anthea, "I will arrange for you to be picked up and brought back at the time Mr. Duke suggests".

She stood up and shaking Mr. and Mrs. Duke by the hand she turned and left the room saying as she went through the door,

"I'll see you about three thirty then, if that is alright".

After she had gone Mr. Duke told David to sit down on the chair on the opposite side of the desk. He looked as stern as a blind man could look and said,

"I am not happy that residents at this establishment make arrangements that do not fit in to the normal pattern during their stay here. I don't like people using their influence through titled persons gaining advantage over other residents. Luckily for you, Lady Howard is a generous benefactor of the NIB and I am willing for you to take up this offer, but I want it made quite clear that this must be the last time and I don't want you bragging around the rest of the residents. Do you understand?"

David was shocked and stunned by this reaction and all he could say was,

"Yes sir".

At a quarter past three he stood by the arched, stone doorway waiting for his lift. He was dressed in his only suit, a clean white shirt and with his shoes highly polished. All available eyes were trained on him from windows and doors as every bit of sight available to the residents was being used to describe to those with no sight what was happening. David had been absolutely astounded that this attractive lady with the broad brimmed hat that he had met on the train was actually a Lady in the true sense of the word. He decided that he must call her Lady Anthea in the future and speak to her with more respect. Another thing dawned on him; the carriage in which he had joined her on the train was nearly empty as it was most probably First Class. He did feel that it was very roomy and the seats were quite plush, perhaps that was what all the fuss was when the ticket inspector came round. She must have paid the extra money at the station, he thought. At precisely twenty past three a large car glided up the drive and drew to a halt just

501

in front of the door. A man in a dark suit and flat, peaked hat got out of the driving seat and came round the back of the car. He came up to David and said,

"Mr. Fellows I presume".

"That is correct" replied David.

Opening the back door of the car he said,

"If you would just like to climb inside and make yourself comfortable we will be at Riviera View in a few minutes. There seemed a lot of room in the back of the car and there was a kind of screen between him and the driver. The glass window behind the driver was open, but he never spoke as they glided down the drive and then onto the road. Within minutes they turned up into a drive which he knew was made up of gravel as he could hear the crunchy sound under the tyres. They came to a halt in front of a large white house with a doorway similar to that of Manor House. David went to open the door, but could not find the handle. The chauffer came round to the door and opened it from the outside. He was met at the door by a pretty young lady in maid's uniform and a little white hat on the head.

"Would you come this way sir" she said.

David was beginning to feel very worried. At first it all seemed very pleasant and a good idea to get out of the Manor House for a while, but now things seemed to be going too far. This was the sort of event that one sees on films and he thought that he was getting out of his depth. Lady Anthea was sitting on a type of long settee with a high back at one end. As David entered the room, which had large windows and a French door overlooking gardens and the sea, she got up and came over to him. She put a hand on both shoulders and kissed him on both cheeks. She seemed to do this each time they met or parted. David had never been kissed on both cheeks before; he thought that this must be what the aristocracy did. They moved to the window area and sat on two white wicker chairs on either side of a small round table, overlooking the garden and sea. They chatted together as if they were old friends and she never stopped asking him questions. After they had had tea and cakes which had been brought in by the maid, Anthea took him by the hand and lead him over to the settee.

"I am sorry said David, I think that I should be calling you Lady Anthea as I believe that is your title".

"Oh, don't be so silly. To my friends I am Anthea".

She told him that her husband was in banking in the City of London and spent nearly the whole week up there only travelling down at weekends.

"Mind you", she said, "Most of his weekends last from Thursday evening till Tuesday morning, so you could say he is down here as much as he is up there. Nevertheless, he spends a lot of time on the phone and seems to do most of his business that way".

She moved up the seat closer to him and began to point out some of the features they had in the garden. David laughed and said,

"I think you have forgotten why I am down here".

She put her arm around his shoulders and said,

"I am sorry. You're right, for that moment I did forget. You see you look as if you can see normally and you look where I point".

"I am getting into the habit of pretending to look at people because if I look in the opposite direction it looks rude".

She gave him an extra hug and David could feel the silkiness of her dress up against him. Being this close he could see that she was an extremely attractive young woman with a very slender figure.

"I know", she said, "I'll find one of William's warmer coats and we can take a closer look around the garden". It was a brilliant idea because he could now see at close hand some of the beauty of the garden and the views of the sea through the trees.

"Of course", she said, "In the summer it is full of beautiful flowers and shrubs, but even at this time of the year it is still very colourful as this part of the coast faces south and is sheltered by the hills to the back of us. In fact it is called the Riviera because many of the trees hold their leaves and palm trees grow along the front".

Anthea held David's hand all the time they were out in the garden and although he was enjoying it tremendously, he knew that it was purely to make sure that he didn't trip over any of the paving. When they came back into the house Anthea offered David a drink. She knew dinner was served at the Manor at seven and promised that she would see that he was back in time. She gave a quiet chuckle and said,

"We don't want to upset that kind little man Mr. Duke, do we? By the way, we are having a little reception as a sort of pre-Christmas get together on Sunday week. It will only be a few fairly close friends, but it will be a good chance for you to meet my husband, William. Do you think Mr. Duke will let you come? I will arrange to pick you up and get you back".

"Sundays are usually free for us to do more or less as we please, but we are encouraged to go to church in the morning. I don't seem to be in Mr. Duke's good books for some unknown reason, but I am sure if you phoned him he would find it difficult to refuse".

"That's fixed then.   Now take care of yourself and I hope all your plans come to fruition".

She then wrapped her arms around his neck and pulled him up close to her.   She held him like that for what seemed like ages and he could feel her pleasant figure tightly up against him.   He didn't know whether to put his arms around her waist, but decided not to as this might spoil the close friendship they had built.

Everybody at the Manor wanted to know how he had got on and what the house was like.   David tried to make little of it as he didn't want those in authority to get the wrong end of the stick. Later on that week he was again summoned to the office and Mr. Duke pointed out to him that he did not like people phoning and asking to visit the residents.   He said,

"You are here for a reason and sometimes I think you purposely forget".

David was quite shocked at this remark as he assumed that it was Lady Howard that had phoned and he was surprised that Mr. Duke would react in such an arrogant fashion to her.

"I have had a phone call from someone who says he is your vicar and would like to come to visit you.   Of course, I had to say that he could and suggested the Sunday after next.   I hope that he is your vicar as I have asked him to take the service in our chapel on that morning.   I take it he is ordained?

"Yes" said David, "I know he is ordained as I went to his ordination service at Chichester Cathedral".

It was only when David was leaving the office that he suddenly realised that that was the same day that Anthea had asked him to go to the reception at her house.   He didn't want to miss either of them.

Charles may have some news of Janet and how she was getting on. Although he had received letters from her every other day which he had got Miss Pope, the craft teacher to read to him, some news from someone who had seen her would ease the ache he had in his heart. On the other hand, he did not want to miss the little lunch party laid on by Anthea. It would be nice to see her again and pay a second visit to that beautiful house. What could he do?

Chapter 53

"Mr. Fellows". It was the rather abrupt voice of Mrs. Duke. "I have just taken a phone call from Lady Howard. I am not in the habit of acting as messenger girl to residents at this establishment, but she asked if you would be allowed to go to her Christmas reception next Sunday. Of course I had no alternative than to accept on your behalf. You seem to be treating this place as a hotel, do remember that you are here to be rehabilitated and not for your amusement".

Although David was required to go on the early morning walks he had grown into the habit of not going with the pack but finding his way along the cliff gardens on his own. He liked to have a little time away from the group so that he could think about Janet, home and the situation down there in Torquay. He had just been coming in the front door when Mrs. Duke spotted him. She was about to turn away when David said,

"Didn't Mr. Duke tell you that I had my vicar coming to see me on that day? I can't accept Lady Howard's invitation".

"I am not here to solve your problems" she said, "I will leave it to you to sort out your diary of events". She made a harsh growling noise a little like a dog who is anticipating attacking a stranger, then she turned and walked away.

David worried nearly the whole day about how he could deal with this awkward situation until late in the afternoon he remembered that Lady Howard had given him a card with her phone number on it. With the help of Miss Pope he extracted the number and went to the hall telephone. A quiet little voice answered the phone, who he assumed was the maid.

"Could I speak to Lady Howard please?"

"She is engaged at the moment, could I give her a message".

"I would rather like to speak to her in person if that is possible. Could you say that David is on the line?"

There was a pause as if the mouthpiece had been covered over then he heard Anthea's voice".

"Hello David, is anything wrong?"

David had not had a lot of practice at speaking on the telephone and stammered,

"No, well I mean yes".

"What is it David, take your time, there is no rush", came the calming voice of Anthea.

David explained how, due to no fault of his own the two Dukes had made a muddle of the arrangements for the next Sunday and although they had accepted her kind invitation, had also booked his friend, Charles, the vicar of their church to come on the same day.

"So what is the problem David? Bring him along with you he will be very welcome and I am sure he will find many of my friends interesting to talk to. That will save me sending the car for you. I take it he is coming by car?"

"Yes, he is coming by car. Well is that alright?", asked David, "Will you mind having another guest?".

"That is no problem. I look forward to seeing you on Sunday about twelve o'clock".

Charles arrived earlier than David had expected that Sunday. He was already dressed in his cassock and dog collar and looked extremely important with his vestments over his arm. He had stayed in a local hotel down in the town for the night so that he could be there in time for the service. David thought that the Duke's were a little taken aback by the pleasant manner that Charles greeted them, although he thought that they were pleased to have, as it were, a visiting clergy. The service went well with more of the residents attending than usual and after Charles changed out of his robes and into a suit, but still retaining the dog collar, they left to visit the Howard's. In the short journey down the road David had to explain about how he had met Anthea on the train and how they had seemed to click. He also explained about the mix up made by Mr. and Mrs. Duke and how it had led to this very pleasant interlude. They were greeted at the door by a man in morning dress, who they took to be the butler and he showed them through into the room in which David had had tea with Anthea. It looked much larger as most of the furniture had been moved to the side and on the right a door was open which David had not seen before. It led into a large conservatory. There were many more people in both rooms than David had imagined and he turned to Charles and said,

"I'm sorry, this seems to be a bigger reception than I was led to believe, I hope you don't mind".

"Don't worry", answered Charles, "I am used to this sort of thing".

Almost immediately Anthea came up to them both and greeted them. David was more than surprised that in that sort of company she put her arms around David's shoulders and kissed him on both cheeks. She looked absolutely radiant in a beautiful silk, powder blue dress which had no sleeves and a moderately low cut "V" at the front. Her hair was wound up in a pile on top of her head which made her look taller than before, or was it the very high heels she was wearing. She shook Charles warmly by the hand and said,

"I have heard a lot about you from David. You have obviously been a very good friend and mentor over a very difficult period of his life and I was so pleased to hear that it had grown into a close friendship which I know he values. Now let me introduce you to my husband, who is also looking forward to meeting David".

They made their way through to the conservatory, being supplied with a drink served on a silver tray by a pretty little maid, until, in an area of small trees they spotted a group of large portly men, some in morning dress but mostly in smart suits. Amongst them was another man with a dog collar and he and Charles greeted each other like old friends, which strangely, they were, having studied together at Chichester, but not in the same year. Anthea's husband, Sir William, was a charming man and naturally used to this sort of occasion. He introduced them both to all the members of the group and then spent some time just talking to David and asking him about his art career, his loss of sight, his prognosis and how he had planned his future. At the end of quite a long interrogation, Anthea took his hand and said,

"If you will excuse us darling, I would like to introduce David to some of my friends", and immediately pulled him out of the group and into the main room leaving Charles, sadly, to fend for himself. He had also been enthralled by the beauty and personality of Anthea and would have preferred to be shown around by her. David went from group to group being introduced to so many people he couldn't really remember any of their names or professions. One of the disadvantages of his loss of central vision was that he couldn't see people's faces, so he could not remember them. Another phenomenon, which was difficult to explain to people one had just met, was that to see them he had to look away from them and when he looked at them, they disappeared. He had to look at a blank space where their face would be when he talked to them otherwise they would think he was talking to someone else. The party was a great success and as they were leaving David having drunk many glasses of what he thought must have been champagne and eaten many small snacks most of which he could not recognise, Sir William invited him to come and have dinner with them one evening in the future. Anthea, after shaking hands with Charles, put her arms right around David and gave him a lingering kiss on just one cheek. He was looking forward to the one on the other cheek, but it did not come.

David said goodbye to Charles at the door of Manor House and felt a very great affection toward this man who had put himself out to try to ease David's sight and career problems. They had made a short tour of the area after leaving the party and had ended up by having dinner at the hotel Charles had stayed in the night before down in the main part of Torquay by the gardens and overlooking the promenade and the sea. They had spent a lot of time talking about Janet and how much she was now helping in the church and youth club, but it only made David feel even more lonely knowing she was so far away and it was going to be such a long time before he saw her again. It was strange how, although he was attracted by many women of all ages, even finding some of them extremely sexually desirable, his heart was tied just to one person and life without her being around was miserable. Nevertheless, he knew that being away from her was unavoidable. He only hoped that she would not go off him in these breaks although to expect a young girl to wait for such a long time had its dangers. He put everything he could into the time he spent down in Torquay. He worked hard in the handicraft section and managed to produce his own original pattern to cover one of the string seated stools. Miss Pope, a curly, ginger haired lady of about thirty five, who was always dressed in a smart, well pressed, green uniform, which showed off the shape of her figure to advantage, was thrilled to see that David had not followed the directions to give him a chequered top to his stool, but had invented a complex pattern using three colours. The little lady that taught Braille was extremely pleased with David's growing abilities to read grade three Braille. She knew that he put a lot of time on his own in the evenings practicing reading and she would encourage him always to move on to the more difficult books. He had typing only twice a week, and that was for one hour at a time. This annoyed him intensely as he had asked if he could do as many hours as possible. Mr. Duke pointed out to him that he wasn't to be treated as a special case and must receive the same as everybody else. However, by typing letters to Janet, Betty and Peter, in the Navy, he was developing more speed and a little more accuracy, but he knew there was still some way to go.

Later that week he was again summoned to the "King and "Queen's" office. This time he expected to get a good reception as all the staff had told him that they were well pleased with his work and how much he had been improving. He also thought that his arranging for Charles to take the service on the Sunday and his connections with the Howard's would stand him in good stead. Not so. He was told to sit down in the chair on the opposite side of the desk from the Duke's. There was a long period of silence then Mr. Duke said,

"I have just received a letter from Mr. Bradshaw, the headmaster of Wallingcester. He tells me that you have already arranged an interview with him at the college. I do not like this sort of behaviour down here at Manor House. I told you when you arrived that I did not like people coming here with predetermined ideas and you have proved my point. You have not accepted the fact that you are now a blind person and you have not taken the guidance which we have given to you".

David was becoming extremely annoyed with this pompous little man telling him what to do and running down all the things that he did. He interrupted,

"That is completely unfair and untrue. I have worked hard at the subjects you set for me and I think that if you spoke to the staff they would agree with me".

"That is not the point", said Mr. Duke, "you have set your goals far above your ability. We", and here he included his wife, "do not think you have the brain to study and qualify as a physiotherapist. We think that you are better suited to being trained as a machine operator where less academic ability is required".

David was now boiling over with anger and felt that they should not get away with this kind of intimidation. He wondered how many others had been treated in this way. He rapped out,

"I have already had an interview with the Principal of the Physiotherapy School and sat in front of the Selection Board. They seem to think that I could make a go of it if I achieve the required subjects, including the Braille and typing, which I have been practicing hard here".

"They saw you for only a short time and anyway, many of them have no idea what physiotherapy is, let alone who should do it. Anyway, I am not here to argue with you. Mr. Bradshaw has asked us to release you for this coming Thursday and it seems that I have no alternative than to let you go. On the other hand I am writing to him and pointing out that I feel that you are poor material to become a physiotherapist and I recommend that you stay on here for another six weeks and complete your three months rehabilitation the same as everybody else. I might add for your information that I was trained as a physiotherapist, so I know the academic requirements".

David was about to respond when he was told that the interview was over and no more discussion must take place. David left the office quite deflated and wandered into the hall. He couldn't go back to his class as he knew questions would be asked and he may react in a violent manner. How could a man with such narrow vision be put in charge of such a centre where peoples' futures depended on him? Then he saw the funny side of his thoughts as this man didn't have narrow vision, but was totally blind. He went out into the garden and began to walk down towards the sea through the pine forest. He made his way out of the bottom gate and across the road down to a rocky shore. He sat looking at the waves crashing over the boulders and was intrigued by the way they smashed onto the rocks. He sat for a long time trying to work out why the Dukes had taken such a dislike to him and why they were so opposed to him trying to gain a profession. He was tempted to walk along the road to Anthea's house and ask for her advice, but he thought that his would put her in an invidious position. He knew that if Mr. Bradshaw had accepted him at Wallingcester his future would be assured. He also knew that if he were accepted he would make sure that he achieved the academic requirements. But what chance had he now when one person in authority gives such a damming report to the next in line. He felt like writing to Mr. Bradshaw himself and putting his case, but he knew that that would sound like "sour grapes" and would do his case no good. Perhaps he should call off the visit as it seemed quite pointless, but again he would be "cutting off his nose to spite his face" as it were. He made his way back up to the Manor and sat in the garden. It was beginning to get very cold, but he knew that the reception inside might be even colder. After about an hour he was aware of Miss Pope coming down the pathway. She sat at the side of him and sat silently for a while. Then she said,

"Have you had bad news David?"

"Not really, I have just had a bit of a fall out with Mr. and Mrs. Duke".

"Is it anything which I can help you with?" she asked.

"Not really" he replied, "They are writing to the Headmaster of Wallingcester to advise him not to take me on. This means that I will not be accepted by the physiotherapy school and that was my goal. I am now undecided as to whether I should waste Mr. Bradshaw's time and go for the interview".

"Well, I really can't get involved with this as all hell will break loose" she said, "But if it were me, I would go and at least have a try at changing the situation, but don't let anyone know that I said so. Now come back in, out of the cold and have some tea and cakes".

He sat at his normal table with Syd and Charlie and they, realising something was wrong told him of a funny occurrence that had happened that afternoon. One of the tests that was carried out at the Manor to check the ability for a blind person to get around on their own was to drop them in Torquay and see if they could make their way back on their own. That afternoon was the turn of two totally blind men who had done the trip several times before and really needed little help. One of the men realised that he was on the west side of the town and made his way along the front to where the main road meets the sea front, in fact right outside the hotel that David went with Charles. It was a busy main road, but at that point there was a zebra crossing. He stood for a while with his white stick held in front of him waiting for assistance. Almost immediately an arm came up against his and slipped inside his. They proceeded across the road and he was surprised to hear the squealing of brakes. When they reached the other side he said to his assistant.

"Thank you for taking me across the road".

"No, thank you. You see I am blind".

It was the other of the two men who had been dropped off in town and the two blind men had crossed the road together. Of course Syd and Charlie burst out laughing and David must admit that he couldn't stop a smile appearing on his face. David did let the two of them know why he was feeling so low, but asked them to keep it to themselves as he thought it would not do him any good if the Dukes thought that he was spreading the story.   He lost most of his drive to practice his Braille and typing and spent a lot of the time in the handicraft room. Miss Pope was very sympathetic and spent much of her time with him, still quietly encouraging him to go on the Wallingcester trip, but he could see no future in it. He felt as if he had lost more independence down there than at any time since he had lost his sight. Why was it that when all seems to be going well and he had overcome one major problem, some one or something would crop up to spoil it?

Chapter 54

It was with a heavy heart that David boarded the train that Thursday morning for the trip to Wallingcester. A taxi had been arranged to pick him up from the Manor House to get him to the station in good time. He had immediately approached the ticket office to buy the ticket and to ask for directions and the number of the platform he required. They were obviously used to blind persons going through the station as the ticket collector took him over the bridge and said that he would return when the train was due, to see that he went off safely. As the train sped through the Devon countryside heading first north then northeast, his mind went back to the trip he had made down to Torquay when he had made the mistake of sitting in a first class carriage, but having the great fortune of meeting Anthea. This time the ticket collector had settled him in the correct carriage with several other people. How he wished that one of them was Anthea. He had grown very fond of her and he had the feeling that she had grown fond of him. That last cuddle and long kiss on one cheek was different front her usual greeting. It was as if she was saying goodbye for good and would not take up the chance of meeting him again. She was a lot older than him and obviously in a position of some influence, but she certainly radiated warmth and love for the people around her.

The journey passed off without any real incident. The ticket inspector had told the guard of his presence and at a station about two hours up the line the guard very kindly escorted him from the train to another platform and told a porter where David was going and to make sure he got on the correct train. At Wallingcester another guard escorted him off the train and left him on the platform. He knew that he was to be picked up at the station and he imagined that an odd job man from the college would be there to meet him. Soon he was approached by a tall, balding man dressed in the loudest of sports jackets and smoking a droopy kind of pipe.   He came up to him and said in a rather rhetorical manner,

"David".

"Yes".

"This way".

He turned and walked sharpishly towards the exit of the station. He must have just had his shoes heeled as they clattered along the pavement like a guardsman until he came abreast of an extremely old, khaki coloured Bull Nosed Morris.   David stood on the pavement trying to see the whole of the car. Then he walked up to the front to check if he was right.

"Wow, a Bull Nosed Morris!"

"Well, you know about cars", the man said. "Have you seen one before?"

"Yes, one of the boys in the youth club bought one and we toured the Isle of Wight in it.

"He must have been a wealthy young man".

"No", said David, "he bought it as an old wreck and rebuilt it".

On the way back to the college, which appeared to be up quite a few steep hills, the car would slow and chug, but always made the top. Little was said at the beginning as the man had to concentrate on heavy, fast traffic and changing gear numerous times.   After a while he said,

"You look a little down in the mouth, was the journey difficult?"

"No, I am sorry, I am just a little worried about meeting Mr. Bradshaw as the man in charge of Torquay, where I am staying, has written telling him that he thinks I am not up to the standard to come to Wallingcester or have the ability to go to the Physiotherapy School".

"Oh dear, that is remiss of me. I am Mr. Bradshaw and, yes, I have received Mr. Duke's letter".

David didn't know what to say. He had been talking to him as if he was the "odd job man" and here he was the Headmaster of the college. He had made his first gaff and probably put another nail in the coffin. He spluttered,

"I am so sorry sir, I didn't know that it would be the Headmaster who would come down and meet me at the station".

"Don't worry, it's not your fault. I should have introduced myself properly. Anyway there was no one else to come to meet you. Two of the staff are blind, two can't drive and one is engaged in refereeing a football match".

The college was set in it's own grounds just outside the city of Wallingcester, up a short tree lined drive. They drew up outside the main, quite small entrance. The building was not what David expected. It was of red brick and must have been built in the nineteen twenties although it looked Victorian. It seemed to have a very flat faced exterior with tall white wooden windows. The front door, although being double, was quite narrow and it led into a short entrance hall which joined another corridor which ran the length of the building. It was quite dark as there was no natural light, but David could see a kind of conservatory built on the far end. The floor was made up of small check tiles and David noticed that Mr. Bradshaw's heels reverberated all the way along to the end and back giving a kind of echo. Mr. Bradshaw turned right and then left into his office.

"Take a seat. Oh by the way, what can you see?"

What a strange question from a man who was the head of a college for the blind.

"Well, I can see to get around, but I can't see anything I look at or any type of writing. I am not too good in the dark unless I give my eyes a long time to adjust".

"Hmm", he mumbled, picking up the phone.

"I'm back. I've got David. I want one of the senior prefects, preferably Paul to come to my office and take David around the college. He will then take him into lunch with the rest of the boys and then bring him back to me in my office".

He put down the phone without listening for the reply and sat down in a large leather armchair.

"You heard what I have arranged. Paul had some sight and like you he applied to come here later on in his schooling. He will show you round the college, then you can make up your mind whether you want to come here". It's not just a matter of whether we will accept you. It is also a matter of whether you will be happy studying here".

He pulled his pipe out of his top pocket and after filling it with tobacco he began a long and lengthy process of trying to light it. There were certainly clouds of smoke which filled the room, but David could hear him drawing on the pipe time and time again and throwing in the occasional, "Drat this pipe".

There came a knock on the door.

"Come in", shouted Mr. Bradshaw.

Into the room came a tall, young man dressed in a blazer and flannels.

"Yes sir, you wanted me".

"Yes", said Mr. Bradshaw, "I want you to show this young man around the college. He is thinking of coming to join us. When you have done that I want you to take him to lunch with the rest of the college and for today he can sit on the senior prefects table. When lunch is over, I would like you to return him here so that I can have a chat with him. Are you happy to do that for me Paul?"

"Yes sir that will be no problem".

They started off down the long corridor looking into some of the doors as they went along. One was the library, where the books were packed from floor to ceiling on large metal racks. David was quite surprised as it was very dull with no colour to any of the books and each volume being the same size as the next.

"This is a drab looking library", said David.

"Of course", said Paul, "All Braille books are the same size and there are no pictures or colours on any of them as no one can see them".

Another stupid observation thought David. He ought to have worked that out for himself before asking such a dim-witted question.

"I am sorry", said David, "I have not had bad sight for long and have not yet adjusted to the changes that I must accept".

"Oh, don't worry", replied Paul, "I haven't had bad sight for that long and I was in the same boat as yourself. Let's push on".

When they reached the end of the corridor David realised that what he thought was a conservatory was a stairway surrounded by glass. It was the beginning of a relatively new wing which housed the study cubicles. They were quite narrow having a window at the far end with most of the space taken up by Braille books, although he noticed than nearly every one had a radio on the table. At the far end of the study cubicles was a corridor that led to the gymnasium. This was quite modern with wall bars, ropes and benches. At the far end was a stage which was curtained off from the rest. He could hear what sounded like a small jazz band rehearsing behind the curtains.

"That is the school band", said Paul, "They are really supposed to be having a music lesson, but the rehearsal is accepted as sufficiently academic. Do you play any instrument?"

"No" said David, "I never really had any chance".

They continued their tour of the college around the inside and then the outside. All the time Paul was asking him questions about his art career, his sight problem, which, strangely, was the same as his and his recent visit to Torquay. David wasn't sure whether Paul had any input in the choosing of pupils for the college, but he certainly tried to give him a good impression. Lunch was strange. After grace was said with them all standing there was an enormous outburst of noise. All of the boys, large and small seemed to want to talk at the same time and even when the food arrived, already on the plates, the din continued. It was some time before Paul could point out to the totally blind boys that there was a stranger sitting on the table. Once he had introduced him, David was bombarded with questions. David was a little shaken as he could now see that he had entered the world of the blind and if he wanted to achieve his goals, must accept that he was now hoping to be one of them. When he finally reached Mr. Bradshaw's office, after thanking Paul for his kindness, he was surprised again by Mr. Bradshaw giving him a Braille book. After pulling a large watch out of his waistcoat pocket and setting it down on the table, asked him to start reading. David started to shake like a leaf and found the reading harder than normal. He had reached about the third line when the phone rang. Mr. Bradshaw went to pick it up and started to speak.

"Just carry on reading David, this won't take long".

He spoke for about five minutes and during that time David slid his fingers along the lines at a speed too fast for him to read. He guessed at most of the words and filled in those that he could not recognise. By the time the phone call was ended, he had covered a page and three quarters. Mr. Bradshaw stopped him reading and measured the pages with a ruler.

"Well that will certainly have to be improved", he said.

He then spent a good hour talking to David about his education, particularly the grammar school and the art college. He was most interested to hear of his paper round, his navvying job with Don and illustrating business that they had set up together. Regularly, whilst they were talking, members of staff in their black gowns, would come into the office and be introduced to David. Each would ask just a few questions on their own subject and then leave. Mr. Bradshaw then took David, at some speed, down to the small garden at the back of the college and then on to the swimming pool.

"Do you swim?" he asked.

"Yes sir".

"Very well?"

"Yes sir. I can swim well over six miles or even more if pushed".

"Fast?"

"Reasonably".

"Can you dive?"

"Yes sir".

"Well?"

"I have dived a lot off the three metre board and can summersault if required".

"Good, now we are going to tea in my house with my wife. I hope you are ready for some bread, jam and cakes".

"Oh my God", thought David, "This will be a testing time. Handling a plate with bread, butter and jam was not easy when you can't see too well."

Although the tea was laid out on a tray perched on a three legged table with a white patterned cloth beneath it, Mrs Bradshaw did not move from her seat by the window.   After being introduced to her he went and sat on the settee nearer to the tea.   Mr. Bradshaw began to pour and when the cups were full, David got up and went over to the table. He took one of the delicate cups and saucers and took it over to Mrs. Bradshaw. She had said little until that time and appeared a little withdrawn.   Now she smiled and said,

"Thank you David, I do like a man with good manners".

David seized the opportunity and went back to get a plate with the bread and butter.   He again returned to Mrs. Bradshaw and offered it to her.   Again he received a nice smile and a polite,

"Thank you".

For himself, he stuck to just bread and butter saying that he didn't eat too much jam and anyway he was quite full after the lunch at the college. He balanced his cup of tea and saucer quite well taking care not to crash it down. It felt as if it was very fine china.

"Is this Royal Worcester?" he asked.

"Yes it is", said Mrs. Bradshaw, "How did you know that?"

"I studied china at the Art College", he replied, "and we covered china from all over the world".

After Mrs. Bradshaw questioned him fully about his work at the Art School, she suddenly interposed,

"By the way, do you dance?"

"Yes", replied David.

"Well?"

"I have just passed my bronze medal and am about to take my silver".

"Oh", she said, "It would be wonderful to have someone decent to dance with".

They were getting close to the time for leaving to catch David's train. Mr. Bradshaw turned to David and said,

"David, we have been impressed by your endeavour to reach the standard to be accepted by the Physiotherapy School. I would have no worry about offering you a place here if you should feel that this is the route you want to take".

David's heart gave a leap, and then he remembered the letter.

"What about the letter from Mr. Duke?" he asked.

"That does pose a slightly difficult question, but I am sure I can overcome that. You see I do not like being told of another's opinion before I see the candidate. I like to make up my own mind. There are certain problems that must be cleared up before I can offer you a place. One is to do with the financing of your stay here, there is the careful handling of Mr. Duke, we must make him feel that he has contributed to your acceptance and there is the verifying of the qualifications required by the Physiotherapy School. Mind you if you do come, and I would expect you to start as soon as possible, I would expect you to take more than one subject. In fact I suggest you have a full timetable and attempt another five to eight subjects. You should at least pass in four or five. Are you willing to do that?"

What was he letting himself in for? It sounded like a marathon to David when all he needed was one subject at "O" level and one at "A". Well, it was all or nothing,

"Yes sir".

"It would be best if you did not say too much to too many people at Torquay. In fact I should keep it under your hat until we have sorted out the finance and other arrangements. I will write to you, personally, nearer to Christmas and if it is good news I should keep it quiet until you go home. It will make your stay at Torquay a little more pleasant. As a famous author once said, "It is best for the left hand not to know what the right hand is doing", eh David!" Oh, and by the way, keep up your Braille and try to read what is on the page and not what you imagine may be there".

As David sat on the train on his way back to Torquay, he pondered the events of the whole day and he felt that all in all he hadn't made too bad an impression. He had made a few gaffs for which he could have kicked himself, but they accepted them as if they were everyday occurrences. He got to know and liked Paul, who treated him as if he were already accepted at the college and he found Mr. Bradshaw a rather daunting and officious type, but honest and generous. He was not sure of Mrs. Bradshaw. It was hard to tell whether she was involved in the decision. It was lucky that he had been out to tea with Charles several times and the youth club had a tradition of being extra polite to the ladies, especially on the dance floor. Yes, he thought that the dancing ability had added to her pleasantness to him. There still seemed to be a few stumbling blocks which needed to be overcome, but it seemed as if it were out of his hands now. Mr. Bradshaw had them in hand and he sounded fairly confident that the problems could be ironed out. The college itself was not quite the grand building that he had anticipated although if it gave him the chance of getting into the Physiotherapy School he was willing to accept it. Mr. Bradshaw had driven him back to the station at break neck speed. It was mainly downhill and he let the old car loose either in top gear or even free-wheeling. It was as he boarded the train that he received his most positive indication of his future. As David said goodbye and thanked him for devoting so much time and energy to his visit, Mr. Bradshaw shook his hand and said,

"Well I hope, with a careful bit of diplomacy, we will see you at the beginning of next term. Goodbye David".

Chapter 55

Back at Manor House the atmosphere grew a little more cordial as the festival of Christmas approached. Although there were no real decorations going up each of the staff made their particular room a little more colourful and the talk was of the festive season which was near the end of the month. David had become much more friendly with most of the other guests and had taken a particular liking to Syd and Charlie. They were always out for a bit of fun, although Syd being in his seventies, liked to be in bed by ten o'clock. One evening all the guests and staff at Manor House were invited to a dance to be held in America Lodge, another National Institute for the Blind establishment a little down the road. It was well within walking distance and most of them decided to attend. The large room was beautifully decorated with Christmas trees and paper chains and they had a fairly modern record player at the far end. After an introductory drink they gathered into groups, those from the Manor mainly sticking together. David noticed that although the music was being played, no one was getting up to dance. He first of all approached the two young ladies that had accompanied him in the handicraft room, but one said that she couldn't dance and the other just shyly refused. After another couple of drinks David went off to find some of the ladies from America Lodge. They had put on the dance so he was sure that they would be only too pleased to get the dancing going, but no, he either was refused or they admitted that they could not dance. Even when David said that he would guide them through the steps they still declined his offer. The evening turned out to be just a drinking session and they all made their way back to the Manor a little worse for wear, but happy.

David kept secret about his interview at Wallingcester for about a week and then quietly let Syd and Charlie know. They promised to tell no one and David felt quite confident that they could both be trusted. The following evening Syd said,

"Charlie and I are going down to the hotel on the front for a meal this evening, we would like you to come. We have let the kitchen know that we will not be in and we have arranged a taxi to take us and pick us up. What do you say?"

"I am sorry", said David, "but I do not have the funds for a meal out in such a nice hotel. I will have to give it a miss".

"Don't be silly", said Syd, "this is our treat to celebrate your good news. We have told the others that it is to celebrate my birthday which is the week before Christmas so no one will ask any questions".

David knew that to refuse such a kind invitation would be insulting. He also knew that both men could easily afford it. Syd used to own a rubber plantation in Ceylon and Charlie owned several stalls in a Fair Ground which toured the Midlands. The evening was a great success and they plied David with more drink than he normally could handle. Mr. Duke, who met them at the door was not amused by their joviality, but as he could not see the state they were in, said nothing. They had all received royal treatment at the hotel and David being the only one who could see his way around was thought to be the member of staff sent down to take care of the two old boys, so he was especially well looked after.

As the days of the month passed, David was more and more tempted to let Anthea know of his visit to Wallingcester and the possibility of his acceptance there. He thought that if he jumped the gun and told her too early and he was turned down, it would be very embarrassing, but if he waited too long, or until the letter came, he may not have time to tell her. After a lot of thought he decided to phone her and tell her of his partial success, but let her know that it would all depend on the letter from Mr. Bradshaw and the consequences of such a letter at the Manor.   He decided to phone her during the tea break of the following afternoon.

"Hello, the Howard residence", came the answer at the end of the phone.

"May I speak to Lady Howard, it is David Fellows".

"I am afraid that Lady Howard is not here at the moment. Could you call back after five o'clock?"

"Yes, thank you" answered David feeling that after all the build up to making the call and the excitement and anticipation of hearing her voice again, he would have to repeat the same build up later.

It was during the final session of the day when an announcement came over the speakers.   It was Mr. Duke,

"At five o'clock this afternoon I would like to speak to all of the residents and staff in the lounge.   It is of some importance, so I will expect everyone to attend.   Five o'clock in the lounge".

"Damn", thought David, "It is just the time I wanted to phone Anthea, I hope it will not take too long".   He wondered why Mr. Duke needed to speak to all the residents at the same time and to have the staff there as well was a little strange.

At five o'clock precisely, Mr. Duke was led into the lounge by his wife and took up a prominent position by the fireplace.   The room was full to overflowing as it was unusual for all the residents to congregate in the lounge, but this time their numbers were added to by the staff, not only the teachers, but also the cleaners and those from the kitchen.

"I have called this meeting as I believe that I must make something clear about the forthcoming Christmas holiday. You will all understand that most of you are here on a Minister of Labour grant and therefore must abide by the rules laid down by that body. Only Christmas Day, Boxing Day and one other day are considered to be holiday entitlement. Because of this ruling, unless your period of rehabilitation ends before Christmas you will be expected to stay on over those days. All the staff have been informed of their duties and we will therefore be fully staffed for the period. Fares for travel will only be available to those finishing their course at that time. Are there any questions?"

There was a gasp from many of the residents and a lot of noise broke out as people complained to each other. Syd stood up. He was particularly looking forward to going home as he had a young wife whom he was desperate to see.

"I intend going home", he said, "Will you tell me what day I may leave and what day I need to return".

"I am very sorry to hear that", said Mr. Duke, "I hope you realise that it is against my recommendation. We intend to put on a very pleasant Christmas here with carol singing in the morning, a full Christmas dinner with turkey, stuffing, roast potatoes and all the trimmings, followed by Christmas pudding and mince pies. In the afternoon we intend to have tea and presents and a festive dinner in the evening".

"Yes Mr. Duke, but that does not answer my question. What date may I leave and what date must I return?"

Mrs. Duke then spoke with some authority, "We can allow you to leave on the day before Christmas Eve and you must return the day after Boxing Day. Now if any more of you wish to absent yourselves for that period you must come to see us in the office".

She then took Mr. Duke's arm and led him out of the room. The noise grew so loud that it was difficult to hear anyone speak. Some of them were getting into groups and discussing what they should do about the situation. David was quite surprised to hear that some of them were more than pleased that Christmas would be laid on at the Manor as they obviously had nowhere else to go, or perhaps no family at home. David knew that this put him in some sort of predicament as he remembered what Mr. Bradshaw had said, not to upset Mr. Drake, but he couldn't imagine spending Christmas here when he knew that it would be a fantastic holiday at home visiting Janet's house, singing in the church and all the time spent with his own family. He was dying to see Janet and he knew that he would give anything to be in her company all over Christmas.If he went to Mr. Duke to ask to be absent he knew that would go down badly for him and if he didn't go he would miss the wonderful Christmas at home.

By the time they began to leave the lounge he noticed that it had turned six o'clock and he had promised to phone Anthea just after five. The phone was blocked for some time with residents phoning home and most probably giving them the bad news. It must have been at least half an hour before he could get into the phone box. The same little voice of the maid answered the phone. David again requested to speak to Anthea.

"I am sorry, Lady Howard is at dinner at the moment, could you call again later".

David knew that this would be difficult as there was already a queue of people waiting outside the box.

"Could you just let her know that it is David on the phone and I have some news for her which won't take a minute".

There was a pause for about a minute, then Anthea's voice came over the phone.

"David. How nice to hear from you. Have you any news?"

"Yes, well I think so. Mr. Bradshaw gave me every indication that as long as the grants and the requirements can be sorted out he is willing to take me on at the beginning of next term".

"Oh, that is wonderful. When will you know that things are definite?"

"He will write to me shortly and tell me if all is set in place and he will also write to Mr. Duke confirming my place".

"This is wonderful news, David. I must go now, but will you phone me as soon as you hear the result whether it is good or bad?"

"Yes, of course. I am sorry to interrupt your meal, but I thought you would just like to know".

David wrote to Janet and Mum telling them of the sad news that he was expected to stay down in Torquay for Christmas, but also let them know that there was a good possibility that he would be accepted by Wallingcester College. He received very sad letters from Janet and Mum saying that Christmas would not be the same without him. Janet even suggested that she may be able to come down to see him for a couple of days as she missed him so much. The days went by and there was no sign of a letter from Mr. Bradshaw. David was beginning to feel that he may have forgotten or was unable to secure the grant needed. It was not until the twenty first of December that a letter came. The only one he could trust to read the letter was Miss Pope, the craft teacher. She had read all of his letters from Janet and he was sure that she never disclosed anything that was in them to anyone. Some things Janet wrote made him feel quite embarrassed when Miss Pope read them, but she made no comment. They went to one of the small quiet rooms that was empty and closed the door. She opened the letter and began to read,

"Dear David,

You will be pleased to hear that I managed to persuade your local authority to cover the cost of your tuition at this college. I have also been in touch with Mr. Jeskinson of the Physiotherapy School and he confirms that if you pass out from here with the required subjects there will be a place available for you at their school to do the three year course.

I have also written to Mr. Duke thanking him for his cooperation in your education and application, so I am sure that he will be supportive of your future career.

We look forward to seeing you on the ninth of January. The school bus will meet the five fifteen train from London. Have a happy Christmas and prepare yourself for a period of hard work.

Yours sincerely,

Bob Bradshaw,
Headmaster.

Miss Pope put her arms around him and gave him a great hug.

"Congratulations! It sounds as if your future is secure and all your worries are now over. Well done David, I couldn't be more pleased".

There was a tap on the door which immediately opened. It was Mrs. Duke. David and Miss Pope moved away from each other quickly, but David had the same feeling of dread that he had experienced at the Art School when the Principal walked in on he and Donna. Mind you, this time they were fully clothed and had not been up to anything unacceptable, but one never knew what misunderstandings can be drawn form walking in to a room too quickly.

"David will you come to the office immediately?" she said and then turned and closed the door.

"Oh no", said David, "I hope I have not blotted my copy book at this late stage, especially as I have just received this wonderful news.   I think Mr. Duke is in a position where he could spoil the whole thing if he wanted to".

Chapter 56

David walked across the hall to the office door, which was already closed although he knew that Mrs. Duke had just gone in. He stood for a while remembering the time at the Art School when he stood outside the Principal's office with Donna in tears. Oh how he could have done with her company now and the positive approach she had to the situation. He must now face the music on his own, after all, he wasn't doing anything wrong and he was sure that Miss Pope would back him up if necessary. He tapped gently on the door and heard Mr. Duke call,

"Come in".

This time he was told to sit in the chair on the other side of the desk while Mrs. Duke read something from a page she was holding in her hand. There was a short pause and then Mr. Duke said,

"Well David." This surprised David as up until now he had always called him Mr. Fellows, "We have just received a very nice letter from Mr. Bradshaw, the headmaster of Wallingcester College for the Blind. He gives a glowing report of your visit to the College and says that he is sure that he can bring you up to the standard required for your entry to the Physiotherapy School. He congratulates us on bringing your Braille up to such a standard in such a short time and feels that your rehabilitation has been a great success. We, of course, are extremely pleased with your achievement and have noticed how you have befriended the older and the younger guests. We have also been informed of your kindness in trying to involve our young ladies and those of America Lodge in learning to dance. The Director of America Lodge wrote to us on that particular point. Mr. Bradshaw also makes the observation that you will begin a three month term starting early in

January, so he suggests that you are released from Manor House at the Christmas break and after a period at home go straight to Wallingcester. We are only too happy to comply with his wishes and you should be ready to leave the day before Christmas Eve. We hope that you have enjoyed your stay at Manor House and we both wish you good luck for the future".

David didn't know what to say. It felt as if a great burden had been lifted from his shoulders and he couldn't decide who he would tell first. What had produced this sudden change in their attitude towards him? It must have been the letter from that very clever and thoughtful Mr. Bradshaw. He stood up, knowing that the interview was ended and said,

"I am absolutely delighted with your news, Mr. Duke, I am so pleased that I managed to rise to your expectations and I think that your boost when I first came made me work even harder. I know that you will be pleased with my efforts at Wallingcester and the Physiotherapy School and I hope that I will be like yourself and qualify in the three years".

David almost made himself sick by saying these things because he knew that they were not true, but Mr. Bradshaw's words came back to him, "Never let the right hand know what the left hand is doing".

"Now you go off and make the best of your last few days here, but try to avoid celebrating too much, especially with Syd and Charlie".

It was the first time he had seen both of them laugh. They had obviously had some earlier dealings with the two elder guests before David arrived. His first thoughts were to write to his family and Janet, but he realised that he had promised Anthea he would let her know. As he had already let Mum and Janet know that he would not be home for Christmas he thought that a short note to both of them would be the first move. After he had typed both letters with envelopes he stuck stamps on ready for posting. He then phoned the Howard's,

"Hello, this is David Fellows, may I speak to Lady Howard please".

"Hold the line, I will call her", came the reply. This was unusual as the maid nearly always said that she was not available.

"Hello David", came the beautiful radio announcer's voice, "have you any news?"

"Yes", replied David, "I have just received a letter from the Head of Wallingcester offering me a place and explaining that all the problems over finance have been solved. He must have also put in a good word to Mr. Duke as he was all over me at the interview and wished me good luck".

"Oh David, that is absolutely marvellous news. Is it possible for you to come down here about five o'clock and we will have a glass of champagne to celebrate your success".

"Yes, I will arrange that with the people here, I am sure they will be only too pleased to see the back of me for a short time".

After clearing it with the kitchen staff that he may not be back in time for his supper, he set off down the road to Riviera View. Although it was dark there were enough lights down the road to find his way easily and the front of the house was almost flood lit. The little maid in her black and white uniform showed him into the large room overlooking the rear of the property. There seemed to be lights everywhere, all over the gardens and even over the sea, which must have been due to shipping making its way up the Channel. The door at the far end of the room opened and Anthea dressed in a long, pale blue, silk dress came in. She walked elegantly across the room to him and threw her arms around his neck.

538

"Congratulations David, I am so pleased".

She pulled him up close to her and kissed him on the cheek. He could feel the whole of her body close up against him and as she tightened her hold around his neck he could feel himself reacting to the warmth and shapeliness of her body. He was beginning to feel a little embarrassed, but instead of pulling away he could feel her pelvis pressing harder against him. They stood like that for some time and then she pulled away, but not before she kissed David on the lips. It was just an ordinary kiss, but from her he knew that it meant something special. She led him over to the chaise longue and they sat down together with her still holding his hands. He told her of the events of the day including the Miss Pope incident and she seemed to laugh at his innocence.

"Sir William would like to join us for this celebratory drink, so would you mind waiting until he has changed. He only arrived home about twenty minutes ago and wanted to take a bath to get rid of the London grime".

David felt a little dismayed at this last piece of news because he thought that he would have a little time with Anthea on her own especially as she looked so beautiful and had been so welcoming. Never mind, he realised that it was a great privilege to be invited to have a drink with her, but even more of a privilege to be joined by Sir William. Although he was always very polite David had the impression that he was kind to Anthea's friends to please her. He appeared to be about ten years older than Anthea and had slightly greying hair, or so it seemed to David. He was tall and quite broad and looked as if he had been either a rugby player or an oarsman at some time. He spoke very clearly and precisely and seemed to form opinions on the spot which one would not dare contradict. Anthea took David's hand and asked him to run through the interview that had taken place at the Manor with Mr. Duke. David told the story this time putting in some asides of what he thought at the time and each time it was greeted by Anthea's musical laugh. She then wanted to know more about the trip to Wallingcester and his meeting with Mr. Bradshaw. She asked him what he thought of the College and, not wishing to spoil her mental picture, he made it sound a lot better than his first impression.

The door at the end of the long room opened and the maid entered with a trolley carrying glasses, a bottle of champagne and a plate of canopies. She placed the plate on the table in front of the chaise longue. At close quarters David could see that the bottle was in a silver ice cooler and the glasses were those with a tall stem and a wide brim. The maid stepped back from the table and did a slight curtsey before heading back to the door. Anthea took very little notice of these proceedings except to just say,

"Thank you Molly".

Almost immediately the door opened again and Sir William entered the room. He was one of those persons who seemed to take over the whole room as he entered and both David and Anthea turned to face him. He walked briskly towards them with his arm and hand outstretched in front of him saying,

"Congratulations David. Lady Howard tells me that you have been accepted by the College and you will be leaving Torquay for your further education in that lovely City of Wallingcester. I know the Bishop well and I have had many dealings with the Head Master of the King's School, in fact as a school boy I rowed against them".

He took David's hand and shook it firmly continuing to hold on to it while he said,

"You have had a remarkable life so far and you have already had to face up to situations which many of us never have to encounter. I think that you have handled your difficulties very well and I am perfectly sure that you will make a success of which ever profession you enter".

He then picked up the bottle of champagne, wiped it with the clean, white towel that the maid had provided and began to pull back the soft metal cover over the wired cork.

"I love doing this part of the proceedings", he said, "I always feel that it is a test of my barman's training to get the cork out without too much of a bang and without too much mess".

He played with the wire and the cork for some time and began to turn the cork in the top of the bottle.   There was a sudden bang and the cork went flying over to the other side of the room missing the windows by inches and hitting the curtains.   All three of them burst into laughter and David at last felt the warmth coming from Sir William as it did from Anthea.   After the drinks were poured by Sir. William, which David found quite strange as he thought it was the sort of thing that the butler would do, he gave a glass to Anthea and then to David.   They clinked their glasses and sipped the contents of the glass.

"Come over to the window and gaze at the wonderful panorama of the lights in the gardens and the boats out at sea" said Sir William as he strolled across to the large windows at the end of the room.

"Darling, you seem to forget why David has had to come down to Torquay and the reason for him staying at the Manor House".

"Oh, good lord!" exclaimed Sir William, "I am so sorry, I had completely forgotten. Never mind come over here and I am sure you will get a feeling of the beauty of the scene".

David was aware of the maid appearing at his side and handing him small morsels from the tray and all three of them spent some time gazing out on the panoramic scene of the lights of Torquay. It was a wonderful evening and a perfect celebration. After their good byes at the front door Anthea again embraced him and kissed him on both cheeks. There was just a hint of lingering slightly longer that on previous occasion and Sir William held on to his hand a little longer than before. They had arranged for the car, which David now saw was a Rolls Royce, to drive him back to the Manor House and David felt a little sad at leaving the Howard's and knowing that this was nearly the end. He knew that he had one treat left before heading for home. Anthea had said that he was not to call a taxi to take him to the station, she would send up the car and he could leave Torquay in luxury. She also offered him an invitation to come to visit them at any time, he had only to phone the number she had given him on the card.

The day before Christmas Eve he found himself sitting in a luxurious first class compartment on his way back to Paddington. He sat and reminisced at the sadness of leaving all the new friends he had got to know so well at the Manor House and how sad they all were at the parting of good friends. They had all wished him all the luck in the world in his future career and many assumed that they would meet up again in a few years time. He had felt like a million dollars when the Rolls Royce had turned up at the front door. Anthea had arranged the car to arrive half an hour early as she had said that she wanted to call in at the house and give him a small gift in memory of his visit to Torquay. When the chauffeur opened the door of the car he was pleased to see that Anthea was seated inside. When they reached the Riviera View she led him into the small study, just on the right of the main door. From the desk drawer she withdrew a small blue box about six inches by two and handed it to David.

"We wanted to give you this before you went home and although it might seem inappropriate at this time, we felt that in the future you could use it for signing documents, cheques and letters."

David took the box and opened it to find a gold pen and pencil inside. He took out the pen which was held in place by a small loop of elastic and pretended to write his name in mid air. They both laughed at the flamboyant waving of his arm and then he replaced the pen in the box. He stepped forward and taking Anthea by the hand pulled her towards him to give her a kiss on the cheek. He suddenly found her arms around his neck and she kissed him fully on the mouth. As her hands slipped up to the back of his head he ran both of his hands down her back to just below her waist. He pulled her up tight against him and began to feel his head swim as she pressed her pelvis hard onto his uncontrollable body. They moved gently up against each other for several minutes and then she pulled away and dropping her head as if to look at the floor she said,

"I am sorry David, I didn't mean to do that. I thought of you as just a young man needing help at first, but as I got to know you more and more I grew fond of you. I now realise that we may never meet again and if we do, circumstances will be quite different. Now, we must get you to your train".

David was unable to speak. Here was a mature, beautiful, and obviously wealthy woman opening herself up to him and even allowing her feelings to grow so much that she would kiss him in that way. If she had suggested going upstairs and making love he knew that he would not be able to resist, but luckily, or perhaps, unluckily, she knew when to stop. She took him by the hand and led him to the door, but just before she opened it she again, took him in her arms and kissed him on the mouth. Even as he sat on the train he could feel the passion rising in him at the memory of that goodbye and how he now wished that he had taken a later train and spent more time with her.

At the station she was much more reserved and as they walked up the platform she handed him a small sheet of paper.

"Keep this with your ticket and show it to the ticket inspector on the journey", she said.

As the train drew to a halt the guard had opened the door and taking David's case climbed back into the carriage. Anthea gave him a quick peck on the cheek and pushed him towards the door. She said,

"Follow the guard, I have reserved a first class seat for you to travel back home to remind you of our initial journey down here and our first encounter".

As he sat watching the beautiful green fields and trees fly past the windows his mind went back to the time he was sitting on the step of his front door with a feeling of great depression realising that his art career was over and not knowing what lay ahead. He thought back on the meeting with Polly and the sexual attraction she oozed with her well developed figure and the silky clothes she always wore. Was it only about six months ago that he sat there reminiscing over his earlier years, the events of the war and the changes in direction of his education. Was it just the sitting on the step which jogged his memory about Donna, her beauty and ability to handle difficult situations, or the lovely Janet who had come in and out of his love life and now held a permanent position. It seemed that every time he pulled himself up a rung on the ladder, he was suddenly dragged down by another ill turn of events. Even now, as he sat in this first class compartment of his train home he could feel a profound loss and hollowness in his heart. The trip to Torquay had led to more than just the entry to Wallingcester, it had proved to be a development in his personality, a meeting of wonderful friends and a knowledge that he must strive to achieve his final aim. Overriding this however was a pain of moving rapidly away from someone he had grown to love and he knew that there was no way he could stop the train and go back. He also knew that to go back would spoil the whole period of enjoyment. He turned his mind to what lay ahead and how he had longed for this day for nearly two months. He had already had a letter to tell him that Janet, Mum and Charles were coming to the station to meet him. He knew that this Christmas was going to be the best he had ever had, visiting Janet's family and accompanying her to church, the youth club and any dances that were going on. He also knew that Mum would put on a wonderful spread on Christmas Day and he would accompany Dad and Jack to the St. Anthony's Arms to join the heaving mass of drinkers swilling back pints of mild and bitter and heaving themselves through the throng spilling beer all over their new clothes. There may also be the joy of Janet staying the night at David's house and coming to visit him in the morning, sitting on the side of the bed and giving him a good morning kiss.

They would see in the New Year in a similar manner and he knew that there would be about another week before he would again pack and head for his new college at Wallingcester. This was the beginning of a new life and although his art career was finished he knew that the lessons he had learnt there would be of great benefit in the future. This was set. All he had to do now was to endure a year and a half at Wallingcester, where he would study hard, pass the necessary examinations and be admitted to the Physiotherapy School in London. He would strive to pass all the exams first time and in four and a half years time he should become a qualified physiotherapist able to work in a hospital and possibly pay back to the community some of the debt acquired by his education. As long as he could come up to standard and pass the examinations required, he felt that his future would now be assured.

THE END